The Alternate Captain

Elite Hockey Book Three

Alys J. Clarke

Cover Art by Tom Drake
Additional Art by Caroline Taylor
Editing: Katie at Between the Covers Editing & Anthony G. Muller MBE
Proofreading by Open Eye Editing

ISBN: 978-1-7384632-3-7
Independently Published First Edition: September 2024

A Note from the Author

This is a work of fiction. I have done my utmost to align the content with real British hockey; however, there may be differences, and this is intentional.

I purposefully haven't given the team a name. This is because I wanted any of my UK readers who are also hockey fans, to imagine it is their team, if they so wish.

If you need support with any issues raised in this book, please reach out to someone. It's okay not to be okay and help is available. www.mind.org.uk is a great place to start.

As always, #justiceforBettsy.

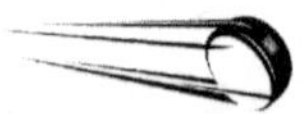

This book is written in British English, however, I have used terminology more aligned to Canadian English (e.g. Mom instead of Mum/Mam).

Trigger & Content Warning

This story has mention of the following with no graphic detail:

Pregnancy
Mental Health Issues
Domestic Abuse
Child Abuse (single sentence where it is passively mentioned)

Timeline of Events

This book starts during the playoffs, which occurs at the end of Ryan's first season in the UK in April. This is before Liam has joined.

Liam joins at the start of the season in chapter ten, and that's when the timelines between The Tape Job and The Alternate Captain run in parallel. I would recommend that you read The Import Slot and The Tape Job prior to reading this book for full context, though this can be read as a standalone.

Definitions

Home Grown:

THE DEFINITION OF A "homegrown" player is a player, who irrespective of their nationality or age, has been registered with either:

1. Their current club (who is a member of the EIHL); and/or

2. A club and/or any other Ice Hockey club affiliated with Ice Hockey UK ("IHUK"), English Ice Hockey Association ("EIHA") or Scottish Ice Hockey ("SIH") for a period, continuous or non-continuous, of two seasons or 24 months prior to his 18th birthday (or the end of the season during which they turn 18).

A non home grown player is usually classified as an import. A team is allowed a maximum number of imports as decided by the league.

The roster spots for imports to consume are known as 'import slots'.

Tape Job (or, T.J.):

Act of applying tape to a hockey stick to:
a) Protect the stick from wear and tear
b) Change the way the stick feels
Alternatively:
A job involving a tape

Alternate Captain

Each team must appoint a captain and not more than two alternate captains from among the skaters listed on the game line up. When the captain is off the ice or unavailable for the game, any alternate captain on the ice is responsible for fulfilling the captain's official role as liaison to the referees.

Alternatively:

Another version of Johnny Koenig.

Slap Shot – powerful, fast-moving shot of the puck on goal made with a full backswing of the stick and an extended follow-through.

One Timer – a shot that occurs when a player meets a teammate's pass with an immediate slapshot.

Celly – Celebration after scoring a goal.

Offside – when any member of the attacking team precedes the puck over the defending team's blueline

D-Man – Defenceman

Icing – when a player on his team's side of the red center line shoots the puck all the way down the ice and it crosses the red goal line at any point (other than the goal).

Power Play (or PP)– a period of play where one team has a numerical advantage in players, usually because an opposing team member is in the penalty box.

Penalty Kill (or PK) – a period of play where your team is down a player, or maybe two and you're playing with less players than the opposition.

Green Biscuit – Puck for off-ice use.

The Point – The point is an area just inside the blue line of the attacking zone. It is normally occupied by the attacking team's defensive players.

The Slot – A prime scoring area located between the faceoff circles in the O-Zone

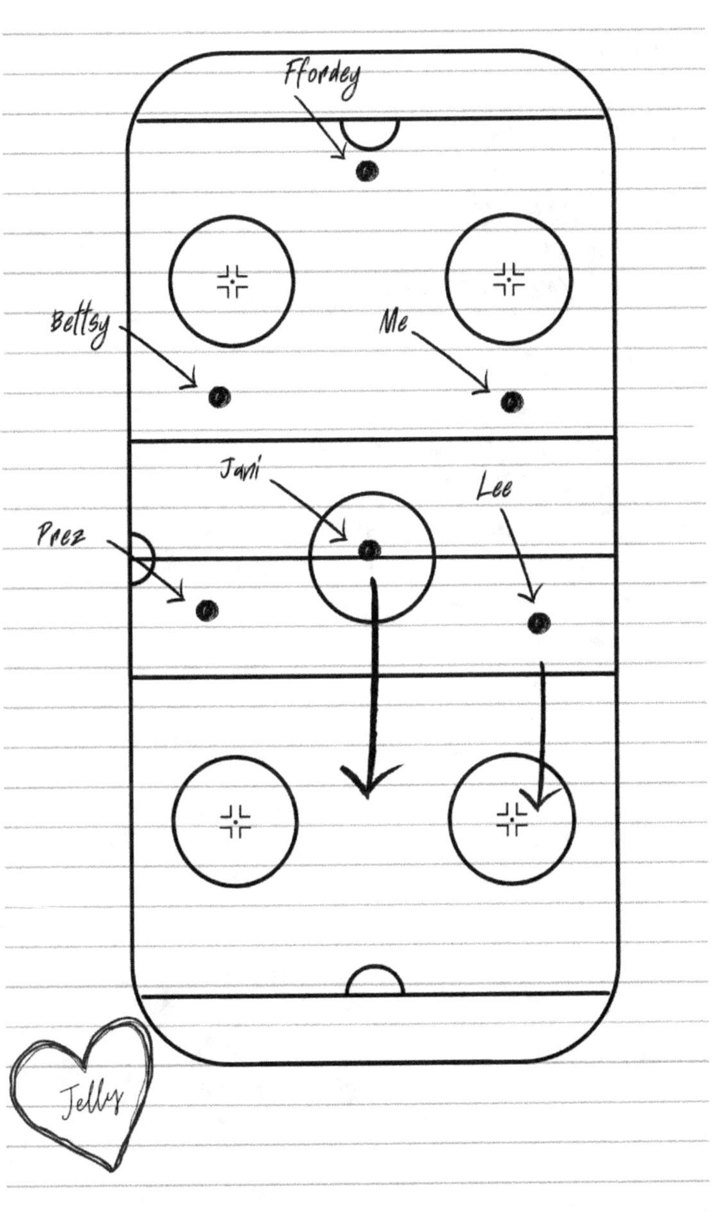
Ffordey
Bettsy
Me
Javi
Lee
Prez
Jelly

Last Season Stats

Games Played (GP) 54
Goals (G) 15
Assists (A) 35
Points (P) 50
Plus/Minus (+/-) +22
Penalty Minutes (PIM) 40
Power Play Goals (PPG) 6
Short-Handed Goals (SHG) 2
Game-Winning Goals (GWG) 4
Shots on Goal (SOG) 160
Shot Percentage (S%) 9.4%
Hits 105
Blocked Shots 140
Takeaways 42
Giveaways 20
Average Time on Ice (ATOI) 24:15

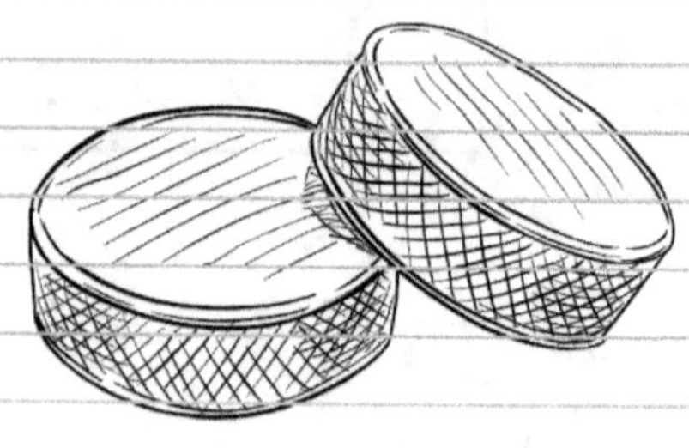

Chapter 1

Kelly

HE'S BEEN FIGHTING AGAIN. There's a fresh wound above his eyebrow, which tells me it wasn't just a scrap. It was a full-on fight—helmet and gloves removed.

"How did you get that scar?" I ask him. We're both aware of my stance on fighting, but I want to hear him say it. I want him to tell me he's being reckless. "Mike? Answer me."

"It's just part of the game," he says, turning and moving to the fridge. He rummages around in the salad drawers before returning to the counter with a pile of pre-chopped vegetables and a pack of chicken. He reaches for a wok that's lying upside down on the draining board, then he sets it on the hob before lighting the gas. "You're singing to yourself again. People will think you're crazy."

"Don't change the subject."

"Okay, fine. It's a paper cut," he says. I scowl at his reply. "What do you want me to say?" I cock my head to the side and stare at him. He'll back down before I do. "Okay, fine. We were down a goal and I needed to apply some pressure. Get the guys riled up. That's how it is."

Sadly, I understand, but this hasn't always been the case. I'd never known him to fight before he joined his current team. In fact, I'd say he was more of a peacekeeper.

"The captain put you up to it, didn't he?" I say, widening my eyes.

"Not really."

"What do you mean, not really?" I stand up from the barstool and step around the counter, pulling his face towards me so I can inspect it.

"Get off me, damn it." Mike wriggles free before grabbing a spatula from the drawer under the hob.

"Have you had it checked?"

"It's a cut. Calm your tits."

Sighing, I make my way back to the counter, accepting defeat. "I just don't like it."

"It's part of the game." He chuckles softly, which pisses me off even more.

He calls himself 'The Enforcer'. I call him an idiot.

"Anyway," he says, tossing some chicken into the wok, "I thought since you were on my side of town, you'd want to come to the game."

"It's still a no," I say.

My usual excuse sits along the line of not wanting to get the bus all the way across the city to freeze my ass off and watch him fight a grown man over the possession of a piece of rubber. I can think of better things to do with my Saturday night.

He stirs and shakes the wok before setting it down. He reaches for an envelope that's stashed next to the microwave and tosses it towards me.

"Would you hate me if I didn't come?" I ask.

"Nah, I already hate you, so it makes no difference." He smirks.

I haven't been to one of Mike's games in a long time. Not since he took a check to the head a few years back. I hold his linemate fully responsible for it since he was the one the check was intended for. I'm certain of this because I re-watched the footage repeatedly. I wanted closure. Instead, I got more riled up. Mike was out for two weeks. And he ended up losing two teeth that game.

He clears his throat. "It's a big game, though, Kel. I mean, it's been a few years since we've made the playoff finals. I think we've got a chance this year." His tone is serious, and I watch him as he tosses veggies into the wok, an intense expression on his face.

"You say that every single year," I say, taking a gulp of my water.

"And you say that every single year."

I roll my eyes. "I need to prep for tomorrow."

"No, you don't. It wouldn't surprise me if you could play those pieces without even looking at the sheet music."

But I'm an over-preparer. At least I try to be. And I couldn't live with myself if I spent the evening before my audition chilling—or turning into a block of ice—with no preparation.

I watch Mike cook as I consider my options. I mean, I could watch his game, but I'd be going alone since I don't know anyone else and the likelihood of Tom or Sally making their way across the city at short notice is slim to none.

I open my mouth to speak, but Mike answers the question I haven't asked.

"That ticket is next to Scottsy's wife. She's cool."

"I don't know Scottsy nor his wife," I say.

"Do you pay any attention when I talk? Scott McCoy? The winger."

"Oh, yeah, him." I roll my eyes. I have no idea.

"Look. The ticket is in the envelope. I won't be mad if you don't come, but I will be pissed if we advance and you don't come to the finals."

Mike shuts off the hob and grabs some plates, filling the air with the clattering of crockery. He glances at his watch, then reaches for his phone just as the front door swings open.

In walks a guy a few inches shorter than my brother, but wearing an identical outfit of sweats, a team hoodie, and a baseball cap.

"Well, look who crawled home," he says, without looking up. "Hutch, this is my sister, Kelly."

Hutch pauses, scanning me quickly before placing his gear bag on the floor.

"Shit, I didn't realise you had a sister, Betts." He grins.

"If you weren't gay, I'd say to keep your fucking eyes off her. Why do you think I haven't introduced her or Stacey to any of you fuckers?" my brother says. "Besides, she's got a boyfriend."

"I don't—"

"I'm bi. But whatever. Is that your guitar in the hall?" Hutch says, grabbing a plate from Mike.

I don't have a boyfriend. Mike's friends were always told that my sister and I had boyfriends. To him, it was a firm sign of our unavailability.

"It's a cello," my brother interjects, jabbing his friend in the ribs.

"A cello? I have no fucking clue..." Hutch says, sitting at the counter next to me. "Is that like a big violin?"

Mike scoffs.

"Yes, it's exactly like a big violin," I say.

"So, how long are you here for?" Hutch asks.

I awkwardly perch myself on the next available stool and reach for a fork. "Just the night. I've got an audition tomorrow at the music college so I'm crashing here—I mean, if it's okay with you?"

"Of course it's okay," Mike cuts across. "Kelly will have my room, and I'll get in with you," he tells Hutch.

"Like fuck you will," Hutch says.

"Don't be mean."

"Don't give me a reason to be. You can take the sofa. You snore."

"I'll take the sofa, I don't mind," I say. The thought of what could lurk in my brother's sheets grosses me out.

"I'm changing my sheets for you," Mike says, pointing his fork in the air towards me. "You're taking the bed. I don't want you going back to Mam moaning about your bad back from sleeping on the sofa."

I roll my eyes and eat my meal. Knowing Mike, he'll be back here this evening either shit-faced from celebrating a win, or shit-faced from commiserating a loss. Either way, the sleeping situation will sort itself out when I will inevitably put him to bed, in his bed.

Mike and Hutch both glance up from their plates.

"Are you nervous?" Hutch asks Mike, as he finishes his food.

"No. Are you?" he replies.

They lock eyes briefly, devoid of any emotion.

The buzz of my phone on the counter breaks the silence and my brother's eyes snap to mine. Then it pings a few more times in close succession, causing Mike to strain his neck to check the screen. I grab my phone and slide it into the pocket of my jacket, hoping he didn't get a good enough view.

"What's that you're hiding, Kel?" he asks, and I can feel my cheeks flame red.

"Nothing. Just people checking in about tomorrow," I lie.

But it's Hutch who saves the day.

"Nap time," he announces, dropping his plate into the sink. He says goodbye and disappears through the door at the far end of the hall.

"I best get my head down, too. You going to be okay here? Make yourself at home or whatever."

I reassure him I'll be fine, and he disappears into his room, leaving his dirty plate where he was eating. I clean the kitchen up and retreat to the sofa, waiting until a gentle snore emits from my brother's bedroom, telling me it's now safe to check my phone.

John.

Excitement bubbles in the pit of my stomach.

Johnny

Ffordey grins at me as I open the door to my apartment. He steps inside, narrowing his eyes as he assesses my chin.

"Has your beard grown an inch since this morning? I mean, I understand you have to shave every day, but that's ridiculous."

He pushes past me and walks towards my kitchen. Just as I'm about to close the door, Ryan and Danny emerge from their apartment next door, so I hold the door open for them.

I texted the guys after waking up from a nap, rounding them up for pre-game prep. Only three bothered to show up. Ffordey, our starting goalie, is only here for the good coffee. Ryan is here because he's the only other person who cares about the playoffs as much as me, and since he shares with Danny, he was likely dragged along.

"Is it itching yet?" Danny asks as he walks past me, pointing at my beard.

I shut the door and follow them through to the living room. "Hell yeah, but it's a small price to pay."

Honestly, I don't even recognise myself. I only wear a full beard during playoffs for superstitious reasons. It easily adds ten years to my appearance.

"Did you see that message your sister sent, Cap?" Ffordey asks from the kitchen. He rummages in the cupboard before setting a bag of coffee beans on the counter. Moments later, the coffee machine grinds away.

I roll my eyes. "About the sunglasses?"

"Yeah. I mean, it's a bit extreme, right?"

"Nah, it's standard," Ryan says. "In juniors, we always did the playoff glasses tradition. It's just a bit of fun."

"Well, you know Vicky. Anything for the socials," I say.

Later this evening, she'll have uploaded a photo burst, including each guy on the team wearing a pair of sunglasses with the word 'playoffs' written across the lenses. She claims that the fans love it, but I think she wants to make us all look like idiots.

"I still haven't got over the hot wing challenge," Danny says weakly.

"Well, forget about the socials. How are you guys feeling about tonight?"

I know I'm overly passionate, but tonight's game could make or break us. Quarterfinals, leg two. We're drawn one-all, so we need the win tonight—and the good news is, since we got the choice, Coach opted for us to play at home for the second game.

"Fine," Ffordey says, bringing his coffee into the living room, and joining me on the sofa.

"Yeah? Well, I thought we could have a final look at game one," I say, grabbing my notebook.

"Are you sure you want to do that?" Ffordey says.

"Fail to prepare and prepare to fail," I say to an audible groan from my teammates. Except Ryan, who sits next to me.

"We've watched this like twenty times, Cap. We're ready. We've got this," Danny says.

Ffordey extends his legs so he can prop his shoeless feet up on my coffee table. I bat them away. The fucker's got two inches on me and it's all leg. I don't need him snapping my coffee table in two.

"What are you worried about?" Ryan asks.

"We need to be ready, you know? I mean, there are so many things that could happen."

"Yeah, but we don't know how things *will* happen, John. We're familiar with how these guys play—and let's face it, their PK is terrible. We'll draw out a few penalties. Ffordey won't let himself make any silly mistakes. We're good," Ryan says.

"But—"

"Yeah, the last game. I remember. And I take full responsibility for my mistake," Danny says.

"Stop it." I point my finger towards Danny. "That could happen to anyone."

Ryan cranes his neck to look at me. "We out-shot them, John. I just need Scottsy to be playing his best and we'll be fine."

It's evident that Ryan has found the past season difficult. Having transferred from the NHL, his pace of game is a lot quicker than how we play, but he's been working hard with the other winger on his line, Scottsy, to get into a good rhythm. And they've been owning it, in all honesty.

"Let's just chill out," Ffordey says. "Honestly, Cap, you need to take it easy. You'll wind yourself up and that's no good for you."

I know the only reason they came over was to keep me level-headed. If I was on my own, I'd be pacing my apartment, making a visible path on the hardwood floor. I'm trying, I really am, but on game day, I just simmer with energy and determination, and I can't relax. My brain tells me that relaxing is a waste of time. It gives me a rundown of every single thing I could be doing instead.

I press play on the remote control and watch the playback. The guys don't protest. And soon, the only sound in the room is coming from the TV, and Ffordey, slurping his coffee. I glue my eyes to the screen. I'm fully immersed, only breaking eye contact to refer to my notes.

"Pause it a moment," Ryan says from the kitchen. "Hello?"

Ffordey and I shuffle in our seats to look at him. I can tell straight away that it's his twin brother, Liam, on the other end of the phone.

There's half a conversation before Ryan steps towards the sofa and holds his phone out to me.

"Hey bud, what's going on?" I say.

"I've got some news," Liam says.

"Let's hear it—wait, good news? Bad news?"

"Well, I guess it depends on who you are. I expect you'll think it's good news."

"I'm hoping you're going to tell me you've got Ronnie figuring out your contract," I say, praying to whatever hockey god is listening that Liam's agent will finally make headway with his aspiration to join me and Ryan.

"Well, yeah, she's figuring stuff out. On the condition that I find a new agent after this season, but of course, we know that this is my last—"

"You're still going with that line?" I cut him off, because I don't want to hear his crap. At Christmas, he told me he had one season left in him before he was calling it a day.

"Yeah, I am."

"What does your dad think?" I ask.

Liam laughs down the line. "You're forgetting something, Johnny. I'm not Ryan."

He's right, of course. The twins' dad went berserk when Ryan came here to play. But Liam and I are both aware that was purely because of Ryan's elite status in the hockey world. The same rules don't apply to Liam.

"I'll keep you posted. But do me a favour, please, bud? Not a word to Vicky—not until I learn what's happening. For the record, she says she's cool with me coming there, but... yeah."

I agree and then pass the phone back to Ryan, who starts pacing the hallway, his phone to his ear.

"Good news?" Ffordey asks.

"Hopefully we'll get both Preston brothers here next season. But not a word to my sister."

"Well, shit. Then we won't need to watch these replays ever again," he says.

"Of course we will. Preparation is no joke."

"You take yourself too seriously," he says. "But, speaking of preparation, we've got ten minutes until we need to head to the rink."

My phone, Ffordey's, and Danny's all ping in unison. Ffordey grins as he checks his screen.

"Vicky's filming entrances. Better warn Bettsy to put his teeth in." He taps at his screen before sliding his phone back into his pocket.

"Speaking of Bettsy—where the fuck is he? Not like him to miss a beckon from you, Cap," Danny says.

I frown at him. "He said he had another engagement. I mean, he's probably sleeping until he needs to leave."

Ryan strides back into the living room. "Suits on then, boys."

Ten minutes. Ten minutes and here starts what could be the biggest evening of my life. Ten minutes and I'll be readying myself to win.

Chapter 2

Kelly

I can't describe how much I hate hockey. Yet here I am, in a crowd of people, all cheering as my brother smashes an opposing forward into the boards. The entire section of plexiglass vibrates with the impact as the guy falls to the ice.

Mike wrists the puck towards one of his teammates, who clears it from the defensive zone before skating towards the bench. Just before he reaches the door, his whole body flies backwards as he's hit from the front.

"Oh, my God," I gasp, covering my eyes. I've seen this happen a thousand times before, but I still hate it. I've watched him pick teeth up from the ice. It's brutal and the whole thing makes me sick with worry.

"Are you okay?" The woman next to me leans in and offers a smile. This must be Lauren.

"Not really," I squeak, letting my hands sink back to my lap. I watch Mike clamber to his skates. He's off the ice in a flash and back on the bench with the rest of his teammates as if nothing happened.

"First time?"

"Sadly not."

"Boyfriend?" she asks.

"Brother," I say.

"Ah, I thought I hadn't seen you before. That's my husband," she says, pointing towards a guy on the ice.

"I hate hockey," I say.

"I sort of understand that," she says. "It's the stench for me. Scott's hands always stink, no matter how hard he scrubs them."

I chuckle. Thankfully, I don't have to smell my brother's hands, but the lingering sweaty-hockey-player aroma is not one anyone can forget.

"Who's your brother?" she asks.

"Mike Betts. But I don't make a habit of coming to his games. I'm just in town for an audition tomorrow and—" I stop talking because I doubt she wants to hear about that.

"Bettsy is hilarious," she laughs. "I didn't realise he had a sister."

Three thousand people let out a sigh of disappointment as our number nineteen's shot hits the crossbar and sails out of play.

"There's two of us. I'm the youngest," I say.

"Well, it's nice to meet you. I'm Lauren."

"Kelly," I say.

"Well, Kelly, I'm sure Bettsy appreciates you coming."

"I told him I wasn't going to, but I felt guilty since it's a big game."

"Of course. It's Scott's last chance at the playoff cup before we move to Germany."

By the time the first period break rolls around, I know all about Lauren's plans to move to Ingolstadt.

"I think someone is already earmarked to take Scott's spot. How well do you know the guys?" She refers to the team, but I shake my head. Mike talks about them at family events, sure, but I've paid no attention to the details. "Well, number nineteen, he's a twin. His brother is likely going to be joining the team."

As we leave our seats, I smile and nod in all the right places whilst she talks, and we follow a small crowd of people towards the bar.

"So, what makes you hate hockey so much?"

"I remember Mike taking this hit that literally knocked him out cold, and it's stuck with me since. I was only a kid and I remember him just lying there, face down on the ice. He was just lying there like he was... dead." I clear my throat, trying to hold back the tears that are desperate to make an appearance. I can't bring myself to tell Lauren the full reason why. "He says it's part of his game, and I know that, but still. I just don't like it."

My brother's a powerful guy. And until that hit, I loved watching him play. I loved the joy and concentration on his face as he soared across the ice. I know all the rules, all the calls, all the play styles—I guess I was obsessed to some degree. But seeing him like that turned it into something I dreaded to watch. I know his 'stay-at-home' defensive style serves a purpose. And his style compliments his defensive pairing—an offensive-defencemen. He says he needs to protect and enable him. He makes it sound like he's his guard dog or something, which is ridiculous.

"I'm sorry you had to see that. That must have been tough."

"Yeah, it was." I swallow down the emotion pushing to the surface.

We grab a beer each and head back to our seats, just as the Zamboni finishes its last lap of the ice.

By the time the teams skate back out for the second period, my single beer has calmed me down enough so I can enjoy the game. I'm not a big drinker, so it goes straight to my head. I sing to the music, joining in the claps and cheers, and I even jump to my feet when we score. It's all good until Mike and the rest of the guys position themselves, ready to take a face-off. He shouts something over to the guy wearing the captain's badge, then indistinguishable words fly back and forth between the pair. The captain shouts and signals across the ice, motioning to someone, and as soon as the face-off is taken, Mike is charging towards the target.

I've seen nothing like it before.

"Why is he spurring him on?" I ask Lauren, splitting my attention between her and the ice.

"It's just part of the game. Try not to worry," she soothes.

But I don't like it. The next moment, Mike gets elbowed in the face as the captain skates off unscathed with the puck. Prick. He should have been the target for that elbow.

To heighten my anxiety, a commotion occurs right against the boards and, of course, my surname flashes into view briefly as the opposing defenceman elbows Mike for a second time and pulls his shirt. The noise of the crowd ramps up as two sets of gloves are dropped. I have to adopt the brace position, practically folded in half on my seat as queasiness washes over me. I can't watch.

"He's fine, he's fine," Lauren says. "I'll tell you when you can look."

Everyone around me gets to their feet. The music starts and cheers erupt from the spectators. I stay in my seat until Lauren flicks her chair back down and sits again.

"Is he okay?" I ask.

"Yeah, he's fine. I think he'll get a major for that, though. But he's got the energy going."

"I don't think I can stay," I say, defeated. The happy, post-beer sensation I had less than five minutes before has vanished.

I take the opportunity to thank Lauren for being so friendly before I grab my bag and squeeze out of my row, scrambling up the steps towards the upper-level lobby, which opens out into a large area with banners and memorabilia scattered around.

I'm just catching my breath when I glance up and double-take the eight-foot banner draped overhead. An action shot of the captain celebrating. It hits me square in the chest.

Oh my God.

John.

No. Not John. Johnny. Johnny Koenig. The same guy I've heard Mike refer to as 'Cap' a hundred times.

Confusion sets in after a full minute of standing there, mouth wide open. I reach for my phone and pull up the message thread I've got with John. We've been chatting on an app for almost three months now, and we've exchanged a few photos.

I pull up the most recent picture from three weeks ago and compare it with the banner overhead. The same blue eyes and unmistakable jawline. He's wearing a helmet in the banner, but I can tell it's the same dirty blond hair, freshly cut in the photo.

Fuck. I'm being catfished.

Shame sets in next, and my skin prickles with heat. Part of me wants to message him and demand to know who the hell he is. Because I deserve to know who I've shared intimate details of my life with. I deserve to know who I've confided in about my anxiety over my music career. I deserve to know who I've been flirting with. And I definitely deserve to know who I've talked to about Jeremy.

I blink away the tears as I hold down the icon for the app and tap the little 'x' next to it in an attempt to erase it all.

Because I'm too embarrassed to call this stranger out.

Johnny

I CAN'T FUCKING BELIEVE it. Now, of all times.

My jaw hits the ice as I watch my second line centre get carted to the box by the stripes.

"How can you say that was a hook?" I ask, tapping my stick on the ice.

"I call what I see. He's got two minutes," the ref says, dismissing me with a wave of his hand as he turns away.

I let out a groan. "But it doesn't make any sense," I say, trying my luck. "There wasn't any contact."

He spins on his skates and faces me. "Fifty-six," he yells. "Get your ass back to your bench or you can join him."

Well, shit. A fucking ridiculous call if you ask me—and the crowd, booing in protest. We're in the last minute of play with a score of 2-to-1 in our favour. I can't afford for us to be three on five, now of all times.

I skate back to the bench, stepping in through the door that Springy, the assistant coach, holds open for me. He pats my shoulder as I sit down and says something in my ear, which I don't catch. All my effort is focused on not breaking my twig. My fingers flex against the carbon fiber, but I take a breath as I run myself through five things I can see, four things I can touch—I don't get much further before I'm drawn back into the game.

We just need to win this face-off and get the puck back to the neutral zone. I know it, the guys know it, and most of all, the fans know it. The entire crowd is on their feet now as the referee sets up for the face-off, and I lean forward to get a better view, resting my elbows on the shelf in front of me.

My own damn heartbeat drowns out the noise from the rink, and as soon as the puck is dropped, I let out a low whistle in relief as Hutch, one of our wingers, receives it.

"Yes, boys," I yell, shifting my gaze between the jumbotron and the ice.

I want to watch, but I also don't want to either. As much as I trust the guys, this is fucking terrifying.

40 seconds.

The puck sails toward Jonesy, the second line defenceman who plays left. He passes it back to Hutch, who does a figure of eight in the neutral zone before he saucer-passes it to Danny.

32 seconds.

Danny skates with the puck for a few seconds, narrowly avoiding a poke check from an opposing forward before he backhands the puck back to Jonesy. They pass it between themselves a few times, moving back toward our defensive zone.

25 seconds.

Jonesy trails the puck along to the defensive zone, skating to the back of the net and hovering behind Ffordey, our starting goalie.

20 seconds.

He leaves the puck, and his defensive pair picks it up. They both hastily skate forward, but just after they cross the blue line, Jonesy gets checked, and the puck sails free.

15 seconds.

There's a scramble for it against the boards on the opposite side of the ice, and I hear Jonesy calling for Hutch to get his stick in.

10 seconds.

I think it's Hutch who gets the biscuit, but before I can fully comprehend what's going on, their number twenty-three comes skating out of the huddle, the puck on the end of his stick as he powers towards Ffordey.

5 seconds.

The next thing I know, Ffordey's dropping to the ice as he dives for the puck, taking care not to let it slip past him as the buzzer sounds.

0 seconds.

We did it. We've made the playoff finals.

Swinging my legs over the boards, I hit the ice, tossing my helmet and gloves behind me. I don't give a single shit where they go today—and my stick? Fuck it. Anyone can touch it. The whole team crowds around Ffordey as we jump up and down on the ice. The crowd is almost deafening, and music plays out through the speakers, only elating us further.

"We fucking did it," Bettsy screams in my ear. And I pull him into a hug, just as another set of arms wrap around me.

"This is all thanks to you, Prez," I shout, trying to project my voice toward Ryan. We've been friends since we were kids, and playing with him this past season has meant we've been able to power ahead and secure more wins with his experience.

We've still got the playoff semi-finals to go, but getting to the playoff weekend was such a fucking dream. Just four teams heading to the finals. I'd been trying to get this far since I arrived here, and now we've finally done it.

I round the guys up, signalling for us to do a victory lap ahead of the 'Man of the Match' awards, but protocol is abandoned this evening with all the excitement.

We group together, some guys tossing their excess gear to the ice before we skate around to the benches, showing our appreciation to the support staff first, before we turn our attention to the crowd.

It's loud. And I'm on top of the fucking world. But only for the time we take to complete a full lap of the ice. Once we're back at the benches, I've got that knot of dread tight in my chest. And when I spot Prez, pulling his girlfriend Jenna up into the air as her hands wind around his neck—jealousy. Would Kelly come to my games and support me like Jenna does Ryan? Christ. I haven't even met her in person yet, and I'm already fabricating scenarios. Besides, she doesn't even know I play hockey—what if she hates it? I should probably drop that into the conversation soon.

I stop where my sister stands, her camera up to her face as she looks through the viewfinder. I can tell she's snapping pictures, so I give her a few photo opportunities before she drops the camera. She's beaming. At least she's here for me.

"Well done, Johnny. You guys were awesome," she says. "How do you feel?" An expectant look crosses her face, but then her smile drops. "Give yourself this evening to celebrate your win. Then you can go back to being 'serious Johnny', right?" She walks toward the door, pushing it open so she can step onto the ice.

There's talking over the loudspeaker, but I can't make out a word of it. Between the crowd and the guys chatting excitedly around me—I'm struggling to focus. It's only when Vicky beckons me with her hand, and a kid no older than ten steps tentatively onto the ice, that I realise I need to present my jersey to tonight's 'Shirt Off His Back' winner.

"What's your name, kid?" I say, dropping to my knee and holding my sweater out in front of us.

His mouth drops open as if he's trying to speak, but Vicky's call to look at her pulls his attention away.

"Smile," she sings, clicking her fingers above her head to get him to focus on her. We both pose, then I hand my jersey over, patting him on the shoulder as he steps off the ice.

Once the rest of the match night awards have been dished out, Vicky disappears, leaving me and the guys to clear the ice, with a little help from the equipment guys.

We file towards the dressing room, our spirits high. Bettsy sings 'We Are The Champions,' and most of the team joins in, but I can't bring myself to. Not yet. Not when we've still got games to play and games to win.

"I can't even say that was a challenge," says Danny, collapsing in his cubby.

I sit down in my spot and grab a towel, rubbing it over my head before leaving it draped over my neck. I listen to the guys chat as I get to work unlacing my skates.

I clear my throat as I stand up, looking around at the guys now, all of them beaming. "The hard work starts now, boys," I say, looking around the dressing room. "I don't need to tell you I've been waiting for this moment for a long fucking time. If we can beat these guys, then we can sure as hell make it to the final."

A chorus of cheers erupts around the dressing room just as the door swings open. Coach strides in, followed by Springy, the assistant coach. They stop just before they reach the team logo in the middle of the room. Coach's face is stony—hard, even. His mouth is fixed in a straight line as if he's about to deliver bad news, and everyone's holding in a breath as we wait. But his face breaks into a wide smile.

"We did it, boys. We did it." He claps his hands together and beams around the room as everyone feels at ease enough to breathe again. "But don't let their shit performance fool you into a false sense of security. Before anyone asks, I'm not saying you didn't deserve that 'W,' because you did, but they didn't play like they usually do. We've got a mountain to climb yet." He pauses, taking his baseball cap from his head and spinning it on his finger before continuing. "Rest up tomorrow. It's been a busy weekend. Do some dry land or research, whatever, but on Tuesday we go hard." Coach sets his hat back on his head. "Now hit the showers. It fucking stinks in here." He paces out of the room, chuckling to himself.

Bettsy strides over to the stereo and turns the volume up, forcing almost everyone to join in the singing.

"Come on, Cap. Join in, won't you?" He moves right next to me so I can hear him over the noise.

"Nah. I'm going to hit the shower," I say, getting out of my gear.

"Yeah, but we can celebrate a little."

"We're only past the first hurdle, Betts. Now is not the time to get excited."

"What did Coach say, John? Tomorrow—" Bettsy begins.

"Tomorrow—my place at 8am. We're going to watch old games and get as ready as we can be," I say, grabbing another towel.

There's no way anyone is slacking off now. I pull out my notebook from my gear bag and make a note of our score and my plus/minus before slipping it back into the pocket it came from.

Bettsy catches my eyes before I can turn away, his face set in a deep frown, as if he's been told Santa wasn't coming. "Fine," I sigh. Then, readying my voice, I shout into the room. "Anyone up for a game of poker?"

Chapter 3

Kelly

AFTER WANDERING THROUGH THE city for the past hour, I return to my brother's apartment, letting the tears flow as soon as the door is closed.

I don't even bother to turn the light on, hiding my shame in the darkness of the empty hallway. I slump down to the floor and hug my knees to my chest, letting go completely. How many hours did I spend talking to him? Or her. It could literally be anyone.

Through blurry eyes, I download the app again, carefully tapping in my username and password, sighing with relief when the conversation history loads. There must be something here showing this guy is a fraud.

I spend ages scrolling right to the top, to the start of our conversation, based on a post I'd put up. It had been a desperate plea after receiving my sixth dick pic of the day. I should've deleted the app right then.

"Are guys only on here for one thing?"

Him

No, we're not.

Me

I've had so many dick pics today and I'm not okay!

Him

I can safely say I've never sent a dick pic in my entire life.

Me

Ha. Well, that's actually refreshing to hear.

Him

Granted, I don't know the etiquette of this app yet. It's my first time.

Me

I definitely wouldn't go around telling people that. People will take advantage of you.

Him

Like penis related advantage?

Me

Exactly that. What are you here for, then?

Him

Honestly, I don't know. Conversation, I guess. You?

Me

Same. Obviously, it's not been a success. I'm close to uninstalling.

Him

But I have so much to offer.

Me

Oh God, you're going to send me a dick pic now, aren't you?

Him

Haha, no. I'd set the bar too high.

Me

You couldn't see, but I just rolled my eyes.

Him

I could sense it, don't worry.

Me

Sense it? That's very intuitive of you.

Him

Well, apparently, you're less than ten miles away, so maybe I could feel the eye-rolling in the air?

Me

Okay, did you hear that laugh you just mustered?

I freeze. That's the red flag. The reddest flag flapping in the internet's wind. I should have seen it. Who even says that? It screams 'fake name'.

I keep scrolling, flicking my eyes past the snippets of conversation.

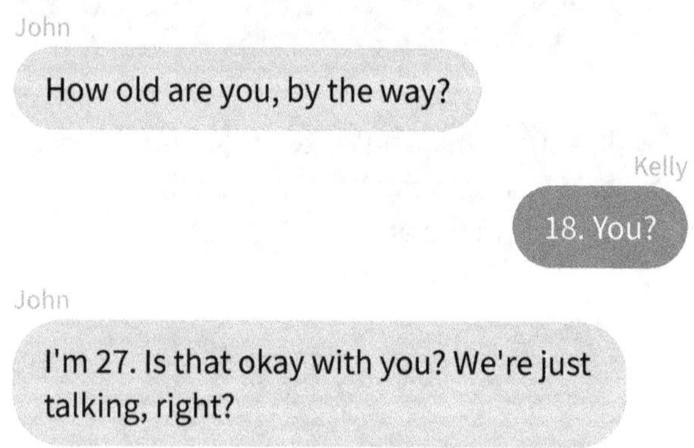

Kelly

It depends. Do you still have all your hair?

John

Ha. Ha. Yes. I do. And I'm confident that male pattern baldness does not run in my family.

Kelly

I think it runs in mine. My brother is definitely thinning on top.

John

Just the one brother?

Kelly

Now, yes. I had an older brother who died when he was my age. And I have a sister who's 3 years older than me.

John

I'm really sorry for your loss. That must have been difficult for you all.

Kelly

It wasn't great. My parents are still convinced that he could have survived. He went on a night out with some friends and fell over drunk in a bar. He whacked his head on the way down and the group of boys he was with just thought he was sleeping and left him outside of his flat.

I didn't really understand what was going on at the time, but then when it clicked that he wasn't ever coming home, I just felt this sadness settle that never properly left. I think that's why I latched on to my other brother so much.

Sorry. You don't need my pity story.

John

Honestly, don't apologise. I'm glad that you feel comfortable enough to talk to me. I am really sorry that your family went through that.

Kelly

Thanks, John. Do you have any siblings?

John

One sister. She's a year younger than me and we're probably more alike than we care to admit. Though she's much more outgoing than me. We get on most of the time.

Kelly

It's difficult being the youngest. You should cut her some slack.

John

Trust me. She's hard work.

Kelly

Sounds like my sister, actually. My brother and I sort of feel sorry for her boyfriend, even if he is a complete prick.

John

You know, some men like a woman to take charge.

Kelly

Do you like that sort of thing?

John

Is this bordering on inappropriate?

Kelly

Inappropriate how?

John

Well, you're only 18.

Kelly

Okay, well, if you think you'll put your back out... I understand.

John

Less of the old jokes.

Kelly

Well, I guess even those pushing thirty still need a good time.

Ha. You're funny.

I tell myself enough is enough when the flirting starts, because it's embarrassing to re-read, even more so when I'm so unclear about who I was flirting with.

I stalk the real Johnny Koenig's social media next, and it only takes me a few minutes to find all three of the photos *you can call me John'* sent me.

There's that one of him in a ball cap, fitted T-shirt hugging his chest, which is clearly the chest of someone who works out a lot. One of him at a driving range, not particularly posed or anything, but he knows someone's taking the photo. And the third photo of him with a cat. A standard picture, I guess, to show that you're a 'nice guy' who loves animals. Of course, there are loads of photos he hadn't shared with me, mostly hockey. And a note at the top saying it's an account managed by '@vkphotography'.

I close it down as I catch someone fumbling with the lock on the door. Scrambling to my feet, I move in time to see the door creak open and Mike's head peer at me by the light of the corridor.

"Kel? What are you doing in the dark?" he says, hitting the light switch. It's so bright I have to cover my eyes, but I'm not quick enough to hide that I've been crying. "What's going on?"

I step aside to let Mike through, and he dumps his gear down on the floor before studying my face.

"I'm just excited that you won your game." I take a punt, considering he looks relatively happy.

"Bullshit. You don't give a shit about that. What's going on?"

I hesitate for a moment, wondering if I should come clean and tell him I've been deep in conversation with someone who's been pretending to be the captain of his hockey team, but it sounds completely ridiculous, so I opt for another explanation.

"I'm just nervous about my audition tomorrow," I lie. "And I have a confession. I came to your game and saw that hit. I'm done with hockey, Mike."

To my relief, his eyebrows relax, and he pulls me into a hug.

"Ah, you'll be fine. And I'm fine. Look at me. Hey, want to come up and play some cards with the boys? We're having a little celebration thing. Johnny's a stickler for the rules, but he's relaxing them for tonight since we're practically champions."

I have to stifle a yelp at the mention of Johnny's name. But Mike takes my reaction another way, thank God.

"No need to panic. I know they can be a bit much... but they understand you're off-limits."

I roll my eyes. "Actually, I think I'll get an early night after I have a quick play-through." I move into the apartment and grab my cello, a little too eagerly, but Mike shrugs and tells me he'll see me later.

Once he's gone, I set my cello back down and slump onto the sofa, because there's no way in hell I can concentrate right now. My whole body is tense, so I dig some headphones out of my overnight bag and settle them over my ears, desperate to zone out.

I get through one track before my phone starts ringing, Tom's name flashing up on the screen, and he knows straight away that something is up when I answer.

"What's wrong and don't lie to me," he says, his tone flat.

"I'm really anxious about tomorrow," I say. Even though I know, deep down, that if there's anyone I could confide in, it's Tom. We've shared a music stand since we started at the university last year, but I can't bear the thought of anyone else knowing how foolish I'd been.

"Well, you don't need to be. Obviously, I want you to do terribly because I don't want you to leave me, but—"

"How was the rehearsal?" I cut him off, hoping to distract him.

And it works. I let him ramble on and on, listening intently as he talks. Except, after he wishes me good luck and hangs up, Johnny's back on my mind and the sadness takes over again.

Johnny

I'M A LIAR.

"I swear to God, if you have the three of clubs, I'll be pissed." Ryan drums his fingers on the impromptu table he and Danny have set up in their living room. He furrows his brow and studies the flop. The three cards on the table made everyone groan when they were dealt, except for me. I know how to keep a straight face.

"I've told you before, Prez. You'll have to pay to see my cards."

I flick my eyes down at my hand and then back up at him, letting a smirk form on my face. Watching him squirm under the uncertainty of the cards I'm holding is priceless. I love how irate he gets.

"Fine. Check," he says, tapping the table.

"Check," Bettsy says.

"Check," Danny agrees.

"Oh hell, no," Ffordey says, reaching for his pile of chips. He plucks two from the top and tosses them towards the centre of the table. "I call."

"I raise," I say, adding to the stash.

"Nah, I fold," Hutch says, sliding his cards away.

"What you going to do, Ryan?" I tease.

Everyone swivels their heads in his direction, waiting for his next move. He peers down at his hand again then back to the flop—as if the cards may spontaneously change if he wills them hard enough.

We're all still in our post-game suits, shirt sleeves rolled up. Ryan fidgets with the knot of his tie before letting out an exaggerated sigh. He flings his cards towards the ones Hutch abandoned a moment earlier. Then Bettsy and Danny follow.

There's only me and Ffordey left.

Ffordey continues his deal, burning the top card in the deck before flipping over the turn card. "Shit. It's the four," he says.

The room goes silent. Everyone's eyes are on me. It's my turn to play and I reach for my chips, stopping halfway as Ffordey pushes his chair back.

"I'm done," he says.

I scrape the chips towards me and set my cards down on the table.

"So, what did you have?" Ryan asks.

"I told you, Prez. You'll have to pay to see my cards," I say, slapping my hand on the table for effect.

I had fuck all. I probably didn't even have the highest card, but that's how I play.

"Could you imagine if we were playing for real money?" Bettsy says to Ffordey. "Because I know Cap would have cleaned up."

"I live to pay another bill," Ffordey sighs, getting to his feet. "Anyone up for another drink?" He makes his way to the kitchen and starts rummaging through the fridge.

I'm ready to call it a night, deciding to head to the bathroom before I say my official farewell.

Closing the door behind me, I slide the lock into place and pull my phone out, finally getting the chance to check my messages.

Nothing. I collapse down to sit on the edge of the bathtub, checking again just in case.

Yep, nothing.

Instead of sliding my phone away, I start doomscrolling social media, probably out of habit more than anything.

I scroll past it at first, then do a double take, flicking my thumb upwards to revisit the post to check if I saw what I think I saw. Then it clicks into place. It's Sarah's hand. Sarah's hand, with a rock the size of Bettsy's fist, gleaming back at me. Caption: 'I said Yes'.

I swallow hard and wait for that gut-wrenching feeling to surface, but it doesn't. The longer I stare at the photo, the more I will myself to feel something. But nothing comes.

No feelings.

Nothing.

It's as if I'm dead inside.

I don't even know why we're still friends. As I navigate to her profile, my thumb hovers over the 'Remove Friend' button. Counting down, I command myself to do it. To finally cut the cord and remove her for good, but I don't. Instead, I flick through her photos, hoping to see something that draws emotion. Not even a snap of the oh-so-lucky guy entices me.

Nothing. Nada. Zilch.

No feelings, except that of being completely broken, which has been sitting like a heavy weight on my chest for as long as I can remember. The only thing I feel is... interrupted when there's a banging on the bathroom door, followed by a plea to be let in.

With my phone back in my pocket, I take a leak, then wash my hands before heading back out. Hutch is in the hallway, dancing on the spot, but his face drops into a frown when he sees me.

"Did your face not get the memo? You're winning, Johnny. Playoffs, cards—"

I stalk away, uninterested in talking to anyone. Why the fuck don't I feel anything? What's wrong with me?

"I'm calling it a night," I say.

I reach for my jacket, plucking it from the back of my seat. The guys groan and protest, but I'm not in the mood. I wave my hand, dismissing their pleas for 'just one more'. "I'll see you tomorrow," I say solemnly, eyes down towards the floor.

"Nah, c'mon, Johnny. We're off tomorrow. Live a little," Bettsy says, trying to coax me. There's jeering of encouragement behind him, but the last thing I want to do is spend more time with people. I'm all done for the day.

"You finish up here, then take it easy," I say. But the grin on his face tells me he's got other ideas. "I mean it, Betts. We've got shit to do tomorrow, and if I have to drag you out of bed, I'll be pissed."

I head towards the front door of the apartment, only stopping to put my shoes on before slipping out into the hallway. The door closes behind me and I lean against the frame, willing my brain to kick into action and tell me what the hell I should do next.

I check my phone again. Still nothing.

I walk to my apartment door, keen to find a stick I can snap. But as soon as I'm looking for my keys, I change my mind.

Eight flights down, I pull my phone out and order a taxi to pick me up from the fuel station a few streets away. Loitering outside my building probably won't do me any favours if someone spots me. Questions will be asked. Questions I know I won't want to answer. I mean, I don't even know what the fuck I'm doing, but I'm convinced a whisky on the rocks will help.

But the longer I wait for the cab, the more logical my thoughts become. What the hell am I doing? I've got a huge weekend coming up, and I can't afford to be cloudy-headed and hungover.

By the time the cab pulls to a stop in front of me, I can't bring myself to get in. My moral compass has taken over.

"Are you getting in, mate?" the taxi driver says, winding down the window.

"Sorry, I've had a change of plan," I say, handing the driver a twenty.

Defeated, I make the short walk back to my building, swiping in and climbing the stairs, still refusing to get back in the goddamn elevator. Luckily, I don't meet anyone, and before I know it, I'm in my bedroom, stripping down to my underwear and climbing into bed.

I stare at the ceiling for the longest time before reaching for my phone and checking my messages again.

But something's different this time. Not only do I have no new messages, but the entire conversation thread has disappeared. Shit.

At least I'm feeling something—devastation.

An ache forms in my chest, and it grows through my body. What the fuck did I do wrong? I rack my brain, trying to come up with something, anything.

Did I come on too strong? Flirt too much? Perhaps the age gap was a problem, after all. But, shit. There's a stranger walking around this city who knows things about me. Things I've told no one else.

I guess this is more evidence of what a huge fucking failure I am.

Physical dating is one thing, but being rejected on an app after three months? That's something fucking else. I thought we were hitting it off.

But just like that, the conversation has disappeared like it never fucking happened.

Chapter 4

Kelly

"Mike? Is that you?" I peer into the darkness from my makeshift bed on the sofa. Then, without warning, the light in the hallway breaks the darkness and I witness my brother face-planting the floor. "Oh, my... what the hell is going on?" I say, throwing the blanket off my legs and hurrying over.

"Fuck," he groans, rolling onto his side. He pauses before collapsing onto his back.

"How much has he drunk?" I ask Hutch, but he just stares at me, eyes glassy and unfocused.

"Hiya, Kel. Did we wake you?" Mike says. I study the huge grin plastered across his face.

"Do I need to put you to bed?" I ask.

"No, I'll be fine right here."

Hutch's face sinks into a frown and he lurches into action, stepping over my brother and practically falling into the bathroom. He aligns his head with the pan of the toilet, just in time for the contents of his stomach to make an appearance.

Shit. I didn't sign up for this.

"Do you think you're going to be sick too, Mike?" I ask. I offer him my hand, and he clasps my palm, pulling himself up into a sitting position. He shuffles himself to lean against the wall.

"No, I need a banana and a pint of water. Maybe two paracetamol, if you can find any."

The classic attempt to avoid hangovers is hit-and-miss, but Dad always insisted on it.

I coax him to his feet and shuffle him into his bedroom, where I lay him down on his side, pull his shoes off, and drape his duvet over him. I draw the line there. There's no way in hell I'm undressing him.

"I'll be right back," I say, slipping out of his bedroom and towards the kitchen. I don't know what Mike and Hutch do in such a circumstance, but I go for the classic solution of emptying the washing-up bowl and grabbing a tea towel. There are a few bananas on the worktop, so I take one, along with a bottle of water and a blister pack of painkillers I find in the cupboard.

The moon illuminates Mike's bedroom, which makes him appear even paler than he normally is, and there's a bruise forming under his eye from tonight's game. Setting the items down on the floor next to his bed, I check he's breathing before backing away.

"Kel?"

"Yeah?"

"Kel. I need to tell you something," Mike slurs. "Are you listening?"

"Yes, I'm right here," I say.

"Kel, you understand I'm proud of you, right? You'll be fucking brilliant tomorrow. I wish I could come and see it." He ends the sentence with a 'woo,' and hiccups loudly.

"Uh, thanks."

Christ, he must be drunk. He's never, in my entire life, paid me a compliment. Nor has he ever seen me play outside of our childhood home, and even then, he used to complain about it. I turn to leave again, but Mike's voice stops me in my tracks.

"Kel?"

"Yeah?"

"I love you."

The snoring starts after that. And once I make sure he's still lying on his side, I leave the door ajar so I can listen out for him.

"It was the pizza," Hutch says from the bathroom. His cheek rests on the toilet rim, arms clutching the porcelain for dear life.

"Can I get you anything?"

"It needs to come out," he says. "It was that pizza we had, Kelly. Someone ordered a pizza, and it must have been bad. The cheese. It must have been the cheese."

I wince as he vomits. I haven't long met the guy and I'm standing here in my pyjamas watching him puke, with no clue how I can help him.

"Are you okay?" I ask.

But he gags again, and I take that as my cue to leave, heading back to my makeshift bed to settle myself down for a night of terrible sleep.

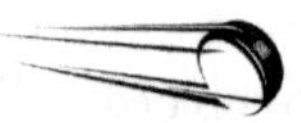

THERE'S A BANGING ON the door that jolts me awake. It's an 'I'm pissed off' sort of banging that grows louder and firmer with every knock. It takes me a few moments to realise where I am and what I'm doing here. My back aches and I struggle to sit up, so I roll over and hug my pillow, willing myself to move.

Then the shouting starts. I can't make it out, but there's a scrambling from the hallway and then I hear the door fling open.

Footsteps.

"Ah, shit," Hutch says, then my brother's name is called out in a yell. "Betts? Johnny's here."

My heart virtually stops in my chest. I lay perfectly still, hoping he doesn't move any further into the apartment. I mean, it wouldn't make any difference if he did see me here. It's not like he knows me. But the shame sits heavy in my chest.

"Fuck's sake. What did I tell you?" A deep and authoritative voice causes my skin to prickle. Is he talking with an accent? I can't quite tell.

"What's the shouting for?" Mike's voice this time.

Then there are more footsteps.

"I told you we had an early start. How much did you guys drink last night?"

Canadian, I think, by the sound of the vowels. But I'm not a linguist, so I can't be sure.

"Yeah, yeah, we're coming," Hutch says, then more footsteps ring out, as if someone's moving further into the apartment, and my heart picks up speed.

"Nah, no way are you coming upstairs like that. You have dried puke on your face. Take a damn shower."

"Hey, calm down, Cap. We just had a bit of fun and—"

"I knew I couldn't trust you," Johnny says.

More footsteps, then my brother speaks again, his voice closer this time. "Do you want a coffee or something?"

"No, I don't want a damn coffee—" That's when the ranting starts. Back-and-forth between Johnny and my brother. It's as if Mike has played outside too late and Dad is telling him off.

Who is this guy? I get he's the team captain, but what right does he have to barge in here and shout at the guys? I guess it's a good thing that this Johnny isn't the same person I was speaking with, because he's a complete dick.

"You need to chill," Mike says firmly.

"You need to realise what's at stake here—because we sure as hell aren't going to win with the way you guys are acting. You're not just letting yourself down, you're letting the whole team down."

I can almost feel Mike wincing at that one. The words cut through the air, but Mike snaps back straight away.

"It was one night."

"Save it, Betts. Just get your shit together and get your ass upstairs. Pronto," Johnny says.

A few seconds later, footsteps retreat, and the front door slams.

I sit up, looking over the sofa to see Mike in the kitchen. His eyes widen when he catches sight of me.

"Sorry, Kel. I forgot you were here. Don't mind Johnny. He's wound up at the moment. I hope he didn't wake you up."

I get up from the sofa. "Does he always talk to you like that? Because he sounds like a dick."

"Nah, he's fine—look, I need to get going, but good luck today. Text me later and let me know how you do."

Grabbing his mug, he heads back into his bedroom, disappearing out of view.

"Why do I get the impression you're more pissed off than usual?" Ffordey takes a seat next to me on the sofa. The entire team, except for Bettsy and Hutch, cram into my living room, occupying every inch of seating available. Thank Christ we're all freshly showered.

"The usual," I say. My notebook rests on the coffee table in front of me and I reach for it, using it as a distraction.

"Nah, Ffordey's right. Is it Betts and Hutch?" Danny says.

What am I supposed to say? I'm pissed that someone I was chatting with online has disappeared off the face of the earth? I shouldn't be the slightest bit emotionally invested, but I thought we were getting along okay. Age difference aside, we chatted, and we were flirting and stuff. And our conversations were a place where I didn't have to be Johnny the Captain, Johnny the Defenceman, Johnny the Big Brother, Johnny the Failure of a Son.

They were a place where I could be myself.

"I'm fine. Can we get going, please? We've got a lot to cover." I reach for the remote, but before I press play, there's a buzz at the front door.

Someone shouts that they'll get it, and I expect it to be the stragglers, but my sister's chirpy tone fills the air and I groan inwardly.

"Does Coach know you're doing this?" she says, pushing her way through the crowd and coming to a stop behind me. "I'm pretty sure he's keen for you guys to rest."

"What do you want, Vicky?" I crane my neck to look at her.

"Can I have a quick word—in private?" she says.

"Can it wait?"

"It'll only take a moment," she says.

I hand Ffordey the remote and stand up, making my way towards the hallway where there's enough space to talk.

"I've been wondering if I should mention it or not, but I've been thinking about it and—"

"Just spit it out, Vic, we've got a shit-tonne to get through today."

"Right, sure. I saw Sarah post online that she's engaged. I was adding a new post to your socials, and I didn't realise you were still following her. I didn't want you seeing it and..."

Well, shit. Of course, Vicky would see.

"Thanks for telling me," I say.

"That's it?" Her voice flicks to a pitch at least three levels higher than usual.

"That's it."

"Johnny. You can't be serious." Her eyebrows pop upward.

I don't know what to say to her. I'm completely done feeling anything for that woman after all she put me through. And with a rested head, I make the decision I should have arrived at last night.

"Do me a favour, remove her from my feeds, and never utter her name again."

Vicky steps forward and places her hand on my arm. "It's okay. I mean, I can contact him and tell him what she's—"

"Vicky. Promise me you'll forget all about it and leave this the hell alone." I raise my voice this time, my captain's tone coming into use outside of the dressing room. She knows I mean business, and she knows I sure as hell won't back down.

"Okay. I promise."

"Good. Now I need to—"

"Oh, and I've booked you a spot on the radio. You're doing a fan call in and it's all set for Wednesday."

I scowl at her, but her face breaks into a smile. She's loving every minute of this. I understand it's part of the deal, and this week will be about drumming up the excitement for the fans too. I tell her to text me the details and turn to walk away, just as Bettsy and Hutch decide to show up.

"Oh, now the full party is here… do you mind if I hang back and take some photos for socials?" Vicky's teeth gleam at me and I stare at her, unblinking. "Okay, another time then? Bye, boys."

Vicky departs, leaving me alone with Bettsy and Hutch.

"Johnny—look, I'm sorry about earlier, but my sister is here and—"

"Honestly, Betts. Save it. Because I don't give a shit about your sister, but I know she wasn't handing you shots last night." I meet his eyes, softening my tone. "Please tell me you've got it out of your system and you're fully invested, because I need you, bud."

Bettsy locks eyes with me and nods. I know it. He knows it. Our synergy is crucial.

We head back into the living area, and I'm relieved to see that Ryan has taken the wheel. He's standing next to the TV, pointing at something, then rewinding the video.

"This guy," he says, jabbing his finger towards a familiar face on the screen. I'd say half of the room let out groans of disapproval. "Have you noticed how much further forward he is when he plays the puck back to the neutral? It's a risk he's taking, but we need to make sure he's cut off at every single opportunity. They've got at least three breakaways this season from that play alone."

It's times like these where my feelings are conflicted. Because Ryan delivers this stuff so well, maybe Sarah was right all along. Perhaps I'm not the right guy to be wearing the 'C'. Ryan's got his shit together. He's in love, he's got hockey, and I highly doubt he has to have a weekly therapy session to keep his anger under control.

Ffordey nudges my arm. "Cap?"

I take a breath. "Yeah, Prez knows what he's talking about. Let's consider how we can keep him in our focus."

Ryan winks, then hands me the remote control as if it's a talisman. I peer around at the faces of my teammates, all looking at me expectantly. But the truth is, they already know everything I can show and tell them.

Instead of resuming the playback, I toss the remote onto the coffee table. "Let's sack this off and hit the range. Because we're ready."

Cheers and enthusiastic chatter fills the room and the guys gather their things.

"You okay, bud?" Prez makes a beeline for me.

"Yeah, I'm fine."

He can see right through me. His expression hardens, but to my relief, he misses the mark. "We've got this, Johnny. Scottsy and I are on fucking fire. Don't worry about it."

"Yeah, I know, but it's been such a build-up."

It's not a lie, except we're not talking about the same thing.

Chapter 5

Kelly

My emotions are in turmoil. I don't know how I'll get through the next two hours. I lied to my mother this morning when she called to check in. I'm not chilled. In fact, I'm so far from chilled I'm lava and it's all my fault. My concentration is at an all-time low because I'm repeating the carnage of yesterday over and over in my mind. Top it off with a horrible night of broken sleep, and it's a whole shit show waiting to happen.

I arrive at the music college in time to freshen up. Then I wait in the auditorium lobby until my name is called, before walking through to yet another waiting room. This time, there are six more wannabe students lined up in seats against the wall with an assortment of instruments. I believe I'm the only cellist. Is this a good sign? How many spots do they have?

Before I can over-analyse the situation more than I already have, I pull my phone out, seeing a flurry of messages wishing me luck for today, but I don't get a chance to reply. A door opens in the distance, and a woman with a clipboard calls my name, gesturing for me to follow.

I grab my instrument and follow her through to the auditorium, where I'm greeted by four stern-looking assessors sitting behind a long table.

This is when my nerves fully hit.

I'm shaking as I unpack my cello, taking care to haul my bow out of the case without snagging the hairs. I give it four turns on the screw to tighten it before I take a deep breath.

"We will give you a few moments to set up before we get started." I notice the name plates sitting in front of each assessor and skim over them, trying to commit them to memory. "When you're ready, come and sit here and we'll get the interview underway." Dr Robertson, the woman who called me through, points at a chair practically sat under a spotlight.

I set my scores out on the music stand, lay my cello on its side, and make my way over to the chair.

Everyone is staring at me.

Staring.

Eyes burning into my soul.

"Why don't you start by telling us a bit about yourself? Why would you like to study here?"

A trick question, of course. I know from asking around that they literally just want your name and how long you've been playing for. They aren't even interested in where you're from or what your qualifications are. They know all that.

I take a moment before replying.

"I'm Kelly. I've played the cello for eleven years, switching from the violin at age seven."

Blank faces stare back at me. But I really have nothing to lose. I either get in, or I don't. If I do, happy days, dream come true, yippee. If I don't, Plan B. Which is still a viable plan—staying in the university and studying music there, except the course doesn't carry the same amount of prestige.

I clear my throat before continuing.

"I am interested in studying here because of the college's distinguished reputation as a world-leading institution in music education. The talent that has emerged from here has influenced my journey as a musician, and I am eager to immerse myself in this inspiring environment.

"The college is all about nurturing artistic excellence and inspiring creativity and innovation, which is exciting. The chance to be instructed by highly esteemed faculty members, who excel both as performers and educators, is an incredibly appealing prospect for me. Their expertise and mentorship will undoubtedly shape my musical progress."

How I manage to drone on for a few more minutes, is anyone's guess. I talk about the varying range of programs and resources, how I want to make myself a better soloist and group musician, blah blah blah. I'm pretty sure I even mention the state-of-the-art facilities. Standard jargon that I've been half-coached to say by my music teacher and the course director, Patrick.

And I don't stop there.

"Beyond academics, I am impressed by the sense of community and camaraderie that encompasses the college." I pause, shifting in my seat before continuing. "The opportunity to collaborate with musicians from different countries, exchange ideas, and push the boundaries of artistic expression is appealing. Ultimately, my goal is not only to become a proficient musician, but to contribute meaningfully to the world of music."

What am I even saying? I hope and pray that I'll never have to hear that played back because it was pure and utter cringe. But, moving on. I smile to signal that my speech has ended. All four of the assessors nod approvingly and take a few moments to scribble in their notebooks, which is when the panic creeps back.

Did I say enough? Did I say too much? Is my accent too strong? Did they even understand what I was saying? My palms sweat.

"Kelly? Would you mind telling us about which composers and pieces hold importance to you?"

I have an answer lined up: *'Tchaikovsky's Pezzo Capriccioso holds a significant appeal to me. It demonstrates an intense showcase of the cello's technical prowess.'*

That's what I should have said. I had rehearsed this answer repeatedly. But, of course, I say something completely off-plan.

"Dvořák's Cello Concerto in B minor is great."

I experience a wave of despair. I can't believe I just said that. Describing Dvořák's cello concerto as 'great' is blasphemy. If I could, I would slump down in my chair, but years and years of sitting with a straight back has waived any chance of me slouching. I still have lingering memories of my first cello teacher sitting behind me with a sharp pencil pointed at my lower back. Any slouch, even just a minor amount, would result in a sharp poke. It only took a few weeks to condition me.

Assessor number two looks at me with raised brows, so I dig deep to redeem myself.

"Shostakovich shows a high emotional integrity with his concertos."

Shit. Another crap answer, which doesn't help in the slightest. But I have a feeling that was my last chance.

"Let's move on, shall we?"

And that was that.

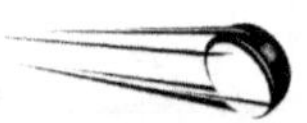

TOM MEETS ME BACK in my dorm room a few hours later. He's let himself in and is sitting on the end of my bed, flicking through a magazine, which he tosses aside as soon as I flop down on my bed.

"Do I need to ask?"

"I referred to Dvořák's Cello Concerto in B minor as 'great,'" I groan into my pillow.

He doesn't say anything. He doesn't need to. The sharp intake of breath he draws in is enough to validate that it was a completely ridiculous thing to say.

"And I droned on about camaraderie and crap."

"Oh, shit. Well, I'm sure they won't even take notice of that."

I crane my head to look at him. "I'm not talking about it anymore."

Tom pushes his glasses up his nose and leans closer. "The others will be back soon. Let's go for drinks."

"Can't. I'm working tonight."

"Ah, yeah. Well, I'll go for drinks to commiserate on your behalf."

I nudge him off my bed and climb under the covers, desperate to hide away from the world and pretend like the past twenty-four hours never happened. But after Tom pecks me on the forehead and pulls the curtains closed like the best friend he is, all I can think about is John. Because if we were still chatting, I would have told him all about it and he'd say the right thing to brighten my mood.

And that memory alone has me bawling into my pillow.

Johnny

WE SPENT ALMOST ALL day at the driving range before piling into our cars. I drove mine so I wouldn't have to be seen in Ryan's team-branded Ford; even on this side of the city, it attracts unwanted attention. I slide behind the wheel, waiting for Prez to ride shotgun and for Bettsy, Danny, and Hutch to pile into the back.

"Ffordey and Jonesy are going to shoot some pool. I told them we're in." Ryan tugs the passenger door closed and pulls on his seat belt. "Is it alright if Jen comes along too?" There's a shuffling from the backseat as Danny wrestles with his own belt. "She's not bringing anyone else," Ryan says, probably for Danny's sake.

Danny and Jen's friend Becca were hooking up for a while at the start of the season, but from what I gather, it's over.

"I was going to hit the gym," I say. "But I can drop you off before heading home."

Ryan chuckles. "You're not getting out of this, bud. You can do that later. Take a left at the lights." He taps the console and I pull out of the parking lot as we follow Jonesy's car.

"Hey, did anyone notice the rookie's shot today? It's definitely improved. I mean, for a D-man, he could have taken the last few swings blindfolded." Hutch leans forward, resting his elbows on his knees. Even with a large backseat, three guys crammed in the back looks ridiculous.

Ryan grins like a proud parent. Ever since Simon Pearce, one of the home-grown guys, announced his imminent retirement, it's given Coach the chance to call up one of the kids waiting for his chance, and adjust the roster a little bit. Harrison Yates, or as we call him, the kid, the rookie, or 'Yatesy the kid' if he's having a good day. He's sharp and he's got potential.

"I've been helping him with his wrist control," Ryan says.

"I feel for the kid, though. I mean, he'll spend most of the playoffs sitting on the bench. Been there, done that," Danny says.

"Nah, he'll get a few shifts. We've all gotta start somewhere, right?" Bettsy nudges Hutch aside. "Cap, can you drop me off on the corner? I think my sister's working tonight and—"

"You have a sister?" Danny asks.

"Yes, and before you get any ideas, no."

"She's cute," Hutch says.

"Fuck off," Bettsy says. "Whatever anyone is thinking, it ends now. I'm not afraid to break legs."

"Here?" I pull over and put my hazard lights on.

"I'll meet you at the pool hall." Bettsy hops out, closes the door behind him, and rounds the back of the car, heading into a high street supermarket store.

I drive on, taking the next left when Ryan gives me the direction and I pull into a parking lot at the end of the street. Jen's waiting outside the pool hall.

"Hey, Johnny. How are you feeling?" she asks as we approach.

"Why is everyone asking me this?"

"It's just a question," she says, raising an eyebrow.

I appease her, engaging in a little small talk as we head inside.

I've known Jen for a few years, long before Ryan arrived on the scene. And I'd probably consider her a friend. She's good to Ryan, and he's besotted. That's all I could ask for.

We choose a table in the rear. It looks private, but by the time Bettsy joins us twenty minutes later, we've got a small crowd gathered, asking for pictures and autographs. It's exactly what I didn't want to happen today.

It takes right up to our second game of pool before the crowd eases off and we're left to our games. And this match is between me and Prez.

"You're up, bud," I call, chalking my cue. But instead of joining me at the table, he beckons me towards where he and Jen are standing.

"Jen wants to run something by you," he says.

"No, forget about it," Jen says, her cheeks flushing red. "It's a bad idea."

"We should consider it," Prez says, cocking his head towards me. "Vicky and Liam."

My sister and Ryan's twin brother have had this off-and-on relationship for as long as I can remember. Except right now they're off. Very much off. But we're all inwardly worried about how things will be if Liam joins the team next season, all being well.

"What're you thinking, Jen?" I ask.

"Well, it's just a thought," she says, looking between her boyfriend and me. "But forget it." Jen lives with my sister, so she knows how Vicky's mind works.

"No, no. I'm intrigued."

"Well, it's just an idea. If Liam does end up coming here. We all know that he and Vicky will—well, you can guess the rest, but given how stubborn they both are... have you thought of trying out a bit of reverse psychology? All you have to do is lay it on thick that they shouldn't be together. If you both do it, it'll have a greater impact. How do you think Liam will react if you tell him he absolutely shouldn't do something, babe?" She looks at Ryan, already knowing the answer.

"Ha!" Ryan laughs.

"This is my point. Tell him to keep away and he'll be drawn in even more if he's really interested in making things work. It's simple."

I crack a half-smile. "You think Vicky is going to listen to me?"

"No, Johnny. I don't think she will, which is exactly why it's the perfect idea. You tell her she shouldn't go there, throw in a few 'stay away from Vicky' comments to Liam, and leave them to figure it out for themselves."

The more she talks, the more I realise it makes perfect sense, but then again, I'm not one to condone that my sister enters any sort of relationship, especially since theirs was such a mess.

"I think it's best that we keep our noses out," I say.

"Johnny, we both know that Liam's focus will be on Vicky. Even if it's him trying to stay away from her. Yeah, he'll play hockey and give us chances..." Prez frowns. "But you know what I'm saying."

I get it. Liam is a skilful player, and when he's on the ice, he's focused. But as soon as he steps off, it's a completely different matter. The entire world could go to shit around him, but when it comes to Vicky? Well...

"Forget about it for now. Next season is next season. We haven't finished this one yet." I step back to the table and set up the play.

I'm acting like I'm some sort of saint, but my concentration is also being tested at the moment. Because I'm dying to know where the fuck Kelly went and why she's ghosting me.

Chapter 6

Kelly

As I use a kick stool to reach the top shelf, I catch sight of my brother's crew cut, longer on top than it usually is, bobbing up the aisle across from me.

I've worked every single evening, practically begging my manager to give me the extra shifts so I can keep myself occupied. It's been three long days since my audition, and I still haven't got over the embarrassment. It's stuck on repeat in my head, and I cringe at the memory. There's little solace in that I played my pieces well, because the questions overshadow the entire event. I'm in a state of constant worry, and I'm checking my emails every five minutes, just in case.

"Back again?" I ask my brother as he turns into my aisle. "How did you know I was working?"

"You haven't answered any of my calls. I figured I'd just check on my way past."

"Where've you been?" I ask.

"Just came to shoot some pool again after a late practice," Mike says, and I busy myself with shelf-stacking because I cannot be bothered with the shift manager tonight. "I take it you haven't heard anything about your audition, yet?"

I shake my head. I knew he'd ask, but I don't want to talk about it. I was practically forced to replay the whole audition to him when he came in on Monday night. That was after I'd run through it with our parents.

"No." My voice comes out weird, so I clear my throat.

"You okay?" Mike asks.

I nod this time. But I can tell he's not convinced. He gives me a look that I can't read, but not wanting to give him the opportunity to press any further, I change the subject.

"What's up anyway?" I ask, trying to push things along. I doubt he came solely for an update. He could have texted me that.

He absentmindedly picks up a tin of sweetcorn and rolls it in his hands. "We got asked to confirm our ticket requests for the weekend. I told them I need an extra two: one for Mam and Dad, and one for you and Tom, I guess?"

"This weekend?"

"Yes. You promised me, remember?" He sets the tin down amongst the peas and frowns at me.

"Promised?"

"Okay, so you didn't promise, but I said I'd be pissed, and I will be. C'mon, Kel. Mam and Dad are making an effort, and it'll be nice to have people cheering me on."

"You'll have an entire block of fans cheering you on." I step down and replace the sweetcorn, pushing the bitterness towards our parents away. They always attend Mike's big events, but never attend anything for me. "Are you making Stacey go?"

Mike scrunches his nose. "Nah, she'll insist on bringing that clown." That's one thing Mike and I both agree on at least—our sister's fiancé is a dick. "C'mon, Kel... I'll even let you have the better seats for the semifinal."

I know what he's doing. In case they don't make it to the final, I'll at least have got to see him play up close.

"Go away. I'm working." I swat the air as if I'm shooing away a fly.

He doesn't let up. He follows me around the shop floor while I work, nagging me every single step of the way. I enter the aisle leading to the back room, hoping he won't follow me. But before I reach the double swing doors, I'm distracted by a tall figure facing slightly away from me.

Shit. Is that...?

My mouth dries and my whole body buzzes with nerves. My brain screams at me to get the hell out of here.

"Kel? Are you even listening to me?"

"Yes, of course I am. I'm just thinking," I lie, stepping around Mike so I can get a better view of Johnny. I try to act casual as I flick my focus between Mike and the figure behind him.

Johnny adjusts himself so I can see his profile. I'm surprised to see that he's got a beard. It looks thick, but it's neat for what I can only assume is a playoff special. The complete opposite of the bird's nest taking over Mike's face.

Even from this angle, I can see the familiarity in the photos I'd spent so long examining, which is obvious, I guess since they were his pictures. A strong jaw, broad chest that fills the suit he's wearing, and my knees quiver a little when he smiles.

I must force myself to remember that this person isn't *John*. I was talking to the alternate captain, and this is very much the real, fully-fledged captain that could get any woman in the world.

Johnny is standing next to the main entrance, talking to a woman who flicks her hair and giggles as he speaks. He hands her a pen and notebook, and she bursts into laughter, catching Mike's attention.

"Oh my God. I can't go anywhere with him, honestly. J—"

"Okay, I'll come," I say, cutting Mike off and reaching for his arm.

I can't bring myself to stand face-to-face with Johnny. I've never met him before, and Mike will probably introduce me, and I'll turn into the colour of a beetroot and probably keel over and die of embarrassment.

"Really?" Mike asks.

"Yes. But I need to get on."

I hear him call out that he'll text me tomorrow as I disappear into the back room. Without hesitation, I walk towards the freezer door, closing it behind me, and sit on a box of chicken nuggets nearby.

This is all too much. Every presentation I've seen of Johnny has reinforced one thing—I was catfished. The real Johnny has a presence about him; he stands tall, and carries himself with confidence. But his expression stayed stony and guarded, probably as cold as this freezer.

I finish my wallowing, then I head back out to the shop floor, tentatively checking outside the swing doors before stepping out.

The coast is clear. There's no Mike and there's no Johnny. But there is an angry-looking queue of customers forming at the tills.

Johnny

Bettsy's late again. I try calling him, but it goes to voicemail, and there's no word from him on the group chat.

I can't say I'm surprised, since his punctuality leaves a lot to be desired, but for him to be completely unresponsive is new. There's a clock that hangs on the wall above the dressing room door that I keep checking. Every second that ticks further away from eight, the more I nibble my fingernails.

I turn and walk back to my cubby, just as the door to the dressing room opens, and Bettsy fills the doorway as he heaves his gear bag off his shoulder.

"Sorry, mate. I got a fucking parking ticket. Ending up having a fight with a traffic warden. Complete nightmare. Here's a tip for you. Don't park outside the railway station." He wags his finger at me in a warning.

"I'd never park there. It's pickup only," I say, grabbing my gloves.

"Well, I wish you'd told me," he says.

He settles himself in his cubby and is out of his clothes at lightning speed.

"I'm pretty sure it's sign-posted everywhere," I say.

"They should make the signs bigger."

I tell him that the yellow hatchings painted on the road, labelled 'No Parking' are another giveaway, but he's fighting with his underlayer, not listening to anything I'm saying.

"What were you doing there, anyway?"

"Just dropping off a friend."

"A girlfriend?"

"Nah. Someone I had a fumble with last night. Definitely not a girlfriend." He doesn't make eye contact with me as he's suiting up, but I can read him like a book.

"Rochelle?"

He clears his throat and nods once, keeping his eyes low. My immediate thought is to lecture him, ask him what he's playing at. But I know Bettsy, and can tell he's already feeling the judgement, so I drop it, telling him I'll meet him on the ice.

It's just us at the rink, except for the guys up in the office. I sweet-talked Bettsy into coming in thirty minutes early so we could have some quality practice time. All I care about is the upcoming weekend, until I skate past the advert for the university and my mind shifts to Kelly. She's a student, and I wonder if she goes there too.

I circle around and spot Bettsy at the home bench, fixing his gloves, so I skate back to him and hop off the ice to grab my stick.

He reaches into a bucket of pucks, stacking them neatly on the shelf, making an upside-down heart shape. For God's sake. He finishes up before reaching for his own stick, then smashes the stack of pucks towards the ice, causing them to scatter and bounce across the surface.

"You okay, bud?" I ask.

"I'm done with her for good," he says.

I don't know what to say because I'm shit at relationships, even online ones, apparently. Besides, that's assuming you can call whatever he and Rochelle were doing a relationship. She was sleeping with him and at least one other guy; I honestly don't understand why he put up with it.

"If it's meant to be, it'll be," I say.

"Anyway, playoffs," Bettsy says, shrugging.

"Let's get started," I say.

Bettsy and I skate towards the boards at the far end, where the nets have been pushed aside for the Zamboni to finish up. We grab opposite ends of the first net and drag it into place. He slips the peg in his end, and I do mine, then we fix the posts in place.

"How's your cardio been?" I ask.

"Fine. How's yours been?" He wiggles his eyebrows at me.

"How's your cardio, Betts?" I ask again. "I'm not talking about your body count."

"Yeah, that's been fine. Danny and I have been running, and I was thinking about going swimming with you in the mornings. I won't even look at your lane, I promise."

He smirks at me, but the idea of it makes me tetchy. His coming along would likely fuck up my routine and knock my whole day out—I don't think I can deal with it.

"You're good with the running. Liam will probably run with Prez when he gets here. Maybe you can start a group."

"How'd you feel about him coming here? It'll be like you're kids again, I bet. But with better skills. Oh shit..."

I snap my head up and look at him. "What?"

"Him and Vicky. That's going to be a show I'll want tickets for."

"Forget about that. They're done. That's it."

Jen's reverse psychology idea swims to the forefront of my mind, and I consider telling Bettsy, but since he can't keep his trap shut, I decide otherwise.

"It must be so nice to have that with someone though—I mean, they've been together since they were kids. I bet that's..." He trails off and I head towards the blue line.

"Enough. We need to get started. Time is ticking away. Remember, I want to hear you. None of that 'I thought you could read my mind' shit."

"Fine." Bettsy positions the pucks to use as markers before getting into place either side of the spot in the face-off circle.

I stay back at the point, readying myself. He skates backwards and I send him the pass, giving him a verbal cue. He receives it, and circles around the left puck before sending it back my way. As he loops back to complete the figure of eight around the second puck, he calls for the pass and receives it, then he returns it before we switch positions. It's pretty basic, but it gets us started and works well for defensive pairs.

We carry on until we change things up and make use of the net. Bettsy's got a good slap-slot, so we position ourselves so I can keep passing him pucks to one-time into the net, with me calling out his aim as I sail the puck towards him. We're probably only halfway into our session, but a familiar whistle blows from the bench, halting us on the spot.

"My office, Koenig," Coach bellows.

"I guess we're done for now, Betts."

"You better be finding out who's replacing Simon Pearce," Bettsy calls after me, but that's the least of my worries.

I leave my stick, helmet, and gloves on the bench and follow Coach to his door, leaning against the frame while I wait for him to beckon me inside.

"Close the door behind you," he says.

I expect the rest of the guys will be arriving soon, so his request makes me anxious. But I can guess what this is about.

He gestures for me to sit down, so I perch myself on the edge of the chair opposite.

"Talk to me about Liam Preston. Should I trust that he's going to turn up if I tell the GM he can sign the paperwork?"

I've spoken with Liam a few times since he first told me his plans. He seems hell set on coming here, even if it won't be the best idea he's ever had. But since I know how good he can be when he's on form, I give Coach a rundown of his strengths on the ice.

"How's the therapy sessions?" Coach spins the conversation once he's learnt enough about Lee.

"Good. I mean, they're helping."

I know I'm lying to Coach, but the words come out and I can't take them back. Although I want to believe these sessions are helpful, it honestly feels like we're just discussing how terrible my childhood was. Apparently, things have to get worse before they can get better, but I don't believe it.

"I'm glad to hear it. I know you're trying to keep your temper in check, too. These guys are looking up to you, Johnny, and I know you can do it," Coach says. Well, at least he has faith in me. "Anyway, I just wanted to reiterate—yes, this is a big game for you guys, but you've worked hard all season. You need to enjoy it, too. Don't put too much pressure on yourself. Enjoy the moment. Take a breath."

I listen to Coach's speech, trying to let the words sink in, but all I can think about is that I'll be a complete and utter failure if we don't win. A failure like I've always been. Almost good enough.

"You got this, Johnny," he says before dismissing me.

But I'm not convinced.

Chapter 7

Kelly

Tom looks completely ridiculous in his get-up. We're wearing matching 'Betts' jerseys, which Mike dropped off yesterday, but Tom's taken things to another level with the face paint and bobble hat he found in my wardrobe. I mean, I thought he was extreme with the hat, but the team's logo slapped on his cheeks makes his entire ensemble look even more... spirited.

"Where's the bar?" he asks, craning his neck.

I lead the way.

There's a whole rainbow of colour in the rink's atrium, supporters from every single team. Even the ones who didn't make it this far. Some fans proudly display homemade medallions, signifying their allegiance to one of the final four teams.

Tom stops to take a selfie with a mascot before we make our way to our block with our beers and 50/50 tickets.

"What row are we?" Tom asks.

"B."

As agreed, we're here today. Tomorrow, my parents will sit here, and Tom and I are relegated to the top row. It's only a problem if Mike's team make the final.

"Do you think your brother will spot us?"

"I hope not," I say, following Tom down the steps to our row.

It's almost full and we're arriving a little later than I wanted, but Tom insisted on a few beers in the Wetherspoons across the road beforehand.

"Do you think people realise you're his sister? I mean, you really do look alike."

"No, we don't," I say, my jaw dropping.

He lets out an evil laugh and we shuffle into our seats halfway across the row. We're on the left side of the benches.

"Mike's team will be in front of us, so it's very unlikely that he'll spot me."

Famous last words, though, because when the teams finally make it on the ice ten minutes later, Mike looks up at me, flashing me a toothless grin.

"Why didn't you tell me there's so many good-looking men on his team? I mean, I'll take up hockey if it means..."

"Can you even skate?"

"No, but I can learn. Can you?" Tom asks.

"Well, yeah, but only because I played hockey a little when I was a kid."

Tom glares at me. "I'm sorry, I don't buy it."

I roll my eyes, using the remaining warm-up time to give Tom a rundown of my very limited hockey career, which involved playing for twenty minutes on a Sunday afternoon, and watching my brother the rest of the time.

"Well, I still think I should take it up," Tom says, getting to his feet as the buzzer sounds, signalling the end of warm-ups. "I'll get us some more beers."

I fan myself with the programme as Tom leaves, settling my gaze on my brother, who circles the net and joins number fifty-six, Johnny.

There's a nervous energy in my stomach as I watch their conversation as they glide back towards the benches. Mike says something directly into Johnny's ear and he nods, just before his head pops up and he looks me directly in the eyes. He's not that far away, really. One row and then the bench. But there's no mistaking that the gaze he holds is for a second longer than would be expected of someone who's glancing in your general direction. His expression hardens slightly before his eyebrows knit together.

I shiver involuntarily, and a warmth fills my whole body. I stand up quickly, quaking on the spot as I excuse myself to the other fans in my row as I shuffle past them.

"I need to use the bathroom," I say to Tom as I pass him on the steps.

There's a queue, but I join the back, chewing on my fingernails as the line shuffles forward. What did Mike say to him?

I wait until I'm safely in a cubicle to freak out. And once I'm out, I splash my face with water, disregarding my make-up.

I grab two more beers from the concession stand before heading back to my seat, thrusting the plastic pint cup into Tom's hand. Because I'm taking him down with me.

"What's going on?" he asks, accepting it without question.

There's a flurry of activity as skaters take to the ice, a flag representing each team held high and fluttering as they skate. The whole arena comes alive with noise, and the buzz of excitement in the air makes this a unique feeling, different than anything I've experienced before.

"I just fancy a drink. Shall we make a weekend of it?"

"See, this is why we're friends. I just hope to Christ that they don't pan across us when this is on TV."

I swig my beer, hoping the same, because we're both meant to be at rehearsal today, and we made up a story about us both getting hit with the same stomach bug after a meal at a questionable Chinese buffet. Apparently, we're never allowed to dine together again, but we're taking that as a win.

The whole arena erupts in applause as they announce the teams. We stand up and join the cheering, shouting a bit louder when my brother skates on. Honestly, despite my feelings, I am so proud of him, and seeing him out there brings a tear to my eye—or it may be the beer making me emotional. Who knows?

When the guys are out, they skate a few laps of their defensive zones and I catch sight of Johnny again. As if he's planned it, he loops around, and looks toward our block as he raises his stick, stretching his arms out behind him so his chest puffs out.

Then his eyes lock onto mine again.

"Oh my God. Did you see the way he just looked at me?" Tom says, nudging me so hard I fight to keep hold of my beer.

But I didn't. I saw the way he was looking at *me*.

Johnny

For once, my notebook yields zero comfort. Sixty minutes. It all comes down to sixty minutes.

"Boys," Coach's voice cuts through the air, and I automatically stand up from where I'm sitting in my cubby.

"Coach," I say, timed with the rest of the guys.

"Right. I won't drag this out. We all know why we're here, how much work we've put in. There's every chance that we'll be advancing to the finals—and I sure as hell know you deserve it. But of course, hockey is not a predictable sport. Anything could happen, and every second counts." Coach takes a breath and casts his eyes around the room. "Now, we've studied how these guys play, and we know that they're in that other dressing room talking about how good their penalty kill is. They have the best PK in the league—but remember, we have the best damn power play. That being said, I don't want anyone taking stupid penalties." His eyes flick towards Bettsy briefly before he reverts to a neutral gaze. "Discipline. Communication and 99% effort. Every shift," he says. 99% purely because he's convinced there's always room for improvement, but we all read between the lines—we know the deal. "Koenig. You're up."

The number of pre-game speeches I've delivered hasn't prepared me for this. This is different. This is playoff hockey. Whatever I say now will be in the forefront of everyone's mind as we step onto the ice. But I slip into captain mode and make my way over to stand next to Coach.

"How are we feeling, boys?" I ask, looking around at the guys cheering back at me. Since becoming captain, I vowed to prioritise these boys. Willing to do anything to give them the best chance at success. And that sure as hell hasn't changed. "All I want to say is we do nothing special here tonight. We play hockey. It's as simple as that. Our focus should be solely on the next goal." There's a murmur of approval from the guys. "We've got this, boys."

The guys fill the room with cheers and excited calls and Springy, the assistant coach, hands me a piece of paper denoting the starting roster before I stride back to my cubby.

"Let's hear the energy. We've got Jonesy and Sonny starting us on 'D'." A roar of applause fills the room. "Hutch, Nics, and Owens as forwards. And between the pipes—" I pause for effect, "Ffordey." A chorus of cheers and whooping follow the goalie's introduction and then Coach exits the dressing room, leaving us to finish our prep.

As soon as everyone is busying themselves, I pull my phone out of my bag and check my messages. One from my sister, warning me she's tagging around with the camera crew to get some footage for social media, a few others I skip, and one from my dad.

Dad

Call me.

Well, shit. Maybe he remembered? I haven't told him we made the semi-final, but I'm guessing Vicky probably did. Before I can reply, Bettsy's hand slaps my shoulder and I toss my phone away as if it's burnt me.

"We've got this, Cap. I'll scale it back like we discussed, but just so you know, I won't have any problems going hard if one of those fuckers—"

"TIME."

"That's the call, Betts," I say, cutting him off. "It's showtime."

We file out of the dressing room and towards the tunnels. We only get halfway to the ice as the crowd above us hypes up. There's an unmistakable rhythm of a beating drum, and then our mascot springs out of nowhere and starts fist-bumping us as we walk past. My sister pops up from behind him with her phone pointed right at me.

The atmosphere is everything when we're announced. The crowd is loud and the music thumps over the speakers. But there's only one thing on my mind.

I need to get another look.

"Have you seen my number one fan?" Bettsy had said after warm-ups earlier. And when I looked, I'd caught sight of her—at least, I think it was her. My heart almost fell right out of my chest.

I'm practically shaking as I round the corner and skate towards the benches. I glance up, and there she is. She's looking right back at me, and then I notice her jersey. *Our* team. *My* team.

My heart pounds.

I have to force myself to pull my eyes away as I keep moving around the ice.

Shit.

Bettsy and I finally settle down on our bench and I set myself up for a stop right at the far end. It gives me a chance to see what everyone's doing and how they're reacting to plays. Initially, my focus is on Jonesy and Sonny, who are taking the first shift, but once the puck moves into the offensive zone, I shift my attention to Bettsy, who's as eager as I am to get out there.

"Remember, bud, keep it cool, yeah?"

"I got this," he says, swinging his legs over, readying himself. As soon as Sonny touches up, Bettsy's away and I quickly fall in line behind him just as the puck sails into our defensive zone. I call it, and check my area, giving myself permission to sail it across to Bettsy, now sitting at our D-zone point. Out of nowhere, an opposing forward sails right into him, practically crushing him against the door to the penalty box. I'd argue an interference call since Bettsy had passed the puck, but it's borderline.

There's a mix of jeers and boos as Bettsy scrambles to his skates, but he must see something I don't because he motions across the ice for me to follow his lead, something we've done a million times. I have a good idea of what's coming next.

It starts off with a push into the offensive zone, with one of the opposing 'D' men clearly out of position. It's their enforcer—a huge guy, bigger than me and Bettsy, for sure. His name is Patrick Langdon, and he's the definition of a brute. Hell knows what's going on, but he's distracted. He doesn't even track the puck, which is currently with Ryan, hustling behind the net.

Bettsy slides into place and calls back to me, and as soon as Ryan flicks it to Bettsy, I one-time it, sending it right below the glove of the goalie.

Red light and buzzer.

I point at Bettsy, a smile illuminating his face, and he sails right into me, knocking me into the arms of Ryan and Jani, our first line centre.

"Excellent play, Johnny-boy," someone shouts, but that was all on Bettsy.

His intuition and awareness of the puck made that play happen. I'm not a big goal scorer, but for a defenceman, I don't do bad. Bettsy is like the magic ingredient, and I love him for it. We're the perfect combination of defensive styles for our team and it makes things happen. I've never had this synergy with a linemate before and I'm here, living for it.

"Look at the face of that prick," Bettsy says, nodding his head towards Langdon as we head back to the bench.

"He was the one out of place—wait, don't tell me you've fucked his girlfriend?" Langdon looks out for blood, but Bettsy reassures me he has nothing to do with the wrath directed at us.

"It's probably just because he wasn't concentrating, and he'll be getting it in the neck from his coach."

We dash through the open door to the bench and take a seat.

"Nice work, boys," Coach says, leaning down between us. The crowd has recovered, and the ref is setting up for a face-off.

"All Bettsy," I say. Coach smirks at me before grabbing his clipboard and leaning into Springy.

"This is our game, Cap," Bettsy whispers, and you know what? I think I believe him.

Chapter 8

Kelly

TOM IS UNDER STRICT instructions not to mention who my brother is when we tag along to a bar with a load of other fans after the game. It's my favourite sort of place. Music pumping from a loudspeaker in the corner, but not so much that you can't hear yourself think, and decent drinks with actual glasses—not the plastic ones they force on you after big events.

We all gravitate towards the back where there are a few tables free, and get some drinks ordered. Tom sticks to beer, but I decide to mix things up with a gin and tonic that I'll probably regret later–but it may add weight to the fake stomach bug. My throat is hoarse from cheering, and I know I'll be feeling as rough as sandpaper tomorrow, but the excitement and buzz from the game has everyone on a high.

We're going to the final.

I text my brother, congratulating him on their win and he replies with a single 'thumbs up' emoji. And I guess he's probably celebrating somewhere until he texts me a few hours later.

Mike

Sorry, Kel. Cap's been riding our asses tonight. The pressure is getting to him.

"Is he talking about Johnny?" Tom says, reading over my shoulder.

"Yes," I say, slipping my phone away. "I think he's a bit of an authoritarian on and off the ice."

And straight away, the vision of Johnny's eyes on mine is back at the forefront of my mind.

"He can ride my ass as much as he wants," Tom swoons.

"You're disgusting."

"All I'm saying is, he can do whatever the hell he likes to me." And I don't know if it's disgust or shock, but my mouth hangs open when Tom pulls his phone out and flashes me his new lock screen. "Look at him, Kel. He's beautiful."

He is.

In fact, looking at him makes my whole body ache. He won the gene pool lottery for sure. It's a pity he's not got the shining personality to match—not like...

"It's not all about looks. From what I know, he's not a very nice person. He's always shouting at the guys, constantly angry about something."

"And how do you know this?" Tom says indignantly.

"It's just what I've picked up on." It's half a lie. Obviously, he didn't make a good impression when I overheard him last Monday morning when I was on Mike's sofa, but when I saw Mike on Monday evening, he seemed unsettled by the encounter earlier in the day. I outright asked him if it was because of Johnny, and he shrugged, dismissing my question.

"Well, I don't buy it. He looks too sweet. Anyway, do you fancy another, or are you ready to call it a night?"

"Let's go. I just need to use the bathroom first."

I excuse myself, and when I return to our seats, Tom is in a deep conversation with two other fans but signals that we're leaving when he spots me.

"So, I've done some recon and everyone loves Johnny. Told you. I'm right." We link arms and start the walk back to our hotel.

"I didn't say that everyone didn't love him. I just said that he's not a nice person. That's different."

"How is it?"

"It just is. Now leave it," I snap.

Tom comes to an abrupt halt, causing me to stumble a little to regain my footing. "Why are you being a bitch?"

"I'm not."

"You bloody are. Now tell me what's going on."

I frown at him. "Nothing. Well, not really, anyway." I think I have to come clean and tell Tom why I'm so uppity towards Johnny. He won't let it rest otherwise. "Okay, fine. But let me finish before you butt in with your opinion."

"Agreed," Tom says, pulling me back into a walking pace. It's chilly, and neither of us wants to be standing outside in the cold.

"I was talking to someone on that app you put me on to. Three months, altogether. He said his name was John, and that he was a mature student. He sent me some pictures, and I sent pictures..."

"Oh my God. What sort of pictures?"

"Nothing like that. Just selfies or whatever. But he used Johnny Koenig's pictures. And—"

"Oh, my God. You were talking to Johnny? My Johnny? What happened?" Tom comes to a stop again, turning towards me with his jaw on the floor.

"You said you'd let me finish," I say. "But, no. I was catfished."

Tom's eyes are like saucers. "How do you know?"

"I just do," I say, tugging at his arm, prompting him to walk again.

"You have the worst luck. How did you find out?" I tell him about the huge Johnny Koenig action shot in the upper lobby of the rink. "Right. And what does that prove?"

"I'm sorry, but the likelihood of the real Johnny Koenig being on a social sharing app to meet new people is wild. You've said so yourself—look at him."

"Yeah, but he could be. Did you ask him?"

"No. I deleted my account," I say.

"Without asking him?"

We turn the corner and make our way into the lobby of the hotel.

"Yes. I freaked out. I mean, if it *is* Johnny, which I'm pretty certain it's not... He plays hockey with my brother and it's just a bit—"

"So?" Tom pushes the button for the lift, and we climb in when the doors spring open. I hit the button for our floor.

"Mike would kill me. And him for that matter. Besides, I'm me, and he's an athlete—"

"Stop it. There's nothing wrong with you," he says as the lift comes to a stop. A single 'ding' and the doors open.

Tom hovers the key card over the lock of the hotel room door and it makes a mechanical unlatching sound before he pushes it open.

"I'm not having this discussion with you right now," I say.

I put my bag down on the desk, then take off my shoes before collapsing down on the bed.

"For once, Kelly, do me a favour and realise that you don't have to settle for people like Darren. What if that really was Johnny, and he really was interested in you? Because there's no way someone would carry on a conversation for three whole months if they weren't."

"Well, it wasn't. And in the unlikely event that it was, I'm not interested. He's a complete dick to my brother and—"

Tom cuts me off. "You never know. Maybe he can be himself behind a screen?"

I wave him off and busy myself getting ready for bed.

I'm feeling surprisingly sober now I'm in a different head space, reeling over the way Johnny looked at me. It couldn't have been him, could it?

Johnny

THE FINAL. THE THIRD period. And there's less than five minutes remaining when Coach calls a time-out. We're leading by a goal but as everyone knows, it isn't won until it's won.

Until the final buzzer sounds through the arena.

Until there's no time left on the clock.

Bettsy and I are ready to take to the ice for our shift, hopping over the boards after Jonesy and Sonny make their way back to the bench. We don't get very far though, because the puck goes out of play, sailing into the netting, and the ref blows his whistle.

Coach uses the opportunity for a little impromptu time-out, pulling us all into a huddle and giving Springy, the assistant coach, the nod to give us an address.

"You've got this. We do nothing special here. We just hold our own and keep the puck moving. Steady does it. No big moves. No chaos. Get the puck up towards the slot and give yourselves another chance." Springy flashes his eyes in my direction. "Let's go, boys."

We position ourselves back on the offensive face-off circle, to the left of the netminder, and Prez lines up, ready to take the face-off. I check Bettsy's positioning, catching him nudging shoulders with the guy he's marking. His lips move and his eyebrows furrow—an argument brewing, I can tell.

The puck drops and Ryan scrambles for it, passing it across to Scottsy, but he loses possession when it's poke-checked from him.

That's when it happens.

Everything moves in slow motion. The puck. The end of my stick. The end of Bettsy's stick. Bettsy himself, and that fucker from the opposition who's fired a puck toward me that I know I won't be able to catch. I yell at Bettsy, urging him to duck, but

Perrott, a defenceman from the other team, changes direction and charges towards him instead, taking him out and into the air. The air leaves my lungs as Bettsy ricochets forwards. The force of the check has him landing on the ice, headfirst.

Thud.

The arena, which was buzzing with noise moments before, is quiet enough to hear a skate slice through the ice.

Silence everywhere.

The crowd.

Every man on the ice.

And Bettsy.

I scream his name. Tossing my stick to the side and hitting the deck. His left cheek presses against the ice, his helmet askew from the impact.

Then I see the blood.

There are guys all around me and I'm yelling. Yelling for someone to get the medic.

"Betts? Bettsy?" I try again.

Voices behind me tell me to move aside, then the ref is next to me, urging me to conform.

"Mike? Mike?" Penny, the team medic, places her hand gently on Bettsy's gloved one.

Then he groans.

I expel a breath.

Fuck.

"Betts, can you hear us?" I ask.

Another groan. Thank fuck.

Penny signals behind her and I spot a stretcher moving towards us.

"You're going to need to back up a bit, Johnny," Penny says firmly as she springs into action.

I've seen nothing like it in all my years of hockey. I force myself to swallow hard, staving off the creeping sense of nausea washing over me as I make my way to the rest of my teammates.

"He groaned. That's a good sign, right?" I ask Ryan. His face is hard, but he forces a nod.

"Yeah, he's in the right hands, John." He pats me on the back as we watch Bettsy getting carried off the ice, the crowd applauding respectfully and the opposition tapping their sticks on the ice.

"That fucker though," I spit through gritted teeth at the ref. "What are you going to do about him?"

"Hey, let me deal with this, Cap," Danny says, attempting to placate me as he steers me towards the bench.

It's definitely the right thing for me right now because my temper is right up there with the rest of my emotions. I try to push my energy toward the first coping strategy that comes to mind: the ten parts of my body that I'm supposed to focus on.

But it's all overwhelming.

Danny joins the opposition captain next to the officials and then an iPad appears in the hands of the ref. All their heads cram together as they watch the screen, and I note Danny wince as they watch the replay. His eyes flick to mine for a split second before he involves himself in the conversation on the ice.

We wait for the call. I think at least two different songs boom from the loudspeaker, which cuts mid-chorus when one of the refs finally skates up to the announcement box.

"After assessing the play, we determine that the call on the ice is a ten-minute major..."

Grabbing my stick, I hold it across my knee and push hard on each end of the shaft. The tension builds before it gives and breaks in two. Then I grab the next one on the rack, not giving a shit who it belongs to.

I feel sick.

Coach is leaning over the boards shouting something towards the stripes, but I don't pay attention to the words. I'm using all the will I possess to sit myself back down.

I don't even complain when Coach tells me I'm not returning to the game for the final few shifts. I sit spaced out, not even concentrating properly. Not even noticing that the final score is in our favour as the final buzzer sounds.

I can't even bring myself to celebrate with the guys. It's a moment I've desired for a long time, but right now, the last thing I want to do is party.

There's one thing I always thought I'd be sure of—victory. Well, the feeling of victory. But I couldn't give less of a shit right now.

Chapter 9

Kelly

M IKE'S FACE RESEMBLES THAT of a champion, not someone who recently suffered a concussion and was sent to the hospital. He's grinning from ear to ear, and he radiates excitement. Our mother, on the other hand, does not appear impressed at all.

"We won, Mam. We won." He beams.

"And we're ecstatic for you, love. But how are you feeling?"

"You know when you wake up on Christmas morning and you really hope you got—"

"Not about the game, Michael. How's your head?" Mam moves closer and starts fussing with his bed sheets.

When they took him to the dressing room, he seemed completely disoriented and unaware of his surroundings, or the game still being played on the ice. Mike only found out they're playoff champions ten minutes ago.

"Ah, it's fine. Where's Dad?"

"He's parking the car," I say, sitting down in the plastic visitor chair next to his bed.

Mam steps aside and forces a cup of water in Mike's direction before stepping to the end of the bed and pulling out the clipboard from the holder.

I know for a fact she can't read hospital notes properly; she works in finance. She flicks through the sheets before putting it back and excusing herself to go and find the nurse. Now it's only us.

"I feel terrible," he says.

"I'm not surprised."

"No, I mean, forcing them to come here."

"You didn't force them, they wouldn't have not come," I say.

"Yeah, but hospitals and all that."

I nod, then quickly change the subject back to the game that Mike is so excited to have won. At least this will help keep his attention away from the worry of bringing our parents to a hospital. Luckily, this isn't the same hospital in which they had their last moments with our brother, Jeremy.

"Just try to relax. Don't let yourself get worked up with worry."

"Stop babying me, Kel. I mean it."

The door squeaks as it swings inward, and Dad steps into the room, followed closely by Mam.

They both stop at the foot of the bed, solemn expressions on their faces.

"Dad, we w—"

"I think it's best for you to come home and spend the off-season with us, son," Dad says, hands deep in his pockets.

Mike's brows pull together. "You think? Or Mam?"

"I do. I mean, we can keep an eye on you. Make sure you're well and—"

"But I have a summer plan. I'm supposed to work with Danny at his old man's construction site."

"Well, you can tell Danny thanks, but no thanks," Dad says. "I'm sure he'll understand, given the circumstances."

I look at Mike, but his eyes flick towards our mother and I see it—the plea. But she shakes her head.

"This is for the best, Michael. Please. We need to make sure you're safe. If you want to play again next season—"

"What do you mean, 'if I want to play again?'" My brother's voice becomes hoarse.

"Mike," I say, moving to his bedside. "You need to rest. Don't let yourself get worked up."

"Well, tell them they need to go. Can you get me my phone please, Kel? I need to speak with Johnny."

My stomach drops. But I grab Mike's phone from the windowsill and hand it to him.

"Thanks." He looks to Mam and Dad. "Can you give me some space, please? I need to rest, after all."

I'm stuck in the middle. I know what Mike is like, and I also know our parents are in a state of 'cotton wool' deployment. If Mam had her way, she'd let none of us leave the house.

"I'll be back in half an hour to check on you. In the meantime, please try to get some rest, Michael," Mam says. Then she gives me the nod to follow her, and like a puppy, I do.

We leave him and Dad to talk for a few minutes, heading down to the coffee shop. The same place where Johnny Koenig and a few of the other guys are waiting, Styrofoam cups in hand, around a large circular table. Luckily, he doesn't see us, but he pulls his phone out of his pocket and sticks it to his ear, before sliding his chair to stand up.

We join the queue as Dad strides in.

"Did you bring my handbag, Tony?" Mam says, looking him up and down.

"Does it look like I have your handbag, love?" Dad huffs before he turns to me. "Kelly, be a star and fetch Mam's handbag, will you?"

I turn on the spot and stalk back towards Mike's room, the anxiety of bumping into Johnny sitting in my chest.

As soon as Mike's room comes into view, I see Johnny through the window of the door, standing next to his bed as they talk.

The silence from the corridor allows me to pick up a mumbling of raised voices from within the room. Hesitantly, I push the door open. There's no avoiding him this time.

"Just leave it, will you? For Christ's sake. Quit nagging me about it," my brother snaps, his ire aimed towards Johnny.

But they both turn their heads towards me, and Johnny's eyes lock with mine, his face softening for a fraction of a second before he looks away again.

Mike's room suddenly seems cramped. It's as if the walls are closing in on me. Johnny's six-foot-whatever frame makes me feel fun-sized and I can't help but stare at him. Tom was right, of course. He is handsome.

"Alright, Kel? How's it going?" Mike adjusts himself in bed and offers me a warm smile.

"I need to grab Mam's bag," I say, bending slightly to reach down and grab it from the floor next to his bed. My face flames. Is this my very own 'I carried a watermelon' moment?

My knees wobble a little, but I use all my strength to stand up straight again.

"No worries. Oh, have you met Johnny? Johnny, this is my sister, Kelly. Kelly, this is Johnny, the team captain."

He bows his head slightly, so he's not looking directly at me.

"Hi, Johnny. It's nice to meet you," I say.

My voice doesn't sound like mine when the words are in the air. I sound frail and pathetic.

Then he looks at me. Fully this time, relaxing his face again as he shoves his hands in his pockets. He looks older in person with a beard. Nervous, too. But confidence oozes from his voice when he speaks.

"Hi Kelly, I'm Johnny. But you can call me John."

And just like that, my heart stops. It couldn't be... could it?

Mike bursts out laughing. "You can call me John? Are you expecting her to call you captain, too?"

Johnny doesn't answer him. Instead, he pulls his phone out of his pocket and glares at the screen, his cheeks turning pink. "Shit, I need to get going, Betts. I'll call you later, yeah?"

He strides out of the room, leaving nothing but the scent of cologne behind him. I make a mental note to tell Tom that even though Johnny is a douche, he at least smells good.

"That was fucking weird," Mike says, looking at the door Johnny closed behind him.

But our conversation ends there, thankfully, when the door creaks open, and a nurse comes in, wheeling a machine. She announces that it's time to check his observations, so I use that as my cue to leave. But I don't make it back to the café. I get to the end of the corridor and come face-to-face with Johnny Koenig.

Johnny

THERE ARE A MILLION questions running around in my head as I process what just happened.

Kelly.

Kelly is Bettsy's sister?

She can't be.

But she is.

I'm doubting myself for a moment until she rounds the corner, and our eyes meet. Those are the same shade of green that I remember from the crowd. *That's* who Bettsy was pointing at. Not the guy covered in face paint next to her.

Does she realise it's me?

The questions fly around in my head as she stops in front of me.

Talk, Johnny. Say something.

"Hi."

"Hello," she says, her eyes dipping to admire a spot on the floor in front of her.

"You're Bettsy's sister," I say.

It's almost a whisper, and at first, I wonder if she's heard me. But she nods.

Fuck.

His eighteen-year-old sister.

If someone almost ten years older was sniffing around my sister at her age, I'd have cut his balls off.

"Kelly," I say. "Can I—did you know?"

She shakes her head.

"But—you ghosted me."

"Stop. Please. I'm so embarrassed. Please don't make this even worse for me." Tears form in her eyes, and I have to hold myself back. Because she's Bettsy's damn sister.

Bettsy's sister. She knows stuff. And I know stuff. And we flirted and... fuck.

This is one big mess.

A door opens in the distance, and I catch the last of the laugh. Bettsy's laugh. Probably flirting with the nurse or something.

And then it all comes flooding back. All the talk of his sister... and leg breaking. I mean, he wouldn't actually break anyone's legs, would he? Mine especially...

A queasy feeling washes over me.

I've thought about Kelly. I've thought about her in ways that someone should not be thinking about his linemate's sister.

"He can never find out about..." I blurt out as Kelly's eyes meet mine for a split second. I realise I have zero emotional intelligence "...us. He can never find out; you understand that, right?"

She raises her head slightly and finds my eyes. "Yes. Let's pretend I don't know you and you definitely don't know me."

"Fine."

"Fine."

"But what the hell happened, Kelly? Did I—"

"Let's just forget about it. Please."

I'm reeling. Overwhelmed with thoughts and emotions, and I have no idea what to do.

"Kelly—"

"It's for the best, right? Besides, I don't even know who you are." She cocks her head to look at me.

"You know who I am."

"No, I don't. I was talking to John. But from what I've seen, you're nothing like John. You're controlling, bossy, and emotionally unavailable."

She winces, muttering something else under her breath.

"What the hell is that supposed to mean?" I ask, aware that my pulse is skyrocketing. "Emotionally unavailable?"

"Forget it," she says, stepping forwards but stopping before she moves away.

"That's not fair," I say, but she's already cutting across me.

"Let's just forget this whole thing ever happened, please. You don't have to keep pretending to be someone you're not."

"Kelly—"

I step forward, but she takes a step back, raising her arm slightly.

"Please. Leave me alone."

"What did I do wrong?" I ask.

"Please, leave me alone and we'll pretend this never happened. I won't mention it to Mike or anyone. Honestly, forget it."

She pleads with me, her eyes full of tears, and I have no choice but to back down as footsteps fill the corridor.

"Kelly, love. I wondered where you'd got to. Is everything okay?" Bettsy's dad comes into view, and I acknowledge him with a nod.

"Coming, Dad," she says, then she looks at me. "It was nice to meet you, Johnny."

A statement that sounds so final.

Then she's gone.

I take a breath. Count to ten. I give myself a moment, but I'm too frustrated. Then I'm angry. Turning around, I kick a chair across the corridor; the noise echoing through the empty space. What the fuck just happened?

That wasn't how I envisioned my evening turning out.

Setting my hands on the back of my head, I stretch out, willing myself to think about my next step. Gently does it.

I think what pissed me off the most was getting called 'emotionally unavailable' by one of the few people I've let my barriers down for.

I pace the corridor a few times before the vibrating of my phone in my pocket interrupts me. I pull it out and check the screen before answering, carefully considering if I'm able to speak to my sister right now.

I let it dial off, but when it vibrates for a second time, I answer and shove my phone against my ear.

"What?" I snap.

"How's Bettsy?" Vicky asks.

"Fine. He'll be home tomorrow. They're keeping him in tonight as a precaution as he came round all confused," I say.

"That's great news," she chirps. "Are you going to be around tomorrow morning? I wondered if you could give me a ride to the airport."

"Airport? Which one?"

"Heathrow. I'm flying back home for a few weeks."

Her admission takes me by surprise. I never thought she'd be planning on flying back to Canada this soon after the season ends. I'm running it over in my head when Vicky prompts me for an answer.

"What time is your flight? Because I've got an appointment at ten."

"Oh, shit. No worries. I'll see if someone else can."

"Have you booked your ticket yet?" I ask.

"Yeah, look, I need to go," she says.

The line goes dead.

But I can't worry about Vicky right now. I'm confused as I return to the café. Maybe I can catch Kelly before...

"Where the hell have you been?" Prez comes into view, and I halt. "Is Bettsy okay?"

"Yeah, he's fine. Sorry—got a bit carried away, then Vicky called me."

"Yeah, no worries. We're just heading out since we can't do much more here. Fancy a few drinks back in the hotel? Bettsy wouldn't want us wallowing here when we're playoff champions."

I'm compelled to agree. When we make it back to the hotel, I get the guys a round of drinks and force myself to be in a better mood than I actually am. Of course, Prez sees through it straight away, but knows better than to ask me in front of the rest of the team. In fact, I think I do a pretty good job of faking it until someone mentions their plans for the off-season and my heart weighs heavy in my chest.

The off-season.

They say everything bad comes in threes and there is the third thing. First Bettsy, then Kelly, then the harsh reality of months stretched out ahead of me which veer me away from my routine.

"Bettsy's supposed to be coming to work with me and my dad on site," Danny says. "What about you, Johnny? Are you going home?"

"I am home," I say, draining my beer. Despite my birthplace being Canada, I feel more at home here than I ever did there. "But I am going with Scottsy to help him settle in before Ffordey and I hit the golf course."

"Ah, of course. Well, if you're looking for work, we always need extra muscle," Danny says.

But my mood deflates even further when Prez says that he's got Jenna tickets to the Senator's playoff games. He called me out earlier in the season for being jealous and it hasn't gone away. It's the whole reason I resulted to downloading an app to meet someone. And I met a few people, but none of them held my attention like Kelly.

My low mood continues through the night, and even when I'm sitting opposite Justine, my therapist, the following morning, I'm simmering, ready to burst into flames.

Chapter 10

Johnny

4 Months Later

MY NERVES ARE OFF the chart as we pull up outside Bettsy's family home, a large detached new-build off the motorway near his hometown.

Ffordey and I returned from France yesterday, and Bettsy thought it'd be nice to have a barbecue this evening before we drive him back to the city tomorrow.

"I'm starving. I hope there's not a long wait for food," Ffordey says as we climb out of my car. The smell of a freshly lit grill wafts through the air, then the front door flings open.

"Thank fuck you guys are here," Bettsy says, running out of the house like a dog who's been home alone all day. He pulls me into a hug and pats heavily on my back. "I'm so glad you could make it. I'm going insane here."

"How's your summer been?" Ffordey asks.

"Shit. Please tell me all your golfing stories because I need to live vicariously through you."

We spent three weeks touring Southern France before settling on a golf course for a week. And it's been great. Except, it hasn't been great, either. I've had too much time to think about Kelly. And since there's every chance I could bump into her today, the anxiety is almost too much to bear.

"It was pretty uneventful," I say. "But Ffordey and I had a blast."

He's my favourite travel companion. He doesn't make idle conversation, and he doesn't procrastinate with plans. I say ten, and he's ready five minutes before. He's perfect.

I grab our bags from the trunk, and we follow Bettsy inside. I'm a wreck. I can feel my body trembling. Is she here? What will I say? What will she say? What if…

"Mam and Kelly have gone to see Stacey. Something about wedding planning or whatever." We follow Bettsy into the kitchen where he stops at the fridge to grab a few beers.

"Who's getting married?" Ffordey asks, saving me the job.

"Stacey. The guy she's seeing is a dick though. I can't even believe Dad said she could marry the guy."

"It's not the nineteen hundreds, dude. I'm pretty sure that's not a thing anymore," I say.

"I think it's proper. I guess I'm a traditional guy."

Ffordey almost chokes on his beer. "Traditional? You? You realise back in the day, most people didn't have sex before marriage."

Bettsy rolls his eyes. "I'm just saying. The guy is a prick."

"Who's a prick?" Bettsy's dad, Tony, steps into the kitchen from the patio. He's wearing an apron that says 'Prick with a fork' which coaxes a snicker from me and Ffordey.

"Who do you think?" Bettsy says.

"Ah," Tony says.

"See. Say no more."

"I hope you boys like steak," Tony says, rummaging in the fridge. He pulls out a tray of meat and gestures for us to follow him outside.

We gather around the barbecue, chatting about the upcoming season and Bettsy's incident. Once Tony serves the food, our conversation flows so smoothly that I completely forget about my concerns for Kelly.

I'm relaxed. Until a distant car door slams, followed by the front door opening and closing, accompanied by a musical call, signifying someone's return.

Shit.

Bettsy's mom, Judith, appears at the patio door, waving at us before asking if we're good for drinks.

"How was it?" Tony calls.

"Don't ask." Judith waves her hand dismissively, disappearing back into the kitchen. There's a clattering of kitchenware, then she returns, carrying a tray of fresh drinks into the yard. "But that aside, Kelly had an email when we were driving home, Tony. It's not good news."

"What email?" Tony asks, wrinkling his brow.

"Kelly, love. The music college emailed to say she didn't get a spot. She's upset, as you can imagine. I'm going to take her a cuppa now." Judith disappears again.

Bettsy exhales. "That sucks. I bet she's gutted." He pulls his phone out and taps the screen a few times, then holds it to his ear. "Get your arse down here, Kel. Come and have a beer."

My pulse thunders in my ears and the nerves kick in. Without fully understanding the situation I'm putting myself in, I excuse myself to use the bathroom, hoping I can have a moment alone.

Judith points me towards the washroom, and as I round the corner, I lock eyes with Kelly, who's making her way down the stairs.

My heart practically falls out of my chest.

She smooths the front of her sundress, and I can see she's been crying. Her face is red and blotchy, and her eyes, big and green, look puffy.

"Johnny—" She wipes her eyes, stopping at the last step.

"Are you okay?" I ask.

Stupid really, because obviously she's not.

"Yeah," she says, giving her face another pass with the back of her hand.

I dip into the bathroom and grab some toilet paper, since that's all I can think of, and hand it to her.

"Thanks," she sniffs, moving off the stairs.

The whole thing breaks my heart. Seeing Vicky cry is one thing, but this is completely different. She looks so fucking sad, and I want to comfort her. I want to make her feel better. I want to see her smile.

I wrap my arms around her, her head fitting into the crook of my neck with ease. For a moment, I think I've over-stepped the mark, but then her arms snake around me and she squeezes me gently.

"It's okay," I soothe, catching myself breathing in the smell of her shampoo.

And despite what happened in April, this doesn't feel weird. It feels...

Her mom's footsteps pull us apart. Kelly discreetly moves back two steps to avoid any obvious sign of our hug. Judith hands her a mug and slips away, not even commenting on my loitering spot.

"I heard about the email," I say. "I'm sorry." I regret it as soon as it's out. But for some reason, I keep fucking talking. "I'd love to tell you it wasn't meant to be or whatever, but you probably don't want to hear that yet. I know I didn't want to hear it when I didn't get—"

"No, I know. I... you know what? It doesn't matter." She sniffs loudly and dabs her eyes with the tissue. A carriage clock on the wall ticks away the seconds before Kelly speaks again.

"Mam said Mike was having some friends over. I guess I should have known it'd be you."

"Yeah. I guess I'd have told you, but I don't have your number or anything."

"Right."

"I suppose I could have tried to message you on socials, but my sister looks after my accounts and she's nosier than Bettsy."

She smiles, ever so subtly. "It's fine. I mean, I wouldn't have stopped you coming over or whatever."

"Well, I was, uh... actually hoping I'd bump into you."

"You were?" Her eyes are full and sad, but there's a flash of excitement on her face. I shove my hands into the pockets of my chinos, contemplating what I should say next, but me being me, I fuck it up.

"You didn't tell Mike about my, uh, problem, did you?"

Her face turns cold again. She stares at me, blank at first, as if she's processing what I've asked, but then she blinks and purses her lips. "No, Johnny. I didn't. In fact, you haven't come up once in conversation," she snaps, setting her mug down on a sideboard.

Shit.

She steps forward, with purpose this time, and I'm forced to step aside and let her pass.

"Kelly, wait—I'm sorry I didn't mean to—"

I grit my teeth and follow her. But instead of stepping out into the garden, where everyone else is, she disappears behind a door at the far end of the kitchen.

"Johnny? Come on, man. Are you playing or what?" Ffordey calls as he waves a deck of cards at me.

Just as I'm about to step outside, the door Kelly went through flings open, and she strides out with her jacket on.

"I'm going out," she shouts into the garden before brushing past me towards the front door.

I turn to follow her, but the slam of the front door tells me all I need to know.

Kelly

WHEN CHARLOTTE TEXTED ME earlier, asking if I was keen for a few drinks in a beer garden, it was a firm no. But, because of recent events, sitting in a beer garden with people I don't really know nor do I want to socialise with, is a lot more appealing than sitting at home with Johnny, listening to Mike swoon over him.

I get the bus to town, making it all the way there before Mam calls me, demanding to know where I am.

"Out."

"Out where?" she says.

"The pub."

I hear her suck in a breath. "The pub?"

"I'm seeing some friends," I say.

"Who?" she snaps.

"Some old friends from school. You remember Charlotte? I'll be home before eleven, don't worry."

The fact that I have to say this makes me wish I hadn't come home for the summer. Since Jeremy, she's been overly cautious about anything that may result in a drunken night out.

"Fine. Send a live location to your brother, and Dad will pick you up. I'll tell him he can't have a drink."

"You don't need to do that," I say.

"It's fine. Send the location."

End of conversation. But I send my location anyway, to save the hassle later, before shoving my phone away.

The chatter from the beer garden has me wanting to turn around and head home. Because I'm socially awkward at the best of the times, and since I only know a few people, I regret my decision. But then Johnny's question pops back into my head, and I take a breath and head inside to the bar where I order a drink.

The audacity of him. To think I'd be blabbing his secrets. And to my brother of all people.

I order a gin and tonic and glug it back, readying myself for social awkwardness, which kicks in straight away when I join Charlotte and a few others I remember from sixth form outside.

Charlotte does a round of intros to the faces I've not seen before, and once that's over, she settles into conversation like we're picking up from our text thread.

"Kelly had some crap news today," she says. "So, we need to make sure we cheer her up."

"Oh, really? What was the bad news?" Harry, a friend of Charlotte's from uni, asks.

He's sitting next to me and attempts to listen when I speak, which I find quite refreshing. He's got a kind face and a mop of brown curly hair, which he's brushed back with his sunglasses.

"I didn't get a spot at this music school I auditioned for. But it doesn't matter." I shrug.

"You could always transfer to our uni," Harry says. "We're probably going to drag you down, but you're welcome."

"I'll just stick where I am, but thank you anyway," I say jovially.

"Is Darren still sniffing about?" Charlotte asks.

I nod before taking a sip of my drink. "Sadly, yes. So, I guess I'm stuck with him for another two years."

Charlotte scowls, which prompts Harry to ask questions about Darren.

I'm about to tell him I don't want to talk about Darren tonight, when Charlotte takes out her invisible megaphone and tells Harry all about how he followed me around for years, begging me to give him a chance and got into the same university as me only to cheat on me once we'd started seeing each other.

"Oh my, God. Really?" Meg, one of the other girls from school, says. She knows Darren, of course, but she didn't realise that we'd become official not long after starting uni. "He was always a creep, Kel. You're better off without him."

"That sucks. I'm sorry," Harry says.

"Well, it's done now," I say.

Meg asks how I found out he was cheating on me, and thankfully, I don't have to recount that story as Charlotte does it for me. I let her do all the talking, and I jump at the chance to get another drink when Harry offers to get a round in.

"I'll come with you," I say, and he holds out his arm for me to walk ahead.

He's chatty, and I like that at first, but the more he talks, the more I realise he likes the sound of his own voice. He talks and talks at me. And, for the rest of the evening, every time I go to the bar, he follows me.

An hour later, I send my mam a discreet message asking for a ride home, since I've well and truly had enough.

I excuse myself to use the bathroom and get some water, coming face-to-face with Harry as I leave the ladies' room. He's giving me Darren vibes. It's that over familiarity and it's making me uncomfortable.

"So, when are you leaving?" he asks, leaning up against the wall next to me. "I'd love to see you again before you go back."

Now the nice Kelly inside is telling me to agree, not to hurt his feelings, but the rational Kelly is telling me not to lead him on like I probably did with Darren.

"I'm sort of seeing someone. I'm sorry," I say.

The lie comes out of nowhere, but once it's out, I can't take it back.

"You're seeing someone? I thought—"

"Oh, hey, beautiful. There you are."

Beautiful?

The back of my neck tingles and Johnny's cologne catches in the breeze. My stomach turns upside down. Of course. Johnny bloody Koenig would pick the perfect conversation to overhear.

I spin around and come face to chest with him, and he leans forward and brushes my cheek ever so slightly with his lips. It makes me shiver. Actually shiver.

"Hi, it's nice to meet you..."

"Harry."

"Harry. It's nice to meet you. How's it going?"

I try my hardest to mask my confusion as I turn to face Harry again. All I can think is 'who is this guy and what has he done with Johnny?' But the way Johnny smiles and engages with Harry, I can see that he's slipped into 'Johnny the Captain, out meeting fans' mode.

God, how many versions of him are there?

"Good, thanks. You must be Kelly's boyfriend?"

"Yes, Johnny. But you can call me John." I pivot my head and roll my eyes, which Johnny catches. He smirks his most smirkiest of smirks and holds his hand out for Harry to shake.

"Kelly didn't mention she had a boyfriend?" Harry says, looking between me and Johnny.

"We don't want to be *that* couple who always talk about their partner, do we, grumpy-pants?" I say.

"Grumpy-pants?" Johnny says, widening his eyes. "I, uh, thought we decided against that?" The confusion hits his face and I stifle a laugh. I don't even know where that came from but since it's out now, I have to roll with it.

"No. No we didn't. See Harry, Johnny here can be grumpy sometimes, so I say it to make light of it. You know, if the skate fits." Without thinking, I reach up and pinch his cheek, and though I thought Johnny would flip out, he doesn't. He grabs my hand and laces my fingers in his.

Staring at our hands, I look up to his cobalt stare, which is surprisingly warm. Maybe it's hot in here.

"Right," Harry frowns. "Whatever suits you guys, I guess."

Annoyingly, Johnny grins. "Actually, I changed my mind. I think it fits."

Damn him to hell.

"What part of America are you from?" Harry asks, and I stiffen slightly as I suppress a laugh.

"Oh, you know Seattle?" Johnny says.

"Yeah, I've always wanted to visit."

"Yeah, well, I'm from a place about one hundred and eight kilometres north of Seattle. A place called Abbotsford, British Columbia."

I can't keep it in this time, I snigger into my hand.

"Oh. I'm sorry, I didn't—"

"It's no problem," Johnny says, holding his hand out for Harry to walk past. "After you."

I wait until Harry reaches the threshold of the beer garden before I turn to Johnny, halting him in his path.

"You okay, beautiful?" he says, coolly.

"What the hell was that?"

"He looked like he was getting too close. It didn't sit right with me."

"It didn't sit right with you." I pace my words like I'm trying to decipher a secret code.

"He was too close. And he looked like he was about to eat you alive."

"It's none of your business."

"It is when your mom has tasked me with bringing you home."

"I—"

I let my jaw hang open, then I snap it shut. If Johnny wants to play games, let's see how far I can push him.

He looks completely ridiculous crammed onto the picnic table in the beer garden, right next to me, where I made a show of patting the empty space. I half expected him to tell me we're leaving, but he didn't. He slipped onto the bench and now we're so close our legs are touching. There's a buzz of energy between us. I can't deny it. But that's probably because I'm fired up for a fight of the wits.

"Who's this?" Charlotte says, her eyes widening.

"Oh, this is my boyfriend," I say, casually. "Johnny, this is everyone."

Charlotte and Meg gawk at me.

"You didn't mention a boyfriend," Meg gasps.

"It didn't come up, really. And it's pretty new, isn't that right, babe?" I grab his arm, pulling it around me, and snuggling into him, all the while plastering the fakest of smiles on my face.

Or at least I think it's a fake smile even though my face obliged so quickly.

I expected Johnny to tense up and pull away, but his arm relaxes around me, and it feels… nice.

"Oh, so you're still in the honeymoon phase," Charlotte says. "That's cute. Where are you from, Johnny? How did you guys meet? I want to know absolutely everything."

"It's a funny story, actually—"

"It's not that funny," Johnny cuts in. "We met online, but we found out that I play hockey with Kelly's brother, Mike."

"Oh, yeah, I forgot Mike played hockey. Has he gone pro?" One of the boys asks.

"Yeah. We play for the—"

"I know who you are," another says, pulling his phone out. Then there's a flurry of conversation as everyone scrambles to see his screen.

"Oh my God," Charlotte says, her eyes almost bulging out of her eye sockets. "You're so lucky, Kelly."

"No, I'm the lucky one," Johnny says, and my heart stops in my chest.

I honestly have zero idea who this guy is. And then he twists his head to look at me, still snuggled into his hard deltoid. His eyes twinkle as he grins at me. I didn't realise how blue they were—are they contact lenses? Because they are really pretty. And he's staring back at me, giving me ample opportunity to keep looking. Then he wets his lips the smallest amount, but it's enough to have me leaning in a little.

It must be happening in a blink of an eye, but it's like everything has slowed down to a trickle as he leans in, too. I draw a breath, feeling the heat of his own. He tilts his head a smidge, and then we're kissing.

I'd love to say that it's a terrible kiss and that I'll push him away any moment now, but it's as if we've done it a hundred times before. It's natural and easy. Like we're in sync with our movements.

His lips are surprisingly soft. He parts them slightly, and I go for it, as if he's the only oasis in the desert for a million miles. I kiss him, and he kisses me back, and everyone is watching, and I don't even care.

'*That's enough*' and '*get a room*' ring through the air, and when we finally break apart, his eyes lock on mine as if he's seeing me for the first time, a crooked smile creeping across his face.

Shit. This isn't good.

"I—"

"Yeah, we'll have a good season if last year was anything to go by," Johnny says, jumping back into the conversation like nothing happened. But his arm is still wrapped around me, and I'm convinced he pulls me a little bit closer.

Chapter 11

Kelly

I slide into Johnny's BMW and buckle my seat belt.

I've never been stunned into silence before, but there's a first time for everything. The sizzling tension spanning between us as we sat together in the beer garden was something I'd never experienced before. Not even with Darren, or that time I kissed the boy I'd been crushing on for years when I was in primary school.

Johnny's performance was worthy of an Oscar. And when he climbs in the car, I can't even look at him. That sensation, completely alien to me, floods back as soon as his hand moves close to my leg as he reaches for a cable to plug his phone in.

I pull my own phone out of my bag as a distraction, groaning to myself when I see it's dead.

"Do you need to charge your phone?" Johnny asks, gesturing to the wire.

"No. It's fine, thanks," I say, letting my stubborn attitude win.

And what infuriates me is he says nothing more. It's like I've got the alternate version of Johnny again. Which is the precise moment I realise I'd spent my evening with *John*.

He belts himself up and pushes a few buttons on the console of his car. It's a warm evening, so he gets the air-conditioning blasting through the vents, and within a few seconds, the cool air whips at my hair and blows his delicious scent around the cabin of his car.

I have to force myself to concentrate on the view outside.

He pulls out of the car park, and we ride in silence. It's probably a full ten minutes before Johnny speaks again.

"How was the rest of your evening?"

"Fine," I say, keeping my eyes fixed outside the window.

"I'm glad."

That's it.

That's all he says. And that's all I say.

And I think he's going to never utter another word, ever again, but he clears his throat as we turn into my street. He pulls up outside and kills the engine, not making any effort to move. So I don't either.

"I'm sorry. I am fucking terrible with words, and emotions and—"

"You were a completely different person back there," I say. "Who are you, Johnny?"

All I get is a stunned silence.

He shifts in his seat. "I'm trying here, Kelly. But I am sorry about earlier. I didn't mean for it to sound as if I don't trust you, but honestly, I was panicking because if that comes out—"

He genuinely looks pained. But I'm reminded of how much he *had* trusted me when he told me about his issues finishing during sex.

"I get it, Johnny. I understand what guys are like in groups. Believe it or not, the orchestra isn't too dissimilar. People talk and news travels fast. But your secret is safe with me. Don't worry."

"Thanks."

His eyes drift over to my seat and his arm flexes, as if he's about to do something, when the front door of my house opens and light spills out onto the path. Johnny flinches, unbuckles his seat belt, and clambers out of the car.

"What took you so long?" Mike asks.

I'm out of his car in time to catch Johnny's explanation.

"Kelly didn't answer her phone, so I went to look for her. Some creeper was looking like he was about to eat her alive, so I told him I was her boyfriend. Naturally, I had to stay for a drink. But there wasn't any drama."

Well, colour me surprised.

I gape at Johnny. And he's so casual about it.

My heart pounds so loud, my pulse is strong in my ears. I'm waiting for Mike to react. I'm waiting for Mike to say something... waiting for him to freak out. He holds his fist up, offering it to Johnny, who bumps it.

"Cheers, man. Who was he, Kel? Anyone we know?"

I stutter over my words. "A friend of Charlotte's, that's all. No one I'll likely see again."

"Good, because remember what I said—no dating. After that fucking loser—"

"Okay, Mike. I get it."

I glare at Johnny.

Mike nods and turns his attention back to his friend, offering him a drink.

I get the hell out of there, in case Mike asks any more questions.

Pushing past them both, I don't even bother saying good night. I head upstairs and knock on my parents' door, which Mam opens in a flash—I knew she'd be waiting up to make sure I was home safe.

"How are you feeling now, love?" she says.

"Yeah, fine, thanks. I had a good evening."

"Good. I knew Johnny would get you back safe. Dad had a few drinks, see."

"Yeah, it's fine, Mam. Just going to bed."

She pecks me on the cheek and wishes me a good night before closing her bedroom door.

I get myself ready for bed, plugging my phone in to charge before I climb under my duvet. Laying in the darkness, my mind is working overtime.

Who is Johnny, really? Like deep down. Who is he?

I absentmindedly run my fingers along my lips. Because whichever version of Johnny kissed me—that was something else. I'm wondering if he always kisses like that as my phone vibrates on my bedside table when it comes back to life.

Charlotte

> Oh my God. You owe me the full story regarding your fella. He is *flame emoji*

I also have an unread message from earlier.

Unknown

> It's Johnny. I'm on my way to pick you up.

I stare at it for a moment, then close my messages, trying to push everything out of my mind.

I have so much to say and nothing to say at the same time. The turmoil of emotions twist and turn not only in my head, but in my heart, too. There's something about Johnny that has me wondering, and I want to understand.

I tap out a message to him and hit send before I change my mind.

Kelly

Why did you kiss me?

He doesn't reply. At least, not until I'm dropping off to sleep and my phone vibrates upon my chest, pulling me back. I scramble for it, blinking vigorously to clear my eyes.

Johnny

Why did you kiss me back?

He is infuriating.

Though, I'm not sure what I was expecting. Him to tell me it was a mistake? That it shouldn't have happened? But I fume in the darkness of my bedroom. Why *did* I have to kiss him back? Why was this the best kiss I'd ever had—I mean, stuff like that doesn't happen to me.

The more I think about it, the more confused I get. Does he like me? Do I like him? I can't say I fully understand how I feel about him, but that stupid kiss has added nothing but confusion to my uncertainty.

I toss my phone aside and roll over, pulling my pillow over my head, willing myself to sleep. But all I can think about is Johnny.

BETTSY RIDES SHOTGUN ON the way home. Ffordey is in the backseat complaining about not having enough legroom, but I'm hardly listening to his rant. I'm too busy thinking about the whirlwind that was yesterday.

I hardly slept last night knowing Kelly was upstairs, probably half naked, with her pouty lips I can't stop thinking about. I'm really fucking grateful Bettsy can't actually read my mind like he says he can on the ice, because I'd have both of my legs broken in an instant.

"When is Prez back then?" We hit the motorway as Bettsy sparks up a conversation. He fiddles with the buttons on my console. I swat his hand away and reset the temperature.

"Next week. Liam will be coming too, so you'll get a chance to meet him once he's settled in."

"What's he like?" Bettsy asks.

"He's decent. Strong at face-offs."

"See, that's why I became a goalie. Because I sucked ass at face-offs," Ffordey adds.

"That's logic for you, right there," Bettsy says. "Can't take a face-off, so opting to get pucks slapped at your head instead. Sounds wild, mate."

"If you D's do your job, then it's all good," Ffordey says.

"Well, I cannot wait for the new season to start," Bettsy says. "That was the longest off-season I've ever experienced. My mam was bustling around like a mother hen.

"She cares about you, bud," I say.

"Too much." Bettsy stills in his seat, gazing out of the window. I'm wondering if something's on his mind, but he answers the question for me, turning back to address me and Ffordey as best he can. "I don't think I've ever told you this, but I have—or had, I guess—a brother." He blinks a few times, then looks towards the roof of the car as he talks. "He was older than me. Basically, he had a head injury someone could have prevented. Drunken night out. You can probably guess why my parents and Kelly behave like they do."

As Bettsy recounts his story, all I want to do is give him and Kelly a huge squeeze—because that's brutal. I can't even imagine how either of them were feeling. I know Vicky pisses me off at times, and I her, but I'd be lost without her.

"Shit. That's rough. Sorry, man," Ffordey says, patting Bettsy on the shoulder. I offer my condolences, and Bettsy clears his throat.

"Yeah, well—that's probably why Kelly hates hockey," he says.

"I guess it makes sense." Ffordey leans forward.

"Yeah, she didn't handle it well when I was in the hospital. She was behaving strangely." He pauses and my heart thunders. "She came to the quarterfinals back in April—the home game we had. Ended up leaving halfway through the second period after I took that hit. She said she'll never step foot in a rink again. I had to beg her to come to the playoffs—but she's definitely checked out for good this time."

I hide my disappointment, giving my driver's side wing mirror lots of attention because it actually sucks that she feels like that.

Bettsy's phone trills from the confines of his pocket. He stretches his leg out to dig deep in his jeans, and he frowns at the screen.

"Rochelle," he says, declining the call.

"What's going on with her? Are you seeing her again or..." Ffordey asks.

"Fuck no. We're done for good. Not that we were official or anything, but she played the pregnancy card."

I'm forced to swerve back into my lane, narrowly avoiding causing a collision on the motorway.

"What the fuck?" I say, catching Ffordey in my rear-view mirror, who's staring back at me with his jaw on his knees. "When she called you at the hospital, you told me it was over." Kelly had entered the room during the argument which interrupted the conversation.

"It is over. And before you ask—she isn't. Or wasn't."

"What's the deal then?"

Bettsy sighs heavily. "So, a week after I got to my Mam's, she called me and asked for three hundred quid. Usually, I'd hand it over but—"

"Wait, wait, wait," I say, holding my hand up to stop him from talking. "What do you mean you'd hand it over? Have you been giving her money? Like money for sex?"

"No. It was nothing like that. It was just, you know, for her to get her hair done or whatever. But yeah, she's never asked me for that much typically, so I asked her what she needed it for. She told me she was pregnant and needed to get some things to make her pregnancy more comfortable or something.

"Now, I may be slow on the uptake sometimes, but I remember her having her period because... actually, forget it. Anyway," he clears his throat, "I know that finding out you're pregnant that soon after your period is not usually how it works."

"How the hell do you know that?" Ffordey asks.

"It is basic biology. It's all about a woman's cycle," Bettsy says. Ffordey looks baffled, but I have a decent knowledge of this stuff, too, because of a stunt Sarah pulled back in the day. I'd spent all day googling it.

Bettsy continues. "Basically, I called her out and asked her if she was defying mother nature, because I get that these things happen, of course, rarely. She sent me a picture of a pregnancy test. Positive. But I noticed straight away it wasn't even a picture she took."

"How?"

"Because it was the first one that came up when I googled 'Positive pregnancy test picture.'"

"Well, fuck me," Ffordey says.

"After dragging it out for another two days, she finally came clean and I told her I wasn't interested in seeing her again."

"That's it?" I ask.

"That's it. I don't want to associate with someone who lies about that. Even if it means I wank myself off three times a day."

Christ. I've heard enough after that.

We pull over at the service station to grab some lunch and I check my phone. There are a few messages from Ryan and Liam, giving me info on their flight time since I'm picking them up, and one from Kelly, which I can't open quick enough.

Kelly

You left your hoodie here.

Johnny

Look after it for me.

Kelly

I'll pass it to Mike to give back to you.

Yep, she hates me.

Disappointment trickles through me. Maybe it was only me who thought our kiss was something else. Until now, a kiss held no significance.

"Earth to Johnny," Bettsy says. "I think you've got a slow puncture."

But something that'd usually piss me the hell off doesn't make me falter at all, because the speck of emotion I allow myself has already been spent on Kelly.

Chapter 12

Kelly

THE PICKUP ZONE OUTSIDE the railway station is busy, but everyone falls into a deathly silence as my brother's car comes screeching around the corner like it needs a new exhaust. If I slowly back away from the curb, I can sink into the depths of the station, and he'll never see me—except I'm far too slow. Mike honks his horn and sticks his head out the window.

"Jump in then, Kel," he says, resting his elbow on the window frame. "I can't afford to get another ticket." He's grinning, revelling in how embarrassed I am.

I hang my bag over my shoulder and grab my cello case, careful not to swing it at anyone, then I clasp the handle of my suitcase so I can wheel it behind me. Mike's car is a three-door hatchback so, ideally, I'd put my cello in the front seat, but I'm keen to get the hell away from here. I open the passenger door and stuff it into the backseat, careful to wedge it in just enough to stop it rocking during the drive.

"How was the journey?" Mike asks as I climb in next to him.

At least he waits until I've buckled up before speeding off toward the town centre.

"Probably more relaxing than this," I say, not taking my eyes off the road. His driving is erratic, and if I look away, I know I'll vomit.

He taps the dashboard impatiently as he waits at a red light.

The route from the railway station to my new student house would usually take a full ten minutes in the car with this amount of traffic, but Mike squeals to a stop outside in eight minutes flat.

"Are you sure this is the right place?" he asks, cutting the engine.

It's a Victorian townhouse, which has seen better days, and because Tom and I left it until the last minute, hoping I would need to live closer to the music college, we were left with the dregs of available accommodation. Luckily, Sally and Marie, two girls from our orchestra, were also looking for a place, so we pitched together and wound up with this.

"Yes. I know it's not a palace, but it's a good price—and within walking distance and all that, so I don't need my car." I wanted my car, of course, but it wasn't practical to be paying out to keep it going when I didn't actually need it. Besides, Tom is bringing his car because he refuses to use public transport.

Mike helps me inside with my things and scrunches his nose up when he navigates the entrance hallway to my bedroom, which is at the very front of the house. It was clearly a sitting room at some point, with an aged bay window. But the room itself is large and bright, so I was happy that I picked it out of the baseball cap Tom had commandeered.

"Do you have your landlord's number handy?" he says, moving towards the hearth. It doesn't serve as a real fireplace, but Mike peers at it sceptically.

"Why?"

"I need to call him."

"It's a her."

"Don't care." He moves over to the window. "Someone needs to sort this out—it looks like it's leaking."

I sigh, flinging my suitcase onto my bare bed so I can unpack. "It's fine."

"No. It's not. Did you even view this place?"

"Yeah. We all did."

He makes an audible 'hmph,' then scratches his head. "Does Mam know?"

"You're done here. Thank you for the ride," I say, ushering him out the door.

"Wait—I thought you needed me to take you shopping? How are you going to manage for bedding and stuff?"

Damn him to pieces.

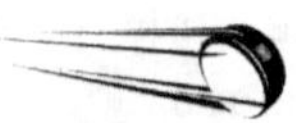

WE SPEND THREE HOURS in IKEA, and by the time we're emptying his car of things, I never want to see another giant blue bag again.

"You've got my schedule, right? Because if you need anything, I can get over here in, like, fifteen minutes, depending on traffic," Mike says after he dumps the last of the shopping bags on my bedroom floor.

It's at least twenty minutes by car back to his place, but I don't correct him.

"Yes, but I'll be fine, honest."

He gives me a hug, squeezing my shoulders, before thumping me in the ribs. Finally, he agrees to leave me to the mammoth task of unpacking, making my bed, and getting my kitchen stuff put away.

I finish making my bed up when the front door clatters open and Tom's sing-song tone calls out.

"In here," I say, moving to hang my clothes up in a rickety wardrobe opposite the fireplace.

Tom bounds in, dropping a holdall in my doorway before collapsing on the bed.

"I've just finished making that."

"I can tell. It's been a long day," he says. "Can I sleep here?"

I eye his bag. "Is that all you've brought?"

Tom props himself up on his elbow, facing me as I stand at my wardrobe.

"No. My car is crammed full of stuff. I'm going to need some help—wait..."

He scrambles to his feet and strides towards me, pulling Johnny's hoodie from my hands, examining it.

"Did your brother make captain?" His eyebrows pinch together, and he looks as if he's trying to work out a complex maths problem.

Shit.

I open my mouth to reply, but Tom's eyes widen as the answer comes to him. "This is Johnny's hoodie," he gasps, slapping a hand over his mouth. "Number '56.' That's not your brother's number."

"Yeah," I say, reaching for it.

But Tom turns away and moves it out of reach. Then, to my horror, he pulls it to his nose and inhales.

"Don't you dare. You'll take all the smell." I fight him for it, and thankfully, he releases his grasp.

"Why do you have Johnny Koenig's hoodie? And that's one of those team-issue ones. And it smells divine, so there's no way you bought that online."

He's right. It smells incredible, and despite my efforts to resist, I've been giving it daily sniffs. I had no intention of handing it back to Mike to pass to Johnny. And I figured, worst case, Johnny would have to message me and ask for it if he wanted it back.

I wanted him to message me.

The memory of the last time I saw him appears like a movie in my head. The kiss. His arm wrapped around me. The clean, fresh scent that is so distinctly... Johnny.

Tom catches my eye, looking at me with an expression of complete bemusement.

"Okay, so something happened," I say, moving to my bedroom door and dragging Tom's holdall inside.

I close it, then turn to face him. He's like a child waiting for someone to open the sweet wrapper.

"Tell. Me. Everything," he says, kicking his shoes off and making himself comfortable on my bed.

ONE THING I'M EXCITED about is the new hockey season. One thing I'm dreading is the new academic year. And since I've been back in town, it's all I've been worrying about. I've spent the past few years working on my master's degree and I'm left with my final year to get through.

Except I've been too relaxed. I completely forgot about my pending thesis until an email popped into my inbox, inviting me to a meeting to discuss my topic. And now I'm here, it's more horrific than I could have imagined. This room is so damn hot I can't wait to get the hell out of here.

"So, any further thoughts about your thesis? Because you really don't have long. I need your proposal by this Wednesday."

Dr Wells is the lecturer I've been assigned to support me with my final year assignment, and the way he's looking at me right now gives me the idea that he doesn't give a shit about it.

"Yeah, I'm just getting it down on paper. You know, get it presented properly for your consideration," I say, but I can tell by his eyes he doesn't believe me.

He averts his attention to the clock over the door and purses his lips before reaching for a pen he has stowed inside his jacket pocket.

"Johnathan, I can help you flesh some ideas out if you need the support. But I can't do it all for you. Do you not have a single idea?"

"Well, I have a few vague ideas noted," I say, reaching for my notebook.

It's full to the brim of hockey content, bar a small space toward the back reserved for university work. Flipping pages cautiously, I find the bullet points I scribbled in anticipation of today.

"Okay, well, that's good. Do you care to share?" His eyes twinkle with expectation and I shift in my seat.

My master's is in leadership and management, but I'm not sure it was the right pick for me anymore.

The list I've made is garbage. It seems like such a simple task—pick a topic, research, and write about it, job done. But right now, it seems like I'm up against the top team in the league on my own.

I take a breath and begin to read the top line of writing. "So, my first idea is around leadership skills for professional hockey"—I stop once I see the look on his face—"or understanding team dynamics that feed into a formal management plan." I list off a few more, but Dr Wells furrows his brow.

"Anything not hockey-related? I understand that's your vocation, and you're already acting in a leadership role there, but I think it'd be useful for you to expand your view on things."

"So, what you're saying is—no hockey?"

"I think it'd be a good idea. It'll be a great demonstration of your skills. Highlighting how you can lead in a variety of situations."

"But..." I don't even know what to say. Hockey is the focus of my day-to-day life and I have no idea what a suitable suggestion could be.

"Since I'm feeling generous, come back and see me a week today. Same time. Talk me through what you've come up with and we'll go from there. But, Johnathan, I suggest you visit the library and consider the theses readily available to you."

"The library?" I blink at him.

The majority of my course has been a week in the classroom, then using internet resources through university provision. Most of my course books are available online. I've never needed to step foot in the library.

Dr Wells scribbles something on his notebook then tears the page, passing me a sheet of paper.

"Here. I need you to research a few topics. Review theses covering similar subjects and write down six further studies or alternative ideas relating to the topic."

The whole thing is giving me anxiety and all I can think about is going home and taking a nap, hoping to wake up in a world where my thesis isn't a problem. But I nod in agreement and gather my things.

I head downstairs to the main atrium and join the queue for coffee. A few people ask me for autographs as I wait to order. Flashing my most charming grin, I accept random bits of paper and Sharpies thrust at me, giving a quick whizz of my surname and number before handing the items back. When it's my turn to order, the barista flashes me her widest grin as she bats her eyelashes at me.

"Oh, I know who you are," she says, tapping my order in on the touchscreen monitor in front of her. "Are you looking forward to the new season?"

"Sure." I smile.

And it's all I can manage. I still haven't mastered the art of conversing with women face-to-face. Lucky for me, the barista doesn't seem to notice because she chats to me as if we're old friends.

When she eventually slides my order to me with a wink, I spot the marker jotted along the side of the cup.

It's not the first time I've got a number written on the side of my coffee cup, and I've never paid it much attention, but a thought crosses my mind—maybe I should text her. Except, it's not *her* that I want to be texting. I haven't heard from Kelly since I saw her back at her parents' house at the start of August. And I doubt she'd want to hear from me anyway, after how I acted.

"Cap?" I turn around to spot Ffordey waving from across the atrium. I stride over to meet him. "How was your session?" he asks. "Mine was fucking awful. Nothing hockey-related—would you believe it?"

"Same, bud. Same. And I've got homework already."

I give him a rundown of my task and he blows out a breath.

"Are these professors in cahoots, because I've got to do the same thing. And we've got a full schedule this weekend."

He's not wrong. There's the season opener on Saturday, and then we're on the road Sunday, returning late. This year is going to suck. I don't know how I'm going to get through it.

We grab some food then decide to find the library, because neither of us has ever stepped foot in the place.

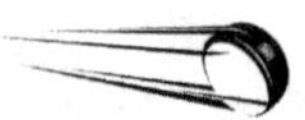

"Any ideas yet, Cap?"

"I'd be lying if I said I had," I say, moving through the ranks of the Dewey Decimal System, looking for anything I can latch on to. I've already reviewed the theses Dr. Wells told me about and come up with no ideas.

"I'm really fucking jealous of Ryan right now. And Liam. I mean, once they retire, that's it, isn't it? They've got a buttload of money," Ffordey says. "And there's us regular folk, having to rely on a Plan B."

I'd be lying if I said I wasn't jealous, too. If I had an NHL or a decent AHL hockey career behind me, I wouldn't have to worry about paying the bills when I'm forced to retire from hockey. I can almost hear my dad's disappointment speech when I got drafted in the sixth round. And the pressure he put on me after that only made things worse.

"I feel like I need a Plan C at this point," I say.

Ffordey's got his nose buried in a book. He and I are in a similar situation—relying on our degrees to see us past our hockey career. His time in the AHL was akin to mine: short and sweet, and we're bonded over our Canadian roots—except he's from Alberta.

"I think I'm going to write about 'Risk management in the Era of Uncertainty,'" Ffordey says, flicking through the textbook.

I raise an eyebrow at him. "How did you do on the risk management module?" I ask, but he waves me off, tossing the book back on a pile before standing up.

The guy's six foot six and towers over the shelves in the library, which is cramped and overcrowded. Also, the freshers are filtering in, book lists in hand, trying to work out where to find their reading material. He's intimidating.

Checking his watch, he pulls his phone out and then grabs his backpack and swings it over his shoulder. "I'm done for now. Are you coming?"

I tell him I'll see him later and he bumps my fist before striding toward the exit.

The thought of writing a thesis has my palms sweating. I mean, I could think of better things to do with my time, but it's the last push before I can graduate and be done with it. I only manage another twenty minutes of scouring the shelves, finally giving up and throwing all my things into my bag before leaving the library.

My focus is on my rumbling stomach, and I'm so engrossed in the group chat blowing up on my phone about the plans for after the season opener, that I don't realise someone is coming straight towards me until there's a clatter of items on the floor in front of me.

Instinctively, I reach down to help them up, but then those green eyes meet mine and my heart stops for the briefest of moments.

Chapter 13

Kelly

I'VE HAD THE MORNING from hell.

Just when I think it can't get any worse, Darren spots me when I walk into the music room. He moves towards me, weaving through a cluster of students, and comes to a stop right in front of me.

"I hear you didn't get in, Kelly. I'm sorry," he says, leaning close so I can see my reflection in his saxophone, which he has slung over his torso.

There's a faint trace of a smile on his lips. Twat.

I hesitate for a moment, taking a step back.

"No, but I understand they didn't take any cellists."

I'm not sure if it's one hundred per cent true, but I've been telling myself that, based on the intel I've gathered.

Darren raises an eyebrow. "Are you sure? Well, regardless, it's a shame for you, of course. But obviously, I'm glad you're still here." I give him a weak smile and move to step around him, but he holds his arm out to stop me. "Do you fancy catching up at some point? We can get a coffee or something."

I shove his arm aside. "I'm busy. Sorry."

"Already? We just started back."

"Yes. I'm very busy."

"Oh, right." A smile creeps onto his face and he cocks an eyebrow up. "Busy with your new boyfriend, right?"

I guess news travels fast through a friendship group that's hardly in contact anymore. Shit, shit, shit.

"There you are, Kelly." Tom appears from behind me and steers me over to our seats.

I slip past Darren, inwardly apologising to my cello as I give him a gentle whack on the legs with it on my way past.

Tom scowls at Darren. "What the hell did he want?"

"I think his original intention was to gloat, but then he asked me if I fancied catching up."

Tom lets out a yelp of disgust. "You're joking, right?"

I shake my head, unclipping my cello case and prying it open.

"And then he asked me about my new boyfriend," I whisper, right into Tom's ear, since the room is getting busy.

"Your boyfriend?" Tom says, not getting the hint that I whispered for a reason before the penny drops into the slot.

"Say it louder, Tom. Dale didn't hear you." Tom swivels his head towards the drum kit at the very back of the room but relaxes when he sees Dale deep in conversation with someone. "Sorry. Did you tell him you don't have a boyfriend?" Tom asks.

"No, you interrupted me."

"Well, what's the harm in letting him think you're seeing someone? I mean, I'm sure Johnny wouldn't mind." Tom shrugs.

"It's completely ridiculous."

Tom smirks and heaves his cello out of its case.

I'm tightening my bow as the course director, Patrick, saunters into the room, slightly late but not giving a damn about it.

"Welcome back, everyone," he says, dumping his music bag down at his desk. He moves behind the conductor's podium and surveys the room.

Patrick runs through a start-of-term speech, giving us an outline of what we can expect in the new academic year, while I tune out. I'm thinking about whether I should give in and wash Johnny's hoodie when Tom nudges me in the arm.

I pull myself back into the room in time to learn of a recital booked for Christmas.

"So, to confirm, Kelly and Darren will play a duet. I'm keen to experiment with some pieces that Darren has written, which bring together the alto sax and the cello. Kelly, I would also like you to work with Darren on the piece and ensure that it works well. In addition, I have something prepared, so we'll be looking to present three ensembles."

It takes a few seconds to sink in, but when it does, I'm ready to crawl back into bed and never come out. Ever.

You can't make this stuff up.

I avert my eyes to the woodwind section, where Darren sits at the front with a shit-eating grin on his face. He mouths something that I can't quite work out, but I flick my eyes back towards Patrick, pretending to hang on his every word.

Ultimately, this is unavoidable. Not only will it give me an enormous boost in credits, it'll get me out of two writing assignments. But I never expected Patrick to pair me with Darren. I wonder if I can call the music college and beg them for a place.

"I'll provide updates via the online portal when more information becomes available. Anyway, we have a lot to do this year and we need to get going. I assume everyone has printed out their sheet music?"

At least I did that. I grab them out of my music folder and place them onto the music stand that Tom and I are sharing. We wait for a further brief, and of course, only in the last ten minutes of our rehearsal do we play a single note. It's not a piece I'm familiar with, and most of the orchestra is given instructions to run things over with their section lead during the week before we're dismissed.

I waste no time packing my stuff up, and tell Tom that I'll meet him back home, out of pure desperation to get the hell out of here. Frustratingly, I'm so engrossed in my efforts to avoid Darren, I don't realise that the hard chest my face comes into direct contact with as I round the corner near the library, is Johnny, until I'm flat on my ass, looking up at him.

"Kelly, hi." His freshly shaven face highlights the squareness of his jaw, and oh my God, I can't even look at him.

"I'm sorry, I didn't see you."

He chuckles, extending his arm to help me up. "I guess I am difficult to miss. Are you in a rush?"

"No, it's—"

"Kelly. Wait up," Darren calls from behind me.

Johnny glances towards him before looking back at me. "Who—"

"You disappeared before I could talk to you," Darren says, coming to a stop at my side. He sets his saxophone case at his feet and fixes his gaze on Johnny, looking him up and down. "Is this your boyfriend?"

I figure now is my time to come clean. I can either admit that this isn't my boyfriend—implying that someone else is, or say it isn't my boyfriend because I don't have one. I open my mouth to speak but Johnny slips right into character, holding his hand out to Darren.

"Johnny Koenig. Nice to meet you."

Darren wearily shakes Johnny's hand and then pulls his arm back as if he's been electrocuted. He shifts his attention to me.

"Can we chat, Kelly?"

"No, sorry. I have plans," I say. "We can catch up another day."

And Johnny, my knight in hockey gear, or a training tracksuit, swoops in. "Yeah, sorry, bud. We've got a reservation. Are you ready to go, beautiful?" His eyes land on mine as he waits for my reply.

"Yes. Sure, okay." I pick my cello up and turn towards Darren briefly. "I'll catch up with you soon, yeah?"

Johnny is quick to swipe my cello from me, holding it carefully as he walks towards the car park. And since Darren is watching, I have no choice but to follow him.

WE COME TO A stop at my car, and I instinctively open the passenger door.

"He's gone," Kelly says, checking behind her. "Thanks, Johnny. I'll tell him we've broken up next time I see him."

I offer her half a smile. "How've you been?"

"Fine. I mean, same old crap, really." She adjusts her eyes so she's looking at me, and bites her lower lip, a pensive look on her face. "You?"

"Yeah, I guess, all good. Just the same old crap for me too, I guess. Season opener is coming up and I've got to come up with some ideas for my thesis by this time next week." I lean on the open passenger door. "Do you want a ride home or something?"

"No, it's fine. Thanks. I live ages away."

"Is it? Because you don't know where I'm going next." My tone comes out as teasing, and I'm rewarded with a smile.

"Fine. But only because it's warm and I can't be arsed carrying my cello that far," she says, reaching for it as I do. Our hands meet, and that zing I felt when we kissed all those weeks ago shoots right up my arm. "Are you okay with it?"

"It's like half the size of my gear bag," I say, opening the rear passenger door.

I slide her cello in and strap it down using the seat belt.

"Have you done that before?" she asks, arching an eyebrow.

I wink at her, not even knowing who I am anymore. Am I flirting? Because I don't know what the hell I'm doing.

I round the car and climb into the driver's side.

"So, who was that douche, then?"

"Darren," she says, and immediately her voice changes. I rack my brain, wondering if she's mentioned a Darren before.

"Darren?"

"Yeah. I don't think I mentioned him before. He's my ex."

"Ah. Right. Well, looks like you dodged a puck to the head there," I say.

"Yeah, well, sadly I have to work on a duet piece with him and I have no choice about it," she says, chewing her bottom lip.

"Shit, I'm sorry," I say.

She shrugs and nibbles her thumbnail.

"I've been meaning to give your hoodie to Mike to give back to you. I keep forgetting, sorry," she says, belting up.

"I'm surprised you haven't burned it yet, as some sort of 'I hate Johnny ritual'," I snigger as I get myself comfortable.

"Oh, I don't need your hoodie to do that. I have a voodoo doll."

I roll my eyes at her. "If you can kill me off before next week, please do. Because this shit is stressful, and I'd rather play goalie for a day with no pads. Address?"

She reels off her postcode as I tap it into my sat-nav, then I find her house number on the list.

"What's the deal with that, then? Why are you finding it so stressful?"

I give her an overview of my conversation with Dr Wells.

"I have no idea what topic to choose. I've got to present six high-level ideas, and I have half an idea after my four hours in the library. The worst part? It can't be anything to do with hockey."

"Have you checked the stored theses there? It is common for people to add a section at the end discussing potential future research. You could use those for ideas. And you could consider leadership of an orchestra, or another sports team or something."

I light up. "Well, shit. That's what the Prof meant. Thanks. You're a genius."

As soon as we hit the main road outside the university campus, we're stuck in a whole load of traffic, which means that Kelly is stuck in a car with me for longer than she probably wants to be.

But I'm nervous and I have no idea what to say to break the tension that hangs in the air. Kelly must be feeling it, too, because she turns in her seat to look at me before twisting back to gaze out of her window again. She does this at least three times before I catch her looking, getting her right in the eyes with a glare that could only say one thing—tell me what's on your mind.

"I was hoping I wouldn't bump into you. I didn't see you at all during the last school year. I thought I may get lucky again."

"Am I that bad?" I ask.

"I can't work you out, John. Or Johnny. Or whatever the hell you want to be called."

"I was hoping you'd call me grumpy-pants again, to be honest."

She gapes at me. "See. This is exactly what I mean. Who are you? Because I've never been this confused in my entire life."

Now I'm confused.

"Do you want my stock answer? Johnny Koenig, twenty-seven—"

"No, I mean... who are you? Because those three months I spent talking to you were... then the way you are around the guys, and when we were at the pub with my friends, you were... I have no words, Johnny."

"How would it appear if I was all nicey-nicey to the guys when I'm trying to lead by example? I mean, using your brother as an example, if I let Bettsy do whatever the hell he wanted, we'd never be where we are now," I say, keeping my voice surprisingly level for me.

"Okay, fine. I sort of understand that. But..."

"Yeah?"

"I really liked the Johnny I was getting to know."

"Are you forgetting that you were the one who blocked me?"

Silence falls between us. And I'm very much aware that we're still moving at a snail's pace through the rush hour traffic.

"Well, it's all a moot point anyway, right? Because you've got such a bromance with my brother—"

"Don't say that," I say, almost pleadingly, even though part of me knows she's probably right. My loyalty lies with her brother. And what would people say if they knew I was dating an eighteen-year-old?

"Fine. End of conversation."

I search every corner of my brain for something to say for the rest of the drive to her place. And instead of coming up with something sensible, I go completely off-piste.

"Well, you hate me anyway, so what does it matter?"

"Why do you think I hate you?"

"I haven't heard from you since I saw you last," I say, coming to a stop outside of a townhouse.

"But how does that mean I hate you? You have my number. You could have texted me. Besides, I don't think I've ever hated anyone in my life. Apart from—actually, forget it."

She undoes her seat belt and climbs out of the car. I'm out, too, getting around to the back door before she can unbuckle her cello. And since I don't want to be *that guy*, I help her and walk her to her front door in silence.

Rummaging in her bag for her keys, she fishes them out, then turns to look at me.

I swear to God I've never understood anything until this moment. Because the way she's looking at me makes me want to spill my heart out. All those messages come flooding back to me, and I remember how much I was into this girl. And then there was that kiss.

When I won man of the match for the first time, I felt pure euphoria. Being recognised as the best on the ice—it became one of my life's greatest memories.

But kissing Kelly for the first time completely shits all over that.

"Johnny, I—"

"Yeah?"

Eyes locked. Breath held. And we're fucking kissing. In broad daylight. On her doorstep. And you know what? I don't do a damn thing to stop it. I kiss her back.

Bettsy could drive past right now, and I wouldn't pull away.

She nibbles my lip and moans in such an erotic way I cannot stop myself from leaning into her. I want more. I want to hear what she sounds like when...

But she pulls away and stares at me for a moment before bringing her hand to her lip and brushing her fingertips over her almost-a-smile-but-not-a-smile.

"Oh, shit."

"Huh?"

"Thanks for the ride, Johnny."

Then she's gone.

Chapter 14

Johnny

"How many sticks did you break last season, Cap?" Bettsy says from the passenger seat.

He's got his phone clutched in his hands, his thumbs hovering in midair as he waits for my answer.

"I don't know, why?" I say, flicking my gaze sideways.

"I'm starting a pool. But I need something to go off. A starting point."

My phone pings in my pocket, and Bettsy chuckles to himself. I suspect he's dropped something in the team chat.

"A pool?"

"Yeah, like a wager. A bet. A dabble."

"Fuck's sake, Betts. You're wasting your time," I say.

"So how many was it? Six? Seven?"

Shit. I'd be lying if I said I actually knew, but it's definitely over seven. "Forget it."

"Fine. I'll get the guys to guess this year's number. Forget last season."

"If you want to keep your ass away from your head, you'll drop it," I say, using my sternest voice.

"Okay, okay, I won't mention it again," he says. But he twists in his seat and stares at me. "Alright, who blunted your blades because you're more tetchy than usual."

I sigh heavily, not wanting to admit that I can't even look at him properly since I've been having very impure thoughts about what I want to do with his sister. But since I have other shit in my head, I decide to tell him about that.

"My dad's got this new girlfriend. He called me yesterday to tell me he's planning a visit since *she* wants to meet me and Vic." I half expect Bettsy to make a MILF joke, but he doesn't.

"Well, I take it you're not interested in meeting her?"

"Not particularly, but if she makes him happy, whatever. It'll keep him out of my business." I always know when my dad isn't seeing anyone, because he becomes fully invested in my hockey career again. Safe to say, I prefer it when he butts the hell out.

"I'm sure she's a lovely lady. Maybe she's hot. Have you seen a picture?" And there it is.

"No, and nor am I going to ask for one."

I park my car in the players' parking lot and cut the engine. We both climb out, and I head to the trunk, pulling out our gear and handing Bettsy his bag.

It's the season opener, and the first game of the Challenge Cup. I'm bursting with anticipation. And since Prez's twin brother, Liam, is here, I think we have a high chance of pushing all the way. But I can't get too excited about that now. My stomach sinks when I spot my sister making her way in through the double doors at the back of the rink. This is another problem I'm having to deal with.

"Have you two made up yet?" Bettsy says as the door closes behind her.

"Well, she's still pissed at me, if that's what you mean."

"I'm still pissed at you, too, but I'll get over it." Bettsy pauses for a moment. "Did you honestly not know about Matt? Because if you did and you didn't give me the heads-up—"

Everyone is pissed at me for sure. The team for thinking that I had some prior knowledge that Matt Rodgers, an ex-forward from another league team, had signed with us. Something that I had no idea about until I saw his name plate last week. And my sister, for thinking I had something to do with her ex-boyfriend, Liam, calling it a day once and for all—and that's on top of her general pissed-off mood at the moment.

"I honestly found out like half an hour before you guys did. And Coach told me he would brief everyone. I'm sorry, bud. I really am."

He blows out a breath and nods at me, but I know he's not fully convinced.

"And Matt has said nothing to you?" I ask.

"You think we're on speaking terms? Hell no. I still hate that fucker and the team he came from." I'll give him that—he's passionate. "And before you ask, Rochelle is still out of the picture."

Rochelle also happens to be Matt's ex. She's the one thing Bettsy and he have in common, well, two now, if you include the fact that they're wearing the same team jersey this season.

We swipe our access cards on the double doors and head through to the dressing room. We're amongst the first to arrive, and Vicky gives us some crap about being too early for her to catch the 'arriving in suits' shot for social media. But of course, Bettsy loves to appease her, so he heads back out and pretends to do his walk in again.

I refuse because I've got shit to do.

And it's the right decision, because as soon as I'm left alone, Coach pulls me into his office briefly for a chat about the lines, then I'm readying up and trying to keep myself in the right headspace by consulting my notebook. I remind myself of the reason I'm here. To lead this team into a victory.

And that's what I do—well, it's not all me but we come away from the ice later that evening with a W and I'm absolutely buzzing. Even my worry about the state of Liam Preston's knee turned out to be nothing.

Once we're done showering, I give the guys an overview on the plans for the evening.

"We'll start at a bar before going to my place. Nothing heavy guys, because we're on the road tomorrow." I have this tradition of throwing a little house gathering when it comes to the season opener, and tonight is no different.

I wait for Bettsy to be ready to leave before we say our goodbyes to the guys, heading out towards the players' parking lot.

"Have you bumped into Kelly yet?" he says, causing me to choke on the air I just inhaled.

"What?"

"Well, Ffordey mentioned you guys have to use the library more, now. So, I figured you may see her."

"Oh, yeah. Just the once. I said 'hi'," I say.

And to my complete relief, Bettsy says no more about it. Once we're on the road, he plays on his phone and casually hums along to the music from my car stereo.

But the mention of her name again has my brain ticking over. My mind has been on the game all day, but now it's over, it's gravitating back to that kiss and how she left things.

Once we get to the bar, I check in for our reservation and order a round of drinks as the team starts trickling in. I stick to water, a tactical plan so I don't feel like shit tomorrow, and once I'm sure everyone is paying me zero attention, I take my phone out and scroll back through the text messages from the last few days, wondering what the hell to do next.

Kelly

Can I ask you a question?

Johnny

Sure.

Kelly

The times we've kissed. How was it for you?

Johnny

I liked it.

Kelly

Right.

Johnny

You should know by now I'm terrible at articulating my feelings. But I really liked it, Kelly.

Kelly

Shit.

Johnny

What?

Kelly

Nothing.

Johnny

Come on, tell me.

Kelly

It's fine.

I'm not oblivious to the fact that 'fine' means the opposite of fine, considering I grew up with Vicky. And seeing as she sent me a string of one-word answers, there's something going on.

What's she not telling me?

I've drawn a few conclusions—she likes me, or she dislikes me. If she likes me, she may be worried about her brother's reaction, or the age gap between us. If she dislikes me, well, she's probably wanting me to leave her the hell alone.

But I end up re-reading the message thread a few more times. And I land on option one—she likes me. But that's my wishful thinking, because I really fucking like her.

But the other things: my age, my affiliation to her brother; they are a problem.

How can I make this right? I can't fix my age, or that she's related to my linemate... perhaps this is a complete waste of time, and I should forget about her.

But I can't. The more I try to push her out of my mind, the more I'm thinking about her lips and how beautiful she is.

Because kissing her was like some weird out-of-body experience. I felt exhilarated. I didn't even know kissing could be like that—it's literally just touching lips with someone else. But... fuck.

I hear Bettsy laugh from a short distance away, where he's chatting with a group of girls, and I watch him for a moment, thinking how things would be if the roles were reversed. Would he try it on with Vicky—Liam aside of course, and would I be okay with it? Probably not actually, but that's because Bettsy is a fuck boy.

But Kelly being eighteen—we're both adults here...

I roll it all over in my head for a while before acting on impulse.

I drop a new message to Kelly, keeping it casual but instantly regretting how lame I sound after I've hit send.

Johnny

What are you up to?

I stare at my phone for a while, and when no reply comes through, I get antsy. Is she working tonight? Is she out with her friends? Is she just hanging out at home, watching a movie or whatever? Is she on a date?

I put my phone away, pull it back out again, then shove it away, telling myself I won't look anymore, and she'll text back when she can. But thirty minutes later, I'm wondering if anyone would really notice if I was here or not.

I figure the best place to check first is the store, as I'd easily be able to see if she's working or not. But when I'm a few minutes away, I wonder if I'm being a complete asshat.

However, something has me pulling into the parking lot and taking a spot that allows me a glance through the huge window that, luckily, affords a clear view of the aisles. My heart thuds as I spot her at the checkout pouring coins into one of those counting machines. She's tied her hair back in a loose bun that has bits of hair escaping around her face, and she looks so damn adorable in her uniform.

A few moments later, I decide that it'll be worse if I sit in my car and watch her, so I get out and head towards the entrance, telling myself that I'll wait until she's free before I try to talk to her ... before trying to find out where we go from here.

Kelly

"Do you think I should call the police?" Linda, the other woman on my shift, says as she comes to a stop at my till.

The shop floor is completely dead, so I have no idea who she's talking about, until she nods her head towards the shop front.

"Him. The blond guy in the suit, filling our doorway."

I step backwards a few paces and crane my neck to align my sight to the front door, and my stomach contracts with a tingle of emotion.

Oh, my God. What's he doing here? Perhaps he's with Mike. Mike could have come by for whatever reason and not made himself known yet.

I glance towards the CCTV monitor in the far corner behind the tills, squinting my eyes to check the aisles, but there really is no one else in the shop right now.

"He's a friend of my brother's. I should see if everything's okay. Can you take over, please?"

I shift aside, letting Linda take my place, and I grab my fleece, slipping my arms into it before heading to where Johnny is standing. He watches me as I approach but doesn't acknowledge me until I stop directly in front of him.

"Hi," he says, straightening up.

Johnny's suit makes me feel significantly underdressed. My uniform is scratchy, polyester most likely, and I have a name badge on. I can't even.

"Are you looking for Mike?" I say, trying to swallow the lump that's rising into my throat.

He puts his hands in his pockets and looks around before setting his gaze back on me. "No, actually. I came to see you."

My pulse thumps in my ears. "Oh."

"You didn't reply to my text and usually I'd just wait, but I'm overthinking."

A group of students, luckily no one I know, come bundling through the shop door, forcing Johnny to step aside as they pass, and his body brushes mine ever so slightly.

My knees actually quiver and I'm so embarrassed—I'm literally saved by the bell as a buzzer sounds, telling me I'm needed at the tills.

"I need to get that, sorry."

"No problem. Sorry to just turn up." He shifts on the spot and shoves his hands deeper into the pockets of his trousers.

"Are you okay, Johnny?"

"Yeah. I was just hoping to catch you, that's all. I've just been thinking about—"

I can tell it's about the kiss. There's a burning in his eyes that I remember vividly from the moment we broke contact on my doorstep when he dropped me home.

"Right."

"I'll wait for you," he says. "If you can talk when you're done."

"I probably won't have a chance to chat after work. I'll miss my bus home. It's the last one."

"I'll drive you home. Or I'll call you a cab, on me, if you'd prefer."

There's a moment when our eyes meet, and I find myself telling him we close at eleven.

"I'll be here," he says, disappearing outside.

Linda is like a dog with a bone for the rest of the shift, giving me a look of complete and utter disgust when I refuse to tell her anything other than that it's my brother's teammate who was wondering if I knew what Mike wanted for his birthday. Complete and utter bullshit, obviously, but she doesn't need to know that.

We finish cashing up the tills just as I spot Johnny's black BMW pulling back into the car park. My heart pounds in my chest. I'm running over potential conversation scenarios, wondering what he's going to say, how I'm going to react. What if...

"I'm setting the alarm," Linda says, beckoning me through the small gap in the shop doors that we slip through.

She pushes the doors closed the rest of the way and I swear I can feel him watching us.

Linda draws the shutters down and works her way through the rest of the locks, all while Johnny's car sits stagnant in the car park, a few cars away from Linda's old Vauxhall Corsa.

Johnny has the common sense not to sit with the engine running and lights on. This helps him go unnoticed when Linda walks over to her car and I pretend to walk to the bus stop, waiting until she's pulled out of the car park before I double back and head towards Johnny's car.

He jumps out and rounds to the passenger side, opening the door for me, and I climb in, my chest tight with nerves.

"Do you want to grab something to eat or whatever? Are you hungry after your shift?" he says, getting back into the driver's seat.

"I'm fine, thanks."

Honestly, I'm usually ravenous, but the thought of eating anything right now is more than I can bear. My stomach twists with nerves.

"Are you sure, because—"

"I'm fine. Thank you for asking, though. I appreciate it," I say.

"Right."

"So, what's up?" I ask him after a few beats of silence.

"I've been thinking about you, Kelly. And I wanted to see you," he says.

"Oh."

"Yeah."

I can tell straight away that the dynamic has changed between us. And Johnny is probably just as nervous as me, because he's running his massive hand up and down his left thigh, and his right thigh jiggles, making the car feel like it's shaking a little.

"I saw you won your first game of the season. Congratulations," I say, trying to offer him a distraction from the tension that hangs in the air.

"Thanks. I'm glad we're back in it. Your brother was good tonight," Johnny says, flinching.

"Did he start any fights?" I ask.

"Not tonight. But, shit. I told myself I'd leave Bettsy at the bar. Physically and mentally."

"Oh, sorry."

"Not your fault. I brought him up." He brings his hand to his mouth and rubs the stubble on his face, then he takes a breath before twisting in his seat to look at me. "Let's say Bettsy was out of the picture. And I wasn't such a jerk with my inability to make good conversation choices. And you didn't ghost me. Where would we be now?"

"Wow. That's a long list of things to scratch out," I say.

"Yeah, but go with it," he says, and I watch his fingers drum gently on his knees.

"I guess I'd be hoping that we'd be seeing how things went. I haven't really thought about it."

A huge lie of course. I mean, I haven't been planning our wedding or anything, but I've definitely thought about what it would be like if we were seeing each other. Properly.

"And the age gap?"

"Well, I-I mean, it wasn't a problem before, was it?" I say.

He looks at me, and I swallow.

Things had started out as 'just a conversation,' with us pushing it aside. But when the flirting began, all mention of it was quickly forgotten.

"And my dick problem?" he says, looking straight ahead again.

I flame red, and Johnny's body language tells me he's not overly enamoured by his question, either.

"I don't know the entire story I guess, but from what you told me, it seems quite focused on your ex—but it doesn't bother me, if that's what you're asking. It's something I could, I don't know, maybe help you with. Try to overcome it together."

I'm mortified. Completely and utterly. But I've said it now.

"You'd want to do that?" he asks, keeping his eyes forward.

Honestly, I'm so relieved that we're having this conversation in the low light of his car. "If you're implying that I would only want single-sided fun in bed, then..."

"Sorry. I guess that's what I've had in the past—"

"Are you telling me none of your ex-partners have wanted to even try to give you a good time?" I say.

"I guess I've been with selfish lovers," he says, dropping his voice, and I reach over the console to grab his hand, squeezing it in mine.

"Sorry, my hands are rough as—"

"Feel these," I say, passing him my left hand. The tips of my fingers are tough and calloused from the years I've spent pressing into the fingerboard of my cello.

"Damn," he says, and then he brings my hand up to his lips and kisses it so gently, it sends a tickle through my bones.

He lets out a breath, then the screen of his console lights up with an incoming call. 'Ryan Preston'. Not a minute passes before 'Liam Preston' calls, then, 'Paul Hutchinson'.

"Ah, shit. I'm sorry about this," he says, pulling his phone out of his pocket. "Shit."

"No, it's fine."

"I'm supposed to be hosting an afterparty. And some of the guys have gone to my place and I'm obviously not there." He frowns at the screen of his phone before looking back up at me. "I'm going to have to head back. I'm sorry."

"That's okay. We can talk another time. Or you can just text me or whatever. If you want to."

I nod. Because I *do* want to.

"We're on the road tomorrow but—I'll call you, okay?"

"Sure."

He takes me back to my place, and he stops outside, looking right at me for a second before his attention is steered away.

"Wait. Is someone coming to fix those windows?" he asks.

"Not you, too," I sigh.

"What?" He gets out of the car, moving closer to get a better look. I scramble out and follow him.

"Mike said the same thing."

"I'm not surprised. Have you spoken with your landlord?"

"Sort of. It's on the 'things to fix' list," I say.

"Do you want me to call him?"

"You can quit the boyfriend act now," I say, and he frowns.

"I wasn't—" And his phone blows up in his pocket again. "I'm sorry, I need to go." And he leans towards me and pecks my cheek ever so slightly.

He waits until I've closed my front door before driving away.

Chapter 15

Johnny

I TAKE MY USUAL Sunday morning swim and go home via my sister's place since we're supposed to be going for brunch. Prez has moved in with Jenna, who was sharing a place with my sister, so I'm not surprised that it's him who answers the door.

"Vicky's not here. She said she'd meet you at brunch," he says.

"No problem," I say.

But even I realise that my voice comes out way too chirpy. Prez looks at me as if I've offered to do the guy's laundry for a month.

"What the hell is going on?" he asks.

"Nothing."

"I don't buy it," he says, leading the way through to the kitchen.

"I'm in a good mood. I had a good swim and I'm feeling positive about our win last night. And let's face it, we're in a good spot to beat these guys later."

"I have to agree but..." Ryan looks at me then shrugs, dropping it luckily and I'm glad because I don't want to tell him I'm into someone.

"Hey, I'm glad I caught you, anyway. Remember when Jen had that idea to do the reverse psychology thing?"

"Yeah?" he says.

"Well, I've been thinking about it. And I really think we should leave them to it," I say.

"Well, maybe, but think of what Lee can actually bring to the game if he's fully focused. And if he's laden with distractions, it'll seep into every aspect of things. Obviously, I'm not going to force you to do anything, Johnny, but consider it. He and Vicky—"

"Yeah. I know."

In the times I've hung out with Liam since he's been back, he's never mentioned Vicky. Which I've seen as a positive, anyway. But then last night he was acting weird. Something's going on, but my attention is too busy elsewhere to put much thought into it.

I decide not to press it with Ryan, either. I leave it there, because my sister's face will probably tell me all I need to know.

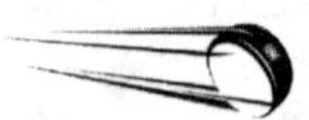

THE COFFEE PLACE IS busy when I get there, and Vicky has already got us a table. I weave through the room and sit down opposite her.

She pounces on me.

"What's made you so happy?"

"Nothing," I lie.

When the truth is, I'm still buzzing about Kelly.

I've only sat down for a moment before a pen and napkin are thrust under my nose.

"You stayed out of sight last night." I scan the QR code to look at the menu. "I was wondering what crap you'd be asking us."

She shrugs, and as soon as I notice her complete avoidance of any eye contact, I decide to play the game.

"At least you did nothing to annoy Liam," I say.

"I didn't come here to talk about Liam," she says.

"I know Liam. I can tell when he's pissed. He wasn't himself during the opening game, nor at the bar last week, and he's been snappy ever since he got here. He's been fighting for Christ's sake. We're talking about Liam. What's going on with you two? Please enlighten me, Victoria." I can't quite believe I threw out her full name, but it flows so well.

"What's it got to do with you?" she asks.

I can feel my cheeks turning pink, and I suck in a breath through my teeth. "It's frustrating when my best face-off guy is constantly in the penalty box and not taking any face-offs."

"Fine. We briefly spoke last week. I told him I wanted him to keep away, and he obviously didn't take it very well."

"Oh. Well, I'm not surprised. I understand you two are no longer a thing, and I've told you before, it's probably for the best, but you need to remain professional, Vic. What the fuck are you playing at?" It comes out a little harsher than it should have, but once it's out, I decide to ride with it.

"Nothing. I tried to keep away last night. I—"

I cut in. "When is this going to stop? When will you stop throwing your toys out of your crib and get your fucking act together?" She busies herself with the menu on her phone and I know I've hit a spot. "Someday, Vic, he'll move on for good and you'll have to cope."

"He can do what he wants. He's a single guy."

But the way her face changes tells me that's the complete opposite of what she wants him to do.

"Could you bear the thought of him properly moving on?" But her silence says it all. "Thought so," I mutter.

"None of this is easy, Johnny," she says.

But that's when I question everything. Because there's no way in hell that anyone can go from being madly in love with someone to the point of getting married to complete disconnection.

"I don't get it. You were going to marry the guy and then suddenly, poof. Nothing. Not to mention that stunt you pulled before Lois passed away."

She fumbles in her purse and pulls out a small tin of lip balm. "If you must know, I didn't want to end up like Mom and Dad. Or Mr and Mrs Preston."

My heart lurches at those names.

Deep down, I knew Mom and Dad would never work out with their different life paths and whatever, but Mr and Mrs Preston were end game and it devastated everyone, and it probably got Vicky more than I appreciated, given her admission.

"Fuck," I say, "I didn't realise that hit you so hard, Sis."

"You can't tell Liam. Promise me?" She points her finger at me.

"Why not?" I ask.

"He'll want to be the hero and try to fix it, but he can't. It is what it is. He can't fix it."

The server sets a mug of coffee in front of Vicky before returning with my brunch.

"Aren't you eating?" I ask.

"Not hungry."

"Well, God knows I can't force you to eat," I say. Because she's the second most stubborn person I've met, after Liam.

Vicky looks like she's deep in thought, so I leave her to it while I eat. Then she snaps back to reality, asking me what I'd do if I didn't play hockey.

I pause and decide to try to lighten the mood.

"Huh. Random, but I'd probably be a vet," I chuckle to myself before giving her my actual answer. "Nah, probably a chef." She gives me a weak smile, and I figure now is the time to bring up Dad. I ask her if he's called and told her about visiting with his new girlfriend.

"When is he coming?" she asks.

"Not sure yet," I say.

"Excuse me, can I—" a voice to the left of us says.

"Sure, do you have a pen?" I turn on autopilot, but it takes me a second to realise that it's not my autograph she wants.

"What? Sorry, I was after the salt, may I?" She reaches over and grabs the shaker from the centre of the table.

"Are you done?" I ask Vicky, eager to get the hell out of here. And we shuffle out of the coffee place onto the busy street. "Vic, could you not mention that? I mean, you know what the guys are like."

"Fine, you keep quiet to Liam, and I'll keep quiet to everyone about that," she says.

I tell her I'm heading into the bookstore before going home, and she replies that she'll see me later, before strutting out of view.

I'm about to walk away myself, when the door to the coffee place flings open and someone calls my name.

I lock eyes with the girl who asked me for the salt, as a familiar face steps out from behind her. What are the damn chances?

"I thought it was you, Johnny." Charlotte beams. "I spotted you once Lyla grabbed the salt but didn't want to interrupt, in case that was a date or whatever. I didn't want to assume that you and Kelly are still together. I mean, she has a poor track record for relationships."

"That was my sister," I say flatly. Slightly pissed off that Kelly's so-called friend would have such a negative outlook on her.

"Oh, my gosh. That makes sense. I mean, I was worried about it after the stuff with Darren and her trust issues, but—oh, sorry, I'm rambling."

Kelly told me that she planned to nip this whole thing in the bud at the next opportunity, but since Charlotte's shown her vote of no-confidence in Kelly's dating ability, I have no choice but to keep the torch burning.

"Yeah, we're doing good."

"I'm so happy for you guys, honestly." Her reaction sounds fake as fuck, but I let it go. "Listen, I'm in the city for a few nights. Long story, I won't bore you. Do you fancy a double date? Or shall I text her and check? I know what you guys are like with social calendars." She nudges me with her elbow, a smirk slipping across her face.

I must have an out-of-body experience because I see myself nodding in agreement. "Yes, we'd love to."

"What's your schedule like?" Charlotte asks, pulling her phone out.

I surprise myself by knowing that Kelly always works on Tuesdays and Thursdays, so I tell her we'll be free tomorrow night.

Now all I need to do is tell Kelly.

WHEN JOHNNY SAID HE'D call me, I wasn't expecting him to actually call me.

I'm setting up my cello when my phone buzzes in my pocket, and when I see 'JK' flash up on the screen, my heart pounds a little harder in my chest.

"How's it going?" he says.

I'm not sure what I was expecting, but his phone voice sounds exactly the same as his regular voice. We talk about our mornings briefly, then Johnny tells me he bumped into Charlotte.

"So, here's the thing. We're going on a double date."

"A double date?"

"Yeah. Charlotte and her girlfriend are in town and—"

"A double date?" I ask again, then I'm stunned into silence.

"Say something," he says down the line, and a prickle of tension runs through me, straight to my stomach. An actual date with Johnny? Where we have to... be on a date? Or pretend to be on a date.

"I didn't realise she was seeing anyone," I say, trying to sound breezy. "Did she tell you her name?"

Johnny scoffs, "I don't know any more than what I've told you." Typical. "I told her we're free tomorrow evening, since I remembered you're not scheduled to work..."

This sends me into a frenzy. Because pretending to be my boyfriend to get me out of a shitty situation is one thing, doing it twice is a step beyond, but accepting a double date—this is wild. I want to ask him why he didn't tell Charlotte we'd broken up, but my heart is screaming at me to accept my fate and shut the hell up. But I try not to sound overly keen.

"Well, I guess we can go. But I can't promise I'll be in a good mood."

Three times this weekend, Darren has called me to find out when we can meet, and since I couldn't think of any other excuse, I agreed to meet him after my last lecture on Monday in the campus library. I tell Johnny and he says that he'll also be in the library tomorrow.

"And I know you said something about mentioning to him that we 'broke up,' but do what you need to do to keep him where you need him to be," he says.

"Are you sure?"

"Yeah."

"Thanks, Johnny. So, how are things going there? I guess you're on the road now?"

I hear him take a sharp intake of breath. "I had this argument with my sister, that's all. About my dad coming to visit. He's got his new girlfriend and apparently, she's keen to meet us both, so he's flying her over to have dinner. And he'll probably want to check out a game or whatever. My sister isn't overly excited about it, and she said I was taking sides and then started crying and it was awful. I ended up yelling at her and it all turned to shit."

As I listen to him, I can hear the sorrow in his voice. A rare show of Johnny's emotions swims down the phone line, and all I can do is listen.

"Do you think she'll be okay?" I ask.

"Hopefully. I mean, I guess we're not overly different in that respect. We get on with things."

"When people hurt, they push away the people nearest to them," I say.

It sounded better in my head, but Johnny seems relieved to hear it.

"Are you sure you're only eighteen because—"

"Uh, no. I'm nineteen now. I had my birthday in July."

"Shit. I'm sorry I missed that," he says, and my heart thumps in my chest. Would he even care about a birthday? Most guys don't. "I'll—shit. I gotta go. But I'll pick you up for the date? Text me the plan."

I hear someone calling his name in the distance, and then he's gone.

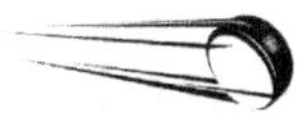

ANOTHER TERRIBLE NIGHT'S SLEEP, thanks to the draughty window from hell, and some horrible one-on-one time in the library with Darren has me simmering on pissed off. But by the time I'm getting ready to meet Johnny for our fake double date, I'm in such a bad mood, I need to get myself a pre-drink.

"How did it go today?" Tom asks when I enter the kitchen.

"Terrible. He's given me the most basic of basic scores to play. It's something that a child could have written on one of those tiny xylophones." Tom sucks a breath in through his teeth while he watches me pour a large gin into a glass. "Six notes. He's given me a grand total of six notes to play."

"Really?"

I tip some lemonade in with my gin, since we're out of tonic, then I indicate for Tom to follow me to my room, where I dig out the score and hand it over.

"He's supposed to be presenting it Friday. I told him he can't."

Tom flicks through the pages. "Yeah, this is embarrassing. I'd let him, Kel. It'll only show to Patrick that he doesn't know what the fuck he's doing. Maybe you'll get assigned a new partner."

"I live in hope. I guess I'll see what happens. Oh, and Darren told me that Lydia broke up with him."

I take a gulp of my drink, setting it down on my side table so I can root through my wardrobe for something to wear. I've already got my hair fixed, so I pick a dress that doesn't involve any over-head action and I make sure Tom is engrossed in the score before slipping into it.

"Can you zip me up?" I ask, moving to where he's sitting on the bed.

"Roll back a second. What the hell happened with Darren and Lydia?" he says, gripping the zip of my dress and pulling it up.

"He told me she cheated on him."

Tom can't contain his laughter. "In this instance, karma is a queen, not a bitch." I turn to face him and blink. "You look hot," Tom says, lounging back onto my bed.

I finish my make-up, and take another large gulp of my drink.

"Do you think it's a bit much?" I ask, twirling on the spot.

"I think it's perfect. It's the right amount of slutty without being overly slutty—if that makes sense."

"I'm changing," I say, moving towards my wardrobe.

"No. Don't," Tom says, hopping up from the bed. "Green is definitely your colour. And your boobs look huge—did you get a new bra?"

I roll my eyes at him, then grab a jacket.

The sound of a car pulling up outside has Tom moving to the window to peer out. "Oh, my God. He's here."

I down the last of my drink and check myself in the mirror for a final time, wondering if I did the right thing by curling my hair a little. Let's hope it doesn't rain.

"I'll get it," Tom says, almost falling over himself to answer the front door that Johnny hasn't even got to yet.

I grab my bag, stuffing my phone and bank card inside, then follow his path to the front door.

Tom swings the front door open before I get there, and Johnny stands on our doorstep, wearing a suit that makes my knees buckle slightly; he's been causing that effect a lot lately. I always thought I was immune to hockey players in fancy suits, but Johnny is, apparently, an exception to the rule. And by the sound of Tom's breathing, he thinks so, too.

"Your ride is here," Johnny says.

"Oh, she loves a ride." Tom grins.

I throw my hand out to smack Tom's arm. "Ignore him. He doesn't get out much," I say to Johnny. "Let's go."

But, of course, Johnny extends his arm out to Tom and introduces himself. "Johnny Koenig."

"I know," Tom says, practically drooling. "I'm a huge fan."

"Oh, great. Do you come to many games?" Johnny asks.

"Oh, I don't. I'm not really a hockey fan."

Johnny's eyebrows furrow. "Oh?"

"I'm a *you* fan, Johnny." His voice is sultry, like he's waiting to pounce on him, so I have no choice but to hurry along and get the hell out of there.

"Okay, let's go," I say. "Don't wait up, Tom. Bye."

I nudge Johnny away from our door as I shut it behind me.

"I'm sorry about him. He's a strange boy."

"It's always nice to meet a fan," Johnny says, opening the passenger door for me as if he's done it a million times. He leans in and pushes my hair away from my ear, his fingers gently brushing my neck, causing goosebumps to rise all over my skin. "You're beautiful, by the way."

What the hell? I slip into the passenger seat and try to compose myself. It's his choice of words that got me. 'You're beautiful,' not 'you look beautiful,' or 'your dress is beautiful.'

I feel so awkward about taking a compliment. I ignore it then he climbs into the driver's side. Instead, I ask him how he's getting on with his thesis and I listen to him talk, dragging it out all the way to the restaurant; the restaurant which I have no idea how I'm going to pay for and eat regularly all week, but I guess that's something for tomorrow Kelly to worry about.

Johnny finds a parking spot and jumps out to pay at the parking meter, just as I get a text from Charlotte, telling me they're waiting for us inside. Which means it's time to act again.

Chapter 16

Kelly

THIS IS THE MOST awkward date I've ever been on. And it's got nothing to do with Johnny.

We're squeezed into a booth, opposite Charlotte and her date, Lyla, watching them quarrel about everything and anything. At first, I think it's playful banter, but it heats pretty quickly. All Johnny and I can do is talk between us whilst we pretend that there isn't a full-blown catfight happening less than a metre away.

"Shall we leave, or...?" Johnny whispers right in my ear since he's taking up about eighty per cent of the space.

"Oh, shut up, will you? I can't believe you're bringing this up now." Charlotte's voice reaches a tone of frustration and Lyla rolls her eyes before pulling out her phone.

"I knew you'd act like this," Lyla says, and she shifts out of the booth, storming off towards the bathrooms.

"Is everything okay, Char?" I ask.

"Obviously not, Kelly," she snaps. But she changes her tone quickly to apologise. "I'm sorry. It's been stressful. Lyla's grandmother isn't well—which is why we're in the city. She lives in a care home right on the outskirts."

"Oh, that's not good," I say.

"Can we do anything to help?" Johnny asks.

"No, no. It's fine. Thanks. Anyway—you two. You literally make my heart leap with excitement. I can see the honeymoon phase is still going strong."

"It sure is," Johnny says, wrapping his arm around my shoulders.

I stumble over my words. "Well, we're doing okay."

He leans down and kisses my cheek.

All for show, of course.

Charlotte's phone buzzes on the table, and she's quick to snap her attention to the screen, reading for a second before letting out a sigh of contempt.

"I'm going to check on Lyla," she says, slipping out of the booth.

I expect Johnny's arm to slip away, since we're no longer being watched, but he keeps it firmly set while he checks the menu.

"What are you thinking of getting?" he asks, flicking through the pages of the menu. "The chicken looks good."

I skim down the list, surveying the prices. "I, uh, the salad."

"Get what you want, and I'll square it up," he says.

"It's fine. I'm trying to lose a few pounds anyway," I say.

"The heck you are. You're perfect. Now do as you're told and get what you want, Kelly."

I stare at him, aghast, and I watch his face break into a smile that has my whole body buzzing.

"Do you love telling people what to do, Johnny?"

It just comes out. And a warm, flushed feeling washes over me.

Johnny's Adam's apple quivers as he swallows. Hard. Then he clears his throat and shifts in his seat, attention back on the menu.

"I'm only asking if you really want the salad." He angles himself towards me and sets his eyes right on mine. "Look at me now and tell me you really want the salad. And only the salad."

Well, crap. I can't even keep a straight face. I laugh softly and pull the menu towards me to check it again. He leans right into me, his mouth by my ear as he lists other things he likes from the menu. Then, in a slight movement, his lips brush my neck.

"You smell really good, by the way," he says and I shiver, inadvertently squeezing his thigh in the process. "And I'm sure you'd love for me to—"

Charlotte's return to the table pulls us out of our whispering, and I'm giggling uncontrollably, probably set off by the giddiness I'm feeling.

She doesn't scoot back into the booth. Instead, she leans across and grabs her coat.

"I'm sorry to do this, but I'm taking off. I've literally had enough. Can you text me and let me know what I owe you for the drinks? Thanks, Kel."

"Is everything okay?" I ask.

"I'll text you," she says, retreating towards the exit.

She stops to let a server pass as Lyla comes skidding out from the direction of the bathrooms a few seconds later.

"Wow," Johnny says, looking at me with a raised eyebrow. "Shall we—"

"Sure," I say, shuffling in the space I have to reach for my coat, but Johnny knits his brows together.

"Oh, did you want to leave?"

"I thought—"

"I was just going to ask if we should order," he says, tapping the menu that's open in front of me. "I'm starving. Unless you want to go home?"

"I don't."

"Good," he says.

I'm not sure what he's going to do next. He doesn't have to pretend anymore, but he's still pressed right up against me. I can see his jaw tighten and then he leans closer, our eyes locking. And for a moment, I think he's going to kiss me.

Someone clears their throat to the side of us, and we both dart our heads towards the noise.

"Are you guys ready to order—or are you waiting for the rest of your party?" the server asks.

"Just us and—are you ready, beautiful?" Johnny's hand runs gently along my arm and my skin prickles with goosebumps. I can't even remember my own name right now, let alone my order. "Kelly?"

"Yes. Right."

The server pulls out a little notepad from a front pocket but doesn't take her eyes off Johnny. She stares at him for a beat before tilting her head to the side, recognition dawning on her face.

"Oh, wait—are you Johnny Koenig?" she asks, widening her eyes slightly, and to my complete surprise, Johnny shakes his head.

"Nah, but I get that all the time."

I have to bite my lip to hold in a laugh, managing right up to the point where the server walks away after taking our order.

Once it's just us again, I giggle. Johnny laughs too, a deep, rumbly chuckle that has me wondering how often he lets his guard down, allowing the less serious side of him to come out to play.

He takes a sip of water then clears his throat.

"Want to hear something funny but also very embarrassing?" he asks, lips tightening into a straight line. "Aw, man. I can't even think about it, really."

"Okay, now I need to know," I say, grinning at him.

He runs his hands through his hair, then grins at me.

"When I bumped into Charlotte the other day, I was having brunch with my sister. When we first got there, I had a few fans ask me for autographs and whatever. And I have this thing where I feel obliged to say yes, even if I'm eating or whatever.

They pay our wages when you think about it, so it's the least I can do."

"Right…"

"Anyway, someone who turned out to be Lyla wanted to borrow the salt from our table, but I thought she was asking for my autograph, and…" Johnny's shoulders start shaking as he laughs. "I was so embarrassed."

"Oh my God," I say, clamping my hand over my mouth.

"Yeah—honestly, I thought she was going to bring it up. I've been worrying about it since we got here, but they were obviously too busy doing whatever they were doing. My sister's face was a picture. She loved seeing me make a complete idiot of myself."

Johnny talks about his sister with a glimmer of something in his eyes. And from what he told me about his upbringing during the three months we spent chatting, they were there for each other. It's endearing.

"I'd love to meet her someday," I say.

"Why? So, you can ask her about more embarrassing moments? I'm sure she's captured most of them on camera, to be honest."

There's that deep chuckle again.

"Can I get you any more drinks?" The server is back with a beaming smile, and she looks like she's checking Johnny out again.

"Do you want another drink, babe?" he asks, the same hand dancing gently over my skin.

Babe. That's a new one.

"I'm fine, thanks," I say.

She ambles away, keeping her eyes locked on Johnny.

"That was awkward, right?" I say once she's out of earshot.

Johnny's brow furrows as he scoffs in disbelief. "Just a little."

"She was undressing you with her eyes, Johnny."

"Nah," he scoffs, suddenly very interested in the dessert menu.

And I realise there are people looking at us. Staring even. Perhaps they recognise Johnny, or they're possibly wondering why we're sitting here together. Because let's face it—right now, I'm punching.

"Why were you on that app, Johnny?"

"I could say the same thing about you," he says sharply before taking in a breath.

"Well, obvious reasons—but look at you. You're really good-looking."

"I don't think that about myself, Kelly. In fact, I see a therapist and that's partly why. My self-esteem was so low at one point."

He shifts away from me, and I realise that I've said the wrong thing.

"I'm sorry. I didn't mean for it to sound like that," I say, feeling like my whole body is crushing itself with the pressure of my poor assumption.

His arm, which was casually draped over the back of my seat, drops to his side.

"Women want the dark and handsome types, Kelly. Not the blue-eyed, blond guys. I mean, it's the hand I've been dealt, and it sucks."

My jaw drops, because I'm in complete disbelief that Johnny would see himself any different from what I see—and what Tom sees. I could ramble on about how handsome I think he is, and tell him he's wrong about himself, but it seems like he's already decided. I try another angle.

"Do you not trust my judgement, Johnny? Because I can't even look at you sometimes," I say with a smirk. "You're really fucking handsome."

"Oh."

I can't even believe I said it out loud. My whole face burns with embarrassment.

Of course, this is the time when the server brings our food, setting the plates down on the table. Johnny insisted on ordering starters and mains to arrive together, so the table fills quickly.

Johnny waits until the server's left before speaking again.

"How're your studies going?"

Okay, I'm definitely embarrassed now. And my heart sinks because he's changed the subject so quickly. The sternness of his voice, indicating that 'Johnny the Captain' is back.

But I'm not settling this time. Despite the anxiety building in my chest, there's no way I'm sitting here, eating a meal with *this* version of him.

"Please don't do this," I say, looking into his eyes. "Please don't switch the conversation or shy away or whatever, whenever things get difficult."

"You're right, I'm sorry. I just don't know how to deal with compliments."

"Well, nor do I, but you'll have to deal with it. Because you're special, Johnny. And I think you should remember that."

Johnny

I'VE NEVER ACTUALLY BEEN on a date. Not like this, anyway.

I don't even realise the time passing, and my face aches from smiling so much. Yes, it got a bit awkward earlier, and my low self-confidence came out to bite me on the ass, but we've moved past it. And now things are easy.

I'm relaxed.

"How do you not know this song?" Kelly says, leaning into me slightly.

"I can hardly make out the tune. If you were quiet for a second, I may be able to catch it."

She looks at me, eyes wide, and presses a finger to her lips, but mouths the lyrics, anyway. I steal another glance at her, because the dress she's wearing shows off her hips and her curves in a way I haven't seen before. I'm intrigued.

I'm watching the way she sways to the music, and I can't help myself; I'm thinking about how her body would feel under mine, how she'd sound when she comes.

Impure thoughts.

A load of impure thoughts about Bettsy's nineteen-year-old sister has my dick coming to life.

"Nope. Don't have a clue."

"It's one of my favourite songs," she says.

"You've said that about every single song that's been played," I say. "How many favourite songs do you have?"

"Okay, confession time." She tucks her hair behind her ear and puts a serious expression on. "If I like a song, it's officially classed as a favourite."

I roll my eyes. "Yeah, but I swear you told me your favourite song was—"

"Shh!" She stops me mid-sentence. "Don't say it out loud. It's one of those guilty pleasure songs that I only listen to when I'm in the comfort of my own car, or my own shower. You weren't supposed to remember I told you that."

But I did. I remember everything she's told me, including the details of her sex toy drawer.

And the dirty thoughts keep coming.

"You never did tell me your favourite song, Johnny. Or does it depend on which version of Johnny you're being at the time?" There's a playful grin on her face and a twinkle in her eye that tells me she won't let up.

"You're funny, Kelly. I like music, but I don't have a favourite song," I say.

"That's wild."

"Nah, it's fine. However, when it comes to genres, it has to be..."

"—classic rock." She finishes my sentence for me and rolls her eyes. "But isn't that a hockey thing? Standard locker room tunes."

"How do you know about locker room music?"

She rolls her eyes at me. "Honestly. Don't make me say his name."

"Right."

Bettsy's face appears in my mind's eye, followed by an image of him snapping my legs in two.

"Don't disappear on me, Johnny. Come back." She laughs and shifts closer so our eyes meet.

Live in the moment, Johnny.

"I'm here," I say.

Her face is inches away from me now, and I lean in and kiss her. Without even thinking about how it's going to be perceived, or if she'd even kiss me back.

But she does.

Tenderly at first, then she shifts closer to deepen it. And I can't even believe how I could forget how good this feels. She opens her mouth slightly and I have to hold myself back from ravishing her.

She does this thing with her teeth, the sort of nibble on my lip that's not a nibble. But it drives me wild. And my kiss turns hungry. I want more. And I want her.

It gets me rock hard, and I'm so conscious that she'll notice, I consider shifting away. But I can't. It's just like how I remembered it to be, except this time, I cup her face with one hand, and my other slips around her waist to pull her closer. If she feels it, she feels it. Whatever.

"I'm here," I say again, breaking away. Our noses touch, and she looks at me differently.

"You didn't have to do that, Johnny," she says. "Charlotte and Lyla are gone. There's nobody watching."

"Well, damn. If I'd remembered that..." I grin at her. "I wanted to. Was that okay? I mean, I didn't mean—"

She kisses me this time. She shifts in her seat to get closer before she breaks away with a gasp as her hand brushes the bulge in my pants.

"Oh."

I clear my throat and shift away; my cheeks burn with embarrassment.

Someone clears their throat behind me, and I disconnect from the moment to find a different server smiling at me.

"Can I get you anything else?"

These fucking servers, honestly.

Kelly shakes her head, so I ask for the bill, pulling out my wallet from my inside pocket as the server slides the receipt onto the table. She tells us she'll be back with the card machine.

"Let me see," Kelly says, reaching for the bill.

"Nah, I've got this."

"No, it's fine. We'll split it."

"Like hell we will." I hand the server my credit card and wait for her to process it.

"Johnny—"

"I had a nice time, Kelly."

"Well, thank—ah shit."

"What?" I turn around and follow her line of sight.

Shit indeed. Hutch and Jani are standing on the pavement outside, which could mean that Bettsy is close.

"Do you think Mike is here?" she says.

"Who knows? I'll be pissed if he is, because that means it's a gathering that I wasn't invited to."

My attention is snatched to my phone when it vibrates in my pocket.

Bettsy.

And there he is. Standing right outside the restaurant with his phone pressed up against his ear as my phone rings in my hand. I swallow hard. I bet he saw my car.

"Grab your stuff," Kelly says, indicating for me to slide out of the booth. She shimmies across and grabs my hand. "Follow me."

She leads the way, right towards the back of the restaurant, towards a patio door that opens out onto a terrace. A string of large, bare lightbulbs decorates the veranda overhead.

"Oh, we should have sat out here. It's lovely." She turns to face me, just as a server comes rushing through the door, knocking Kelly forward into me. I stumble to catch her as the server makes a half-assed attempt at an apology, but neither of us is listening.

She's right here in my arms, her body pressed tight against mine.

"Shit, sorry," she says, straightening up. Turning towards me, we lock eyes for a second and I lean down, pecking at her lips.

"You are so beautiful. I mean, you always are beautiful, but tonight—that dress is something else."

Her jaw drops just a little, as if she's going to say something, but she leans in and kisses me, lingering her lips on mine for a moment, before tickling my bottom lip with her tongue, sending a shiver down my spine.

"Thanks," she says.

And before I can consider what I'm doing, I'm pushing her hair away from her ear so I can lean down and kiss her neck, just the briefest of touches, before I whisper into her ear.

"Do you want to come back to mine? I mean—that fucking dress is killing me."

She giggles, sending a delicious swell of excitement all the way through me. Then a familiar drawl slices through the air.

"Johnny?"

Kelly and I both turn our heads towards the caller, and I'm not sure if it's the shock or the jelly legs that Kelly has given me, but I lose my balance when Sarah's face comes into view, knocking both Kelly and me to the floor.

"Oh my God," Kelly laughs and because she's got such a huge grin on her face as she flails underneath me, I laugh too.

"Oh, shit. I'm sorry," I say, trying to right myself.

I get to my feet and pull Kelly up so she's flush against me again.

"Did you hurt yourself?" she asks, brushing at my shirt.

"Fuck. No, but did I hurt you? I'm sorry I—"

"Aren't you going to say hi?" Sarah's voice fills the air again.

I haven't encountered Sarah once since we broke up, and now, here she is, popping the bubble on my date. She looks the same. And when I lock eyes with her, I feel sick to my stomach.

"I'm Sarah, Johnny and I used to—"

"Kelly. How's it going?" she says.

Then, to my surprise, Kelly leans in and whispers in my ear, so close that she has me giggling as her breath tickles me. "Do you need me to be your fake girlfriend still?"

But the look on Sarah's face tells me that Kelly doesn't need to say or do anything else, because seeing me standing here with another woman is enough to make her angry. And the giggle probably didn't help.

"We need to go," I say.

I take Kelly by the hand. I pull her away as Sarah calls out again.

"Johnny, wait. Could I talk to you for a moment, please?"

She looks between Kelly and me, and it's obvious that she wants me to step away. She wants to talk to me in private.

"I've got nothing to say to you," I say, gently tugging Kelly's arm again as I pull her along after me.

We exit through the back gate and move around to the front of the restaurant, staying close to the wall.

Fuck.

"Are you okay, Johnny?" Kelly asks.

But I can't find any words. I feel like everything I've been building myself towards, every single thing I've done to get Sarah's harsh words out of my head comes flooding back.

Then, I remember the reason we are leaving via the back entrance, and once I'm confident the coast is clear, I usher Kelly into the passenger seat of my car and walk around to the driver's side.

Instead of getting in, I lean against the door and take a breath, scolding myself for allowing another replay of that encounter with Sarah. Should I have said anything different? Should I have allowed her to talk to me? Should I go back and find out what the hell she's still doing here? Of course, I know the answer to all of these is no.

No, because she's poison. She's an abusive piece of shit.

My mind reels and that familiar surge of tension runs through my body, causing me to kick the front driver's side tyre of my car as I yell into the air. I pace away, running my hands through my hair, then giving my tyre another kick for good measure before placing my arms parallel against the door frame.

Deep breaths, Johnny. Remember your coping strategy.

I completely forget that Kelly is inside the car until she climbs out and tentatively comes around to my side of the car.

"Are you okay?" she says.

Shit.

"Yeah. Sorry. I just needed a moment. I'll take you home."

I'm fully expecting her to run away, or call Bettsy or something, but she doesn't. She looks at me for a moment. I can see her studying me from the corner of my eye. Then she squeezes into the gap between me and the car and wraps her arms around my waist, slipping them underneath my jacket.

Instead of that bubbling feeling growing at a steady rate, it trickles away when she squeezes me and rests her head on my chest.

"I'm here, Johnny. Be in the moment with me," she says.

And I do. I drop my arms and return the hug and we stand there on a sidewalk for at least ten minutes, in each other's arms.

Chapter 17

Kelly

"Has that happened before?" I ask Johnny.

He pulls out into the flow of traffic and heads for the link road towards my place. The traffic is minimal, so we glide through the streets with ease.

"I struggle with my emotions sometimes. I'm sorry," he says.

"You don't need to be sorry for feeling something, Johnny."

He keeps his eyes on the road, his jaw clenched. Whatever that was back there, has pushed away the Johnny I was having the most incredible time with, and brought out a stranger. Because that wasn't even Captain Johnny.

"I haven't seen Sarah since we broke up. I thought she moved back to Canada. It caught me off guard, that's all."

"Was it a nasty breakup?" I ask, wondering if I'm being too nosey—I mean, he's mentioned her before, but I don't know any details.

"It wasn't great," he says, still looking at the road as he drives.

Since it seems like our conversation is over, I switch my attention to the passing scenery illuminated by the streetlights. I'm not sure how much time passes before Johnny talks again.

"I was playing a road game, and we got all the way there to find that they'd cancelled it because the ice was patchy and unsafe. It was a last-minute thing, but we got back on the coach and headed home. I called her, but she didn't pick up, then I got back to our place, and she was riding the guy who lived across the hall. Fully going at it right there in my goddamn bed. Turned out, it'd been going on for months and I was too dumb to notice it.

"Wanna hear the worst part? I didn't even care. I was glad to have a valid reason to free myself from her—from her ways. And if he wanted her? Then happy fucking days. Ultimately, I ended up moving out that night. I went to stay with your brother, actually, before I moved to where I am now." His hands clench the steering wheel as he talks.

"Did you love her?" For God's sake, Kelly—why did you ask that?

He scoffs. "If you ask her, she'd tell you I'm incapable of love. But I guess I did at one point, at the very beginning, when she made me feel special. When I caught her cheating? No. It was probably the complete opposite. She wasn't a very nice person, Kelly. But I fell for the show she put on. She followed me around for months before we started dating. Came to all my games, made out she was really into me, and I fell for it. But she didn't want me. She wanted money and the status of being a 'WAG' or whatever—except, she didn't want me to play. She didn't want me to have friends. But you probably know yourself, when you're with a guy on a team like ours, you're not just with the guy. It's like one big family. The guys are back and forth, and that's how it is."

"I'm so sorry that happened to you. She must have really broken your trust. No one deserves that," I say.

"Well, I'm a fucking failure, aren't I? So, what does it matter?"

His words hit me hard, knocking the air out of my lungs. "What do you mean by that?"

"Forget it," he says, and he reaches for the dial of the stereo and turns the music up. Volume twenty-five hits different when there's a bad mood in the air.

I twist the dial down again. "You don't get to do that, Johnny," I say. "You can't lay that one on the table, then refuse to talk about it."

"I need some time," he says, setting the volume back to twenty-five.

Volume down.

"Why are you shutting me out?"

I realise I have no right to ask him that. Because, after all, who am I to Johnny?

And as if the evening couldn't get any worse, the console of his car chirps with a new text message.

Sarah

Can we talk?

He glances down at the screen, then straight back at the road, still choosing to say nothing.

As much as things simmer under the surface, I realise he's retreated twenty steps from where we were an hour ago—this is an alternate version of Johnny that I don't know. And by the time we pull up outside my place, I'm on the brink of tears, frustrated and upset that I started to think that Johnny was becoming comfortable with me, and that he was enjoying my company. And I was really starting to like him.

I've got my hand ready on the door handle, so as soon as he stops the car, I'm climbing out.

"You're right, Kelly. I am emotionally unavailable. I'm sorry I ever put you in a position where you thought this may become something. I'm sorry that I led you on."

I hold back the tears. "It was all a show anyway, right?"

I don't wait for him to reply. I climb out of the car, slamming the door shut behind me just in time for the tears to come.

I can't get to my front door quick enough, just like a replay of that night I saw Johnny's poster at the rink. I get inside and press my back up against the door as I sob.

Johnny

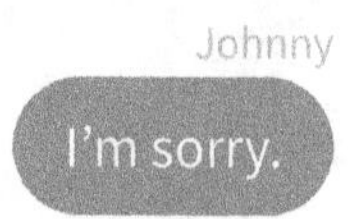

It's one of those times where I don't even remember driving home, but suddenly I'm sitting in the parking lot of my building, and I'm sending Kelly a message. It's all I can muster right now, but I can't *not* say anything.

She reads it but doesn't reply, and I take it as what I deserve.

I'm so angry with myself. And I understand if I go back to her place to speak with her, I'll end up saying a whole load more stuff I shouldn't because I can never find the right words.

"Well, I'm a fucking failure, aren't I? So, what does it matter?"

Sarah used to call me that all the time. And in an instant of seeing her, all the things she used to say to me came flooding back. All those times she told me I was a waste of oxygen, and I wouldn't amount to anything.

My mind quickly becomes overwhelmed, running the events of the evening over in my head, over-analysing every single little detail.

Sarah was the catalyst that fucked it all up.

I head straight upstairs, but instead of going back to my apartment, I stop outside my neighbour's, rapping on Liam's and Danny's apartment door.

What I really want to do is talk to Bettsy–since he's the only one who knows the full extent of Sarah's wrath. But right now, I doubt I'd be able to look at him, let alone talk to him. If he knew the way I reacted in front of his sister, he'd have my balls as well as my legs—I'm sure of it.

But I need to vocalise this, and I hope to God that Liam or Ryan are here.

Danny answers the door and shifts aside to let me in, not even asking why I'm here.

"Alright, Cap?" Danny says, sitting down. "Help yourself to whatever."

"No, Liam?" I ask, moving into the apartment.

Ryan and Jenna are in the living room clutching video game controllers.

"He's in bed," Ryan says, hitting pause and looking up at me. "You okay, bud?"

"I—can I have a word?" I ask. "Out on the balcony."

It's futile really, since he'll only tell Jenna anyway, but whatever. He nods and then shifts to stand up.

I step through the apartment towards the door leading to the seating area outside. It's not a huge balcony, but it'll do.

Ryan follows me outside, closing the door behind him and automatically reaches for a pair of sticks leaning up against the wall. He hands me one, Danny's, and not my usual style, but I accept it. He uses the toe of his stick to flick a Green Biscuit closer, then we stand at opposite sides of the balcony and pass the puck back and forth.

I know what he's doing. He's creating a focus point, since he knows that having something to concentrate on is exactly what I need.

"What's going on, Johnny?" he says after what feels like ten minutes. "You look like you've been out. Anywhere nice?"

"I bumped into Sarah," I say, receiving his pass.

"Shit. I didn't realise she was still here," he says.

"Nor did I. I saw on social media that she's engaged. I guess I figured she'd be back home."

"I thought you got Vicky to look after that stuff for you?" he says.

"Yeah, I do. But I did a bit of scrolling and I came across it."

"Did you wipe it clean?" he says, chuckling to himself, but I'm not in the mood for jokes right now. He clears his throat. "Right, sorry. Sarah. Did you talk to her or anything?"

"Not really. But she asked if she could talk to me, and I told her I had nothing to say to her. Then she texted me when I was driving home, and it sort of hit me hard."

"Didn't you block her number?"

I look at him, and he shrugs.

"Okay, I guess not."

I pull my phone out of my pocket and do what I should have done a long time ago.

"So, what's the problem?" he asks, flicking the biscuit onto the blade of his stick and playing with it in the air a little.

What can I possibly tell him? That I'm fucking terrified that my ex, who said she was moving to another continent, is in fact, still in the same city as me. And that her lingering threat to tell everyone who will listen about my... issues is towering over me—all the way back from when we first broke up.

What if she decides that she's going to the media? I mean, I know I'm not a big deal or anything really, but that doesn't change the fact that I'm in the public eye and people will talk and laugh and... fuck.

"She knows something about me, Prez. Something that I really don't want getting out. I mean—it's nothing crazy or illegal or anything but something—" Shit. How do I phrase this? "It's something that I don't want getting out."

He stops abruptly and looks at me, confusion on his face.

"Isn't it her word against yours?"

"What?"

"Well, if she tells anyone, you can deny it and people will go about their business."

"I'd rather she didn't," I say.

"I'm not sure what else you can do, though. Because if someone wants to talk, they'll talk. Unless you can convince her to sign an NDA or something, but you said it's nothing that bad."

"I honestly wish she'd fuck right off."

"I appreciate you're not ready to tell me the full story, bud... but, does she know where you live now?" he asks.

Shit, that's a good question. She knows I live on this side of the city. But I haven't given her my address or anything, not even for forwarding mail. I asked her to send anything that came through to the rink. The damn rink.

"No, but she obviously knows where I work." I grit my teeth.

"I guess your best bet is to ignore her and hope she goes away," Ryan says, sending the puck over to me.

I leave the conversation there, mulling it over as we play around on the balcony, getting over the initial shock of seeing Sarah, and wondering if telling someone helped.

It hadn't.

"Can I ask a favour?" I say, receiving the puck and stopping play. "Can you not mention this to anyone? I honestly don't need any more fucking drama."

"You bet," Ryan says.

And I take my leave.

The whole thing is stuck in my head for the next few days, and even when I get to the next scheduled practice, I'm hoping that some time on the ice will help my focus.

But when Bettsy rocks up and slinks down in his cubby next to me, I'm reminded of how shit I reacted in front of Kelly. Fucking Kelly. Too-good-for-me Kelly.

I've been so wrapped in my rage towards Sarah, I haven't even reached out to her again.

But Bettsy makes the situation a million times worse.

"What's up?" I ask him as he tosses his phone into his gear bag.

"Nah, nothing, it's all good," he says. But he changes his mind less than six seconds later and turns to look me right in the eyes. "Do you think if you learnt Vicky was seeing someone, and he'd upset her, you'd want to track him down and gut him like a fish?"

"What?"

"Well, probably not Vicky because of all that stuff with Liam, but... I had this feeling that Kelly was seeing someone. She denies it, but I went to her place yesterday to fix something and there's definitely a guy involved. She hadn't been that put out since she found out Darren was cheating. In fact, I think this has hit her harder."

I can hear my pulse beating through my ears. And to make things worse, he goes on and on about it during practice, and since we are linemates, I have no escape.

In fact, the whole thing makes me so nervous, I forget all about Sarah and put all my focus on Kelly. Because, there's a pain in my heart, knowing I made her feel that way.

I text her when I get home from the rink, desperate to figure things out.

Johnny

I'm sorry for acting the way I did. Can I see you?

Kelly

I'm working but I'll message you soon.

That was that.

And of course, I waited to hear from her. But she didn't message me back.

Chapter 18

Johnny

"Shall we set up for deadlifts?" I ask Liam, reaching for a barbell.

I'm in the gym with a few of the guys and we're working our way through the free weights, but I leave Liam to set up the weights when my phone pings.

Unknown

> Please, can we talk? It's Sarah.

I was hoping it was Kelly, but seeing Sarah's name after I've blocked her number is like a kick to the stomach. Why won't she leave me alone?

Liam is staring at me, then he pulls his eyes away as he crouches down to take the dumbbell clamp off the end of the bar, and I know I need to focus on our workout.

"Figured out what you're doing after hockey yet?" I say, tossing my phone down next to my gym bag.

"Why does everyone keep asking me that?" he says, fixing the clamp and stepping up to the barbell.

"Because you should have a plan. Simon Pearce had a side hustle for years before he retired."

"I don't know who that is, but he can kiss my ass," he says.

"He was the guy Rodgers replaced. A benchwarmer, but he had his shit together. He had a plan."

Liam looks at me with a pensive expression. "Actually, I do have a plan—Ryan and I are going to flip houses."

All I can do is stare at him because in all my years of knowing Liam, he's never once shown that he'd be keen to flip houses, that's for sure. I'm about to open my mouth to reply when the light from my phone screen blinks on and ignites curiosity.

Maybe *that's* Kelly.

Then several pings follow.

I try to ignore it, stepping up to the bar and readying myself for my set as my phone buzzes again.

"Want me to get that for you?" Liam asks.

"No. No—just leave it," I snap.

Because if he sees Sarah's, or Kelly's, name for that matter, he'll start asking questions.

He seems to back off, but my phone rings and panic sets in. What the fuck is going on?

"Shut that fucking thing up," Danny shouts from where he's spotting Ryan. And it feels like all eyes are on me, willing me to shut my phone up before someone throws it through the damn window.

"You okay, bud?" Liam asks as I reach for my phone. I take a moment to read the screen before I notice it was Wes Smith, Matt Rodgers' old team captain, who called me. Not Sarah. Not Kelly.

"Um, yeah. Look, I've got to head off," I say, grabbing my things. I've known Wes for a few years and he's not a social-call kind of guy.

A voicemail arrives as I reach the stairs.

"Hey Johnny, it's Wes. I wanted to call you and give you a heads-up. One of the guys here, you don't need his name, said that Rodgers called him a few days ago offering to sell him something. Nothing came of it here, but I wanted you to know, as he may pull the same bullshit with your men. Look after your guys, bud. Catch you in a few weeks."

Well, shit. That's something I wasn't expecting.

I slip my phone away and consider my next move. I feel like I know the guys well enough to know that they wouldn't touch anything like that, but then again, I've been proven wrong in the past. And since we underwent mandatory drug testing last week, it's probably going to be another couple of weeks before we have another, which may be a window of opportunity for someone.

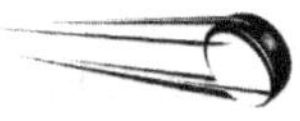

I DON'T MENTION WES' voicemail to Ffordey when he meets me in the library a few hours later.

Since we've both got proposals approved, we're now cycling through a shit ton of textbooks while we gather enough reading material to write literature reviews.

"How many words do we need to write?" he asks, highlighting a load of text on his screen two hours into our studying.

"Dr Wells told me to aim for three thousand words to allow for editing," I say.

"Well, fuck. I've got, like, three hundred. Words are deceptive." Ffordey frowns.

"Wanna grab something to eat? We can come back here after if we go to the coffee shop."

"I'll eat. But I'm done for the day, that's for sure."

We pack up our stuff and head over to the coffee shop to find that it's closed, so we walk towards the parking lot to get my car so we can head somewhere else.

As we round the corner, Bettsy's car comes into view, and my heart stops when I spot Kelly climbing out of the passenger's seat.

I think she hasn't spotted us, but Bettsy sticks his head out and yells, causing everyone in a five-mile radius to turn and stare.

"Hey, swots. How's it going? Wanna grab something to eat?" he says, flashing us a full set of pearly whites.

Kelly meets my eyes for the briefest of moments, then reaches for her cello as the campus warden moves in from behind us.

"You can't park there, mate," he says, gesturing to Bettsy to move.

"I'll park up and come find you," Bettsy shouts, pulling away.

"Oh hey, Parker," Kelly says.

She looks at me with so much hurt in her eyes, I feel damn right ashamed of myself. There's so much I want to say, but Ffordey's standing right next to me.

"How's little Bettsy?" he says.

"Stressed. I'm having to perform a duet with my ex," she says. "And speaking of him—"

Darren's saxophone case bangs me in the shins on his way past, and I stumble into Ffordey.

"Oh, I didn't realise you were bringing your boyfriend. Nice to see you again, Johnny."

He's a dick. Honestly, this guy is something else. And after the second it takes for me to process what he said, I look at Ffordey, who's staring at me as if he's trying to calculate how many rolls of tape he'd need in a season.

He opens his mouth to speak, but I talk over him.

"We're going, aren't we Ffordey?" I say, completely mortified. "We're waiting on—"

"We'll leave you to it," Kelly says, more to Ffordey than to me, nudging Darren towards the entrance of the music building.

Once they disappear, Ffordey rounds on me, and I pray for the ground to open up.

"What the hell was that?" he asks.

"Well..." He stares at me, his stony-grey eyes penetrating mine as if I've got less than a second to talk. "Remember when we went to visit Bettsy, and I picked Kelly up—"

"That was the guy?"

"Not exactly." Well, shit. That would have been a decent lie to tell. "That's her actual ex, who was also giving her shit, so I filled in again. Honestly—it's nothing. But I don't want anyone thinking it's more than it is."

I swallow hard, careful to maintain eye contact with him because there's no way I can tell Ffordey the truth.

"She doesn't think it's more than that, right? You aren't leading her on or anything, Cap? I mean, how old is she again?"

I have to fight back the urge to tell him that despite her age, some of the most mature conversations I've had in a long time have been with her. That'll be me showing my hand. Admitting that I'm actually into her, even if she's not speaking to me right now.

"She's nineteen. But no. It's nothing like that. Just do me a favour, please? Don't tell Bettsy."

The last thing I need is Bettsy putting two and two together and figuring out it was me Kelly's upset with. Besides, I know he's not as dumb as he makes out sometimes.

"I—" Ffordey's eyes widen as he looks straight past me.

"Don't tell Bettsy what?" Bettsy's voice cuts through the air. I spin around and there he is. "What can't you tell me?" He asks again, shifting his eyes between me and Ffordey.

I feel sick. The heat rises through my body as my blood rushes. I have to give him something. What the hell can I say? I ramble for a moment about him needing to keep his mouth shut, then something pops into my head. Vicky's going to kill me, but it's that, or Bettsy breaks my legs.

"I found out that the real reason Liam and Vicky split up was because Vicky couldn't deal with the prospect of divorce. She didn't want to end up like our parents. And—"

"Well, I can't say I blame her. But I don't really give a shit about that, mate."

I flash a glance at Ffordey, who shrugs.

"Are we going to eat then or what?" Bettsy says.

As we head towards my car, I realise I've made a huge mistake.

"He's too old for you, you know," Darren says, loading his saxophone back into its case. "I've seen it before, Kel. He'll realise that you're at different stages in your lives and then call things off and then he'll leave you heartbroken and—"

"Can you stop talking now, please? I really don't give a shit what you think." I've been holding in tears ever since I saw Johnny. Because I'm punishing us both. All I want to do is tell him I forgive him—tell him I understand why he reacted the way he did, but I can't muster the courage. What if he rejects me even more?

Darren gives me a pitiful expression. "Really? Because I know you, Kelly."

"No, you don't."

I rummage through the music in front of me.

"I do. And trust me. Guys like Johnny don't go after girls like you. He probably wants an easy time. I mean, assuming you're sleeping with him?"

I pull my attention away from the score sheets to stare Darren in the eye. "What business do you have asking that?"

"Come on, Kelly. His mate out there thought the same thing. He hadn't even told the guy you were a couple. I saw the look on his face—he's probably embarrassed admitting he's with you."

Oh my God.

Ffordey.

I pull my phone out and navigate to my text thread with Johnny, tuning out the yapping that Darren is still rolling with.

I stare at my screen for a moment, but when it doesn't change to read, I stuff it away and busy myself packing up my cello.

"Are you even listening to me?" Darren says, moving into my personal space.

"No. And unless you have something to say about the composition, please don't speak to me."

He shifts on the spot before backing away, which suits me because my phone vibrates in my pocket, and I fumble to pull it out, hoping to see Johnny's contact information, but it's not him. It's my brother.

Panic hits me in the chest. Because if Parker Fforde knows, he could well have told Mike and then... well, I have no idea what the repercussions of that would be.

I'm driving past, it's cool.

It's fine. I'm not finished yet.

Then why are you texting me?

I put my phone away and grab my cello and backpack, not even bothering to say goodbye to Darren. I'll leave him to fester, knowing that our professional relationship is declining as quickly as our personal one.

Except, I regret leaving as soon as I exit the music building because Mike is waiting for me. Is he angry? Did Johnny have to come clean, or did Parker tell him?

I try to come up with a single reason why I can't accept Mike's lift home, but he's striding towards me at record speed.

Shit. He knows.

Except, he's smiling, and I realise his expression is not that of a man who's recently pummelled his team captain.

"Okay, full disclosure. Mam asked me to check on you. She's been worried," he says.

"I'm fine," I say.

"Are you sure? Because the other day you were a bit off, and both Mam and I think someone's upset you."

"No, Mike. It's because I'm so stressed with work and uni. I haven't been feeling myself." He gives me a sideways glance that tells me he needs more information. "I've been working overtime, and I've had uni work to do on top of my music stuff. I'm trying to keep afloat, but things just got the better of me last week." I pause for a moment and decide to play the ultimate card. "And I got my period so—"

"Okay. Okay. Fine. It's probably a good thing you're so busy, anyway. I don't want you dating until you're in your thirties." There's a hint of humour in his voice.

"That's completely unreasonable, but whatever," I say.

He scoffs. "Jokes aside, you need to make sure you're focusing on your studies, Kel. You don't want to end up like me, do you?"

"You get paid to do something you love," I say.

We start the walk to his car.

"Yeah, but I'm just one injury away from claiming benefits. I mean, I have nothing to fall back on. Not like Johnny and Ffordey with their degrees. And Danny has his dad's company." He unlocks his car and lets out an exasperated sigh before listing off other guys in the team who appear to 'have their shit together'—his words. "I just want to ground myself. Perhaps find a girlfriend, maybe."

My jaw drops open. "You want a girlfriend?"

"No. Yes. No, actually. Pretend I didn't say that."

"Okay—well, you should come up with a plan. See if you can find something to use as a fallback. For life after hockey, I mean."

"On the girlfriend front, I've got that all squared. Remember Ellie?" I remembered Ellie. She lived next to us when we were growing up, before my parents moved to the house they're in now. I nod as Mike quickly glances in my direction. "We had this pact that if we weren't married by the time we're thirty, we'd marry each other."

"I'm sure she probably won't hold you to a school-yard pact, Mike," I say.

"Well, I know that. But it's an option." He checks his phone. "Oh, anyway, how'd you feel about coming speed dating? I saw a flyer on the window of the coffee shop near my building earlier today. Ffordey's coming. And Johnny too."

My stomach flips. Johnny, speed dating?

Now it really is like there was nothing between us. Perhaps my attempt to avoid him had gone too far.

"I thought I wasn't allowed to date until I'm thirty," I say, climbing into his car. A quick glance around confirms that there's no sign of Johnny and Ffordey—thank God. He must have brought them back here for Johnny to get his car.

"Oh, shit. Yeah. Probably not a good idea. Forget I said anything."

I manoeuvre my cello into the back of Mike's car, and he rounds to the driver's side and climbs in.

"Are you hoping to find a girlfriend at this event?" I ask, getting in next to him.

"It's more to prove a point. I can't have Rochelle thinking she can snap her fingers and I'll come running. I need to show her I've moved on," he says.

"Yeah, but you don't need a girlfriend for that. Just block her number," I say.

"If only it was that easy," Mike says, pulling out of the parking space.

It takes him ten minutes of chit-chat to switch it up and ask me when I'm next coming to one of his games. And after I've firmly said no for the third time, he admits Tom messaged him and asked for tickets.

"He's obsessed with Johnny, that's all," I say, diverting my gaze to the window.

I can't risk Mike seeing my face, because even mentioning his name gets me emotional.

Mike bursts out laughing, "Well, tell Tom that I saw Johnny's ex's name flash up on his phone earlier, but she's exactly the reason I'm insisting on him coming speed dating. He doesn't need that crap again. Not after last time."

"Oh, right," I say, literally trying to think of anything else that wouldn't make me sound anything other than normal.

"He'll probably kill me for telling you this, but she was a bit abusive."

"What?" I say, trying to keep my tone even.

"Well, not sure if it was physical, but she definitely used to call him a waste of oxygen and always made a point of telling him he was such a fuckup and a disappointment. She really got in his head, Kel. She controlled his money, wouldn't let him out to socialise... it was all a bit much." He comes to a stop outside my house. "Anyway, those tickets are always an option, Kel. Just text me if you want them."

"I don't, but thanks for the lift."

"Still hate hockey, huh?"

I can just about manage a smile, but this time, it's less about the hockey and more about Johnny.

Chapter 19

Johnny

I OPEN MY DOOR to find Ryan staring at me, grocery bags in hand.

"Prez? What's going on?" I ask.

"Do you mind if I use your kitchen?" he asks, pushing past me. "Vicky's still sick and—"

"I've got plans," I say, and he stops in his tracks, looking down at his watch before catching my eye.

"Plans? What plans?"

The worst thing about being in a team is everyone knowing your plans. Because typically, we're either in practice together, or at the gym. And since I have neither planned...

"I'm off to the store," I say, pulling it out of my ass.

"No need, I've got loads of stuff here," he says, holding a bag up.

"I need shampoo." It's the first thing that pops into my head.

What I'm actually doing is meeting with Justine, my therapist, but I don't need Ryan knowing about her.

"Right—well, can I use your kitchen? I'll clear up after myself."

I guess there's no harm in him cooking here, so I agree, reaching for my keys and my phone to shove them into the pocket of my jacket.

Ryan moves into the kitchen and starts rummaging around in my drawers, and I figure I've got a few minutes to spare since I've got him alone, so I walk back to the living area and stop at the threshold of the kitchen.

"Hey, quick question. Have you heard the guys discussing supplements?" I ask.

"Supplements? Like legal ones, right? Or are we talking about something else?" He pauses on his way to the fridge.

I tell him about the voicemail Wes left me regarding Matt.

"Fuck. That guy is something else. But I haven't heard anything. Though things like that aren't discussed in the dressing room, out in the open."

"Well, no. But keep an ear out, will you? Thanks, bud."

I pat him on the shoulder before heading out, barrelling down the stairs two at a time.

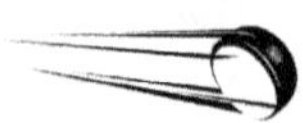

JUSTINE'S SMILE CALMS ME. I don't know how she does it, but she has some sort of magic way about presenting herself that makes me feel relaxed and at ease. But I guess that's part of her job.

Her office is above a bakery in a former terraced house. It's a pretty bizarre set up, but I've got used to it, even the narrow staircase that creaks with every single step I take.

"How have you been, Johnny?" she says, gesturing for me to take a seat opposite her.

The chairs are squishy and comfortable, and it feels like I'm sitting in an old lady's front room. She leans back in her chair. Her body language is unguarded, as if she's talking to an old friend. I wonder how long it took her to get into that habit.

"It's been a while since we spoke last," she says.

Where do I even start?

"Fine, I guess. I've had a lot going on. My dad is coming to visit. I saw Sarah, and I've completely pushed my sister's feelings away. And there's the stuff with Kelly—"

Justine shifts in her seat to sit up straight. I told her all about Kelly last time. And how things went from chatting via an app to being ghosted, to finding out she's one of my teammates' sisters. An emotional rollercoaster, to say the least.

"What's troubling you right now?"

The thing at the forefront of my mind is my date with Kelly. And how I reacted after seeing Sarah.

As I recount the evening to Justine, she nods encouragingly as I talk. Standard, really. Part of me wishes she'd interrupt and tell me what I was supposed to do instead, but apparently, this is all about reflective listening and finding my own way. Bullshit.

"I don't remember the last time I had a date, not one like that, anyway. It was easy, and it was fun and—it wasn't even supposed to be a real date," I say. I don't dig into the details, but I tell Justine about how I bumped into her friend and agreed we'd both go out. "And Sarah was there."

"How was it seeing Sarah?" Justine asks.

"It knocked me a little. In hindsight, I recognise that I was overwhelmed. I did try my steps to calm down and then Kelly hugged me, and it was... odd."

"Odd, how?"

I talk Justine through the events, and she listens, nodding at intervals.

"It felt really calming. Like she was soothing me. It sounds completely stupid, right?"

"Not at all, Johnny," Justine assures.

It's only when she hands me the tissue box that I realise I'm crying. A whole well of emotion, buried so deep I've forgotten what it feels like to let go.

"But ever since, I've been replaying the interaction and how seeing Sarah reminded me of what a fucking failure I am."

"What makes you believe you're a failure, Johnny?"

"My sister fucking hates me right now—she seems to think that our parents didn't want her. I did my best when we were growing up. I tried to make things as good as possible for her. Because we were pretty much left to our own devices. I tried. And hockey. Flitting between pro-teams in North America because there was always someone better to come along and take my roster spot. And my sex issues—I mean, what the hell is that about?"

"Let's consider this, Johnny. When do you feel the least like a failure?"

"I guess when I'm playing, and we win, and the guys are fucking beaming and they're all buzzing with energy."

"And do you think your captaincy has anything to do with that success?" she asks.

"I don't know." I shrug.

Justine settles her hands on her lap. "Who do they tend to look up to? Who do they unload their concerns regarding hockey onto?"

"Me, I guess."

"I think so. From what you've told me before. It sounds like they come to you because they trust you, and they see you as a leader and someone who can carry them forward. Which is why the victories are a little sweeter, most likely. How do you think you could use this information to focus on other aspects of your life that you find troublesome?"

I think for a moment; consider a long line of things that I find frustrating, and what is lacking.

And it's like a lightbulb pings on in my head—I need to be in control of the situation. Sarah belittled me and made me feel fucking tiny and redundant. I wonder if this is why I found it so hard to let go when it came to sex. I always had my guard up. I wasn't willing for her to see me at my most vulnerable because she could do even more damage then.

I replay my view to Justine, who nods thoughtfully.

Then, I remind her of a previous conversation we had. Early on in our sessions. Where I concluded I spent my childhood trying to parent Vicky. And even now, all these years later, I struggle to relinquish control, because it's something I'm so desperate to hold on to.

"See, I think this is something you should consider," she says. "How can you be in control of your orgasm, Johnny?"

Christ, this is embarrassing as hell.

"By doing it myself," I say.

Justine doesn't say anything back. She lets a smile creep over her face.

"So, you're saying I need to be in control to finish?"

"You tell me, Johnny. Do you need to be in control? Or let someone take control, with your full permission. Because when we've discussed Sarah in the past, she took control, but it didn't sound like that was your intention."

"It wasn't. But that doesn't explain my partners before."

"It does, Johnny. Consider it."

She's right. I mean, I wasn't raped, but the times I had sex before were hardly on my terms. It'd be a girl who only wanted sex because of a status thing; an athlete with lots of choice but giving them an ego boost to be picked—the lucky girl for the evening.

They wanted to feel special, except so did I. And I never did.

I wish I knew the answer, because Kelly deserves this. Not a half-assed effort, or, like she's been saying, an alternate version of myself. I need to give her me.

But the sting of potential rejection runs deep.

"Tell me about Kelly." Justine smiles, and from the premise of talking about her, I can't help but copy her. "She makes you smile like that a lot?"

"Like what?" I ask, shifting my eyes to Justine.

"Like you did then."

Well, shit.

"She's beautiful. And she's really smart and funny. She's someone completely different from me, but she's nineteen and my linemate's sister, which is... fuck."

"Do you think he'd disapprove?"

"I know he would. He'd have my balls," I say.

"What makes you think that? Do you know that for sure? Have you tried to date his sister before?" A twinkle in Justine's eye tells me she's probably trying to hold back a grin.

"No, but..."

"Remember, Johnny. The majority of scenarios we make up in our head are just that—made up in our head."

"He mentioned something the other day, that's all."

I roll my eyes, but as always, Justine doesn't react. This reflective listening stuff really pisses me off sometimes.

I'm exhausted by the time I get out of my session, and I sit in my car for an hour, reflecting on the conversation and what I can do next. Because Justine is right. There's something about Kelly that has me drawn to her. Is it because she's forbidden fruit? Or is it because she makes me feel genuinely wanted? Like, she was into me before she knew who I was. Hell knows, but I'm invested.

I pull my phone out to check my notifications and I end up going back to my message thread with Kelly.

Kelly

I realise Ffordey was there when Darren said what he said.

I'm so sorry. Hopefully, you told him the full story, and he doesn't get the wrong idea.

I'll tell Darren we've broken up the next opportunity I get.

Johnny

It's fine. He won't say anything to Bettsy, anyway.

Kelly

Okay.

Johnny

Can I talk to you? Please?

Kelly

I've got a lot of stuff going on with our composition and schoolwork, so I'll text you when I'm free. Thanks for respecting the fact that I need space.

But after my conversation with Justine, and my time reflecting, I know I can't wait around for her to be ready without her knowing how I feel. I need to take control of the situation for once. Even if it makes me appear desperate. But I have no idea what to do. Because I'm fucking terrible with words, and I'll say the wrong thing.

I decide to give myself a few days to think this through. To come up with a plan. And if I can't figure anything out, I'll call Scottsy and ask him how he bagged Lauren.

Kelly

Tom bursts through the door of the music room as I'm putting my cello back in its case. He's waving his phone at me, a grin spread across his face.

"Have you seen this, Kel? You didn't tell me your boyfriend is doing a live today. Oh my God. Look at him in his outfit." Tom drops into a chair, pretending to pass out in the most dramatic Tom-like fashion before righting himself. The grin on his face drops away when he locks eyes with me. "What's wrong with you?"

"Nothing," I say, glancing at Darren, who emerges from the storage room.

Even though Johnny is not my actual boyfriend, I've been thinking about what Darren said before. What the hell does a twenty-seven-year-old hockey captain, underwear-model-looking Johnny Koenig, want with me? And since Darren is back in earshot, I decide that now is the time to come clean. Or end it, anyway.

"We split up. And no, I don't want to talk about it."

Tom pulls out all the stops on his acting since he knows that Johnny and I aren't *really* a couple. He flings his arms around me and squeezes. "Oh, babe. I'm so sorry. When did this happen?"

"Oh, a few days ago," I say. "It's still fresh, so can we not mention it again?"

Tom tries to soothe me. "Do you want to get a drink? Talk about it?"

"No, no, it's fine," I say, my attention pulled to the live stream that's still playing on his phone.

"Let me turn this off," he says, turning the volume up a few notches as he fumbles with the buttons.

I catch a glance of Johnny standing at the edge of the rink with the rest of the team skating around behind him. He's talking about the team's performance on the weekend, and how they're set up for another full weekend of hockey.

"It's not an outfit, by the way," I say, nodding towards Tom's phone when he shuts it off.

"What is your obsession with him, Tom?" Darren asks, bitterness in his tone.

"Look at him," Tom says, flashing his phone screen towards him. He's still got Johnny plastered on the wallpaper of his phone.

"I've seen him. He looks like someone from a Marks and Spencer's catalogue, yes, but don't swoon over him after he's broken up with Kelly."

I couldn't roll my eyes any harder. Like he actually cares.

"How do you know Kelly didn't break up with him?"

That starts an argument I tune out, using this as an excuse to leave. I take my cello and leave through the side entrance, but Patrick, the course director, stops me in my tracks.

"Kelly. I was hoping to catch you. How are things going now that Darren has agreed to adjust the composition?"

Instantly, I switch into schmoozing mode.

I tell him about the re-work I've done, and how I've added depth to the supporting melody. Basically, I tell him what he wants to hear, giving him no reason to make me stay for longer than I need to.

"We're going to run through things on the weekend," I conclude.

"Perfect. That reminds me, please make sure Darren's tie compliments your outfit when you present your pieces."

I nod. "Of course."

"And let me know if there're any issues at all. I shouldn't tell you this officially, but I think there are some casting producers scheduled to attend at least one of your performances."

My heart leaps right into my throat, and I can hardly get parting words out.

If Patrick is right, then this could be an enormous opportunity for me. This could mean getting to play at the next level. It could mean that my future is a little more secure than it is today.

I take my cello to the single use practice rooms, fuelled with a fresh tank of adrenaline to push into practising, grateful to find one free at the end of the corridor. Whilst I unpack my things and ready myself to play, I find my mind drifting back to Johnny because all I want to do right now is call him and tell him the news.

Tom's great, and so are Sally and Marie, our other housemates, but they will probably dull this down, make out it's only another person watching the showcases that Darren and I will be doing.

Johnny will understand.

I set my cello down on its side, then rummage around in my bag for my phone. And I remember his live stream, which I pull up a few moments later. I catch it in time to see him thanking the fans for their continued support before it cuts. And of course, when it loads to playback, I watch the whole thing from the start.

It sounds wild, but Johnny's role as the captain, and my own as the lead cellist, demonstrates how alike yet completely different we both are. And when he talks about his team, it's how I feel about the others in the orchestra—except Darren.

I'm completely fixated on Johnny, watching the way he holds his stick, taking note that he shoots right.

Whoever is interviewing him asks about his feelings on the upcoming season, but I don't listen to his answer, I'm watching his lips. Thinking about how they felt when he kissed me. How they look when they curve into a smile.

The video halts when my phone vibrates in my hand. Charlotte's voice comes ringing through the speaker as soon as I answer. We chit-chat briefly before she reminds me of the failed double date. That night was everything before quickly turning into a shit show.

"How do you feel about a do-over?" she asks.

"Johnny and I broke up," I say, trying to keep my voice level. "So, thanks, but no thanks."

"You're kidding?"

"No. But it's fine. I don't have time for a boyfriend, anyway," I say.

"If you're putting all your effort into your music, then I get it, but you and Johnny—I wish Lyla looked at me the way he looks at you, Kel."

She sounds so enthusiastic; it makes me sick.

"We weren't meant to be," I say.

"What happened?" she asks.

"We weren't in the right place."

There's silence on the other end of the line for a moment before Charlotte talks again.

"I call bullshit, but whatever. I think you guys were perfect together. Most couples never find that level of chemistry."

I let her talk at me for a few moments before hanging up, with the promise that I'll call her soon, but as soon as I take a breath, the tears come, and I'm mourning a relationship that never really existed.

Chapter 20

Johnny

My dad calls as I'm finishing up with the barber and I answer after the first ring, shocked to feel excited to speak to him since it's been a while.

"Johnathan. How are things?"

"Not bad, thanks. You?"

He ignores my question and presses on with the real reason for his call. Safe to say I'm no longer enthused to be speaking with him.

"Dinner plans. I'll give Liam Preston a call, see if he can join us."

I furrow my brow. "You realise Vicky and him broke up, right?"

He avoids that, too. "Jayne is really looking forward to meeting you all. Her son plays junior hockey, you know. He's got lots of potential. Same barn you used to go to. I think this kid has the ability to go big, Johnathan. Like the twins did."

The sinking feeling that sits in my stomach tightens.

Like the twins did.

"Well, if I can offer him any pointers, I'm more than happy to—"

He cuts me off. "Maybe Ryan can give him some advice."

"Right."

"And I'm proud of him. I mean, he works hard, and he listens. Honestly, I can't wait for you to meet him." Like a knife in the chest, Dad's words hurt probably as much now as they did when I was a kid. And now he's proud of someone else's child, but not his own. Fucking brilliant.

"I need to get going. I've got something—"

"Before you go, son. Can you arrange tickets for the game on Saturday? Thanks."

The reminder that I'm a disappointment, a failure, seeps into me, and I fight an inner battle with myself as soon as he hangs up.

All I ever wanted was for my dad to be proud of me.

A heat rises through my muscles, sitting heavy on my chest. I get back to my car, slide into the driver's seat, and count to ten. Attempting to feel every part of my body, concentrating on each of my limbs—trying to ground myself.

But today, it's not helping.

I turn my phone off in case he tries to call back. Then I get out of my car and kick the front driver's side tyre hard, hoping that'll help. It doesn't. It angers me more. So, the only thing left to do is head to the rink, where I can cocoon myself.

I head back to my building to grab my gear, finding Bettsy outside the open door of Danny and Ryan's apartment. His head swivels towards the stairwell when I walk through.

"Why don't you ever answer your phone?" he says.

"I was busy," I snap.

"You okay, Cap?" Danny asks, stepping out of his apartment.

"Yep. I'm off to the rink. If anyone wants to join me, you're not welcome."

"Well, that's rude. Besides, it's out of action today. They're replacing some of the glass and have a load of workmen there," Bettsy says.

"Who told you that?" I ask, unlocking my door.

"If you bothered to check your messages..." He says goodbye to Danny and follows me towards my door. "Question, what are you doing tonight?"

"Not going speed dating, if that's where this is going."

"But Ffordey can't make it. Danny told me he's got plans and I can't go on my own, Johnny. Come on, man."

"Not happening."

"Please, Johnny?"

THREE HOURS LATER, BETTSY and I are standing against the back wall of a social club, sizing up the room. Bettsy's got his new teeth, and he's ironed his shirt; while I've lost my will to live.

"Hey, isn't that the guy who plays field hockey or something?" Bettsy says, pointing towards a gap in the crowd. "Barry, wasn't it?"

"Vicky's date from last Christmas? It looks like, yeah," I say.

"Well, if he's the best of the bunch, we shouldn't have any problems finding someone." Bettsy's grinning when he looks at me, but his expression drops to a frown. "Right, what the fuck is going on with you? I know you're usually in a mood about something, but this is ridiculous."

"I—"

"Alright, or what?" Bettsy says when Vicky and Kirsty, the girl from HR, come to a stop next to us.

"Fancy seeing you here, dear brother," Vicky says.

I honestly don't know how I agreed to this. The embarrassment I felt prior to seeing Vicky was bad enough, and now I'm completely mortified.

"Vicky."

I don't look directly at her, afraid that she'll see right into my bad mood and ask me fifty questions.

"He's not here, if that's what you're wondering," Bettsy says as Vicky glances around.

But all of our attention is pulled to the host, who starts giving us a rundown of the event. We're told the men will rotate seats after each buzzer, allowing us two minutes per person.

"I'll get us a match card each," Bettsy says, as we're ushered towards our seats.

But it's clear that Vicky is on to me when she sits herself opposite me for the first 'date.'

"You don't date," she says.

I shrug. "Bettsy didn't want to come alone."

A buzzer sounds, announcing the start of the session.

"Then why did you get a haircut?" she asks, narrowing her eyes.

"Because I needed a damn haircut. Quit it."

"I don't buy it."

"Well, it's the truth. I have my hair cut every five weeks. Live with it."

We argue back and forth before I cut the conversation and switch it to Dad, since putting the focus on him takes the heat away from me.

"He's due on Friday, you remember?" I say. "He wants to catch my game on Saturday."

"He's never cared about your games, John. Why would he care now?" Vicky drones.

"Jayne's interested by all accounts."

"How much do we know about Jayne?" she asks.

"I think she's younger than him," I say, immediately thinking about Kelly.

Is the look on Vicky's face judgement? Is she judging Dad? Would she judge me?

I don't have time to think about it as the buzzer sounds and I'm getting ushered along to the next seat, opposite Kirsty. At least these two minutes will be relatively easy too. I've known Kirsty since I joined the team, and I don't feel nervous at all.

"Hi, Johnny. Nice haircut," she says.

"How's it going? Were you coerced into coming too?"

"Sort of. But it's fine." She plays with the ends of hair as she talks. "I'm nervous."

"How come? You've always come across as pretty confident."

"Same as you, Johnny. So, are you hoping to meet someone on the off chance? Since you're here?" She raises an eyebrow.

"Can you keep a secret?" I ask, lowering my voice.

"If it's anything work related, maybe not. Since—"

"It's not. I've sort of met someone, and I really like her. But I've fucked up."

"Oh! Well, isn't this a lovely surprise? Care to tell me the name of the lucky lady who's broken through your shell, Johnny?" Kirsty says.

"I can't. Honestly. Just in case. However, saying that... it's probably a complete loss now, considering I was such a dick."

Kirsty tilts her head to the side and studies me. "Want to tell me more about it? I may be able to help. Offer some advice or whatever."

"Really?" I ask, probably sounding too excited.

"Yeah, sure. And I'll keep it to myself," she says. "Tick my box and get my number. Give me a shout when you want to talk."

"Sure. Thanks." I turn my checklist over to tick the box next to her name. Then I spot a list of questions to use as icebreakers, throwing one out at Kirsty for the fun of it.

"What's your favourite sport?" I ask, flashing her a grin.

"Not hockey," she says. "Let's go with rugby."

"Right."

I relax into the conversation after that, using the prompt card to fire off questions as I move around the room. If I ask my dates questions, it means I have little talking to do myself. I use the time to think about Kelly—and what my next move is.

I text Kirsty as soon as I get home and after an hour of back and forth, I've got a plan. Kirsty is a lifesaver.

Kelly

"These came for you." Tom's standing in our kitchen, presenting me with an enormous bouquet.

He's holding it in his arms like he's cradling a baby, a swoony grin plastered all over his face.

I move closer, eyeing the wonder in his arms, confused at first, until I realise they aren't real flowers. They're made of paper, score sheets of music crafted into roses.

"Oh my God," I say, dropping my bag.

"There's a card," he says, pointing to a small envelope taped to the cellophane. "And please don't take it back to your room to read it. Do you know how much effort I've put in to restrain myself? A woman delivered them earlier today and I swear to God it's like you've been at work forever."

I take my work fleece off and drape it over the back of a kitchen chair.

"Is that how long you've been nursing them?"

"Well, no, but they must have sprayed something on them because they smell divine."

He passes the bouquet to me carefully, as if he's handing me a baby.

I sit down and pluck the envelope from the plastic, turning it over in my hands a few times before examining the paper roses.

"*La Gazza ladra*," I whisper.

"If he knows that's your favourite piece, then..."

Of course he's talking about Johnny. I remember telling him how obsessed I was with this after I watched a movie with my brothers that we shouldn't have been watching—it was the last good memory I had with Jeremy. There are few classical pieces I enjoy, but this is one of them.

I try to angle myself away from Tom as I slip the card from the envelope, tucking it into my chest as I read.

> *I'm sorry. Really fucking sorry. And I'm terrible with words, so I hope these do a tiny amount to show you how sorry I am.*
>
> *I really like you, Kelly. And yes, I'm emotionally unavailable, but I want to try not to be. As for leading you on? I'm hoping you'll give me another chance. I can explain everything if you are willing to listen. If you aren't, I understand.*
>
> *I'll call you shortly after you're due home from work. If you don't answer, I'll leave you alone.*
>
> *J x*

"What does he mean he led you on?" Tom cranes his neck to read the card.

"Shush, Tom," I say, waving my hand to swat him away while I read it again.

"No. I need to hear the full story," he says, pulling up a chair and sitting right next to me.

"I told you everything," I say.

"Did you?"

"Yes."

Tom raises an eyebrow at me.

The emotion swells through my chest, and I sniff hard to hold back the tears.

All I want is the Johnny I knew before. The one I spent three months getting to know before I deleted the app.

Maybe this is my fault. Maybe I pushed him too far to open up.

"I need to go to bed," I say, standing up. "I'll take a shower, then call it a night."

"Do you like him, Kelly?" Tom asks.

"I don't know."

"Then why can't you say that and look at me?"

I pull my head up and look Tom right in the eyes. Which is when the floodgates burst open, and I cry the tears I've been trying to hold in for days.

He pulls me into a hug and pats my back, trying to soothe me.

"I don't understand why you're both making this so difficult," he says. "From what you've told me, it's nothing that can't be fixed. Yeah, he got irritable that his ex-girlfriend showed up, but most people would. And he probably told you he led you on because he was feeling embarrassed about how he acted."

"It's more complicated than that," I say.

"Is it?"

"You're really not the right person to talk to about this. Since you're the founding member of the Johnny Koenig fan club."

Tom pulls away from me so I can witness the contempt on his face.

"Tell me you haven't thought about him since you saw him last."

Obviously, I can't. So, I don't bother trying.

"And tell me that the date you went on, real or not, didn't put you into a state of euphoric bliss?"

Again, I can't deny it. There was something there when it was just us two. And I think Johnny felt the same way.

"What about my brother?" I ask.

"Well, that I can't help with. You're on your own there. But we can't help who we fall in love with, Kel."

Hearing the 'L' word is enough for me to call it a night.

"I'm off to bed," I say, and to my relief, Tom nods.

"Think about it," he calls after me as I walk away.

And I do think about it.

I take a shower and sort through some laundry, then I review some coursework, or try to anyway, because all I can do is think about Johnny.

But then my brother's face pops into my mind. And his warning about how I should be concentrating on my studies jingles like a tune through my head.

I take another look at the roses, delicately crafted into shape. Johnny had made an effort to get them for me, even more so since they're not just random score sheets. That must mean something, right?

There's a feeling that I can't deny. A feeling that I can't shake. And when I think about it, trying to pin it down to a specific point in time, I can't. All I know is how I'm feeling now, doesn't come close to how I felt about Darren. And that's what's scaring me. I'm afraid of getting hurt again.

My phone rings just as I put it on charge, Johnny's contact card flashing up on the screen; my heart pounds.

It's almost midnight, but I'm wide awake. I've been waiting for his call.

"Are you home?" he asks when I answer.

"Yes," I say, my breath shaking.

"Can I come in?"

I feel like a nosey neighbour, twitching at the curtains to peek outside, and sure enough, Johnny is leaning against the side of his car, his phone pressed against his ear.

I signal for him to meet me at the front door, and I hang up, giving myself a moment to settle my heart.

Taking in deep breaths, I open the door.

He's dressed in chinos and a button-down shirt which makes his biceps look like they're trying to pop out, which would probably look try-hard on anyone else. But I forgot how fucking effortlessly good-looking he is. He doesn't even need to try. He probably rolled out of bed like that.

"Thanks for the flowers," I say.

"No problem. I remembered you had that pollen thing, so I figured it'd be a better idea." He pauses for a moment, looking down at his feet before he lifts his head and looks me right in the eye. "I know you may not be ready to speak with me yet, but I couldn't take it any longer. I'm sorry, Kelly. I'm honestly so sorry—I'm shit with words and feelings, so I figured trying to show you how sorry I am would be a good idea. I know it's not enough, but... damn. I don't even know what to say."

Everything about him makes me want to melt. I don't even know how to describe it. Seeing him standing here on my doorstep, apologising. I can't.

"Can I take you out?" he asks.

"What?"

"Can I take you out? For real. Not that it wasn't real to me before. But for real, for real. Just us."

"You don't need to do that," I say.

"What? Take you out?" he says.

"Honestly, Johnny, what are we doing? Because I have no idea." I build a scenario in my head before explaining. "Say you take me out and we have fun. What happens when you shut me out again? Another bunch of flowers? Another note of apology?"

"You're right. I don't have an answer. And all I can say is I'm sorry. And that I'll try. I am trying, Kelly. But if that's not good enough, then I understand." He pauses for a moment, and the sadness on his face is so genuine. "I really fucking like you. Like I haven't ever liked anyone before."

He looks down at his feet, then takes a breath before turning away and taking a step back towards his car.

But I don't want him to go.

I want him to stay.

I want him.

"Johnny? Wait, please."

And it's like a Hollywood movie moment. Completely ridiculous, really. And if I was witnessing this as an outsider, I'd probably scoff and pass judgement. But I run towards him, in my pyjamas, and I cup his face in my hands, pulling him towards me to kiss him.

I kiss him like my body relies on it to keep me alive. Hot breath, tongues ever so gentle, touching and caressing. And when his hands move from his sides to cup my ass, I don't even care who's looking—anyone could walk past, but I've gone from zero to one hundred. Gone from not being sure to never being so sure about anything in my entire life. Because some people do this—they have a secret passageway directly into your soul that even you can't block.

I break away, his forehead still touching mine as we fall into a stare. Looking right at each other as we share the same breaths.

Then I ask him a no regrets question. "Do you want to come inside?"

"I don't think that's a good idea," he says, his breath heaving from the kiss.

"What—"

"Not because I don't want to. But because I haven't stopped thinking about you and what I—it's all or nothing for me now, Kelly. No more fucking around with fake dates."

My body burns with a heat for Johnny. "Do you want to come inside?"

Chapter 21

Johnny

"I HAVE A CONFESSION to make," I say ten minutes into our make out session.

Kelly breaks free of my grasp and looks me right in the eyes, terror on her face.

"What? Did something happen at speed dating?"

I cringe. "No, but let's not talk about it."

"Okay... what then?"

"Don't look so scared. Or maybe do, I don't know." I shrug. "But... fuck. You're not helping me here, Kelly. Because I've been having the dirtiest thoughts about you and now your hand is right next to my dick. And I told you, I don't think I can contain myself any longer."

"Oh," she says, biting her lip.

I want to bite her lip too, hear that little quiver of excitement fall from her lips as I work my way into a deeper kiss.

But I don't.

"Yeah." My lips find the crease of her neck and she smells of soap and something else that is distinctly Kelly, and it drives me wild. It's her feminine smell that's sort of like strawberries and vanilla. And I love it.

"Wanna tell me?" she says, leaning her head to the side, giving me more of her neck.

"You know I'm terrible with words," I say, running my lips over her skin.

And she giggles just a little, rubbing her hand through my hair as she whimpers.

"Wanna show me?" Her voice is teasing now, and my throat makes a noise that sounds almost feral.

Lust-filled eyes. From me and from her. Because my body is buzzing with excitement.

I spring into action. Rolling her onto her back, I coax her out of her T-shirt and toy with the fabric of her bra, wondering why the hell she's got one on in the first place.

"Are you a boob or a bum guy?" she asks.

"I'm a you guy," I say, reaching around and fumbling with the clip of her bra.

I'm rewarded after only a minor delay, my fingers gripping the clasp just enough.

She's got curves and creamy skin. And nipples that have my mouth watering—I can't believe it's taken me this long to find her.

"You're beautiful," I say, taking a deep breath.

My fingers dance along her collarbone as I toss her bra across the room. I trace my index finger between her breasts before following the curve of her left boob, working my way in a spiral, ending right at her nipple.

Her chest rises and falls, and I lean down and kiss her again, nibbling on her lip as I tentatively pull at her nipple.

"I've had lots of thoughts about these, Kelly," I whisper into her ear. The lust taking over.

"Yeah?" she breathes.

I nod and shift my body down onto the bed slightly before flicking my tongue right across her left nipple. Watching it get harder by the second. Her breathing deepens as I move my hand over to her other nipple, pulling at it slightly.

She shivers and moans in such an erotic tone. It sends a jolt straight to my already hard dick, which is now fucking painful.

I can't hold back. With one hand pulling and teasing one nipple, I flick and suck the other with my tongue, completely lost in how she writhes and moans beneath me.

She draws in a breath as I move my hand away from her nipple, her skin hot underneath my palm as I move my hand across her chest, then down to her stomach.

"Do you know I'm crazy about you?" I say, watching the path of my hand. I stop right above her waistband, and I can tell she's waiting, waiting for more, because she bucks her hips ever so slightly. Enough for me to notice. "What do you need, Kelly?"

"Johnny—"

"I've been wondering how you'll feel, and how you'll taste, and how I ever went a day without knowing."

"And what if I'd sent you away tonight?" she whispers, a smile playing on her lips.

"Then I'd have spent the rest of my life trying to win you over," I say.

Yeah, the lust is in full force, but I don't care. My head is cloudy with it—and all I want to do is slip my hand down the front of her panties and find out if she's wet for me. If she's feeling the same for me as I am for her.

"Tell me what you need, beautiful?"

"Touch me, Johnny. Please," she says, and my dick flexes in anticipation.

It's fighting against the zipper of my pants.

I roll onto my side, laying tight against her and pushing myself back into position so I can nibble a spot just above the curve of her neck.

"Is that what you want?"

She nods, and I'm living for it.

"You want me to touch you here?" I kiss her neck again, and she groans.

"My pussy, Johnny. I want you to touch my pussy."

I slide my hand right down her stomach and into her panties, not stopping to tease this time. I can't. I'm done waiting.

And by fuck, she's not only wet, she's soaking.

"Fuck, you're wet," I breathe, pushing my body into hers. "Feel that? That's what you're doing to me."

I briefly hold my breath in sync with her as I look down to where my hand is, except I can't see what I want to see.

"Slide your pants off. Let me see you."

The fact she doesn't hesitate has me in a trance. I watch her, and then shift so I can sit up against her headboard, and I pull her with me so her back is against my chest. Completely naked, her head on my shoulder, and I drink her all in. I want access to every part of her. I want her in my arms as she comes apart for me.

"Open your legs," I say, peppering kisses along her neck.

And she does, almost shaking with expectation.

I'm not sure what's more erotic, having her quivering beneath me as I slide my hand up and down her thighs, not quite getting to her pussy, or that she's whimpering in such a way that has me rocking against her.

"Touch me, Johnny. Please," she says, desperation in her voice.

I run two fingers from her clit all the way down to her pussy. She's soaking and I want to feel her. I do another pass from her clit downwards, but this time I slip a finger inside her.

Her left arm shoots up and grabs at my neck, holding herself in place while I push my finger inside her. She's tight and hot and it's even better than I imagined.

I work my way deeper, then press my thumb to her clit and circle, starting off slowly to determine what she likes, to see how she responds to me.

"How does it feel?" I say, right into her ear. "Is that good for you, baby?"

She moans into me and I settle my mouth down on hers, kissing her deeply.

"Don't stop," she says, her breath mixing with mine.

Then, eyes on eyes as she looks at me, almost silently pleading. There's a change in her body. She tenses under me and pushes her head further into my neck. And then she exhales, giving me a warning.

"Oh my God. Johnny I'm—"

"Come for me," I say, and she tumbles over the edge, shaking and writhing and moaning right into my neck. Her nipples are hard, and her pussy slick with wetness, but I can't let go, not yet.

"Fuck," she says, pushing my hand away.

I finally move away, sliding my finger out and bringing it to my lips, tasting her. Honestly, it can't get better than this.

"That was embarrassing," she says into my neck, trying to suppress a laugh. "I'll put it down to it being a while since I got myself off."

"Oh really. When was it?"

She slaps my arm playfully.

"Come on, I want to know. I jerked off to you earlier," I say, right into her ear.

"Oh my God. You did not!"

"I did. All I needed was my memory of you in that green dress."

She hides her face as I prompt her again.

"Okay, fine. On the weekend, but I'm usually a once-a-day girl."

I groan, picturing Kelly on her bed, legs spread while she works herself to climax. "God, you're killing me."

She shifts and turns to face me, reaching for the covers as she does, and I lean down to kiss her. Completely melted into the moment.

"Thanks, Johnny. I mean, for the flowers, for apologising, for... that."

But now I'm fucking terrified of what comes next. And I don't mean with us. I mean, with me.

Kelly

"ARE YOU OKAY, JOHNNY?" I ask, painfully aware I'm completely naked and he's laying here, fully dressed.

"Yeah, I am now," he says, adjusting himself so he can look at me.

"Can I do anything for you?"

My voice doesn't come out as confident as I intended it to, and since the whole subject is a bit awkward, I don't know if it was the right thing to say.

"Honestly, just accepting my apology was enough. I can't say sorry enough—"

"Stop. It's done now. Let's just look ahead."

Johnny nods. "Do you think we should tell Bettsy?"

The elephant in the room neither of us wants to discuss. But I guess there's no time like the present.

"Yes. But also, no."

"Maybe I can tell him I met someone at speed dating," Johnny says. "But that probably wouldn't work since he knows who I met at speed dating."

"You met someone at speed dating?"

"Well, yes, and no. My sister was there with a girl from work, Kirsty. You can thank Kirsty for helping me out with the flowers."

I chuckle. "I will. If I ever meet her. Though Mike mentioned Sarah has been messaging you. Is everything okay on that front?"

Johnny fills me in on the fact that he blocked her, but she's been texting him from random numbers.

"Sounds like she belongs in the same place as Darren," I say.

"How are things going with him?"

"As good as they can be, I suppose." I hesitate for a moment before telling Johnny about the casting directors.

"Well, that's exciting." He grins. "How amazing would that be? It's like when the scouts come around. Not that you need to worry."

"You've never even heard me play," I say playfully.

"I don't need to. I know you're one of the best."

My whole face flushes, but he leans in and kisses me, anyway.

"Okay, I need to tell you something," he says, pulling away but keeping close. "I'm really fucking nervous about—you know. I've got a therapist, I think I mentioned it before, but her name is Justine and I've been seeing her since Sarah and I broke up. She's been helping me through some things. And the problem with my dick being one of them. Honestly, no one knows about that except you. I want to do this right with you. You turn me on so fucking much, Kelly. You know that, right?" He clenches his jaw. "I've had blue balls ever since—actually, never mind. But I'm worried that if I do, we do, whatever, and I can't... I don't know."

"Johnny? There's no pressure at all. I want you to have a good time, but it's not something that'll push me away. We'll take things easy. See how it goes, right? Work things through together."

"I'm so grateful for you," he says, wrapping his arms around me. "I'll let you know when I'm ready. Cross my heart."

We lay looking at each other for a moment.

"Johnny? I think we should hold off telling Mike. Because it's another layer of stress neither of us needs right now. Obviously, if you want to tell him we can, but he's enthusiastic about me not dating and, ugh, I don't have the energy right now. I just need to get past my performances. Besides, I like your face how it is."

"It's actually legs he's threatened to break, not jaws. But no. I get it. Okay, so, once you're done with that, and we see how things are, we tell him?" he says.

"Agreed."

But this feels like it could be the worst idea either of us will ever have.

Chapter 22

Johnny

THE ENTIRE MORNING THROWS my routine out of the window—but that's on me, and the fact that I didn't want to leave Kelly's bed.

I ignored my alarm and, surprisingly, didn't care at all. All I wanted to do was make her come again.

I was completely sated. And I was comfortable, even if her bedroom was fucking freezing.

When I finally dragged my ass away, I had a swim, followed by breakfast, then I met Ryan for coffee and a trip to the bookstore a short walk from our apartment building.

Which is where we are now, browsing the aisles for something he doesn't know he needs until he sees it.

"How're you feeling about tonight?" he asks, skimming through the books in the fantasy section.

"Couldn't be more excited," I say.

Ryan suppresses a laugh.

Dad texted me this morning to say they'd arrived, and they were settling into their hotel. He said he'd see me at seven on the dot at the restaurant. My guess is, he'll be late.

"Liam's going too," Ryan says, reaching for a paperback. He turns it over and skims the blurb. "Apparently, your dad invited him personally."

I let out a breath. "I'm sure that'll delight Vicky."

"I was going to ask you how that's going from your angle, actually," Ryan says, flicking through the pages of the novel in his hands.

"As expected, I guess. I'm not really sure what's going on. I'm a little preoccupied if you must know."

Ryan discards the book before selecting another.

"Sarah? I thought you blocked her?"

"Well, yeah, I did. But she's been texting me from a different number. It's probably time for me to get some new digits."

"Or a restraining order," Ryan says sympathetically.

My phone pings, and I slip it out of my pocket to glance at the screen. Kelly.

I can't even help the smile that creeps across my face, which gives Ryan all the fuel he needs.

"I take it you had success at speed dating?" He wiggles his eyebrows at me.

Now my next move is crucial. Because Vicky knows that Kirsty and I matched, and she probably told either him or Jen. But I don't want to lie to him, not really—I've been doing that enough already.

I keep my response casual. "I guess you could say that."

"Well, I can't wait to hear more about her. Or him, if that's what you're into."

Maybe Vicky didn't mention Kirsty after all.

"Where did you get that impression?"

"I didn't. But it's rude to assume."

I roll my eyes and shove my phone back in my pocket as we move towards the literary fiction section. Ryan plucks a book from the top shelf and turns it over.

"I think Jen would like this," he says, tossing it into his basket.

And it gets me thinking that maybe I should buy a book for Kelly; to show her I notice her. She's got a stack of books on a shelf in her bedroom, and I think they're mostly romance novels. I make a mental note to check next time I'm in her room.

"Speaking of Jenna, how's the house hunting going?"

At the start of the season, Ryan moved in with Jenna, who happens to live in the same apartment as my sister. I know that Ryan and Jenna are looking for a more permanent place to live, which means either Vicky will be looking for a new housemate, or she'll be looking to move out too.

"We've got a few viewings lined up. But I just can't find 'the one', you know?"

I can't say I really *did* know but I nod anyway. As far as I'm concerned, home is wherever my stuff is.

"Right, are you getting anything?" Ryan says, indicating that he's ready to check out.

We pay and leave, and then we grab some coffee, carrying on the conversation about house buying before switching to hockey. Which is when my anxiety creeps in.

Dad coming to watch a game isn't a new thing, but I always feel a heightened level of stress when I know he's in the crowd. Every time I take to the ice, the nerves hit, and I'm desperate for my shift to go well. I'm desperate to impress him.

"What's on your mind?" Ryan asks me after a few moments of silence.

"I feel like I should have tried harder. I feel like I should have done better."

I can't even look him in the eyes as I speak. Because when I do, all I see is the NHL superstar that I could have been.

"We've all got different parts to play, bud," he says. "You're killing it here. The guys love you. They respect you. And yeah, you need to be less serious at times, but you're doing great." He pauses for a moment and studies my expression. "What's brought this on?"

"We both know why my dad has invited Liam tonight. Hell—he probably would have called you if he had your number."

"He did call me," Ryan says. "I told him I'm busy."

I raise an eyebrow at him.

"Date night with Jen. Nothing ever hinders date night. Sorry, bud, but not even your old man." Ryan smiles.

"I respect that."

"Now, let's kick a ball for a bit. Get your mind on something else. Worry about tonight later."

And that's what we do.

Kelly

FOR MY EIGHTEENTH BIRTHDAY, my parents bought me an electric cello.

At first, the idea of playing anything other than my usual acoustic cello unsettled me; I was horrified. But I came around to the idea when I realised it meant that I could play with my headphones in, not having to worry about waking anyone up when I'm in a deep-focus mood at an ungodly hour.

Like I am now.

I've been practising for around two hours this evening. I run through my pieces with the determination to get them fine-tuned, ready for the hours I'll be putting in with Darren.

I'm about to move on to my third piece when I hear a tapping on my window.

Pulling back my curtain, I find Johnny staring at me as he stands in the pouring rain. He's soaking wet and wearing a suit that looks like it's moulded to him.

"Can I come in?" he asks.

Without delay, I motion for him to come to the front door.

"Oh my God, you're soaking," I say, pulling him over the threshold. "What's happened? Are you okay?"

He stares at me, teeth chattering, so I pull him through to my bedroom and turn on the portable heater Mike bought me for emergencies.

"Are you okay, John?" I ask.

"Can I hug you for a moment, please?"

His voice is sombre, and I disregard how wet his clothes are, sacrificing my own in the process as I wrap my arms around him.

He twists his arms around me and pulls me closer.

"I've had such a crap evening," he says after a few minutes.

"Do you want to talk about it?"

"Did I disturb you?" he asks, clearly *not* wanting to talk about it.

"I'm just practising. That's all. Nothing that can't wait."

"Can I listen?" he says, adjusting himself so his eyes meet mine. The piercing cobalt makes my whole body prickle.

"Really?"

"Yeah. I'm interested. How often do you practise?"

"Two to three hours a day when I can. Some days, I can only manage half an hour, if I've got a full day of work or whatever," I say. "You should probably get out of your wet clothes. I caved and washed your hoodie so I can grab that for you, if you like?"

"I'll be fine," he says, kicking off his shoes and stripping right down to his underwear. I can't even bring myself to look at him properly: defined muscles and a bulge in his pants that I probably shouldn't have looked at. I force myself to put all my concentration on my cello. "Do you mind if I lay under the duvet? It's cold and all."

"Go ahead," I say, relief washing over me.

It's the most surreal thing. Johnny Koenig lying almost naked in my bed, whilst I play my cello.

I move back to where I set it down and pull my headphones out. I grab a small amp and set the volume low, then set myself up to play. My back is straight, my left hand on the fingerboard, my right elbow bent at the right spot, and my right hand holding my bow enough to support it, but not so tight that my hand aches.

He watches every single move I make.

I start my third piece, and my eyes slip closed as I play out the first few bars—since I know them so well by now. I always sway gently, flowing along with the music, and even though I start off very much aware that Johnny is watching, by the time I reach the coda, I'm in my own world.

"You're incredible," he says, shifting to sit up a bit.

"It's a work in progress," I say.

He stills for a moment, looking at me intensely, as if he's contemplating.

"I don't even know where to start, Kelly. Dinner with my dad was a complete shit show and I don't understand what's going on with my sister and her ex. Maybe they're screwing around—I don't know, but I didn't have time to think about it because I had this text message from Sarah... she said she was at my place, demanding that I talk with her, or she'd start knocking doors and—fuck."

My jaw drops as I listen to Johnny, and I set my cello down before moving to my bed. "Oh my God. What happened? Did you talk to her?"

"Well, yeah, but only as much as telling her to fuck off and leave me alone. I told her I had nothing to say to her, and then the guy she cheated on me with, Charlie, turned up and had to drag her out of the building. It's been a fucking nightmare, to say the least."

The more he says, the faster he talks.

"I'm going to need another hug, babe," he says.

And I crawl into my bed and snuggle up next to him.

"Your hair smells good," he says, taking a deep breath.

"Thanks. I washed it."

At least he laughs at that.

"I'm sorry to drop this all on you," he says. "I can go?"

"No, no. It's fine."

"It's shitty of me," he says.

"Johnny—look at me," I say, shifting myself so I'm under the blanket too. Face-to-face. "If you need to talk, I'll listen. If you need to think, then that's fine too. I'm here for whatever you need."

His sorrowful eyes tug at my core. And even though it feels like we're moving fast, the way he opened up last night showed a whole different side of him. Like I was meeting the real Johnny for the first time.

"You're something else, you know that, right? And you're so fucking beautiful. I'm sorry I was such a dick to you."

My heart aches with how he's looking at me right now. I want to ask him so many questions, but all I can do is stare.

"Stop saying sorry," I say.

He leans in and presses his forehead to mine.

"You make me forget about all the crap when I'm with you. You make me feel something, Kelly. I mean, I thought I was dead inside."

Fuck me. I was not expecting that.

"Why did you think that?"

"I guess I was told for so long by my dad that I needed to toughen up. I wanted to impress him, make him proud of me." He's silent for a moment, then he inhales deeply, turning his head away so he's staring at the ceiling. "I had these extra practice sessions when I was a kid. My dad arranged them one-on-one with the assistant coach at the club I was in. My dad thought it would help to improve my game, and he was always on at me to get better. Train harder. Do more. But the coach was after a different one-on-one session to what I had in mind. And, well, I was lucky, I guess. Because I got out before anything got too heavy. It makes me sick thinking about it. I pissed off my dad, because the extra sessions stopped, and he said I was falling behind. Then some other boy on the team ratted the guy out. He was asked to leave before they made him leave, but it didn't undo the damage already done. From that one experience, all those years ago, I shut myself down. Told myself that feeling something wasn't an option, and I needed to push ahead and get things done."

I cuddle right into Johnny, sharing my warmth with him.

He presses his lips to mine, and even though we've kissed before, it's like I'm kissing him for the first time. His lips, surprisingly soft, lock on mine as he sets the palm of his right hand on my face. Rough skin. Rough fingertips, just like mine, from years of pressing hard onto strings and the demands of pizzicato.

We spent the rest of the evening snuggled up under my covers, talking about everything and anything. But the more I find out about Johnny, the more I understand. And the more I hate his dad.

Chapter 23

Johnny

I CAN'T EVEN LOOK at Bettsy when he arrives for morning skate. The only thing I can think of is his sister coming on my fingers, that beautiful sound she makes as she comes running through my head.

He ambles into the room with his gear and then tosses his bag down before greeting the rest of the guys, completely oblivious to my antics. Then he looks right at me, and I swear to God he's trying to read my mind.

"Danny and I are going to shoot some pool tonight if you fancy it, Cap?" he says, taking a seat.

I sigh in relief. But before I can reply, one of the equipment managers sticks his head around the door.

"Johnny, your dad is looking for you."

Great.

"Your dad?" Bettsy says. "Shit, how did it go last night?"

"Don't ask," I say, slipping past him half-dressed.

Dad is waiting for me in the tunnel. He doesn't even bother saying hi.

"Have you asked Coach if Cody can join in on your skate?"

Last night, Dad asked me if Jayne's son could join in morning skate, so it doesn't surprise me that is what he's leading with.

"Really?" I ask. "Nothing to say about last night?"

"Come on, son. It was embarrassing for me. How do you think I felt seeing my kids react like that in front of Jayne?"

I can't believe this is the avenue he's taking after the way he reacted to Vicky's upset.

"You need to apologise to Vicky," I say.

"Yeah. Sure. Now, Cody—come on, son. Be a champ and ask." He pats my shoulder, and like a puppy, I chase after the ball he pretended to throw.

I head towards Coach's office to find it already occupied.

Matt Rodgers' voice slips through the crack underneath the door, and I strain to listen; it sounds like an argument. But before I can actually hear anything, he comes bounding out and pushes right past me, veering straight for the dressing room.

"Koenig. In you come," Coach says, gesturing for me to step into his office.

"I need to talk with you," I say, disregarding the Cody conversation for a moment. "I had a call from Wes Jones—about Rodgers. Something about him offering supplements before. He warned me to keep my ear out."

"Thanks, Johnny. I appreciate that because I've heard whisperings myself. Can't find anything amiss though, so I guess he's innocent for now." He takes his cap off and places it on his desk. "Anyway, things okay? All good with—"

Therapy. He's going to ask me about therapy. But since I know how easy it is to eavesdrop, I cut him off.

"Yeah, all good, thanks."

I keep the conversation going for a little, assuring him that I'm doing all I need to be doing, then I ask him for a favour.

"Cody? Sorry, Johnny. We're not insured, anyway." He winks.

I head out to break the news to my dad, only to find he's gone—probably back to Jayne and Cody. So, I call him and tell him it's a no, as my sister powers past me, a smug look on her face.

I want to ask her how she is, but she makes a beeline for a reporter and slips into conversation with him.

I return to the dressing room and finish getting myself ready, but my mood is already sour as hell, and when I finally catch up with Vicky, I'm snappy and irritable. The conversation is one I'm not overly proud of, because all my frustration turns into a lecture on how she needs to stay away from Liam.

To make matters worse, Coach yells out that today we'll be bag skating. Basically, a puck-less practice where we skate back and forth until we're ready to collapse.

At first, I'm hoping it will be an ideal opportunity to work out my frustration, but of course, the universe has other plans today.

One minute, I'm skating towards Hutch, the next, I'm flat on my ass with Liam towering over me.

He tosses his gloves to the side as if he's ready to fight.

"What the fuck, man?" I say.

"Get up!" He grabs my jersey, pulling me to my skates, then he takes a swing at me, but I duck, avoiding the blow.

"Fucking fight back, you fucking…"

But the guys gather around and then Coach yells.

Liam is getting pulled away, Ryan's arms around him as he fights against his brother.

"What the fuck are you doing?" Coach Adams is between Liam and me. "Get him off the damn ice. Now," he says, directing Ryan to take him off.

"What the hell was that about?" I ask, but when no one answers me, I have no other choice but to rush towards the dressing room.

"What the fuck was that?" I ask.

"Sorry. I didn't get a punch in. You're supposed to be bleeding."

"What the fuck is going on, Lee?" I pull my helmet off and shake my head.

"Why wouldn't you tell me you knew why Vicky called off our wedding?"

"Oh. That."

"What do you mean 'Oh, that?'"

"How—"

"Bettsy."

"Fucking, Bettsy," I say.

"No. Atta boy, Bettsy. You should have told me if you knew, because Vicky wasn't going to. I deserve to know!"

"It's not for me to tell. Besides, I promised her I wouldn't," I say.

"It didn't stop you telling Bettsy, though, did it? You're supposed to be my best friend. You know what?" Looking furious, he stands up and for a second I wonder if he's going to swing for me again. "Don't speak to me," he says.

I try to reason with him but he's not listening. Not that I can make things any better. My own selfish behaviour has caused this, and Coach...

"Office. Now," Coach says, and I follow him.

He rounds his desk and pushes his chair away but doesn't sit. Instead, he leans on its back and buries his face in his hands.

"Tell me why I shouldn't book Liam Preston a one-way flight back to Toronto, Johnny? Because whatever the fuck that was—it's interfering with my practice. You guys may think that I'm here for the fun of it but believe me—"

"That was on me, Coach. I'm sorry. We had a misunderstanding, and I can promise you it won't happen again."

"Between you and Tweedle-dee, I had faith in Liam. I trusted that giving him another chance would be a good move for us."

"Coach. Please? Considering that was half my fault, you should consider kicking me off, too."

"Well, that'd be a fucking idea—but I can't, dammit. How's that going to look? There's some shit with Rodgers and—fuck." Coach lets go of his desk chair and slips into it. "Right, Koenig. Here's what's going to happen. I'll bench him—lower body injury if anyone outside our need-to-know circles asks, but you have to promise me that this shit won't happen again."

Like a nodding dog, I agree. Because being benched and having to watch us play tonight will be punishment enough for Liam. The bottom line is, he needs to stay away from Vicky because the two of them are causing an entire load of unnecessary shit.

Before I can leave, I need to address something else. Something that's been sitting heavy on my chest since I got here today.

I wasn't feeling guilty about seeing Kelly until today. Until Bettsy walked into that dressing room and looked right at me with trust and adoration that I'd seen so many times before. There's no way in hell I can have him depending on me when I'm not even able to depend on myself.

"Hey, Coach," I say before I turn to leave. "I think it'd be a good idea to play Betts with the rookie. He's got potential and Bettsy's play style would really compliment him, you know, give him the opportunity to grow."

"Huh? What's brought this on?" Coach says, narrowing his eyes.

"I've been watching him for a while, and I believe it'd be a good call to make. I mean, it's your call obviously, but I wanted to offer some insight—things I see when we're on the ice."

Coach rubs his stubble and then nods to himself before dismissing me. I have no idea what will come out of that, but I've tried.

I'm fully fired up, and my anger boils right to the surface when I return to the dressing room to find Vicky standing outside of the logo in the centre, and I highly suspect she was in here talking to Liam.

"What are you doing in here?" I sneer, borderline ready to punch the damn wall.

"My tri—"

"Were you talking with Liam? Because you need to keep away. You're fucking his game up. Listen to me. I've told him, and now I'm telling you."

Once she's gone, I rush to the showers and scream into a towel.

Patrick, the course director, strides into the music room twenty minutes after he told Darren and me to meet him here. He doesn't even apologise for being late. Honestly, that pisses me off the most. And he's so flippant about it, it makes me wonder why we bother to keep timings if he can't.

"I've had a phone call," he says, dropping a large file on the desk next to the conductor's podium. "And it's good news."

"Oh?" Darren asks, side-eyeing me.

"You two are going on tour. For charity. The university is working with their charity partner, and they want you to do some concerts to raise money and awareness. They had booked in the drama department, but Samantha broke her leg, and it won't be healed in time for her to get enough practice in. But you're lucky I was there to hear the news—I volunteered you both. This will be a fantastic opportunity."

"When is it?" I ask.

"I'm waiting for them to confirm the dates, but it's likely going to be December. Festive shows. But I'll send you the details closer to the time. Now, for today, we're running through our set. I'm thinking Darren's piece will be second, and then I want you, Kelly, to knock something together since this will be quite an event."

I watch as Darren's face falls.

"Can't I write a second piece?" he asks.

"You can, but I won't be using it," Patrick says, putting his attention on the file, and flipping it open before rummaging around inside. "I think we'll go for this. I've adapted 'Tableaux de Provence' to be played by the cello, instead of the piano—unless you'd prefer to play it on the piano, Kelly?"

I've been wondering how long he's been waiting to ask me to flex to the piano. I'm a proficient pianist, but it doesn't do it for me in the same way the cello does, so I tell Patrick I'll stick with the cello.

We start with initial familiarisation. Patrick pulls out a laptop from his satchel and spins it around so Darren and I can see the screen. He hits play and we listen to a full run-through of the piece twice before grabbing some pencils to read through the score. I mark the paper, trying to gauge a feel for it, and Patrick offers some advice on how he thinks we should interpret some of the flow.

We spend a full two hours on this before we even play a note—classic Patrick. And then he calls it a day, giving us homework to chunk out sections for next week.

I feel completely exhausted by the time I get home, and considering I didn't have a full eight hours last night, I'm ready to fall into bed for a nap, except I don't have the option because I'm greeted by a bouncing Marie as soon as the front door closes behind me.

"I won tickets!" she says, waving her phone in my face.

"To what?"

"The ice hockey. At least I think it's the ice hockey—Jake entered a competition on the radio and won four tickets, but he can't go."

Jake, Marie's boyfriend, is now officially off my Christmas card list.

I take her phone and glance at the screen before nodding. "Yeah, it's ice hockey."

"Is this your brother's team?"

"Yeah."

"And her boyfriend's team!" Tom shouts from the living room. His head pops around the door frame and I glare at him.

"He's not my boyfriend," I say.

"Oh, is that why he was leaving in the early hours this morning?"

"What? Who are you seeing, Kel?" Marie asks.

I hand her back her phone. "No one. We're seeing how things go. But you can't mention it to anyone. My brother—"

"Oh, shit. Yeah, Kelly's brother said that she needs to stay single forever," Tom tells Marie.

"That's not entirely true," I say.

"Well, anyway, you're coming right, Kel? Even more reason to now—wait, what's your boyfriend's name? I'll Google him."

"Do not tell her!" I warn Tom.

Marie rolls her eyes at me. "I'll find out eventually. Don't worry. Anyway, it says doors open at six, so get your asses ready," she says, flicking her hair.

"I'm not going." I shrug. "I don't like hockey."

"Here we go again." Tom rolls his eyes at me. "Free tickets though, Kel."

"I can get free tickets anytime," I say.

"Why have I never been told this?" Marie says, dropping her jaw.

"Well, regardless. I'm not going. But you guys have fun."

"But you have to come," Marie says. "Who's going to explain the rules and stuff?"

"You'll have your phones," I say. "Google is your friend."

"What else could you possibly be doing tonight that's more important?" Tom says.

I don't tell him about my own plans with Google. I'm determined to find something I can offer in the way of support or advice to help Johnny become more at ease. To get Johnny a happy ending.

"I don't want to go," I say.

"Look, I know you're probably feeling anxious about it, but, I mean, it's what your brother loves to do. And you'll get to see Johnny." Tom wiggles his eyebrows at me.

"I swore to myself that I'd never set foot inside the rink again," I say.

"Okay, so how about you come, just this once, and see how it goes? It was a bad hit before and Mike is probably being more careful about his play style now."

"It's a no," I say. "Please respect that."

I resign myself to my bedroom, keen to get researching.

I'm deep into reading an article when my phone vibrates on the bed and a message from Johnny comes through.

Johnny

> Beyond stressed today. Without meaning to sound needy as fuck, when can I see you again?

Kelly

> When did you want to see me again?

I consider the article I just read, and I use the opportunity to check something with Johnny.

Kelly

> Also, do you have any boundaries?

Johnny

> What sort of boundaries?

Kelly

> Sexual boundaries.

Johnny

Should I be worried? I guess if you suggest something and it's a hard no, I'll tell you—how's that?

Kelly

Sounds good.

Johnny

Would you like to come over later? Since your room is Baltic.

Kelly

It's not that cold.

Johnny

I could use the ice your window collects to skate on.

I'll drop in a key on my way to the rink. You can let yourself in when we know everyone will be out. Apartment 801.

And… let's explore my boundaries.

Well, that gets me excited. And really fucking anxious.

But an hour later, a small envelope with my name written in black ink slides through the letterbox of our front door.

Chapter 24

Johnny

I STARE AT TOM for at least half a minute before I realise where I know him from. He's beaming, almost in tears, as he steps onto the red carpet to collect my jersey.

"Great game, Johnny," he says, keeping hold of my hand for a little too long as I shake it, then I pull my jersey off and hold it out for him.

"Thanks."

"Kelly says 'hi'," he says, then he leaves the ice, my jersey clutched to his chest, into a crowd of people.

Still avoiding eye contact, my sister gives me the signal that it's time for the post-game awards.

I feel sick with guilt. Throwing her under a bus to protect myself—I mean, I'm a complete and utter dick. Why Kelly gave me a second chance is beyond me.

I turn and skate back to the rest of the guys, taking a quick glance around the crowd, wondering if Kelly is actually here. And if she is, the likelihood of spotting her is pretty much non-existent. But I'm focused on checking anyway whilst I complete a victory lap with the guys, holding my stick in the air in appreciation for the fans before tossing it over the glass to a kid sitting on his dad's shoulders.

That's when I spot Sarah; eyes locked on mine as she stands a few rows up from ice level. For the love of Christ, why won't she leave me alone?

"Is that who I think it is?" Ryan asks as he skates alongside me. I don't even need to answer. "Well, you're having a great day, right, bud?"

We get the hell off the ice and the elated mood I was in from our win is extinguished as soon as Bettsy walks into the dressing room after me.

"What was that about earlier?"

I didn't get much of a chance to talk with him before the game, so it figures that he'd want to talk to me the first chance he got. And all I can think is that I'm standing here, lying to his face to save myself. Because that's who I am right now. And, like the coward I am, I pull the reason I've been running with right out of my ass.

"Nothing, man. I figured you'd be the best guy to pair with Yatesy. Give you a chance to show him how it's done."

"Why didn't you mention it before?" he says, his voice raising a few decibels to talk over the chatter of the guys' post-game conversations. "Is it because I told Liam what you said? I mean... it slipped out. I didn't mean to blab."

"Honestly, no. It's not. You've got a tonne of stuff you can teach him," I say. "Besides, that was on me. I shouldn't have broken Vicky's trust by telling you. I'm not proud of myself at all."

"And did you know about Liam getting the 'A'?"

"Sort of. Coach mentioned it briefly."

"Did you tell him I was interested—I mean, I am. You know that, right?"

"He knows. But it was Jani's idea, forcing some leadership on Lee since he's a bit preoccupied at the moment."

Bettsy considers this for a moment before slouching down into his cubby.

"We're good though, right?" he says, chewing his lip.

"Yeah, man," I say, patting him on the back. "Just give the kid as much support as you can. Show him how it's done. You know Team GB scouts are always watching, right?"

"Yeah, right." He nods.

I leave him at his cubby and get showered and dressed at record speed since I'm not in the mood to socialise anymore. But when I exit through the back door of the rink and close in on my car, I spot my dad leaning up against it with an expression on his face that tells me he's not happy.

Honestly, today can fuck right off.

"Congratulations on your win," he says, his stony-faced expression not budging.

"Thanks," I say, moving to the trunk of my car to toss my bag in.

"Cody enjoyed it. Do you suppose he could spend a bit of time with you before we head home?"

The question hits me in the chest.

"Slim pickings, huh?"

"Don't be like this, Johnathan. I've got enough on my plate with your sister. I don't need you causing any drama."

"Have you apologised to her yet?"

"I have."

"And?" I stare at him, watching his expression.

"She said she needs some space. And she doesn't need my help financially anymore."

That gets my attention. From what I understand, Vicky relies on an allowance from Dad. Which gets me thinking... Ryan and Jenna are moving out soon, how is she going to afford to keep living where she's living if she isn't accepting help from Dad? I know her salary doesn't stretch as far as her expenses demand, and that's before all the shoes and crap she buys.

"Do you want to grab a beer?" Dad asks.

"Can't. I've got plans."

"I've flown all this way, and that's what I get?"

I scoff. "Let's face it, Dad. You didn't come here to see me, nor Vicky."

His face changes, an expression that I can't put my finger on.

"Well, are you surprised? The pair of you are an embarrassment. How do you think that made me feel? You humiliated me in front of Jayne and Cody. She told me she doesn't know if she wants to keep seeing me," he says, shoving his hands into his pockets.

"Probably because she realised you're not a ticket to the NHL," I say.

Then it gets worse.

"If you'd done as you were told and had those extra lessons…"

My jaw drops. "Are you serious right now?"

"Yes, I am. Because you could have done better."

"And you wanted me to suck my coach's dick for the privilege? You're crazy."

"It wasn't like that," Dad says.

But I'm done with this conversation. I can feel myself tensing up with frustration.

Just once, I'd love for my dad to tell me he's proud of me and that he enjoyed my game, without making it all about him.

I move around to the front of my car and reach for the door handle. "I've got to go."

And I'm hoping beyond all hope that Kelly did actually go to my place, because she's like a single flame, burning bright in my world of darkness.

Kelly

I THOUGHT I'D FEEL awkward waiting in Johnny's place, but I don't. It feels homely and cosy, and I can't wait to see him.

I'm half-tempted to look around, nose through his cupboards and drawers and whatever, but I'm also scared about getting caught. I'd be so pissed off if someone went snooping around my stuff.

I do, however, get out my sheet music and work my way through it while I wait. And I check the score of his game every so often just in case I need to prepare myself for a loss.

It's almost half ten by the time I hear the door rattling as someone opens it from the other side, and Johnny comes into view, carrying his gear and wearing a suit that practically makes my eyes pop out of my head.

"Did you win?" I ask, knowing full well that they did.

"We sure did. The next game is a Challenge Cup game but—what? Why are you looking at me like that?" he asks, moving to where I'm sitting on his sofa.

He squats down next to me, putting his elbows on the arm.

"I just think... you look really good in a suit, Johnny."

He laughs, right to his eyes, making the cobalt sparkle.

"I'm actually so glad to see you," he says, tilting his head to the side as he looks at me.

"Yeah? Did you have a good day?"

He stands up and loses his suit jacket. He's wearing a crisp merlot-coloured button-up shirt that hugs every single muscle he has. It makes me wonder if I should start going to the gym or something.

"Honestly? No. I don't even know where to start, or if I even want to talk about it. But by any luck, my dad will be going home tomorrow." He moves towards the kitchen before turning his head back towards me. "Hey, do you want a drink or something, beautiful?"

My heart pumps wildly in my chest and I can't even will myself to speak, so I shake my head.

He steps into the kitchen area and brings back a bottle of water, setting it on the table before taking a seat next to me.

"Your friend Tom won the 'Shirt Off His Back' prize—and guess whose jersey he took home?"

"You're kidding?" I ask, widening my eyes.

"Nah. He was like a kid at Christmas."

"I told you he's a fan," I say.

"What're you up to anyway?" he says, looking at the papers I've got on my lap. I fill him in about the tour and prep that I have to do beforehand. And before I know it, we're sitting right up close to each other, and Johnny is playing with a tress of my hair while he listens to me talk.

"When can I hear you play again?"

"Soon. Once it's ready. I've got three pieces I need to work through, and this is my weakest." He nods, and I bundle up my papers and place them in a neat pile on the coffee table, careful not to make a mess.

"Wanna talk about it?" I ask, rubbing his leg.

"That obvious, huh?"

Johnny tells me that his dad was waiting for him after the game, and they had a brief conversation about his sister.

"I mean, she's pissed at me, anyway. I sort of let out one of her secrets. It's all my fault. Obviously she's not happy, and I don't blame her. But my dad mentioned she told him she doesn't want his help anymore. She's done. Which means I'm now worrying about how she's going to cope with her finances and her apartment."

He tells me about his sister's living situation, and I make a suggestion.

"Could you offer for her to move in here? You've got a spare room, right?"

Johnny thinks for a moment before biting his lip. "I guess I could, yeah. I don't know how long she's going to hold this grudge, though."

"Well, all you can do is to be there for her whenever she needs you. Speaking as a sister, I know that even if I'm pissed off at Mike, I still need to know that he's got my back and he's there for me, no matter what."

"I guess you're right," Johnny says, gazing at me.

"It just makes sense with family. Family that you actually want to associate with, anyway."

"Speaking of family... your family in particular. I spoke with Coach, and Bettsy and I aren't going to play on the same line for a while. It'll give him a chance to build his leadership up."

I gape at Johnny. "What?"

"Yeah, he'll play with Yatesy. The rookie kid. Bettsy will suit him and help him develop. It's a strategic move. A captain does what's right for his guys."

"A strategic move? Or a move because you can't bring yourself to look at him, since you know what his sister looks like when she's coming all over your hand?"

I can't even believe I said that. But Johnny stares at me for a second, then he rubs his stubble.

"Okay, fine. The reason was twofold. However, for the record, I wouldn't change my decision for anything. And I'm hoping soon I can see his sister's face when she comes on something else."

I take the initiative to grab a cushion and whack Johnny across the chest with it.

"Anyway, are you coming to bed or what?" he asks, shifting from his place on the sofa. Honestly, this side of Johnny is something else.

"Do you want me to?" I say.

But of course, we end up in Johnny's bed. Or at least I do. Flat on my back, half-naked while Johnny paws at my leggings to pull them off. Then he stands over me while he undresses himself, his eyes not leaving mine for a second.

"Have you thought any more about your limits?" I ask him.

His eyebrows pull together in confusion.

"No, was I meant to?"

"I've been doing some Googling today, and I was wondering if I could try something? If you're ready, that is."

There's suspicion on his face as I stand up, forgetting I'm now completely naked, and get to work to remove the rest of his clothes.

His skin smells fresh from his post-game shower, and I kiss his lips as I work at the zipper of his trousers, taking him in. His mouth opens as my tongue tickles his bottom lip and he moans, sending a jolt of excitement all the way through me.

"Sit on the bed," I say, pushing at his chest.

"Oh, are you in control now?" he asks, reaching up and snaking his arms around me so he can grab my ass.

"Am I allowed to be? Just this once. But if you want to stop at any time, that's fine, I can..."

I'm nervous as hell. And I think Johnny is, too. But his eyes are locked on mine as he pushes down his boxer shorts and then takes my hand, placing it on his dick. Permission. And I take it.

I sink to my knees, and he watches me with an expression that tells me he's waiting to see what I do next. But what I *see* next takes me by surprise, halting my breath in my throat.

"Oh my God," I say, eyes wide as I get my first proper glimpse of Johnny. All of him.

"What?" he says, but I'm fixed on his dick.

His pierced dick.

"You didn't tell me you have a piercing," I say, swallowing.

And now his dick is right in front of me. I mean, right there. Solid. And... large. And...

"Yeah, well. I read it's supposed to increase the sensitivity, and I thought it may help with my situation."

"And?"

"Well, what do you think?"

"Right. Sorry."

I can't help staring at the small silver bar in his dick. I wonder if it does make it more exciting for him. I wonder if I'll be able to feel it.

"And you can't ever finish?" I ask.

"Well, I can when it's just me or whatever, but not when I'm with a partner. It's like I get stage fright or something."

I cock my head to the side and study him for a moment. "Right, so, when you have a wank or whatever, you're fine?"

"Jeez—yeah."

"Right."

"What about wanking in front of someone?" I ask.

"You're being serious?" he asks. "I've never tried it."

"So, let's try now."

Chapter 25

Johnny

HER FACE IS CENTIMETRES away from my dick. It's so close I can feel the warmth exuding from her mouth. And I'm so damn hard, I think I'm about to pass out.

"So, let's try now," she says. And the nerves hit me like a check, right into the boards. The air leaves my lungs and my body tenses.

"I, umm..."

"I mean, if you want to, that is?"

Oh, I want to. I want everything with this girl.

I reach out and take her chin in my hand, pulling her towards me and kissing her. Parting her lips with my tongue, melting right into her.

"I want you to touch me," I say.

She pauses for a moment, and I wonder if I've gone too far. But she sits back and studies my dick for a second. She's thinking. And I want to know what she's thinking. But I'm so mesmerised by her, I'm watching and waiting.

She leans forward slightly and looks up at me through her eyelashes. Big green eyes on mine as she parts her lips and runs her tongue along the bottom one.

I don't think anything could have prepared me for her tongue. Hot and wanting, right on the tip of my dick, teasing at my piercing. Her hands wrap around the base of my dick as she holds it firm. Then she parts her lips a little, spitting onto me before she wraps her mouth around the head of my dick. Hot and wet and—

"Fuck," I breathe, instinctively running my fingers through her hair and gripping, gently tugging at her locks. It feels really fucking good.

She moves slowly, taking a little more of me as she adjusts her position. Her tongue caresses my dick, right under the head near the piercing, where it's the most sensitive. My eyes roll back in my head. Honestly, it's such an intense experience, my whole body lights up.

She takes me halfway, and I have to use every ounce of self-control I have not to thrust into her, because she feels so good, and I need more.

She slips away with a pop and looks up at me, and I can't help it. I reach for my dick and wrap my hand around my shaft and stroke. Up and down. Slow movements. Because I'm so hard, I could explode at any moment... could I explode?

Her hands run up and down my thighs and my pace quickens. Then she leans forwards and cups my balls in her hand. Caressing them gently. They're tight and heavy—like they're waiting to give her my release.

"Can I try something?" she says.

I stop, giving her my attention. Curious.

"Sure?"

"Put your legs up on the bed," she says, pushing to scoot me back. I do what I'm told, and watch as she disappears, returning a few moments later with a bottle of lube. "Any hard limits?"

"Fuck. I... I don't think so. What are you doing?"

"I want to try something," she says. "I've been doing a bit of research, and... do you trust me?"

I figure I literally have nothing to lose except my load, which I'm willing to rid myself of at this point, so I nod.

She slips between my legs again, and I hear the squelch of the bottle.

"Keep jerking yourself," she says, and I do. Slow and steady. "Does it feel good?"

"Yeah," I breathe, then there's a cold pressure right on my ass. "Christ, what are you doing?"

"If you hate it, I'll stop. But let's try."

I keep up the work on my dick. Long strokes. Pressure building all through my body. And I feel it. Her finger probing at me, then it slips inside just a tiny amount and I exhale.

It's not bad. In fact, it feels—

"Fuck."

"You okay?"

"Yeah, I mean—can you try a little more lube?"

Another squelch of the bottle, then the absence of her hand briefly before she runs her finger around my rim and pushes into me again.

I exhale, shuddering on the spot.

"Is this okay, Johnny?"

I can't even answer her, so I groan. Nodding.

And she slides in a little deeper. And a little deeper.

"Just keep going with your hand," she coaxes.

And I do. Picking up the pace as I jerk myself off. All the while, Kelly's finger is in my ass, and I want more.

"Deeper," I say.

"Are you sure?" she says, not waiting for me to reply.

Pushing into me a little more, I swear to God I'm going to pass out. Because she hits a spot, and it's like everything I've ever wanted has come true. The euphoria and the way my whole body comes alive.

"Fuck, that's good," I pant, picking up my pace.

She presses into me a little more, and I think I'm about to blackout. I can't even keep up the pace of jerking my dick. My hand wilts but it's replaced by another hand. Smaller. Wetter. Slick with lube, I guess.

"Fuck. Right there," I groan, and she keeps it going.

My balls tighten and there's that feeling right in the bottom of my stomach... all the way to the base of my spine. And I know there's no going back as soon as my mind completely clears of anything.

Blackness.

And I come.

I don't even give her a warning. I come hard and I watch in complete awe as she covers me with her mouth. I don't even understand what is going on.

"Fuck, fuck, fuck. Oh, my... fuck."

Her hot, tight lips are wrapped around my dick as I come. I ride out my orgasm, her finger still deep inside me and her lips around my dick. And I realise from this one experience, I'll never be able to jerk off on my own again.

"That was hot," she says before giving my dick another long suck.

I'm quaking. Almost in pieces, and I realise I'm crying. Literal tears are trickling down my face.

"I'm going to pull out now, okay?" she says.

I brace myself, feeling oddly empty once she's gone, and her tongue darts out to lick a bit of cum that dribbled into my naval.

Then she's gone. She vanishes into the bathroom, and I steady my breathing, trying to come round.

I need the moment to compose myself. Because I've never come so hard in my entire life. I've never been so fulfilled.

"Are you okay, Johnny?" Kelly's voice floats through the air, pulling me back into the moment.

I try to settle my breathing, still in the moment, as she leans down and kisses me.

"I came," I say.

"Yeah, you did." She's hovering over me, running her hands up and down my chest. "I sort of managed my own expectation that you may not. But... I hope that was okay."

"Fuck. That was more than okay."

I pull her towards me and kiss her with all the passion I possess. Because that was something else. I can't even find the words to tell her how good that was.

But this is just the beginning. When I wanted to shut myself away, Kelly opened the door.

JUST AS JOHNNY WORKS his dick into a good rhythm, there's a knock at the front door.

We're replaying last night, his legs up on the bed and my finger slipping in and out of him, giving it another shot in case it was a fluke. And I've found that sweet spot inside him again; he's completely engrossed in the moment.

"Yes, beautiful, right there. That's fucking incredible." He throws his head back and groans.

"Uh, Johnny?"

"Fuck."

"Johnny?"

"Huh?" He looks at me this time as I nudge his leg.

"That was the door."

"The door?"

"Yes. Someone's knocking on your door," I say.

And there it is. Another knock, harder this time.

I panic and pull my finger out of him.

Bang, bang, bang.

"Ah, fuck. That *is* the door," he says, clambering to his feet.

I watch him pull on clothes frantically as I dash to the bathroom to wash my hands. I'm still in my night clothes but since we both know there's a good chance it's one of the guys, I can't be found here.

"Wait here," he says. He kisses me gently on the lips before dashing out of the room, closing his bedroom door behind him.

And the next voice I hear is my brother's.

My heart sinks right down to my ass. Fuck. My shoes are out in the hallway, and I get that my brother isn't all that observant, but still. There is a chance of him noticing them.

How foolish of me. What was I thinking coming over here and staying the night? All it takes is for someone to see me for this whole situation to blow up in our faces. What if Mike catches me here, inside Johnny's apartment? He'll kill us both.

"What's going on, bud?" someone asks. I think it's Parker Fforde.

"I was sleeping," Johnny says.

"Like hell you were. You've got company, right?" Hutch's voice rings out.

I bet the whole team is outside Johnny's apartment right now. What if they come in and more than one of them needs to use the bathroom at the same time, and someone opts to wander in here to use the adjoining bathroom?

"Nah, I told you I was sleeping."

Can they smell sex in the air? Will they know?

"Then whose scarf is that?"

That's my brother's voice.

I have to clamp my hand over my mouth to stop myself from yelping. Of all the things he doesn't notice—why the hell would he notice that? Would he guess it's mine?

I take a breath and pace the space between Johnny's bed and his wardrobe. Okay, this is Mike we're talking about. He wouldn't pick it out as my scarf, would he? Has he even seen me wearing it before? Probably not, actually. But my jacket is out there somewhere, and he may recognise that.

"Okay, so I had a girl over," Johnny says. "She must have left a scarf. It's no big deal. You guys have hook-ups over all the time."

There's a moment of silence before Johnny speaks again. His tone is firm and authoritative this time. "Anyway, what's up? Because I'm sure as hell not wanting to spend my downtime standing here."

"Fancy some breakfast?" Hutch asks.

"Wait—what? You had a girl over?" my brother asks. "Who?"

I listen hard for Johnny's reply.

"Just some girl. One time thing. Nothing special."

It's completely ridiculous, but my heart pangs in my chest.

I know he's not actually talking about me. He's generalising the situation so Mike doesn't ask questions. I mean, what was I expecting him to say? *'Oh yeah, I've been seeing your sister, and she was giving my prostate a massage before you knocked on the door'?*

"Well, shit. If you aren't a dark horse. Where did you meet her?" Mike says.

"Forget it. I don't kiss and tell. And you should all know better than to ask."

"Ain't you the gentleman?" Parker says.

"So, breakfast?" Hutch says.

"I can't. I need to get a shower and whatever," Johnny says.

"It's no problem. We'll wait."

"No, thanks," Johnny says. "I'm not having you out here touching my stuff while I'm showering. I'll come knock on your door when I'm ready. Besides, I'm about to spend enough time with you guys later."

"Yeah, but you've got the good coffee," Parker says.

I hear footsteps towards the kitchen, then rummaging. The footsteps move back up the hallway towards the front door.

"Here. You take the bag. I'll see you soon," Johnny says.

Then there's a gasp.

Horror?

Shock?

"She's still here, isn't she?" Mike says.

Shit.

I can hear the grin in his voice. I know he's smirking right at Johnny, eager to show that he's cracked some sort of secret code.

"Could be a he," Hutch says.

"Fuck. Off. All of you," Johnny says, pointedly. "Now, I told you, I'll come downstairs when I'm ready."

There's a shuffling of feet before the door slams, and I sit on the edge of the bed, dipping my head into my hands.

"I thought they'd never leave," Johnny says as he walks back into his bedroom moments later. "Now, where were we?"

I gape at him.

"That can't happen again," I say. "I mean it, Johnny. I can't come here if we're going to play with fire like that. What if Mike had clocked it as my scarf? What if he'd spotted my jacket? What if he'd barged right in here and seen me in your room—in my nightwear?"

"Relax, it's fine," he says.

But I'm shaking.

"It's not fine."

"Okay, it was a close call, but we need to be more careful. Make sure your stuff is out of sight." He kneels down in front of me and takes my hands in his. "Yeah?"

"I don't know, Johnny," I say, meeting his eyes.

"Okay, so we'll lay off for a bit. I'll come to yours or whatever. I mean, the guys already think I've got a secret girlfriend, so I may—"

"What?" I say, probably a little louder than I was expecting. "Why didn't you mention this before?"

"It's no big deal, it's speculation. Now come here," he says, scooping me up into his arms as if I weigh nothing. "I think I can stall for another fifteen minutes before the guys come knocking for me again."

"Johnny—"

"Okay, okay. Well, I'll get a shower and then we'll figure out how we're going to get you home. But you're coming in with me."

Chapter 26

Johnny

My dad texts me on the drive over to Kelly's, telling me he and Jayne have split up. And he has the audacity to blame me.

I don't reply, because I'm so fucking angry at him. I end up putting my stereo on loud, and driving to Kelly's at a speed I should reserve for the highway.

I spot the cardboard covering Kelly's window as soon as I pull into the street. You can't miss it. It's taped over where a single pane of glass should be and it looks like whoever did it rushed the job.

Parking up, I hop out of my car, giving her front door a quick knock before it swings open to reveal a girl I've never seen before carrying empty shopping bags.

"Can I help you?" she asks, raising a brow.

"I'm looking for Kelly," I say.

The girl's eyes widen slightly as she studies me before she turns her head and shouts down the hallway.

Kelly's bedroom door swings open a moment later, and she pads out, wearing her hair up in a messy bun, and my damn hoodie.

Fuck, she's cute.

"Johnny?" she says. "I wasn't expecting you tonight."

"I, uh…"

"I was just heading to the shop," her roommate says. "Do you need anything picking up, Kel?"

"I'm fine, thanks, Sally."

Sally squeezes past us, leaving Kelly and me alone.

"What happened to your window?"

"I got home from uni earlier and the glass had literally fallen inside. I'm not sure if it was deliberate damage, or if it had lost the will to go on. But anyway, I called my landlady, and she sent someone over, but they covered it until they can get a replacement pane."

"The whole damn window needs replacing," I say, raising my tone.

"Well, I agree, but it's not my call to make."

"You can't sleep in there like that," I say.

"It's fine, Johnny."

"It's not. It's too damn cold in there as it is. You'll freeze," I say.

"I'll be fine."

"Get your stuff. You're coming back to mine."

She widens her eyes, then bites her bottom lip.

"We'll be careful. I promise," I say, trying to reassure her.

"Are you sure? I mean, I could ask Mike, I guess. Or stay in Tom's room."

"Kelly—"

"Okay, fine. Just give me a minute."

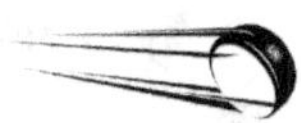

BY THE TIME WE get to my place, we've come up with a plan. Kelly will use the elevator to come and go since most of the guys use the stairs. That's been the case ever since a few of us got stuck in the elevator last season. I tell Kelly that it's the best idea we have, and if she sees anyone when the doors open to the eighth floor, she can say she was looking for Mike's apartment and she pressed the wrong button.

The whole thing is a bit of an effort since she's got her cello and a bag of her essentials. I offered to carry them both, but she assured me she's done it enough times to manage herself, and she pointed out that if someone sees me with both items, more questions will be asked.

When we make it safely into my apartment, we put all her things in my bedroom, just in case.

"Do you still have your key?" I ask.

"My key?"

"Well, yeah. The key I gave you. You can stay here until the glass is replaced."

"Johnny—"

"Well, the offer is there."

She hugs me, and it's something I realised I've been wanting all day—at least since the shit with my sister earlier.

"Are you okay?" she asks, studying my face.

"I guess. Another rough day for me."

I lead Kelly into the living room and we relax on the sofa, sitting close so her legs can lay over my lap.

"Wanna talk about it?" she asks.

"No," I say.

But ten minutes later, I've told her all about the photoshoot at the rink this morning, and how my sister's still pissed at me because she thinks I'm like our dad.

"That pissed me off," I say. "It made me really fucking angry, actually, because there's no way in hell I'd put my son's career prospects ahead of his welfare."

"Do you think he knew?" Kelly asks.

"Of course he fucking knew."

I finish venting about my dad, and then I make Kelly and me some dinner.

After we eat, she offers to wash up while I work for a little while on my thesis.

I don't get much done, because my phone pings in my pocket and I consider if I should bother reading it or not, until I see it's from Vicky, telling me about a side gig she has lined up.

Vicky

If you want to come along, you can.

Johnny

I'm good, thanks.

I show Kelly the message.

"You have to go," she says. "This is a great opportunity to reconcile."

"At a rugby match?" I ask.

"It doesn't matter what it is. It's time with your sister while she has a primary task to focus on. Maybe you should consider it."

"I'm oblivious to rugby," I explain as I hover my thumbs over the keyboard on my phone, readying myself to text Vicky again.

"You don't need to, but you could always Google it to find out."

Which is what I do. Abandoning my uni work, I learn what a scrum and a line-up is; getting myself mildly clued up enough to go with her, so I don't appear like a complete ass. Moments later, I text her back and tell her I'll go.

And because I've mentally checked out of my thesis, I put on an old hockey game to study instead.

"You can turn it off if you like," I say, passing Kelly the remote control once the second period ends.

She's sitting next to me on the sofa with her music book in front of her, cycling through a few of the pages and tapping a beat out on her leg.

"Nah, it's fine," she says, and I notice her eyes drifting to the screen as the game plays on. She moves her book to the floor, putting all her attention on the TV. "That number eleven always goes for the right side in the D-zone. Have you noticed?"

"Yeah. I have actually. And the way the play changes to match his position is always the same," I say. "I thought you hated hockey?"

"I do. But that doesn't mean I'm clueless about it." She chuckles and I stare at her. "What?" she asks.

"You. I just—I'm waiting to figure out what your red flag is. I mean, you know mine, but there's got to be something that isn't—"

"Hey," she says, nudging me playfully on the arm, but I pull her right on top of me, wrapping my arms around her waist as I kiss her.

"I'm feeling stuff for you, Kelly," I admit.

"Oh."

And I lift her up and carry her right into my bedroom, putting her down in the centre of my bed.

All I can think about is how fucking fantastic she made me feel when she—fuck. I can't even think straight.

I want her to come as hard as she made me.

I DON'T TELL JOHNNY that no one has ever gone down on me before. I mean, I've watched enough porn to know what I should do in the moment, but I don't want to admit that this is completely new for me. Not yet anyway.

His head is between my legs and the way he looks up at me has me quivering in anticipation. I've still got my underwear on, but I know how wet I am.

And I'm embarrassed.

"I wonder if you taste as good as you smell," he says.

And honestly, if anyone else had said that to me, I'd be mortified—but there's a lust in his voice that tells me he's absolutely not kidding.

Instead of sliding my underwear down, he scoops up the fabric and pushes it to the side, and I'm so exposed I don't know where to look, so I lock my eyes on the ceiling.

He kisses the insides of my thighs and I melt away, completely oblivious to whatever he's planning on doing. So much so, I don't even realise my hands slipping down and grabbing at his hair until it's beneath my fingertips.

What if I don't taste good? Or what if I laugh? Should I have taken a shower first? What if—oh sweet Jesus.

I don't even know what he's doing with his tongue, but my eyes roll back, and I sink into the bed, holding onto his head. Without thinking, my thighs clamp around his neck and he hums. He hums, and it feels so...

My pussy fills as he slips a finger inside, and he does this thing where he presses a spot inside me while he sucks down on my clit, and I scream. I actually scream.

"Shhh," he says, shifting so I can see his big blue eyes looking up at me.

"I can't—"

"Is it good? Is this okay for you?"

"Mhmm."

He suctions his mouth around my clit again and my orgasm comes out of nowhere. I can't even say I have time to give him a warning, but there's a shiver that runs through my entire body just as I climax.

It's not even a moment later that my underwear is off and he's kneeling between my legs.

I'm still shaking.

"Ready to go again?" he says, grinning down at me.

"There's no way in hell I'm going again. I need a few minutes. Or a few hours."

I'm relaxed and completely engulfed in the moment. And when he pulls me into his arms and tugs the duvet over us, I snuggle into his chest and listen to him breathing steadily.

"That's never happened to me before," I admit, after what feels like an eternity of silence.

"What? You coming like that?"

"Yeah. Thank you." I run my hands over the hard lines of his chest.

"You don't have to thank me, beautiful. I loved it. I want to do it again. I'm just waiting for you to tell me you're ready to go again." I hear the smile in his voice and gaze up at him.

"You're better than my toys," I say. "I think I'll have to retire them."

Johnny laughs.

When we were in our second month of talking, the discussion of sex toys came up. And now I'm thinking about them again. I remember wondering what 'John' would look like using his Fleshlight. I'm not sure why it gets me so excited, but now I'm lying in bed with him, his dick making a tent in the sheets, I'm curious.

"Hey, John, remember ages ago, when you told me about your Fleshlight? Was it a joke?"

I peer up at him from the crook of his arm, eyes locked on his. He grins.

"No, why? Wanna use it on me?"

My cheeks flush pink.

"Do you usually come in it or…?"

"Yeah. Well, actually, it depends."

He fumbles out of bed and heads over to the wardrobe, pulling out a box which contains another box, and there it is.

"I'll freshen it up and we'll give it a go," he says.

This is when the nerves hit. I don't know what to do with myself, so I slip deeper under the covers and take in Johnny's room.

White walls, white ceiling, grey bedsheets. It's such a guy's room. Then I cast my eyes towards his bookshelf. Mainly crime and thriller novels. I wonder if he's the sort of person who lets a friend borrow a book. I'm considering this when he comes back into the room and lays down on the bed, right next to me.

"Come here," he says, placing the toy on the bed next to him and putting all his attention on me.

He cups my face in his hands and kisses me, slow and focused, and my whole body prickles with pleasure. It's hard to believe that just a few months ago I was crying in my brother's apartment because I thought I was being catfished, and now here I am. Naked in Johnny's bed with his pierced dick and a Fleshlight. Honestly.

"I want to see what you do," I say, pulling away.

"Yeah?"

He tugs at his dick a few times, then reaches into his drawer, pulling out a small bottle of lube.

"Well, I usually find something to watch, but since I've got the hottest show around in my bed, I think I'll be fine." I'd usually cringe at such a line, but there's a way he's looking at me, which makes my whole body shiver. "I think you're fucking beautiful. And those freckles… so damn cute."

"Is cute what we're supposed to be going for right now?" I ask, watching him squirt some lube right onto the tip of his dick. He reaches for the Fleshlight and squeezes a bit inside before rubbing it right on the head of his dick.

"Whatever. Just know that this will never be as good as I know you're going to feel." He lets out a breath as he sinks the Fleshlight down onto his length.

"Does the piercing hurt?"

"Nah. It's good, in fact." He closes his eyes for a second. "I'm imagining your pussy grinding right up on it so it rubs your clit." He pops his eyes open, fixing them right on mine. "I think you'll come really hard."

He slides the toy gently up and down himself, building a rhythm. I watch his whole body respond to his movements, his abs flexing as he works it up and down.

I become engrossed, moving to straddle his thighs and get a closer view.

"Is it good?" I ask.

Johnny nods. "Wanna take over?"

Honestly, what I really want to do is whip the toy away and sink down onto him, but that'd be pushing it. Instead, I extend my hand and replace his palm with mine.

"That's it," he says. "Just keep building up the speed, beautiful."

And I do. The sound of the groans coming from Johnny, and the look on his face as it fully engulfs him, is really hot.

"Still good?" I ask, seeking reassurance.

"Yes. Really fucking good." He bites his lip and looks down at my hand, working the toy up and down. "Yes, baby, keep it going like that," he encourages me. And I take it. I watch the movements of his face, right down to the way he clenches his jaw. "Keep fucking me, just like that."

His face changes slightly, and he stiffens. Then he's begging me not to stop.

"I'm so close," he says, then before I jerk anymore, he pulls the Fleshlight off his dick and his eyes roll back as he shoots all over himself. Abs. Chest. Covered. And it's such a sight, I can't bring myself to look away.

I don't even mind when he pulls me onto his chest, wrapping his arms around me and kissing me. My pussy is pretty much right on top of where his dick is, still half-hard under me.

"You did that. You made me fucking come again," he says. And he laughs; a relieved sort of laugh that makes me grin from ear to ear.

"That was the hottest thing I've ever watched," I say.

"When do I get to see you with your rose thing?" he asks, kissing my neck.

Shit. I forgot I told him about that.

We're both sticky, so after a long shower filled with touching, kissing, and laughing, we climb into bed and I fall asleep, right in Johnny's arms, wondering how the hell I'm going to sneak out of his apartment tomorrow.

Chapter 27

Johnny

AT LEAST VICKY AND I are on speaking terms again. Which makes two road games in a row bearable when she's sticking her camera in your face.

I usually love road games, but I've been getting into a routine with Kelly. I'm already excited about getting home and seeing her again.

I left her lying in my bed this morning, fully aware that I wanted to sack off the weekend and spend all day between her legs—but then Bettsy was knocking on my door like the cock-block he is.

If only he knew.

As soon as we get to the rink for the first game, I'm off the coach first and rooting around under the bus for the ball, tossing it towards Hutch who flicks it towards Bettsy. Bettsy sat by me the whole way up, and even though I kept my head buried in my notebook for a huge chunk of time, I couldn't get away with ignoring him the whole trip. I feel so guilty, I can hardly look at the guy. Even when he kicks the ball in my direction, I avoid eye contact with him.

"You know what I found out the other day?" he says to no one in particular. "A strimmer is just a shortened way of saying 'string trimmer'. I mean, what is that about?"

"Where do you come up with this stuff?" Hutch asks.

"I didn't make it up," he says. "But it's sort of blown my mind. I won't be able to garden the same way ever again."

"When have you been gardening?" Danny asks, ducking to head the ball towards Prez.

"That girl I met at speed dating. Her nan has this enormous garden that needed cutting back. I was doing a good deed."

"You've met her nan already?" Hutch says.

"Well, she lives with her nan. Which means it's a nightmare to actually get any alone time. Since you're a creeper, I can't go for it at our place. You'd probably listen to us with a glass against the wall."

"I most definitely would not," Hutch says. "But you're right. Living with someone else always makes sex difficult. Spontaneous sex anyway. I mean, I can hardly bring someone back and get down to it on the sofa, can I? Or the table."

"Our table? Please tell me you haven't."

"No—but I've wanted to."

The ball sails through the air and Liam catches it on his chest, flicking it with his shoulder to delight the crowd of guys watching him. Everyone whoops and cheers. But as I watch him, I wonder how often he and Vicky are sneaking around—if they are. Ryan and Jen moving out is an ideal opportunity for them to keep it up. I tried to gauge her reaction during the rugby match, but I couldn't work it out. Though, on the topic of sneaking around—what if Vicky had to move in with me? I'd never be able to have Kelly stop over...not unless I could guarantee Vicky was out for the night. Regardless, she'd know I'd had a girl over.

I quickly snap out of my thoughts when the ball comes sailing towards me, almost hitting me square in the face. But my reaction time is good enough to head it into the direction of Danny, who knocks it towards Ffordey.

We switch things up and play a game where the first guy to let the ball touch the ground is out, and that takes us right up until we're called through to the dressing room to suit up.

The energy is high again now, all thanks to the game of ball, and Hutch puts the portable stereo in the corner of the room and connects his phone, blasting out a playlist he made at the start of the season.

I take my phone out to text Kelly when someone taps me on the shoulder, and I turn on the spot, coming face-to-face with Robbo, a defenceman who plays in our third pair.

"Hey, Cap, can I have a word?" He's fully dressed, bar his sweater, clutching his bucket in his hand as he chews at his lower lip.

"You okay, bud?" I ask, locking my phone and tossing it into my bag.

I can tell he's anything other than okay, so I cock my head towards the dressing room door and signal for him to follow me.

The tunnels are teeming with activity, mainly the support staff setting up for the game, so I check in a small office-type space that looks empty, making sure no one is inside before stepping in and closing the door behind us.

Robbo stands opposite me, shifting his weight from left to right as he fidgets with the strap of his helmet.

I furrow my brow and give him time to get his words out; I know they're right on the tip of his tongue.

"This is awkward, and I just want you to understand that I'm only telling you because it's the right thing to do. I'm not a grass, though, for the record—and if it was anything else... shit. Cap, can you do me a solid and not tell him I was the one to tell you?"

"What's going on?" I ask, standing tall.

"I think I saw Rodgers with some pills. I mean, they could have been something innocent but—"

"Ah, shit. I was afraid of this," I say, rubbing the stubble on my chin.

"Do you know something?" Robbo asks.

"You remember Wes Smith, right? We played together a few years back, and we sort of keep in touch—I mean, as much as most guys do now we're playing on opposing teams, but anyway. He called me and mentioned something about Rodgers and—actually, I've probably said too much. Let's keep this locked, right, bud?"

"Yeah, of course."

"When did this happen?"

"Earlier today. But I mean, I don't know the full story—he could be on meds or something."

"Leave it with me," I say, patting him on the shoulder before reaching for the door handle.

Instead of heading back to the dressing room, I make my way towards the benches, hoping to find Coach there.

As soon as I round the corner, I spot him standing, heads together, with Springy, the assistant coach, as they study something on Coach's clipboard. He looks up when I approach and beckons me towards him with his hand.

"Come and see this, Koenig," Coach says. "What do you think about changing the power play unit?" He flashes the paper at me.

"What're you thinking?" I ask, trying to keep my tone level.

"Just want to add more net-front presence against these guys, but—what's wrong?" he asks, frowning.

I lower my voice. "I don't know how serious this is, but I just had one of the guys tell me that they saw Rodgers with pills. And I figured you'd have a good idea if he was on anything official from the doc or whatever."

"For Christ's sake." Coach presses the clipboard to Springy's chest before striding away towards the dressing room.

"I had a feeling this would come and bite us in the ass," Springy says. "His stats were good, and he was cheap. The GM told us it was an easy decision. It figures."

I nod, considering it for a moment, but then a flurry of people crowd the benches.

"Finish readying up, Johnny. I'll see you shortly."

I head back towards the dressing room, just in time to see Matt Rodgers coming out of the same office I went into with Robbo, looking nervous as hell.

Kelly

I DRAG TOM ALONG with me when I meet Charlotte for lunch. She called me out of the blue and said she was in town and needed to tell me something. And she'd be coming alone.

We agree to meet at a café in the city centre. Charlotte is already waiting for us; she springs to her feet, waving and gesturing for us to join her, and after all the usual pleasantries, we sit down and browse the tatty menu.

"So, Lyla's pregnant," Charlotte says.

Her tone is so casual, I wonder if I've misheard her.

"Excuse me? Did you say...?"

"Yes. Pregnant. Lyla. She's pregnant. And she's keeping the baby, which is fine and all, but she doesn't know who the father is."

Tom and I gape at one another as if we're featuring in one of those TV shows where someone pops out from behind a screen and tells you that you're being filmed. But when I glance back at Charlotte, I see she's never been more serious in all her life.

"Yep. She cheated on me, and it all came out when we met up for the date with you and Johnny, Kel. It's been a rollercoaster ride since she lied about it. But we've split up for good and she's been trying to get me to forgive her, asking for me back and all that. I can't even look at her, let alone take her back."

"Well, shit. I'm sorry that happened to you, Char," I say.

"Why are we in a café?" Tom says. "Why aren't we drinking? I mean, I could use a drink, and this sounds like a conversation for a drink."

"You could always use a drink," I say.

"No, he's right," Charlotte says, twisting in her seat to pull her coat from the back of the chair. "Let's get out of here. Let's find a bar or something."

I'm practically dragged out of the café by Tom and Charlotte as they lead the way.

We walk up the high street and dip into the first place we walk past that looks open. It's not somewhere I'd usually go, since it looks upmarket, but Charlotte waves a credit card she pertains to be Lyla's and drags us into the bar.

I don't feel overly comfortable having drinks on Lyla's card, but when Charlotte tells me she owes her five hundred quid, I give in.

"Our entire relationship was a complete nightmare, when I think about it," Charlotte says, tapping her card on the reader. "And what makes it worse—she told me she hates men. Like actually hates them. I hate liars."

My cheeks flame red, and I'm just about to open my mouth to come clean to Charlotte—even though now may not be the time to do it—when a blonde I recognise pushes the door open and ambles inside.

I stare at her for a moment, my mind wandering from the conversation as I wonder where I remember her from. Then it clicks. It's Sarah, Johnny's ex.

"... Kel thinks so too." Tom nudges my arm.

"Huh?" I tear my eyes away from Sarah.

"Darren. The whole drama with him and what's-her-face. All a complete shitstorm too."

"Oh, yeah," I say, letting my eyes wander back to Sarah.

She's taking her coat off and draping it over the back of a chair, revealing her tiny figure. My face flushes with embarrassment. What is Johnny thinking getting involved with me?

"You okay, Kel?" Tom wraps his arm around me this time, pulling me in.

I take a gulp of my drink and nod, trying to push Sarah out of my mind. But she's heading towards us, and she double-takes when her eyes land on mine. I do that thing where I pretend not to recognise her, because maybe she'll go away, but her face breaks out into a grin as she edges closer.

"Kerry, right?"

It's hilarious. I want to say something witty back, but I've lost all my nerve. At least, I have for a split second. Until a second wind hits me.

"I'm sorry. Have we met?" I say, cocking my head to the side.

God, she *really* is pretty. I want to throw my drink in her face.

"At least, I think we have? You're seeing Johnathan Koenig, right?" She's got a Canadian accent. And it's sweet, probably sickly, actually. It makes me really self-conscious about my own.

"Oh, right. You're his ex. Of course." There's an audible gasp from Tom's direction, then a gulp as he takes a swig of his drink. "Nice to see you again."

She looks me up and down before smiling at the bartender to get his attention. She orders a drink and then turns back towards me.

"Kerry, actually, I'm glad I bumped into you. Do you mind if we have a quick chat?"

My stomach tightens. I try to respond, but nothing happens. I can't even will myself to shake my head, because I really don't want to be having a chat with her. Quick or otherwise.

Unfortunately, she takes her own initiative and grabs my elbow, steering me away from my friends.

"I just thought you should know," Sarah says, lowering her voice, "Johnny's not the man you think he is. And before you get too excited, he'll never love you. I don't think he's even capable of it, Kerry. He doesn't have a firm grasp on his own emotions, let alone the ability to let anyone else in. I'd say, do yourself a favour now and get out while you can. Before you're forced to seek the love and desire you need from a man elsewhere."

I'm quite literally too shocked to say anything. No witty comment or second wind this time. She grins at me, flicks her hair, then strides back to the bar to grab her drink, joining a dark-haired guy at the table near the window.

"What the hell was that about?" Tom says as I amble back over to them.

I pick up my drink and knock it back, hoping it'll kick me into gear, but it doesn't. I don't even know what to tell Tom and Charlotte. Because they'll both want to march over to where Sarah and her date are sitting and cause a scene.

"Would you believe me if I say it was nothing?" I say.

"No," they say, simultaneously.

"Johnny's ex just asked you for a quick chat... that can't have been nothing."

"Well, can we just leave it?" I ask, digging in my bag for my bank card. "I'll get us another round, yeah?"

But I can't fully relax until Sarah leaves twenty minutes later. My gaze lands on hers one last time as she exits. I'm wondering if I should tell Johnny since his reaction last time pushed him over some invisible edge, and I'm terrified if it happens again, he won't come back.

Chapter 28

Johnny

"I THINK MY SISTER'S coming to the game tonight," Bettsy says, tossing his phone back into his bag.

My heart jerks in my chest.

She didn't mention anything to me, I'm sure she didn't. I pull my phone out from my bag, trying to be discreet as I check my messages. All that's there is the stuff we were chatting about on the coach, which only entailed questions about porn.

Kelly

Random, but what porn do you watch?

Johnny

Is this a trick?

Kelly

No, just wondering.

Johnny

I guess I enjoy watching the usual stuff.

Kelly

Which is? Come on, Johnny. I'm not judging you (unless it's anything illegal).

Johnny

Fine. I guess my favourite is like role play, BJs, a bit of anal sometimes. But I don't need it now. I have you.

Kelly

Ha. Aren't you the sweetest? Maybe we should watch something together sometime. Do you have any favourite videos you could send to me? Just curious.

Johnny

I'll see what I can dig out.

Kelly

Don't pretend you don't have something bookmarked.

Johnny

Want to tell me what you watch?

Kelly

I like dirty talk.

I don't even realise I'm smirking at my phone until someone slaps me on the shoulder, and I have to wipe the look off my face. All our messages have heated up, and since we're still getting to know each other in the bedroom, it's exciting.

"What's got you so happy?" Ffordey says, raising his eyebrows. He's half-dressed, wearing just his underlayer.

"I'm excited that you're about to beat your own personal record for the highest save percentage on the road."

My attempt to distract him fails miserably when he raises an eyebrow at me.

"Who're you texting?" he asks.

"Just a friend."

"Is that the same friend who you met at speed dating?"

"Kirsty?"

"Yeah. I've seen you texting her a few times now," he says.

"Nothing's happening," I say. "Besides, I don't think we're all that compatible anyway. And if Vicky has to move back in with me—"

I cut myself off. Because that issue doesn't go away, regardless. Because Kirsty may not be coming around to stay over, but Kelly certainly has been, and I want her to keep doing it.

"You're a better man than me," he says. "I wouldn't want my sister moving back in with me. I mean, I wouldn't see her homeless or whatever, but I'd rather get into that net without a cup."

I feel a similar way about Vicky. She's hard work, and not to mention the whole Liam thing.

In an ideal world, I know Vicky would want to stay put anyway, but I don't have the spare cash to help her out with her rent, and I really don't want to ask either of my parents, even though I know my mom would probably give it over just to get me off the phone—that's the sad case of it.

But I park that for now, because Coach strides into the dressing room and puts his hands on his hips, ready to give his pre-game speech.

"Challenge Cup, boys. And we're getting it done. I'd like to see more presence in front of the net, and it'd be useful to try out a different power play unit. I've been considering it for a short time, but I think we'll give it a whirl tonight." He looks at me and nods. "Koenig, you're up."

I take a few steps towards the front of the room, and I stop next to Coach, giving the guys a once-over before I talk.

"We've got something special here, guys. And Bettsy is showing us how strong and adaptable he can be, so please show him your support and create those plays. Remember, our focus is always on the next goal."

A chorus of applause rings out, and I step back to my cubby to toss my jersey on and finish taping my stick.

Ultimately, I haven't broken as many as I have done previously at this point in the season, and I don't know if that's down to Kelly or...

Shit, Kelly.

I glance over to the door where Bettsy is having a moment with the kid. Heads together. Laughing. I realise I'm actually jealous—not that it makes much sense. Ultimately, I miss being paired with him. And I'm wondering how long it'll take him to notice how much I've been distancing myself from him.

But Kelly.

Is she here tonight to surprise me? Who knows? I spend time looking for her, wondering if I can spot her in the crowd. I'm scanning the rows to see if—

"Johnny, it's yours!"

I'm checked into the boards, missing the puck entirely because I'm not paying attention. For fuck's sake. Luckily for me, I chase the puck down and then clear it back to Danny, who receives it in the neutral zone. He presses on with a forward attack, so I change it up with Bettsy, my heart sinking a little when he sails past me towards the point.

I try to push Kelly out of my head, putting all my focus on the game, but it's harder than I expect. Since I know she won't be at any home games, this is never usually a problem.

It takes until the end of the second period for me to get a break from the thoughts of Kelly, when Bettsy stops at the end of the bench and waves up into the crowd and I spot not Kelly, but his other sister, Stacey. All that's similar is the deep shade of auburn hair, but otherwise, I probably wouldn't have recognised her.

"Who the hell is that?" Danny says, coming to a stop behind Bettsy.

"My sister, and before you ask, no, she's not available."

"How many sisters do you have again?" Danny says. "Isn't there one called Kelly?"

"Again, she's not available either. In fact, she's more off-limits than Stacey. And I'll break anyone's legs who tries so much as a smile in her direction. She's nineteen and has potential. She doesn't need any losers like you sniffing around."

There's a lump in my throat that I can't swallow down. Guilt.

The same guilt that I carry around the rest of the evening that only slips away, temporarily, when I video call Kelly. I'm happy in that bubble. I even go to sleep with a grin on my face after some unexpected phone sex.

But as soon as I see Bettsy the next day, it bubbles to the surface again.

Morning skate, team brunch, video playback. All I can hear is the voice in the back of my head screaming at me, telling me I'm a disgrace and that he's gearing up to snap my legs in two.

Even a win doesn't put me back in high spirits.

But there's a conflicting thought pushing through.

Kelly is supposed to be waiting for me at my apartment. And I can't fucking wait. I've never been this excited to get back from a road trip before.

As I stand next to the coach after helping to load the gear on, I end up texting Kelly back and forth about my impending arrival home and how I plan to show her how much I missed her. I only slip my phone away when I hear the double doors open, and I see my sister approaching me with her bag. She looks upset.

"Are you alright?" I ask as she pulls me into a hug. "What's going on?" I hug her back, feeling compelled to comfort her. "Is this about Liam? Because I'll kill him."

And that makes me feel even fucking worse. I've been so wrapped up in my own little world, I haven't been looking out for Vicky like I usually would.

I know how Bettsy feels, and here I am, doing whatever the hell I like.

"No, it's nothing. I just wanted to give you a hug," she says, quickly disappearing onto the coach.

But I'm racking my brain. If it's not Liam, what else could it be?

When I board the coach, I spot Ryan and Jenna snuggled up together, and it hits me. I bet Vicky's heart is broken about having to move out of her place once they've bought a place to live. It's a big change, and I know that she'll probably find it difficult. Not to mention, the possibility of living with me isn't likely injecting too much excitement into her day. We've done it before, and we swore not to do it again.

I need to do something.

I need to look after her.

I need to fix this.

Kelly

THE CLOCK TELLS ME that Johnny is likely to be home at any moment now, so I put my cello away, relieved to have gotten a few hours of practice in today before moving all my things to his bedroom—just in case.

I'm mulling over an email I got earlier today from Patrick, addressed to me and Darren, as I get ready for bed. It had details of our 'tour', if that's what you can call it. But regardless, I'll be away for a few weeks.

By the time I climb into my side of Johnny's bed, I'm wondering if Darren is going to be a decent travel companion, and the next thing I know, I'm waking up to Johnny's freezing cold body, pulling me into him.

"Did I wake you?" he whispers.

"Yes." I stir. "But it's fine. I've really missed you."

"Can I show you how much I've missed you?" he says right into my ear before he starts to kiss my neck. Delicate pecks and the stubble from his chin makes me squirm. It actually feels really fucking good.

"Are you sure you're ready?" I ask.

Johnny told me he was ready when we video-called during his road game, and I'm nervous as hell, purely because of his piercing. And also, probably because I don't know how he'll fit.

"I'm really fucking ready," he says, moving to take my mouth in his. He's so tender with his kisses, it's almost teasing. Then he slips his hand under a T-shirt of his that I'm wearing and palms my left boob. "Naked. Now."

Woah. He's got his control hat on, and I'm all for it. I wriggle myself free of the T-shirt, then push my underwear down, sending them to the floor of his bedroom.

I can't help but touch him—his chest, his shoulders, his biceps, as he hovers over me, eyes locked on mine by the light of the bathroom.

He sits back on his calves and then pushes his boxers down, not looking away from me for a single second.

Now, I don't have a lot to compare this with, but I already know this will be different. There's a way he's looking at me, and a tenderness about him, even though there's absolutely nothing tender about him physically.

He reaches over to the bedside table and takes out a condom, and my heart beats wildly. I'm expecting him to put it on and get on with it, but he doesn't. He keeps it in his palm, and he leans down to kiss me again. His tongue is slow, and so relaxed that my legs are shaking around him. I can feel his dick pressed into my lower abdomen as he moves himself on me, thrusting into the space between us.

"Pull your legs back," he says, gripping my thighs himself anyway and pushing them back onto me. I watch him. So intently as he shifts himself down the bed and kisses along the insides of my thighs. "You're already so wet for me, beautiful." His finger runs the whole length from my clit right down to my pussy, and probably a little further, actually, causing me to shiver. The anticipation is killing me.

He adjusts himself and I look down to see what he's doing just as his tongue touches me. Circling my clit. Then sucking deep.

My hands clamp right onto his head, pulling at his hair as I let out a gasp. I can't even believe this is happening to me. I breathe deep to settle myself, but he's driving me wild with the way he circles my clit. Fast and needy. It's like he knows he's getting me close. Because there's nothing else I want more than to come right now.

But he stops. Getting me right to the edge and pulling me away again.

"You're needy for that orgasm, beautiful?" he says in a hoarse voice.

"Yes. I was really close."

"I know," he says. "But I want you to come while I'm deep inside you, Kelly. Are you ready for me?"

I'm tugging at his neck, pulling him right down onto me, and then I hear the fumbling of the condom, so I give him a little leeway to move. Then he's right there. His dick pushing at the entrance of my pussy.

"I'm ready."

He pushes into me, achingly slow. So slow, in fact, I'm bucking my hips to drive him in deeper.

He buries his head in my neck, shaky breaths tickling my collarbone.

"You're really fucking tight," he says.

"Yeah? But it feels really good, Johnny," I say, reaching for his face and pulling his lips down to mine.

"It feels really fucking good. And I love kissing you," he says.

I'm beaming. I'm not sure if it's the right reaction to have, but there's a smile on my face. Even when I'm kissing him, I can't shake it. And when he pulls away and looks at me, he adjusts himself so he's really fucking deep, and I can actually feel my eyes rolling back in my head.

"You're so beautiful like that," he says, chuckling gently.

And I'm laughing right back at him. Even when his lips find mine again, we're laughing softly.

The first time he pulls out and slides back into me, I gasp. And the second time, I moan. And by the third time—I don't even remember what I do because he's building a rhythm now, and his face changes. Putting all his weight on his left arm, he shifts his right to press down on my lower stomach. And fuck knows what it is he's doing, but the noises I'm making must be the effect he's going for because he moans right back at me.

The slow and steady soon becomes hard and fast, and I want more.

"Your pussy feels incredible," he says, slowing down again. He pulls back slightly and watches the space between us. "Do you know why it feels this good, beautiful?" His eyes flick right up to meet mine again—that cobalt burning brightly.

I have no idea where it comes from, but I find myself replying to him, "because it's yours."

He looks at me for a split second longer, before pushing right into me again. Deep. And he leans down, lips hovering over mine again.

"Because it's mine."

Just when I think it couldn't feel any better, and I couldn't feel even more connected to him, his hand disappears and his thumb finds my clit.

I don't even remember when I come but it takes over my whole body. Like nothing I've ever felt before. And I'm moaning right into his mouth as I pull myself up with his movement, wrapping my arms around his neck.

And as I'm coming down, the emptiness of Johnny leaving me overwhelms me for a second, before I realise he's pulled out to whip the condom off, and he finishes himself right on my stomach.

Our bodies are a tangled mess, but we're kissing again. Hot breaths, desperate for each other. And my hands roam all over his chest, feeling him, because I don't quite believe he's real anymore.

"I'm a dead man," he says, pressing his forehead into mine. "I'm a fucking dead man, Kelly. Because there's no way I'm letting you go of my own accord."

"What's going on?" I ask.

He stills for a second before he rolls off of me. His breathing is the only sound to break through the air.

"Johnny?" I prompt again.

"Your sister was at the game. And Bettsy was quick to tell us he'd break legs if anyone even thinks about trying anything with either of you."

"You choose now to tell me that?" I say, letting myself laugh a little. "Well... you realise he wouldn't actually do that, right? I mean, he wouldn't literally break anyone's legs."

"Well, no, but still. I think I'm in too deep, anyway."

I kiss him again, holding my lips to his for a little longer than usual. But I think he knows what I'm getting at. I feel the same way he does.

Chapter 29

Johnny

"I NEED TO TELL you something," Kelly says.

I'll be honest—Kelly was the last person I expected to see when I was drinking coffee with the guys earlier.

Vicky rounded the entire team up to get fitted for suits ahead of Ladies' Night, and since none of us can read an email properly, we all turned up and crammed into the tailors at the same time. Since the place is the same size as the damn penalty box, Vicky dismissed us and told most of us to come back later, which led us to this place.

I've made my way back over to speak to Kelly briefly, since my suit fitting was pretty quick—same as last year.

"Is everything okay?" I ask, confused. "Is this about you coming to a game this weekend? I mean, it shocked me to hear it, but I'm excited."

I'm unsure of how much time we have to talk since the entire team is buzzing around in the area—and if someone spots me having a private conversation with Bettsy's sister, it'll lead to many questions that I'm not ready to answer.

Kelly fidgets with the drawstring of her hoodie, eyes on the floor for a moment before she sets her gaze on mine.

"No, nothing about that—though, that's another story. But listen, remember when you were on your double-header road trip? I met up with Charlotte—she told me that Lyla is pregnant and, never mind that, but I bumped into Sarah and she—"

"Sarah? Wait, what? Lyla's pregnant?"

I'm confused. Probably more confused than I should be, but Kelly presses on with her point.

"Don't worry about that for now. But yeah, Sarah. She wanted to tell me all about you. But I just wanted you to know, I don't believe what she said—I mean, I've heard your side of the story."

I take a few seconds to process what she's telling me. Because Sarah hassling me is one thing, but seeking out Kelly is another. That familiar heat starts creeping up through my body and I tense my jaw.

"Why didn't you tell me sooner?"

"I was trying to find the right time, but it's been chipping away at me." She places her hand on my arm before retracting it quickly. "But try not to worry. You've changed your number, so I'm sure she won't bother us again."

"What did she say to you?" I ask.

But before Kelly can reply, the door to the coffee shop opens and in walks my sister and Jen.

Shit.

"I've got to go," I say, rushing towards my sister.

She's staring at me with mild confusion on her face, and I stumble over what to say, blurting out the first thing that pops into my head.

"Did you know Bettsy had a sister?"

"No?"

"Well, that's her. She said she's coming along to the home game this weekend." I'm digging myself into a hole here, so I cut myself loose. "Anyway, gotta head out. See you later."

Back on the street, I pull my phone out and see a few messages in our group chat, telling me they're in a pub a little further up the street. So, I let my legs carry me there while I pull up the latest message I received from Sarah to my new number. God knows how she got it, but right now, that's not the issue.

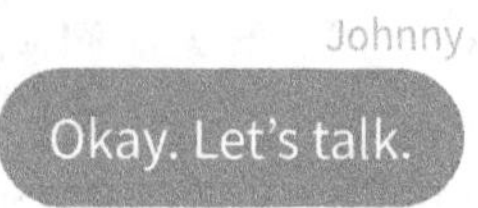

I head into the pub, finding the guys in a corner near the bar, full beers in front of most of them, chatting excitedly about the upcoming Ladies' Night.

I order a water and occupy myself with conversation, all while I wonder how long it'll take Sarah to message me back.

"I think this year will be decent," Ffordey says, shifting into a ramble about the change of venue and how many tickets they've sold, but I'm not listening. I'm way too tense and fired up.

I pull my phone back out to message Kelly, asking if she can give me a full rundown of what Sarah said to her, but just after I hit send, I get a reply from Sarah, giving me the name of a bar across town where she said she'll meet in twenty minutes.

"I need to head off," I tell Ffordey, pushing my way through the crowd of people now filling the bar area.

He calls after me, but I'm out on the street and hurrying away before he can stop me.

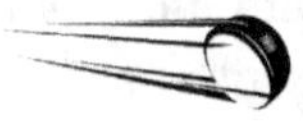

I MAKE IT TO the bar in fifteen minutes, thanks to a cab that drove past as I was debating calling for one, and I'm annoyed that Sarah's here already, giving me zero chance to prepare myself in the new setting.

She gives me a small wave as I head inside, and I meander through the empty tables over to where she's sitting.

"Hi, Johnny," she says, her lips curving into her best fake smile.

I've seen it all before. And I know how she plays these games. She looks evil. Really fucking evil. And as soon as I slide into the seat opposite her, I regret texting her back.

"Do you love her?" she says.

"What's it to you?" I say.

She laughs. Actually laughs, throwing her head back as the shrill sound of her cackle fills the air.

"I called it because you can't love anyone, Johnny. You're incapable. Why do you think I was forced towards Charlie?"

I've already had enough.

"What do you want, Sarah? What's so important that you can't leave me alone?"

"Your dad gave me your new number," she says. "He was incredibly helpful, actually. And I told him all about my problem and that you've left me on my own to struggle."

I scoff. "I left you on your own to struggle?"

"My visa is running out, Johnny. And I'm pregnant."

And just that like I feel sorry for a foetus.

"It's not Charlie's, before you ask."

I wasn't going to, but whatever.

"And what's this got to do with me?" I ask.

"I made a mistake, Johnny. I told Charlie that it was yours and—"

This woman, honestly. "What the hell is wrong with you?"

"I panicked. And I don't know how to fix it. Because he won't believe me, and he wants answers. I think he's going to leave me, Johnny."

"So? Tell him the truth. I literally have no idea what any of this has to do with me."

"I need money, Johnny. And I remember you had savings from your dad, and—"

Ah, yes. The only money I managed to keep from her clutches. It only figures that she'd remember I have it, though.

"I'm done here," I say, moving to slide my chair out.

"Johnny—I don't know what else to do. I told you; my visa is running out and I literally have nothing. Please, I just need some money to get back home, and I'll leave you alone for good—I promise."

That's the icing on the cake for me. Because all the promises she's ever made me have turned into a pile of lies. Instead of acting rationally, I kick the chair I was sitting on and high tail it out of there.

"You'll regret this," she says.

And what pains me the most? A small part of me is actually considering paying up just to get rid of her.

Kelly

"That was weird," Marie says.

I sit down opposite her in the coffee shop.

"I think something came up," I say, casting my eyes back over to the blonde who's standing in the queue with a brunette.

That must be his sister, because he stopped to say something to her briefly before rushing off.

"Anyway, about this tour… we leave on Monday, and Darren is convinced that they'll extend it once we get started. So, I have no idea how long I'll be away for. I'm banking on a week, but I need to get it cleared with work. They should be fine, but it'll mean that I'll probably be working extra shifts when I get back."

"Oh, shit. Sounds like you've got a few things to worry about. How are you feeling about the show, though?"

"Yeah, okay really. I've just got a few things I want to prepare, but it'll be fine."

"Send me your schedule, and I'll make sure Tom can drive us to at least one show," she says.

We dip in and out of conversation, and all the while my eyes keep flicking to Johnny's sister, Vicky, and her friend, who are still waiting in line. At least, they are until Vicky gets her phone out.

"And how will you manage with your classes?" Marie asks, pulling my focus back.

"I think Patrick has cleared it. He said he did, anyway. I just need to keep on top of my coursework."

I'm trying to concentrate on Marie's words, but when I hear Johnny's name mentioned, I chance another look at Vicky.

"She looks pretty pissed off," Marie says, following my gaze to the window where Vicky and her friend storm off up the street.

What do I do? Do I call Johnny and give him the warning? But before I can decide, my own phone is vibrating across the table.

Darren.

"How are things with him?" she asks. "Is he okay with you having a boyfriend?"

"I'm not sure Johnny is my boyfriend," I say, lowering my voice. "Besides, it's none of Darren's business."

"Well, you're spending a lot of time together." Marie raises her eyebrow, but I push the conversation back to the tour.

We visit the high street, and I pick up some new clothes before we head home on the bus, all the while checking my phone at every opportunity to see if Johnny has messaged me. I have no idea if he actually went to see Sarah, and the anxiety is sitting heavy on my chest.

As we pull into our street, I spot Johnny's car straight away.

"Told you," Marie says in a sing-song voice, stepping off the bus.

But I perceive this isn't going to be *that* sort of visit.

He's sitting in the driver's seat, head back on the headrest, and I knock on the passenger window, indicating for him to come inside.

"Talk to me," I say, closing the door behind him, waiting until Marie is out of earshot.

"I'm going to need a hug, beautiful," he says.

And with no hesitation, I wrap my arms around him.

"What's going on?" I say into his chest. He's wearing a jacket over his team hoodie, and he's got his cap peak forward, casting a shadow, so when I glance up, I can't make out the expression on his face.

He doesn't reply. He holds on to me, and all the while his phone is on a constant vibration in his pocket.

He sighs after a moment, then pulls it out of his pocket, tapping a message on the screen before slipping it into the back pocket of his jeans.

"Can we go into your room?" he asks, and I nod, tugging his arm behind me as I go.

I try to clear away the open case I have on my bed, one I've started to pack since I need to plan ahead for Monday, but Johnny looks at me, eyebrows knitted as if he's forgotten about my upcoming schedule.

"What's going on?" he asks. "Where are you going?"

"I told you about the tour with Darren. We're going on Monday." I drop my shopping into the case to sort through later before moving it onto the floor.

"Oh, yeah. Shit. Sorry."

"Forget about that for now. Talk to me."

He takes his cap and jacket off, tossing them on the end of my bed before he settles down onto the mattress, his back against the headboard.

"Come here," he says, pulling me onto his thighs. "I'm feeling really fucking overwhelmed. I don't even know where to begin."

"What's on your mind?" I ask.

"Distract me," he says. "Give me something else to think about for a moment."

"Okay," I say, racking my brain for something. "Do you want me to tell you the reason I ghosted you?"

Johnny's brow furrows. "Go on..."

"I thought someone was catfishing me. Using your photos and pretending to be you."

He laughs, and it makes him sound so *John*-like again, that I give him the whole story. From the game, to seeing his poster, to checking his socials.

He takes a deep breath and kisses me.

"Well, shit."

"Yeah, I know."

I wait for a moment, wondering if it's enough.

Then he comes out with it.

"Sarah wants money. She's pregnant. And her fiancé, or whatever he is, thinks it's mine. And now she wants money to go back home, on the promise that she'll never bother me again."

My mouth hangs open.

"You can't be serious," I say.

"I am. And I won't lie, it's crossed my mind to just give it to her."

"Johnny—"

"And I paid my sister's rent."

"What?"

"Yeah. I paid for it. This morning. I got the details of her landlord after a bit of digging, but I got it and paid off three grand of her upcoming rent."

"I, uh—"

"I borrowed the money off Liam."

"Oh."

"Basically, my dad pays Vicky an allowance. Well, he did. Until she opted not to receive it anymore. And I get one, too, except I can manage okay without it, so I just put whatever he gives me into a trust fund for a kid I don't even have yet. I don't want his money, but I figure it may come in handy. But it's money I can't easily get to. It's money that Sarah knows I have."

I put my arms around him and hug, not having a single word I can say to help.

"How am I going to manage when you're away?" he asks.

And I feel really fucking sad. Because there's a lot going on for Johnny right now, and I'm leaving.

"I'm only going to be on the other end of the phone. And I can give you my schedule. You can see if you can visit or something. Maybe come and watch a show? My parents haven't watched me for years. And Mike would never, so it would be good to see a friendly face."

"Are you serious?"

I wriggle off his lap and grab my phone, intending to go for the calendar app. Without hesitating, Johnny pulls his jacket towards him and roots in the pocket for his own notebook. The trusty notebook.

But when I glance down at the screen, there's a notification that wasn't there when I checked it earlier.

"New Message Request from..."

I don't even have to click it to know who it's from. I have a feeling.

Chapter 30

Johnny

I SUCCESSFULLY FENDED OFF my sister on the road trip yesterday.

But how I go an entire pre-game at home avoiding her is anyone's guess. She's lurking on the edge of the ice, and every time she looks like she's about to speak to me, someone else catches her attention or mine. Since we're making progress in our climb of the league, that's where my focus is tonight.

Hockey.

One hundred per cent hockey.

At least, that's what I tell myself, anyway.

I know Kelly is here. And even though I know where the club seats are, I try my hardest not to look in that direction as we skate onto the ice for the intros. And when we line up for the national anthem, I avoid looking then too.

She said she'd be in the bar, but a tiny piece of me wonders if she is actually here. At her seat. Watching.

Fortunately, the position of the benches is in my favour too, so when the puck drops and the clock counts down, I have zero distractions.

The first defensive pair on the ice tonight are Bettsy and Yatesy, and considering the kid's play style a few weeks ago, I can already see a vast improvement in his game.

I'm watching the play, so I don't notice Matt Rodgers coming to stand directly behind me, leaning down to talk right into my ear.

"What's your fucking problem, mate?" he says, his tone laced with rage.

"I have no idea what you're talking about, but if you're not careful, you'll be my problem soon enough," I growl back, not shifting my attention away from the ice.

The forward line changes and bodies move away from the bench, clearing some space, and Rodgers sits down next to me, popping out his mouthguard to talk.

"I hear it was you who started shit about me," he says.

"Regardless of what you heard, you don't play fucking dirty in my dressing room," I say, dropping my leg over the boards and hopping onto the ice when my change comes in.

The puck goes out of play, but I skate over to the face-off circle and ready myself.

I'm shoulder to shoulder with Prez for a moment as he takes position, and I talk under my breath, telling him to play back into the neutral a little before we push forward, and he nods, getting himself ready to receive the puck from Liam's face-off.

It's a good play for us, resulting in receiving possession of the puck and forcing the opposition to keep their play without a line change. Heavy legs on the ice mean opportunity for us.

By the time my shift is over, I scan the bench for Matt and make sure I hop off the ice at the opposite end of the bench, because I really cannot deal with his attitude right now, considering I'm permanently simmering in a bad mood.

Ever since that day I saw Sarah, I've been a wreck. And for once, Justine wasn't able to help.

I make it the whole way through the first without thinking about Kelly again, or allowing her to be a distraction more like, and luckily for me Vicky is completely absent during the intermission.

When we return to the ice for the second period, I'm in the starting pair on the blue line. Danny takes the opening face-off and wins, sending the puck my way before I pass it over to Hutch, who's ready to receive it. He shoots it straight across the ice to Danny, who's placed himself right at the edge of the ice, and he plucks it up with the blade of his stick and moves it forward.

Hutch has speed, but I've got the position, right at the point, and I see Danny look over his shoulder for a second before he sends it through the gap he's created between his legs. I one-time it in the direction of the net, assuming that Hutch will be ready in time.

But when the red light buzzes, I stare at the opposing netminder for a second, checking that it's actually gone in. He's looking around for it, and the puck is jammed right on the edge of the net, but I spot the stripes pointing at the goal line.

Goal.

"Fucking A," someone shouts, banging my lid, and we hustle around for a group hug.

It's when I'm skating back to the bench that I spot her. My eyes lock onto hers, a grin spreads across her face, and there's fucking evil behind those eyes as she stares at me from a few rows behind the bench. I wouldn't have noticed her, except she's the only person sitting down.

My stomach lurches as I tear my eyes away from Sarah. And then my concentration is stolen by her request, hanging over me like a bad smell.

By the time the clock runs down the second period, I'm buzzing with an anxious energy, and I'm pissed off.

The third period trickles by, but I block six shots in the first ten minutes, and another four in the last eight, making sure I play my game with as much caution as I can. We're leading 2-1 and I'm not in the mood to let this thing go to overtime.

As I'm skating back to the bench, with two minutes left on the clock, I spot Kelly, standing right at the top of the block—at least I think it's her, anyway. She's talking with a blonde—fuck my life. She's talking to Sarah.

When the final buzzer sounds and we have to do all the post-game stuff, my eyes are flicking towards that spot, but neither Kelly nor Sarah is there. When we do the victory lap, I'm skating as slowly as I can so I can keep a lookout, but my blood is boiling with rage. Complete and utter rage.

I step off the ice first, snapping my stick over my knee as I exit, then tossing the remnants of it into the gutter of the bench. I don't pay anyone any attention as I head for the dressing room and no one attempts to talk with me, probably out of their better judgement.

I've never turned myself around so quickly from post-game to fully dressed, but I'm striding past the guys, and past Vicky, who yells after me as I push the double doors open into the chilly December air.

I pull my phone out and immediately dial Kelly, but it goes to voicemail.

It goes to voicemail the following six times I try to call her, all while I'm driving to her place, but when I pull up outside, the lights are off, and the anxiety builds in my chest.

Just as I'm about to leave, my phone rings and Kelly's name flashes up on the screen. Relief floods through me when I answer, but it quickly diminishes when she talks.

"Johnny, I'm at your place and you need to come home. There's someone here to see you."

Kelly

"I'VE ALREADY TOLD YOU, he's on his way," I say.

Though it's clear from his expression that this fella does not want to wait.

I didn't even want to answer the door, but he was pounding on it, probably having tailgated after someone because this building has controlled access and there's no way anyone would willingly let this guy in.

"I've been waiting long enough," he says through gritted teeth.

There's an angry-looking vein on his forehead that looks like it's about to pop.

I'm nervous as hell. He won't tell me what he wants or why he's here, just that he wants to talk to Johnny. Johnny, who should have been here ages ago, clearly didn't remember that we'd arranged to meet here after his game.

"He'll be here soon," I say, my voice shaking.

I attempt to push the door closed, but before it clicks shut, the guy sticks his foot on the threshold and there's no way I'm able to coax it away.

"I'd rather we didn't close the door," he says, leaning against the frame.

I wonder if he's going to force his way inside, but he doesn't. He stands still, foot unmoved, so I remain on the spot, trying not to freak the fuck out.

Mr Foot-in-the-door pulls his phone out of his pocket and taps away at the screen, putting it to his ear before hissing at himself when it rings. He does this several more times before he loses himself and moves away from the door enough, clearly shifting his concentration, and I take the opportunity to slam the door shut. My heart pounds in my chest as I press myself against the wall next to the door.

The pounding starts then, followed by swearing. Then I swear to God the door rattles.

"You better open this fucking door," he yells on the other side.

But I'll be honest, I want to open the door even less now he's said that. I feel sick with fear.

Heavy footsteps. And then a moment later, the pounding resumes.

"If he's in there and you're hiding him... I'll fucking—"

A phone rings. And then Mr Foot grunts. I take a chance and peer through the peephole in the door, and I watch him pace the corridor outside the apartment with his phone pressed against his ear. I can't make out what he's saying, but I'm grateful it's causing him a distraction.

But it's only a distraction for a short time. Because as soon as he slides his phone into his jeans pocket, he's coming right at the peephole again to resume the pounding.

"You tell Johnny to get his fucking ass out here now. You stupid—"

But then there's a banging in the distance, and the attack on the door stops.

Then I hear Johnny's voice.

"What the fuck is going on?" Johnny says.

Mr Foot abandons the door and strides towards Johnny, which is when I recklessly decide that I'm leaving the safety of the apartment.

"You." Mr Foot points his finger at Johnny, and now they're standing face-to-face, it's clear to see that Johnny has a good four inches on this guy. And a lot more bulk.

"What the fuck do you think you're doing here?" Johnny says.

Mr Foot flings himself at Johnny, and all I can do is watch in horror. Except, Johnny reacts quickly enough, grabbing onto the guy's forearms and pushing him against the wall between Johnny's place and next door.

"How fucking dare you," Mr Foot says, fighting against Johnny.

"How dare I? You're fucking kidding, right?" Johnny says, making the task of holding him back look effortless.

"Does she know?" Mr Foot asks, motioning to where I'm standing.

Johnny's gaze drifts over to mine for a split second before his face darkens with concern.

"Kelly, go back inside, please," Johnny says.

"Oh, this is priceless. Don't go anywhere, princess. You need to hear all about this," Mr Foot snarls.

"Johnny? What's going on?" I ask.

"Kelly, please—"

"Did you know he's being fucking my fiancée?"

Johnny drops his hands, releasing the guy, who uses the opportunity to take another dive at Johnny. But Johnny corrects himself, pushing him back into the wall.

"I know all about it," Mr Foot says.

"Really? Because I don't think you do, Charlie," Johnny says.

"You and Sarah. Fucking sneaking around. She told me everything, Johnny. And you've knocked her up and—"

A laugh erupts from Johnny's throat. Wicked and hard. One I haven't heard before.

"You're crazy," Johnny shouts. "Actually, fucking crazy."

Charlie goes right for Johnny's throat, causing him to tumble to the floor after he loses his balance. This is when I panic. Even more than before. What do I even do?

"I'm calling the police," I say, fishing in my pocket for my phone, but Johnny pushes Charlie off and pins him down.

"Get the fuck off me," Charlie says, his face flushing red. I honestly think steam is going to fly out of his ears at this rate.

And then the door at the far end swings open, and Parker Fforde comes into view.

"What the—" Parker pries Johnny off Charlie and stands between them both. "What the hell is going on?"

Parker's eyes find mine and his face drops.

"He got my fiancée pregnant!" Charlie screams, fighting against the wall of Parker's arm.

"Johnny?" Parker says.

"You should ask her who's fathered her child, Charlie—because it wasn't me."

Then Charlie's phone rings, and he answers it quickly then he bolts towards the exit.

Which leaves Parker standing there, looking between me and Johnny. "You want to tell me what's going on here?"

Chapter 31

Johnny

I get to Kelly's place just after one in the morning. She left me a key under an old plant pot near the front door, so I let myself in as quietly as I can before slipping into her room.

I lose my clothes quickly, keeping just my boxers on as I slide into her bed, wrapping my arms around her and kissing her neck.

At least her window's fixed, and it's not completely freezing in here.

"Hey, Johnny," she says, rolling over. "Are you okay?"

"I've been better," I say.

"What happened?" She reaches for the lamp on the table next to her bed, flicking the switch, and letting her eyes adjust to the light. "What did you say to Parker?"

"He's not going to say anything," I say.

"Johnny—"

She's thinking.

Overdrive.

"It'll be okay. He won't say anything. I told him that once things settle down for us, we'll tell Bettsy."

She doesn't look convinced, and she'd be right not to be. I had to beg for his silence, and he insisted on giving me a lecture. Kelly being 'only' nineteen was at the top of his list. According to him, she'll likely fall in love easily and then cling on to me, but I don't believe it.

"Honestly, babe, it's fine. He's a good guy. Besides, once I told him all about Sarah, he shifted his focus. I just have to figure out my next step."

That bit wasn't a lie. Ffordey called Sarah, and I quote, 'a creature'.

"About Sarah. She sent me a message on social media, and she came to find me at your game. I spent the majority of it in the bar area—I'm still not ready to watch. I just thought you should know," Kelly says.

"What did she say?"

"The message on socials was just a general note begging me to see sense and cut you out. And then at the game, she asked me if I needed help getting away from you. Nothing I couldn't handle."

I exhale, thanking the stars that I don't even have to convince Kelly that Sarah is poison and manipulative. I don't have to convince her that she can trust me.

But instead of pushing Sarah out of my head, I move onto my back and lay there, staring at the ceiling.

Thinking.

Thinking about everything she said to me. All the horrible things she would say to get under my skin.

Am I incapable of loving anyone? Because I don't even know what I'm feeling right now. Angry, for sure, but not the same kind of anger I'm used to feeling. In fact, right now, I'm exasperated.

The more I lay here thinking, the more I allow myself to embrace my worries.

Highlight reel for Johnny:

Incapable of loving anyone, even his sister, apparently.

Incapable of having a sex-induced orgasm.

Incapable of having the balls to tell his best friend he's been fucking his sister. That one really hits me.

"Johnny? Stay in the moment with me." Kelly's voice floats right into my ear, and then her hand is on my chest. Warm and calming.

Incapable of getting called up.

Incapable of being the son my dad wanted.

"Remember when we first started chatting, and I called you an old man?" She laughs, probably hoping that I will too. "Remember our first kiss, Johnny? I thought about it for weeks after and I—"

Incapable of being the boyfriend someone wants. And to think—she cheated on me with Charlie. And he had the audacity to accuse me of cheating with her. After all she put me through.

"Johnny?"

And then there's Kelly.

Comforting. Funny. Beautiful inside and out. And driven. I love that she wants to carve her own way in the world—she doesn't need anyone else.

"I thought about it, too," I say, pulling myself back. "And I still think about it now. And... you know I wouldn't cheat on you, right?"

"I know."

"I wouldn't—I..."

"I know, Johnny."

I rub at the stubble on my face. Thinking. Because even if I was the sort of person to cheat, it wouldn't be with her. I can probably list a load of things I'd rather do than go near her again. And one of them has to be taking Ffordey's place. With no pads. Or a cup. I'd rather be pummelled with pucks to the head for sixty minutes than go near her again.

The thought alone has me laughing, well, chuckling to myself.

"Are you okay, Johnny?" she asks.

"What's funny is Sarah being a problem in my life long after I ended things with her. Honestly, Kelly—she made me feel so weak. Even if she was the last person on the planet, I'd play an entire game naked between the pipes rather than go there with her. And she has the audacity to have Charlie thinking that I would. I mean come on."

And that's when my floodgates open. Years of keeping it all locked in. Because I'd told myself it was weak to cry.

I was weak.

"She stopped me from seeing my friends. She used to control all my money, tell me what I could or couldn't spend it on. She used to tell me what I could wear, how I had to have my hair cut, and when I got offered the captaincy first, she told me I wasn't allowed to take it because it meant that I'd be spending more time focusing on hockey. You know what? I even found out she was piercing holes in a stack of condoms. I caught her doing it. And when I first told her I was going to leave, she told me she'd kill herself if I did. What's someone supposed to do with that?"

Kelly stares at me for a moment, then I sigh.

"I'm so sorry that you went through that, Johnny. I can't imagine how that must have felt for you."

"Well, sure. But the worst part is, she told me she loved me. Who does that to someone they love? I don't even believe it exists if I'm being honest."

I wrinkle my nose. "You don't believe what exists?"

"Love."

"Well, I think it does. And you make me feel really loved, Johnny."

Silence takes over me once again. And Kelly, patient and brilliant, lets me cohere my thoughts.

What can I even say to that?

My entire body swims with emotion, and before I know it, I pull at her arm, tugging her onto me so she's straddling my hips. And of course, my dick is nestled right between her legs. But I'm looking right at her. Taking her in. Her pink lips that plump when she kisses me, and those adorable freckles, and her long deep auburn locks that are really fucking smooth and shiny.

And then she sits up straight and pulls off the T-shirt she's wearing. One of mine. The 'C' distorting slightly when she pulls it over her perfect breasts.

"Are you with me, Johnny?" she asks.

And I am.

I'm fixed on her. Everything about her has me in a trance. I'm in the moment, reaching up and cupping her face in my hands for a moment, then tracing them down the smooth skin of her body and cupping her boobs. Watching in complete fascination as her nipples harden under my touch. And she moans on me, and I can feel her rubbing her pussy against the bulge in my pants.

I adjust our position so I can push my boxers down, freeing myself, and feeling completely in the moment. When she moves to shimmy down the bed, knowing that she's likely planning on taking me in her mouth, I pull her back towards me, kissing her deep, letting our tongues meet as I smooth over her ass, feeling her skin hot under my hands.

"I need you," I whisper right into her mouth as I pull back slightly. There's a movement from her, and I feel the wetness of her pussy as her hands take my cock and push me inside her. Her panties are shoved to the side, and it's hot and dirty, like she's just as desperate for me.

My brain stops functioning as she sinks down onto me. The tightness. The heat. The fucking wetness. Everything about her has me prickling with excitement.

"Fuckkk," she whispers as she sits back.

And I glance down between us, seeing our bodies together.

I run my palm all the way down from her neck, over her nipples, and right down to her clit, where I graze it with my thumb. And when she rocks back, shifting her hips slightly, creating a small motion, it's enough to have me seeing stars.

There's nothing about this that could get any better.

"That feels so good, Johnny," she gasps. I grip her hip with my other hand and try to match her rhythm.

"You feel so fucking good riding my dick," I say.

She moans and I feel shivers everywhere. I want to hear it again.

"Tell me how it feels for you," I coax.

"Fuck, Johnny. You're so deep—there. Right there."

And there it is. That moan, just as I thrust up into her at an angle that has her pussy tightening around me.

"I'm going to come for you, Johnny," she says. And those words.

She's going to come.

For me.

Just for me.

"For me?" I find myself asking. "Are you going to come for me?" It's barely a whisper.

"Yes, Johnny. I'm coming for you," she says, just as her voice gives away a moan that causes my balls to pull tight. And then there's a feeling I'm sure I'm familiar with, but I'm not expecting. Her name is on my lips and I'm coming. Right over the edge with her. I'm coming hard, and the way her pussy tightens even more—I'm groaning. Almost crying out in euphoria. Because it's like nothing I've felt before.

"I love you, Johnny."

Then her lips are on mine and we're kissing. I've never been more in the moment than I am right now.

And then I'm crying. While my dick is still inside her. Because the moment is just so much, and I don't know what else to do. Or what else to say. I don't have any words.

Kelly

YOU'VE GOT THIS, BEAUTIFUL.

Johnny's words ring in my head, still crystal clear after the phone call we had several minutes ago. His 'pre-performance pep-talk,' as he called it to prepare me for our tour.

All you need to do is relax and think about your next note.

I guess you can take the captain out of the team...

The entire backstage area is teeming with people. And Patrick fusses around the place like a mother hen, trying to make sure his chicks are on their best behaviour. He moves away from our dressing area and, grateful for the break, I pause only to be smothered a few moments later when he comes striding towards me waving a hairbrush.

"Let me just get this bit, Kelly. Keep still," he says, tugging at my hair.

I'm so nervous I can't even bring myself to protest. I let him do what he needs to, and then he moves away again, returning moments later with a can of hairspray.

"I don't need that," I say, trying to swat him away, but he eyes me nervously.

"Just a quick spritz, Kelly... like that." He steps back and gets me to twirl on the spot before nodding.

The chatter from people makes the place unbearable, and I can't even hear myself think. It's probably why I don't hear someone calling my name until they come to a stop right in front of me.

"You're Kelly, right?" a dark-haired guy with glasses says, and I nod.

He shoves a small box into my chest before spinning on his heel and striding away before I can work out what just happened.

I step away from Darren, turning my back to him before peeking inside the box. There's a single rose inside. It's made of sheet music, but this time, it's one of the pieces we're playing tonight.

There's a small piece of paper with it, and when I unfold it, there's a heart drawn in black pen, and the memory of last night comes flooding back.

I told him I loved him. I told him. Shit.

Stuffing the note back into the box, I tuck it into my bag and turn back to Darren, who's eyeing me suspiciously. Then Patrick appears out of nowhere and gives us our two-minute warning, gesturing for us to follow him up to the edge of the stage.

There's a curtain blocking the view, but when someone slides it open slightly to let the stage crew through, I spot Johnny straight away. And once he catches me looking, he beams at me, his eyes lighting up like a thousand lightbulbs. And seeing him makes my heart pound even harder than it was already.

I told him I loved him.

Do I love him? Do I even know what love is? I don't know, but I've said it. It's out there.

My cheeks grow hot, and I want the stage to open up and consume me whole. Because I cannot right now. First off, he wasn't due to come to opening night. Even when I left him in bed this morning, I'd geared myself up to not see him until Thursday. And second, how can he be here when he's got practice tomorrow morning? It doesn't make any sense.

"What's your ex doing here?" Darren leans in and hisses into my ear.

We're waiting for the previous group to clear the stage, so the curtain keeps flapping open every few seconds.

"I guess he's just here to show his support. You know, in place of Mike or something." I don't know why I lie but it just falls out into the air, and I can't take it back.

He's sat in the third row back, and he's at least a full head taller than everyone else, so it's no surprise that Darren would have spotted him too.

"Right. Are you two ready?" Patrick says, coming to a stop behind me and Darren.

We both nod, and I feel so awkward now, my hands are shaking.

"All you need to do is play like you've been practising. And remember, you're the only ones who really know when you've messed it up."

I love that. A true mark of Patrick's confidence. But whatever.

Patrick strides onto the stage after someone in the distance signals for him to come forward, and he stops in the centre, bending at the waist and giving the introduction spiel that he's been writing all day.

He did run through it with us earlier, but I wasn't concentrating. I'm still not concentrating now, because I'm looking right at Johnny, and I'm thinking about last night. And the complete euphoria I felt when he... oh my God. We didn't use a condom.

I rack my brain, trying to think if I took my pill earlier today, and I'm cut short when the audience starts applauding and Darren nudges me forward.

I get to my chair and pull the spike out of the end of my cello.

I definitely took it, right?

I settle my cello between my knees and tighten my bow a turn.

Yes. I definitely did.

Phew.

And when Patrick slides into my visual path, I switch into performance mode. Pushing everything else out of my head. The auditorium quiets as the lights over the audience dim, and the stage is illuminated. I watch as Patrick brings his arms up, baton in his left hand as he mouths: one, two, three.

I don't even need the music perched on the stand in front of me. I just close my eyes and play, moving my fingers over the fingerboard in the sequence I've been practicing. Fluid movements over the strings, matching the flow with Darren's saxophone rhythm.

My whole body moves and rocks steadily as I play, and by the time we're on our third piece, I'm relaxed and immersed. I'm in my element.

The roar from the crowd pulls me back into the moment when we play the final note, and Darren is quick to stand up, grabbing my left hand just as I manage to move the cello into my right, holding it by the neck as we take a bow.

Patrick spins and bows to the crowd, too, and then he whisks us off the stage.

"One word. Bravo. That was fantastic. Well done."

Darren turns and beams at me, pulling me into an awkward hug as I try to keep my cello safe. And just when I think he's about to release me, his lips almost brush mine, and then there's a wetness on the corner of my mouth that I did not consent to. I'm grateful he missed because I'm furious—and he'd probably end up with less teeth than Mike.

"What the hell are you doing?" I say, shoving him away. I set my cello down on the floor safely on its side before I turn to him again with a seething expression.

"Don't pretend that it doesn't make sense, Kelly. You and me. The true love story."

"You're deluded."

Darren blinks at me.

"Is this about him?" he asks.

"No, but—"

"It is, isn't it?"

"Darren, whatever it is you're doing—stop."

"Why else would he come here? I mean, if you're back together, all you need to do is say—"

"We're not."

"What's going on?" he asks. "Why are you being so evasive?"

I push past him and grab my cello case, rolling it towards the spot where I left my instrument.

"I'm not."

"Wait—does this have anything to do with your brother? Are you—"

"Forget it, Darren."

I pack my cello up quicker than I ever have before and dip behind the screen in the corner to get changed back into casual clothes.

Darren is waiting for me when I exit, and he's holding his phone out, a grin spread across his face.

"So, Kelly. If I were to call Mike right now and tell him how lovely it is that Johnny is filling in for him—what do you think he would say?"

I can almost feel my jaw dropping, but I check myself, straightening up and looking right at Darren.

"He'd probably say 'Yeah, he's a good friend.'"

"Okay, let's find out, shall we?"

I don't even know how Darren has my brother's number, but whatever he just pressed on the screen has a ringing tone emitting from his handset. And that's when I break. I reach over and snatch it from him.

"Ah-ha!" Darren chimes, grinning at me.

"Darren, please."

But then Patrick bursts back into the room and nods his head in my direction.

"Kelly, a word?"

Chapter 32

Johnny

The team group chat is fired up. Texts flying back and forth all day, but I only check my phone after Kelly's show once I'm back in the hotel.

Bettsy

> What the hell just happened?

> Twinnies, where did you go?

Danny

> Jenna just called me. No fucking way @Ryan Preston.

Hutch

> What the hell is going on?

My heart skips in my chest. Married? Ryan got married? I don't even think I can believe it until I tap on the photo and pinch the screen to zoom in. Yeah, it's him and Jen, alright. Donned in casual dress, standing outside the registry office.

Well, shit.

Without thinking, I call Ryan and he answers after the third ring, his voice a buzz of excitement on the line.

"You got married?" I ask. "Well, congratulations are in order."

"Yeah, bud. I mean, it was just for the paperwork stuff for the house. Last-minute cancellation. We're going to have a formal wedding soon. But I'm sorry you weren't there."

"Yeah, don't worry about it. I'm happy for you guys."

An unsettling feeling swims in my stomach, but since I'm so goddamn out of tune with my feelings, I have no clue what to think.

"Look, I know you're in a bit of a place right now, John. But I've got you, you know that, right?"

I'm just relieved he doesn't ask me about why I've been coming and going in the early hours of the morning.

"Yeah, of course. I just needed to take a few days," I say.

I had to. I needed the space from hockey. I think I'm coming to terms with the fact that I may be able to feel something. Because I've been thinking about Kelly's words non-stop. She told me she loved me for one. And I came. Shit, I came, and we didn't use a—

"Johnny?"

"Sorry—I got distracted then."

"Call your sister. She's really worried about you, bud."

That knot sits heavy in my stomach. But I agree and hang up.

Before I call Vicky, I pull out my notebook and jot down the date and time, and pen a few words about the situation and how I'm feeling. Then I check it over before dialling Vicky's number.

"How are you, Johnny?" she asks, her voice shaking.

"I'm okay, Vic. I'm just feeling exhausted, and I need a break," I say.

"Where did you go after the suit fitting?"

"I just needed to get away," I say.

And then she starts flooding me with questions, but I get a notification that there's a call waiting and Kelly's contact card pops up.

"Look, I'll talk to you another time. Just trust me on this, will you? I know I'll miss Ladies' Night, and I'm sorry, but trust me."

Once we hang up, I dial Kelly and she answers straight away. "Where are you?"

"At your hotel. In the lobby," I say.

And then I spot her hurrying towards me, cello in tow.

"Call the lift, quickly," she says, looking behind her.

"What's going on?" I ask, following her inside the elevator that's stopped in front of us.

She nibbles her thumbnail as we ride up to the sixth floor, and as soon as the doors spring open, she leads me down the corridor and pulls inside room '606'.

"Darren is on to us," she says as soon as the door closes behind me. "He started asking me all these questions, wondering why you're here, and then—shit. He made out he was calling my brother and I panicked, Johnny."

I take her cello from her, setting it in the corner, and then I walk forward and wrap my arms around her.

"Okay, so we didn't think it through. We'll figure it out," I say.

She pulls back and looks right up at me. "Johnny—"

I lean down and kiss my name right from her mouth.

"What happened to that dress?" I ask, kissing her neck.

She giggles, and it sends a fucking shiver right through me.

"Johnny... I'm being serious here. I'm worried."

"I'm sorry, I'm distracted," I say, raising an eyebrow.

"Last night?"

"Fucking last night. Wanna see if we can do it again?"

I feel like my hunger for her has pushed all seriousness aside. And I'm fumbling out of my suit quicker than I care to admit. I want to be naked. And I want her naked. In that bed. Or on that dressing table, actually, because that looks good.

"Johnny," she giggles, pushing at my chest.

"You realise seeing you playing today got me excited? You're incredible. Do you know that?"

My hands find the hem of her T-shirt and I pull it over her head eagerly.

And as soon as she's standing there, naked, right in front of me, my lips are on hers. Devouring. I'm desperate to feel her again.

Instead of going to the bed, I settle for the sofa, pulling her onto my lap and taking a nipple into my mouth. Hearing her moaning and running her hands through my hair with need is really fucking hot. I don't even know myself.

"What are you doing to me?" I ask, pulling her mouth down to mine again.

"Johnny—yesterday we didn't—"

"Shit," I say. Halting in my tracks. "Do we need to?"

"No, I'm taking the pill but I just—"

"Well, fuck."

I pull her in closer, so her pussy is right on my dick, and I adjust the position so the tip, right where my piercing is, is rubbing against her clit. I know I get the right spot when she flings her hair back and moans, pushing her perfect nipples right within reach of my tongue.

Honestly, I don't even know how I survived before.

"Johnny, I think—"

I can't help myself. I adjust my position again so I can slip inside her. That tight, hot feeling completely engulfs me and takes my breath away. I grip her hips and thrust into her, fast and hard. I live for this. It takes me a matter of moments to come apart, to fall right over that edge as Kelly comes on top of me. And I'm almost shaking by the time her lips find mine, completely transfixing me in whatever spell she's put over me.

I don't even notice that my phone is ringing. It's vibrating in the pocket of my pants, and I let it ring a few times before the calls get more and more angry sounding. If a phone can sound angry, that is.

"You should get that," Kelly says, kissing my jaw and shifting away from me. The coldness of her tone hits me and I look around for something to clean myself with as she tosses me a pack of tissues from the counter.

When I finally get to my phone, I cover my dick with my boxers because it feels odd to talk to someone fully naked, especially when I see my dad's name on the screen.

I look at Kelly. "It's my dad."

"Oh?" she says, wrapping a robe around herself, then tossing one to me. "I hope everything is okay."

I shove my arms into the robe, which is snugger than snug, and then I answer the next incoming call.

"Hey, son. Just checking in."

"Checking in? You've called me about five times. Is everything okay?"

I take only a few seconds to realise that he's been drinking. I can hear it in his voice.

"Just checking in, that's all. Seeing how my superstar is doing."

"Superstar? You're kidding right?" I let out a burst of a laugh that I genuinely can't contain.

"What? Am I not allowed to miss my son?" he says, and I can hear his tone change slightly.

"Well, sure, but it's out of character."

"I see you're doing well with the Challenge Cup, Johnathan."

"Sure."

"I mean, it's hardly the Stanley Cup, but I guess we'll get what we get."

Kelly sits on the bed and ruffles her hair, her eyes not leaving mine. She mouths 'are you okay' and I nod, but I have no idea where this is going.

"Wow. Okay," I say.

"But you know, Johnny—I expected you to tell me I was going to be a grandfather. I mean, after everything I've done for you and your sister—"

My heart hammers hard in my chest. And here comes the feeling. It creeps all the way through my body, warming my muscles.

"Excuse me?"

"I had to learn from Sarah—how do you think that made me feel?"

Kelly drops to her knees and scoots towards me, rubbing her hands on my thighs as I grit my teeth.

"Thanks for trusting her over me, I guess."

"A man wouldn't disown his child," he says.

But I don't think I want to hear anymore. That response was all I needed. I hang up and toss my phone past Kelly and onto the bed.

"Johnny?" she says, her voice soft, and I pull her onto me, needing the comfort she offers.

"That was the most bizarre conversation I've ever had," I say. "I mean—fuck."

She runs her hands through my hair as I hug her to my chest, and the rage that was building momentum through my body edges away slightly.

"Let's go for a walk, Johnny. Let's get dressed and go for a walk. Get some fresh air and maybe grab something to eat. Yeah?"

That is exactly what I need. And when I look right into her eyes and lean in to kiss her, I don't think I can ever be without this girl.

WHEN CLOSING NIGHT ROLLS around, Patrick pulls me to one side before we head out onto the stage. I half expect him to ask a load of questions, just like Darren did, about the 'good luck' basket of muffins I received half an hour ago, but he doesn't. He looks me right in the eye and takes a dramatic intake of breath, like he's planning to blow out a candle.

"Kelly, the casting directors are here tonight. And I think they've been to one of the previous shows. Just wanted to give you an advanced warning."

He walks away as if he's just delivered bad news but doesn't want the repercussions. But I stand here, agog, while I process the information.

God, I wish Johnny was still here. He'd know what to do. He'd stop me from freaking out.

After the close call with Darren and his massive nose, he stayed with me for a few days but kept to the hotel room—besides the walk we took, and from what I gathered, it actually did him the world of good to checkout from the usual demands on his time.

Considering we spent a lot of time in the hotel room, it meant we had a lot of time together, and Johnny made it his mission to level up his dirty talk.

But right now—I'm regretting letting him leave.

I check the time on my phone and then call him, standing to the side, away from eavesdroppers.

His voice is like music to my ears and after greetings, I ask him how things are back home.

"I feel guilty," he says. "The guys and I sort of broke into the rink."

"And you're feeling guilty about it?" I ask.

"No. Because Bettsy is so fucking nice and he's such a good friend and I'm pissing all over it," he says.

"Oh." Johnny's breath sounds hard. "What do you want to do? Do you think we should just come clean and tell Mike?" I ask.

"Let me think on it," Johnny says. "But for now... good luck, babe. I wish I was there to see you."

"Johnny. They're here. Tonight."

"The scouts?"

I roll my eyes, because I guess, in Johnny's world, that's what they are.

"Sure."

"And you're worried?"

"I don't think I've prepared enough," I say.

"You're ready. Don't overthink it. Just keep the next note in mind. Play like you do for me—when there's no pressure and just ears waiting to hear the music."

I concentrate on his voice, and by the time we say goodbye, I feel fairly normal.

After stowing my phone away, I turn to see Darren beckoning me towards the stage.

"Kelly, we need to stand by the curtains," he says. And I weave through the crowd, over to where I left my cello.

The nerves hit me as soon as we're in our spots and the light is beating down on us. Flashbacks from my audition at the music college roll through my head, and I'm struggling to focus. I don't even think I can keep my cool.

But I'm not afforded any time to freak out, because Patrick's arms raise, and he waves his baton. Shit.

Johnny's face swims into my head, and that laugh he does when he's trying to convince me something's a good idea, then I replay the conversation we just had.

Then we begin, and I revel in that thought as I sway with the music. The Christmassy feeling filling the air and the warmth that spreads through me has me feeling relaxed and confident once we progress through the first piece.

As we come to the end of our composition, I hear Tom whooping and cheering in the crowd in a way that only Tom does, and I have to refrain from bursting into a laugh.

Even when Patrick introduces me to the casting directors after the show, I'm carefree and casual, but completely flabbergasted when they invite me to a formal interview after Christmas.

And the worry creeps back in. Except I don't have time to dwell on it, because Tom bursts through the door of the backstage entrance, ignoring the 'Performers Only' sign.

"You were wonderful!" he says, pulling me into a hug.

Tom draws his attention to the muffin basket sitting in the far corner, next to my cello case.

"Are these from J-Dog? He's such a babe. I love him," Tom says. "Are you official now, and does your brother know yet?"

"Shh," I whisper, pointing towards Darren who's schmoozing someone less than three metres away.

"Oh, shit, yeah. Well, anyway. Are you?"

"I don't know. But we are telling Mike soon. At least, I think we are."

"Well, you can tell him now, if you like—he's out there."

My heart stops in my chest.

He never comes to my shows.

Without hesitating, I rummage for the card that came with the muffin basket and stuff it into my bra. Then I shove the basket towards Tom and tell him that if anyone asks, he was the one who gifted it to me.

I pull Tom in close to whisper in his ear.

"Darren can't see Mike. I know he'll ask him about Johnny, so it's your job to go out there and cause a distraction."

"What? What sort of distraction?"

"I don't know. Maybe tell Mike I'll meet him at the hotel—actually don't because Darren is there too." I think for a minute, catching sight of Darren moving towards me with his saxophone case. "Change of plan. You'll need to distract him," I gesture to Darren, "so I can get Mike out of here. I'll text you and let you know where we're going, and you can meet us there."

"You can't be serious," Tom says indignantly. "I can't."

"You can. I'll owe you. Please, Tom?"

He looks at me with a pained expression, shoving the muffin basket towards my chest before turning to Darren.

"You were brilliant, Daz! Tell me how you got your sax so shiny."

I use that as my cue to slip away, knowing that time is against me and Johnny.

Chapter 33

Johnny

APPARENTLY, THE EQUIPMENT STORAGE room at the far end of the tunnels is a good spot for a little alone time. I hadn't known about it until Danny mentioned it in passing, so I grabbed the key from the key store earlier. It's not usually locked, but I want to be prepared.

As soon as Kelly calls me to say she's outside, I make sure the coast is clear and slip out of the dressing room, navigating to the double doors to let her inside. She's wearing a huge winter coat, and she looks so adorable.

"I'm so glad you're back," I say, pulling her inside.

"Where are we going?" she says as I lead her through the tunnels towards the storage room.

We slip inside and I look around, reaching for a crate and sliding it in front of the door before locking it from the inside—knowing my luck, someone else has a key and they'll be able to push my key out from the other side given the age of these locks.

"I've missed you, beautiful," I say, cupping her face in my hands.

"You can't be serious, Johnny. It stinks in here. It smells like—"

"Don't say it," I say, pressing my finger to her lips. "Forget about everything and come here."

She hums into me as I kiss her, and before I know it, her hands are pushing at the waistband of my sweats. Pre-training kit is handy for this sort of thing.

"You're hard already," she says into my lips.

And when her hand grips my shaft, I let out a shudder.

"I've really fucking missed you," I say.

My breath halts in my throat as she drops to her knees in front of me.

Teasing me, she works her way all the way from the base of my dick, right to the tip, and she moans onto me as she opens her mouth, letting me slip inside a little. I can't stop myself from running my hand through her hair, pushing her face into me a little as I try to coax more of me into her mouth. But when I drop my head back to moan, she stands and kisses my chin.

"Do you have any tape around here?" she says.

I raise a brow at her. "Huh?"

And then she holds out her wrists, tight together. My dick leaks with excitement.

We'd talked about it briefly while she was away. I said I wanted to try a new position, and Kelly agreed that she was interested. And now she mentions it... this is the perfect place, given the circumstances.

"Take your coat off and stand next to the shelf," I say, nudging her towards the steel railing that supports the side of the shelf.

I reach for a roll of tape and find the end, then I tape her wrists around the railing above her head, but with enough flex for her to bend her arms.

My heart is beating so hard, because we also talked about increasing the dirty chat. It is completely new for me, and, to put it bluntly, I'm embarrassed. What if she laughs at me? What if I say the wrong thing and she gets the ick?

But here she is. Waiting for me to take control. And I figure I won't get better at it unless I try and see how she reacts.

I tug the zip of her jeans down and pop the button.

"Are you wet for me?" I whisper into her ear.

"Yes," she pants.

"Have you missed me?"

She nods.

"Good. Now let me give you what you need, beautiful."

She practically purrs as I kiss her neck. I slip her jeans down; she swallows.

"Is this what you need?" I ask, reaching for her underwear and tugging them down.

"Yes," she says.

"Do you need my dick to make you feel good, Kelly?"

Another nod.

"I want you to tell me," I say, kissing her jaw. "Tell me what you want, and I'll give it to you."

"I want you to fuck me, Johnny."

I rub my hand over my dick, still exposed from the blowjob, then rub the head right onto her clit.

"Yeah? Do you want me to make you come, baby? Spread your legs a little wider," I say, nudging them open with my knee.

And with a few adjustments, we find the right angle.

I get her clit with my piercing like before and she writhes against the tape, eyes closing and mouth parting as she moans.

And when I edge myself into her, she gasps, so I slide my hands up under her shirt to toy with her nipples, teasing her even more.

"Hold still and relax for me. I want to go deep," I tell her, eyes locked on each other as I push in.

I take a deep breath in, letting myself adjust to her. Because despite how busy we've been in the bedroom, it never gets old—she always feels fucking incredible.

I watch my dick disappear and I slide out again, before thrusting in slowly, building a steady rhythm, trying to hold back a little, willing the moment to last longer.

"Please, Johnny," she says, biting her lip and looking down between us.

"You want me to make you come?" I say.

"Yes."

"Yeah?"

"Yes," she says.

"If I rub your clit for you, are you going to be a good girl for me, and come on my dick?"

I don't even know where that came from, but I'm going with it. She quivers around me, so that must be a good sign.

"Yes. Please."

Having her practically begging for it is more than enough to entice me. I drop one hand to her clit and move in circles, building up the speed with the rhythm of my fucking. I bury my head in her neck to nibble on her skin; delicate and fresh and just so very *her*.

"Johnny—"

She comes on my dick just as the door rattles.

"Shit," I say, probably a little too loud. And in the panic, I pull out and yank her jeans up, forgetting about my dick.

A moment later, there are footsteps walking away from the room, and I glance back at Kelly, the horror on her face making me feel a little queasy.

"Johnny—ohmigod."

I pull the tape off her wrists and then fix myself, except I'm harder than ever—the thought of getting caught pulling at my balls, and I need to come.

"There's no way I can go out there like this," I say. "I'm going to have to finish."

Kelly fixes her clothes before stepping towards me, lowering her voice. "Do you think they've gone?"

We listen hard for a moment and I nod. "I heard footsteps walking away, so—"

"Okay, but make it quick," she says, dropping to her knees.

It doesn't take me long at all, and I bite my tongue as I come down her throat a moment later.

Then, I get to work cleaning up as best as I can before putting the room back to how we found it.

"How was the dirty talk, by the way? Any feedback is welcome." I grin, trying to push past my embarrassment.

Kelly giggles. "It was fine."

"Just fine? Damn."

"Okay, it was great. I mean, I had a good time."

Pulling her face towards mine, I drop a kiss onto her lips and make a mental note to do more research.

I'm also stalling, because there's something I'm keen to ask her, and I'm feeling really fucking nervous about what she may say.

"Are you okay?" she asks, cocking her head to the side. "Was it okay for you?"

"Oh, heck yeah. I just... how do you feel about spending Christmas in Canada with me?" I ask.

It's been something I've been mulling over ever since I got back from Kelly's tour. Since having those few days together really set me up for wanting more. I'm so keen to have more one-on-one time with her. And I figured, if we go to Canada, we'd have the whole place to ourselves.

"What?" she asks, cocking her head to the side. "Are you kidding?"

"No. How do you feel about it? I mean, you don't have to, but I remember you telling me Christmas hasn't been the same since Jeremy... and I figured that it may be nice to give you a new memory of it. We can stay at my mom's place since she's never there. I can fix your plane ticket."

"I don't know, Johnny. What would I tell my parents?"

"Shit. I guess, just tell them you're spending it with a friend?"

Kelly's expression changes from pensive to something a little more curious.

"And your mom wouldn't be there?"

"Well, she never is. But if you wanted to meet her—"

"Can I think about it?"

"Which part? Coming or meeting her?"

"Both. I just want to make sure it'd be okay. And I have some savings, Johnny. I wouldn't want you paying for my ticket."

She pulls out her phone and curses at the poor signal.

"You do realise we'd only be there for like three days? With your schedule and—"

"I guess you're right," I say, realising that I'm probably talking with my dick. But then she turns to me with a glint in her eye.

"You know what? Fuck it. Let's do it."

The universe is on our side, because whoever was trying to force their way in earlier is nowhere to be seen when I peek around the door to sneak Kelly out.

And when she's safely out of the back door, I wander back to the locker room. It's as if I never left. In fact, I blend right into the background—which is fine by me.

Kelly

He's been fighting.

"It's not what it looks like," Johnny says, standing in the doorway to my room.

"It looks like you've been fighting," I say, rushing over to him. "Have you, or have you not been fighting?"

I give a stern look right into his eyes and the guilt glows hot on his face.

"It was a complete fucking mess. Rodgers came on to my sister and said something hugely inappropriate to Jenna, Ryan's girlfriend. What do you expect? I mean, I didn't ask him to punch me. I got in the way."

His lip is swollen, and there's a tiny cut on the left side of his mouth. And when I reach up to touch his cheek, I can see my hand shaking.

"Oh my God. I hate hockey," I say. "I told you I hate it. And this is why."

"This is why I didn't see you last night—I knew it would upset you," he says. "But in my defence, I wasn't even playing at the time."

I stare blankly at him, taking in his face a centimetre at a time while I survey for further damage.

"Is your head okay?" I ask.

"Yeah, it's fine. Honestly, it's fine."

Johnny leans down and pulls me into a hug.

"You should see the other guy—"

"And my brother? Was he involved?"

"Bettsy's fine, babe. I promise."

Johnny moves towards the end of my bed and sits down, elbows on his knees.

"Turns out he was using."

"Who?" I say, knitting my brows together. "My brother?"

"No, Rodgers. Remember, I—"

"Oh yeah, right. Sorry." The worry has set in. "But I'm confused as to how someone could be using and they didn't pick it up on a drug test. They still do those, right?"

"Well. We had suspicions. But he was micro-dosing and using some sort of masking product—but it's all out now anyway, and the club has dismissed him."

"Well, as long as—"

There's a knock on the front door and I turn to head towards my half-open bedroom door as someone rushes past. There's a clattering of something in the hallway, then Sally's voice sails through the air as she greets the visitor.

"Hey, is Kelly here?"

My brother.

"Oh, yeah, she's just in her room. Do you want to come in?"

I push my door shut, clicking it as quietly as I can before rounding on Johnny.

The panic rises and my head races.

"What do we do?" Johnny mouths.

I point at the space under my bed and motion for Johnny to get under, surveying the room quickly for any other sign that he's been here.

"You can't be serious?" he whisper-hisses, eyes flicking between me and my bed.

There's a knock on my door next.

"Kel? Your brother's here."

Johnny drops to the deck and shuffles under, and I distinctly hear a few grumbles of pain.

Once the coast is clear, I tentatively open the door and give my best fake smile.

"Hi, Mike. How's it going?"

He glides into the room and plonks himself down on the bed, the full weight of his frame pressing into the mattress; I honestly feel so bad for Johnny right now.

"I noticed Cap's car outside. You haven't spotted him coming and going from any of your neighbours' houses, have you?"

Shit. We didn't think about that.

I throw out my best confused expression and hope for the best.

"No, but I don't make a habit of people watching out of my window," I say. "What's up?"

"Just checking in, seeing how you're doing. Mam said you've been distant recently, and she said you're not going home for Christmas. What's that about?"

Of course he'd ask about that.

"I've just got a lot on with music, and Tom invited me to Christmas at his parents' house. I can't go home for the rest of my life, Mike."

"Well, yeah, but it won't be the same without you. Maybe I'll see what Johnny or Hutch are doing if that's the case."

Mike picks up a book from my bedside table and flicks through it before setting it back down again.

"Can you not, please?"

"What?" he says, standing up.

He makes his way around my room, picking up my stuff and surveying it before setting it back down again. It's like being at home, except this time, I don't have Mam to tell him off.

"Well, do you want to get something to eat tomorrow? I'll buy."

He picks up a block of resin and turns it over in his hand before placing it back.

"Okay, sure. That'll be nice."

I move towards the door and hover on the threshold, gearing myself up to see him out.

"Why do I get the impression you're trying to get rid of me?" he says.

"Because you're touching my stuff, and—"

And then he stops dead. His brow furrows as he comes to the paper roses on my desk. My blood is thundering, and I can feel the room getting warmer. I'm positive the note from Johnny is still around there somewhere—

"We're getting takeaway. Is anyone interested?" I've never been so glad to see Tom in my entire life. He cruises through the open door, creating the perfect distraction.

"Yes, I am, Tommy-boy," Mike says, abandoning his position and following Tom out of my bedroom. "What are we getting?"

I wait until he's out of view before crouching and pulling my duvet from the edge of the bed.

Johnny does not look impressed.

"You're going to have to sneak out," I say. "I'll call you once he's gone. But I can't keep doing this Johnny. We have to tell him."

"Okay, after Christmas. Agreed?"

"Agreed."

Chapter 34

Kelly

THIS HAS TO BE the wildest thing I've ever done.

Literally.

I rack my brain for anything that'd come close to this, but I think *this* is actually it; travelling for over half a day to get to Johnny's mother's place all the way on a completely different continent.

I've never been outside of Europe before and here I am, in Canada, for Christmas.

As soon as I saw the mountains—the mountains that are everywhere I look—I knew I'd made the right decision to sack off the holidays at my parents' house, because it's like nothing I've seen before. British Columbia makes the mountains back home look like molehills.

Johnny's mother's house is right on the edge of the mountains, and it's so beautiful, I want to cry. It's comprised of expansive rooms with a log cabin feel I want to tell everyone about. Except, the only person I can tell is Tom, because he's covering for me.

"Why the hell did you pick Britain over this?" I ask, gazing out of his old bedroom window. The scene outside is, of course, the mountains, and countless fir and spruce trees.

Johnny moves behind me and wraps his arms around my shoulders, finding my neck with his lips.

"I'd never have met you if I didn't. I think the logic works out."

I turn around and study his face. His handsome face that I think I've fallen in love with—even though we're not talking about the 'L' bomb I dropped during sex weeks ago; Johnny hasn't brought it up, and nor have I.

"Speaking of home, we need to carry on like we're on UK time. Trust me. It'll make returning a load easier."

I welcome the notion, because I'm ready to pass out from exhaustion.

The first thing we did once we got here was take showers. Then Johnny ordered in some food, and I've been fighting the fatigue ever since.

Nevertheless, I do agree with him, because neither of us has time to adjust back to UK time once we get home, so pushing another hour and setting an alarm to wake up at 'normal' time tomorrow is probably the best idea.

When we finally climb into his bed, he pulls me close, settling on a steady rhythm of stroking my arm while we lie in silence.

My eyes droop closed almost immediately, because I'm tired, I'm really fucking tired. But my head is reeling, and there's only one topic on my mind.

The more I try to push my thoughts away, the harder they root themselves in. And when I try my countdown from one hundred, I get through it twice before Johnny's voice breaks the silence.

"I can hear you thinking," he says.

"I'm sorry."

"Don't be sorry. Do you want to talk about it?"

He shifts in bed, turning towards me. Though I can't see him properly, I can make out the outline of his face.

"I'm just worried about telling Mike," I say.

It's all I've been thinking about, if I'm being honest. Ever since that close call in my bedroom, I've been worrying how he'll react when we tell him. At least I think it'll be a 'we' thing, anyway.

"I understand. But please, try not to worry. I'll talk to him, and he'll understand."

"Will he, John? Because I'm not sure."

Johnny says nothing. Instead, he reaches for my cheek and pulls my face towards him, dropping his lips onto mine.

"If he doesn't, then I'll do all I can to convince him we're a good idea."

My heart dances through my chest, because that's been another thing on my mind—the unrequited 'L' word I said.

He hasn't even mentioned it, and since I know it's probably unlikely that he's there yet, I don't mention it either.

"I think it should be me," I say. "I should be the one to tell him."

Johnny sucks in a breath. "I actually don't agree. I think it needs to come from me."

"But he'll be furious with me—for keeping this to myself."

"Yeah, and he'll be furious with me, but at least I can hold my own."

"He wouldn't attack me, though," I say.

My thought process follows the rationale that Johnny will have broken legs by the end of the interaction, whereas I'll probably end up in tears—which is fixable.

"It'll be fine, babe. Leave your brother to me."

I roll over and snuggle into the pillow, hoping that Johnny is right. Because what's the alternative?

"Kelly?"

"Yeah?"

"I should probably tell you something," Johnny says.

I flip onto my other side and gaze towards him in the darkness. "Is everything okay?"

"Yeah. But I just wanted you to know I told Sarah I wasn't going to give her any money."

I extend my arm, searching for his hand in the dark.

Before we were due to board our flight, Sarah texted him and asked if he'd made a decision. She gave him an ultimatum: either he pay up, or she'd go to the local media about him—alluding that he's a liar and has fathered a child he wants nothing to do with.

Johnny had laughed out loud when he read the message, but I could tell it was playing on his mind. Instead of the chirpy Johnny I'd become accustomed to, he was back to his old ways of short answers and sharp attitude.

But I let him be. I gave him time to think and to stew over it. And rather than try to influence his decision, I held back, knowing that he'd do what was right for him—and I'd support him no matter what. Even if I didn't agree with his decision. Besides, he knew what I thought. I didn't need to remind him.

"And there's a good chance my dad will show up and kick up a fuss. I've told him I want nothing more to do with him, either." Johnny rolls onto his back. "Out with the crap, Kelly. Out with the crap."

"So that's it then?" I ask, tucking myself into the crease of his deltoid.

"Yep. Both Vicky and I. Cutting the rope. He can go fuck himself for all I care."

Johnny

"WOULD YOU LET ME peg you?" Kelly giggles, her cheeks red from the wine she's been drinking. I cooked for us, and Kelly made dessert. And ever since we finished cleaning up, we've been drinking.

I almost spit my drink out for the second time today. "What?"

"Would you let me peg you?" she says again.

For some reason, we thought it would be a good idea to put some porn on the big TV and watch it together after Christmas lunch. And I've got my notebook in hand, making some high-level notes about dirty talk—mainly video references so anyone flicking through it on the off-chance that I leave it unattended, wouldn't work it out.

Kelly reaches for my phone and taps something onto the screen, changing the video on the TV.

"This sort of thing, Johnny," she says. Then she leans in closer and pulls my head towards her mouth. "Because you love it when I—"

"Hello?"

Shit.

I hit the power button on the remote control, killing the TV just in time for my mother to round the corner into the living room. I wouldn't be surprised if she heard us, but she doesn't say anything. Instead, she offers a warm smile.

"Oh, my. Sorry to burst in. Just popping back to grab a change of clothes before I head out."

She spots Kelly then, who's adjusted herself on the sofa so she's sitting up straight, legs no longer tangled with my own.

I stand up, toss my notebook to the side, and move towards my mother, giving her a tight hug before stepping back.

"Mom, this is Kelly."

Kelly walks over, smiling at my mom, dimples in her cheeks. "It's lovely to meet you. Thanks for letting me stay here."

"Oh, no problem, Kelly. Make yourself at home."

Then I see it. The eyes of judgement as Mom averts her gaze back to me. She turns and steps towards the door before calling me to follow her as she sweeps out of the room.

"I'll be a sec," I tell Kelly, dropping a kiss on her cheek before leaving.

I find Mom in the kitchen, rummaging through a stack of papers on the worktop that weren't there previously—probably work files.

"I spoke to Vicky earlier, I said that you said 'hi'."

Mom ignores me and jumps right into the real reason she summoned me to the kitchen.

"How old is she, Johnathan?" she says, not even turning to speak to me.

"Kelly? She's nineteen."

Mom huffs then opens her work satchel, stuffing the papers inside before spinning to address me further. "Please tell me you're not as dumb as your father is."

"What's that supposed to mean?" I say, furrowing my brow.

She stands on the spot and looks right at me. Right in my eyes. And it's the look I know only too well, a lecture is coming.

"Thinking with the contents of your underwear, not your head."

I gape at her.

"Don't you dare compare me to Dad."

"What in God's name are you doing with a nineteen-year-old? And why didn't you tell me?" she says, hushing her tone a little, probably trying to keep Kelly from hearing.

"I didn't think it would be an issue. She's an adult. I'm an adult—"

"Only just, Johnathan. Honestly—I don't even know what to say."

"Because there's nothing to say. We're not hurting anyone."

But as soon as I say it, I realise I should have added 'yet' at the end of that sentence. Because I'm probably more scared about telling Bettsy than I'm letting on. I'm scared of hurting him, and there's a guy code and I'm stamping all over it.

"I just don't want you getting walked all over again. Not after Sa—"

"Don't go there. This is completely different."

"Is it, Johnathan? Because she had her claws in deep—and now someone from... you'll end up staying there for good at this rate."

"Is that a bad thing?"

Mom scowls at me. Her eyes are hard with a range of emotions that I can't pinpoint. "And you're probably at different stages of your life. Is she still at school? What are her plans after she graduates?"

"What does it matter?" I ask, feeling the heat in my muscles rising.

But then a thought slips across my mind—what are Kelly's plans once she graduates? Apart from her pursuit of joining a national orchestra, but I'm not sure how long she'd want to do that for. And how long am I planning on staying in the UK?

"Just think about how reckless you're being," she says, her attention drawn towards the pager vibrating across the counter. She picks it up and glances at the screen. "I have surgery in an hour, so I need to go, but I won't be impressed to learn that things are serious with this girl. Just don't get her pregnant."

Mom gathers her things.

"Have you been speaking to Dad?"

She observes my face. "No. But is there something I should know?"

"No, but—"

Exhaling, she looks up at the ceiling, then back at me. "All I'm saying is you have a different level of emotional maturity, and getting yourself involved with a teenager is not good for your career direction—for life after hockey."

I roll my eyes, but she doesn't see because she's already en route to the front door. Typical Mom. Conversation over before it really began.

"Merry Christmas," I call, and get nothing back in reply.

Kelly's sitting on the sofa, scrolling through her phone when I get back to the sitting room and my heart is in my mouth since it's likely she heard every single word.

"Is everything okay?" she says, looking up at me.

I try to read her face, trying to gauge how much of the conversation she heard, but she gives nothing away.

"Yeah, babe. Fine." I sit back on the sofa and reach for the remote control. Turning the TV back on and beckoning Kelly over to me. "Do you want to pick up where we left off?"

"Johnny—"

"Come here," I say, and she does.

I wrap my arms around her and take in her scent, because I want to make full use of the short spell of time we have away from the reality of our everyday lives.

"Can we just watch a film or something?" she says. "A normal film."

And I figure that tells me all I need to know, so I find something on the TV and pull the blanket over us both.

As with last night, I can hear her thinking again.

"Does the age gap bother you, Johnny?" she says, after around twenty minutes of deep contemplation.

"So, you heard it all, huh?"

"Well, yeah. And I was trying to not think about it, but—it's just another thing, isn't it? Maybe we're not going to work out."

"Don't say that," I say, adjusting myself so I can look at her. She's got her back against my chest, so I prop myself on my elbow. "Please don't say that."

"Well, regardless of what happens, Johnny, I want you to know... I belong to you. My heart belongs to you, but we need to make this right. Family is important, and I don't want anyone falling out because of us."

I feel like the fucking Grinch at this point because my heart swells in size. It's growing in my chest, ready to burst out.

Am I in love?

I mean, I think I am. I don't really know what love is, but I've seen it.

It's the way Liam and Vicky put each other before anyone else.

It's the way Ryan thinks about Jenna's favourite things and puts his all into making her dreams come true.

It's the way Jani, our first line centre, looks at a basket of bread when we're eating at a restaurant.

And I haven't forgotten about when Kelly said she loved me—but I don't know what to do with it, because I can't bring myself to believe I'm capable of love.

I drop my head and kiss her on the lips, locking in the moment with a good memory—her in my arms where it feels like she belongs.

Then I spend the entire movie thinking about it, and trying to find the right thing to say to let Kelly know how I feel—but the issue is, I don't even know how I feel. Not ever.

But I do know that when we're in bed together, later that evening, and I'm looking right into her eyes as I move into her... there's a feeling that runs deeper than any physical connection I've ever had. And when she comes, my name on her lips as she lets go completely—when she's giving herself to me, there's a reason why I'm able to do the same thing back.

A reason why I'm able to give myself to her completely, like I've never been able to do before.

Because I'm in love.

Chapter 35

Kelly

HE STILL HASN'T TOLD him.

And I feel sick with worry because we're now seeing in a New Year. A New Year that was supposed to start with no secrets.

Except Johnny maintains the guise that he hasn't found the right time yet.

And I finish telling Tom all about it just as carnage ensues at the New Year's Eve party which he is throwing in our student house.

And if there's anything I've learnt in my nineteen years, it's that I can't deal with it. I'm physically incapable of confrontation with strangers—even ones that burst into our home.

Not only does Darren show up with a plus one, but someone Tom fooled around with before Christmas turns up with a load of his friends.

"What are we going to do?" Marie asks, eyeing the crowd of delinquents that settle themselves in the corner of the living room.

One of them picks up the lamp and swings it around by the cord, and my stomach tenses with queasiness.

"I'd call Jake, but he's away with the team," Marie says, worrying her lip.

She's onto something, because her rugby-playing boyfriend would definitely get them removed.

She exhales and looks at me, saying, "Can you call your fella?"

"No. But I can call my brother."

Mike, Hutch, Danny, and, of course, Johnny turn up twenty minutes later, all dressed in post-game suits that have girls staring with eyes like pucks as they filter in.

Honestly, this is like something out of James Bond, because all of them are donning expressions that say *'I mean business.'*

"What the hell is going on?" Mike says, coming to a stop next to me.

"It's Johnny," Tom shouts at the top of his voice, turning his head to project his speech over the music. And since I take longer than a second to answer, he's hell-bent on getting a response. "Kelly? Didn't you hear me? Johnny's here."

"Yes, Johnny is here," I say.

I see him. And he sees me. Our eyes lock for a moment before a smile creeps across his face.

Bloody Johnny and his handsome face. Honestly, I could scream at him right now.

"Who the hell are those guys?" Mike says, breaking the gaze between me and Johnny.

"Don't ask. But we can't get them to leave," I say, ignoring Tom's hoots of excitement. "They weren't invited, nor are they welcome."

"J-Dog. Can I call you J-Dog?" Tom says, right in Johnny's face.

Johnny sniggers, patting Tom on the shoulder. "Do you need some water, bud?"

And when I tell you Tom almost faints, I'm not exaggerating, but all the attention shifts to the crowd of boys, who've just spotted the looming hockey players. They slip into the kitchen, leaving a trail of un-plumped cushions and a broken lamp behind them.

Johnny sits Tom down on the sofa before navigating through our living room towards the kitchen, right behind Mike and Danny.

There's shouting, then the smash of something, then the sound of a cupboard slamming, and moments later, cheers erupt in the living room as the intruders are escorted out.

"They made that look so easy," Marie says, downing the rest of her drink. "But I think it's time for a refill."

I follow her into the kitchen, and assess the damage—which is luckily just a few glasses.

Marie and I rummage around in the fridge, looking to see what's left when Darren waltzes in, followed by his new girlfriend.

"You know things are bad when even Darren can get a date," Marie whispers into my ear.

Then the shrill tone of Darren's voice cuts through the air.

"Kelly, I wanted to introduce you to—"

"Kel, a word please?"

Mike pokes his head around the door frame and my stomach drops.

Has Johnny told him?

I study his face, trying to decide if he knows or not, and relief washes over me when I realise this is nothing about Johnny.

But of course, Darren is here, so it's only a matter of time before he sticks his size tens in the mix. He holds his hand out to shake Mike's.

"Nice to see you again, Mike. Hope hockey is treating you well."

Mike stares at him for a moment then shakes his hand, trying to maintain the manners that Mam enforced upon us.

And when Johnny appears behind him, I practically leap in between Darren and Mike—because there's no way in hell that Darren is outing me. Not now. Not ever.

I wiggle through the gap between them and motion for Mike to lead us away from the kitchen.

"Do you mind if we head off? Ryan and Jen are having a little bit of a party back at their place for the team, well, and the WAGs and stuff—I'm just glad I'm not the only single fucker there. Isn't that right, Johnny?"

Mike slaps Johnny on the back and Johnny looks away, just as my eyes meet his.

Because that's the thing about this. I'm just Mike's sister—not in a position to be seen with Johnny outside of the comfort of our own bedrooms, really.

And it's really starting to grate on me.

And what's worse? Johnny stands there and says nothing.

"Yeah, that's fine. Thanks for coming to help."

"See you next week," Mike says, following Hutch and Danny out.

Johnny looks at me for a second, then nods before trailing after my brother.

"Is your boyfriend not staying?" Darren says, coming to a stop behind me. "Because now, more than ever, I'm convinced that there's something going on—something you're keeping from your brother."

"Why are you even here?" I say, turning towards him. "No one invited you. In fact—"

But then there's a vibrating from the pocket of my jeans. And since I'm more invested in that than I am in Darren, I shift away from him and pull my phone out.

Johnny

> I really wish I could see in the New Year with you.

Kelly

> Tell him then.

Johnny

> I will. I just need to find the right time.

Kelly

> Are you having second thoughts?

Johnny

> Not at all. I just need to find the right time.

Kelly

> Will you tell him before my sister's wedding?

We'd had a brief conversation about Johnny being my plus one. But it's seeming more and more unlikely the longer this drags on. And I'm not sure if it's the booze I've drunk, but I'm getting pretty pissed off.

Johnny

> I'm not sure. I hope so. Like I said, I just need to find the right time.

What's the point in being in love with someone—who you think may feel the same, when you can't do the things that couples do together?

Johnny

Can I come see you later tonight?

But I'm too pissed off to reply.

$$Johnny$$

I MAKE IT TO Kelly's a little after two in the morning—all thanks to Bettsy and his inability to take no for an answer.

I ended up playing several hands of poker after we saw in the New Year, and as soon as I could slip out undetected, I did. I headed straight for my car and drove over to Kelly's, seeing the last of the party-goers leaving her house as I pulled onto her street.

I do my usual thing of tapping her window, hoping that she's in her room, because knocking on the front door will probably mean Tom answers and I'm not in the mood for another 'J-Dog' moment.

A glow of light fills a gap at the bottom of the window, then the curtain creeps back just enough so she can see me.

I hold my hand up in a wave, taking in the look on her face.

I woke her up. Shit.

The curtain returns to its usual resting place, then a few moments later, the front door clicks open, and Kelly comes into view, clad in one of my college T-shirts. She turns on her heel and pads up the hallway back into her bedroom, leaving the door ajar.

"Happy New Year," I say, slipping into her bedroom and pushing the door shut behind me.

She's already back in bed. The duvet pulled right up to her neck.

She's pissed.

But I'm on autopilot. I hit the light and undress before slipping into bed next to her.

"Did you tell him yet?"

"Kel—"

"So that's a no, then?"

I feel so fucking disappointed in myself, because I had the chance to tell him earlier. I just needed to come out with it and worry about the consequences later. But I couldn't do it—not after the news I learnt today.

"I told you, I will. I just need to find the right time."

She shifts in bed, turning herself away from me, and I can feel the tension in the air.

Should I tell her what I know? Would it make a difference?

"This is hurting me, too, beautiful. You know that, right?"

I'm desperate for her to understand how much this is killing me, too. Because I wanted her there at the party this evening. I wanted people to see us together, and witness how fucking amazing she is—and how she makes me come alive like no one has done before.

I wanted to kiss her at midnight.

But I'm met with a wall of silence.

Silence.

But she shimmies back into me and pulls my arm around her waist.

Okay, so she still wants to cuddle. Which is something, at least. And I bury my face in her neck, breathing her in, letting her scent settle the anxiety flaming through me.

But the silence is so abnormal for us, I can't handle it.

"Talk to me, please," I prompt.

"What do you want me to say?" she says. "Because I don't know how many other ways I can ask you when you're going to tell him."

"And I will, I just—"

"—need to find the right time," she says, finishing my sentence.

I let out a heavy exhale and pull her just a little bit closer.

"Is this about what your mom said? Are you worried about the judgement we'll get from everyone?"

I close my eyes—now burning with the threat of tears, but I can hear the hurt in her voice. And I'm doing this to her. This is my fault.

"No, it's not. I honestly don't give a shit what she or anyone else thinks." Pathetic. "Look—if I tell you something, you can't tell anyone, okay?"

She reaches up and flicks her lamp on, then rolls over to face me, concern etched over her face. "Johnny—is everything okay?"

"Yeah. But you can't say anything, right? Promise me, please."

"Okay, I promise," she says.

"Coach had a call about the preliminary roster for Team GB. And two of our guys have been listed. Your brother being one of them." I wait for her expression to change but it doesn't. She just stares at me, waiting for me to say something else. "And honestly, it's a fucking huge deal, as you probably know—so I'm just really fucking anxious about telling him now and then having him flip out and cause a drama before they officially announce anything. To be honest, I don't even think Coach should have told me."

"So that's the reason?" she asks after what feels like the longest stretch of silence.

"Yeah. I mean—what happens if he doesn't take the news well? What if he lets it affect his game and—"

"But what about me, Johnny?"

"I—"

"I have an open audition invitation for a national orchestra soon." She sits up in bed and then flicks the duvet off her legs. "What about how much this is affecting my ability to perform?"

"Where're you going?" I ask.

But she's on her feet now, walking towards her closet, pulling out my hoodie. There's complete rage in her eyes, and I half expect her to throw it at me, but she doesn't. She slips it over her head and pulls it down her body, and my eyes linger on my number, and the 'C' mocking me.

Because right now—I'm anything other than a captain.

I'm a coward.

'C' for coward.

And I realise I should say something. I should speak up and try to prove to her that this isn't a case of me picking Bettsy over her. It isn't.

But the fear of being yelled at, called pathetic and useless—all the things Sarah used to do to me, floats right to the surface.

But she doesn't yell, her voice comes out smooth and calm.

"I'm going to see Tom for a bit. Because believe it or not, I kind of understand—though I don't at the same time. I need some space, Johnny. Please don't be here when I get back. I'm asking you this, Johnny—please." I bolt upright in bed, staring at her for a moment, willing my brain to engage and for me to say something—anything at all. "Just let me know as soon as you've told Mike." Then she steps back towards the bed and meets my gaze, her eyes filling with tears that I've caused. "I love you."

Then she slips out of the room before I can process the words fully. My heart thrumming in my chest, my skin hot and clammy as if I'm about to pass out.

There's so much at stake here and my head is swimming with all the possibilities.

What if Kelly gets the opportunity of a lifetime and leaves, after her brother disowns me—not only have I lost her, but I've lost my friendship with Bettsy, too. What if Kelly decides a few months down the line that she can't handle the age difference—that she wants someone ready to tread the same path as her, without knowing the full picture from me. What if—

Then Justine's words float back into my head: *"Remember, Johnny. The majority of scenarios we make up in our head are just that—made up in our head."*

But this, right now, is so real—I can hardly breathe from the pressure.

It appears I am being forced to decide here. Kelly or her brother. And that's exactly what I don't want to do.

I don't think I've been in love until now. But then again, I don't think I've had such a pure friendship as I do with Bettsy. I mean, yeah, the twins are my best friends, but when you're paired with someone, and have the bond that we do—that hits differently.

And after all the times I've failed in my life—I feel like I'm failing him and Kelly, and I'm stuck.

Chapter 36

Kelly

My brother's idea of a wedding is getting pissed and dad-dancing until the DJ calls it a day, but since he's got morning skate at an ungodly hour—his words—he's forced to be sensible.

"Honestly, I can't wait for this to be over," he says, sipping at the glass of water he's clutching. "What is it with weddings? Because this is torture."

"It's not that bad," I say, looking over at Stacey and her new husband—who is still a prick. And I feel it too. This *is* torture.

He follows my gaze and grunts.

My sister's wedding is on a Thursday, to accommodate Mike's schedule and save money since it's cheaper. But although this is supposed to be the happiest day of Stacey's life, Mike and I are both miserable—but for different reasons.

We're hovering near the bar, watching the happy couple travel around the room, thanking people for attending.

"It makes you sick though, doesn't it?" Mike says, glancing around the room.

"The wedding?" I ask.

"No. People being happy. And in love."

"What happened to that girl from speed dating?" I ask, but he scowls at me.

"Honestly, Kel. I'm sick of dating now. Most of the women I meet are trying to tick a box labelled 'hockey player'. They don't actually care about who I am."

"Maybe if you stopped putting yourself out there as much, you'd have more chance," I say, taking another sip of my drink. "You don't want to get a reputation as a fuck boy."

Mike cringes. "I already think that's the case, to be honest, but I don't want to talk about that with you. I'm just glad Johnny is a stone wall and down to be single forever. At least we'll have each other in our old age."

I nod, feeling the guilt settle in my stomach. Because Johnny still hasn't told him. And there's no way in hell I can either.

"What about Ellie?" I ask, trying to shift Mike's thoughts away from Johnny.

"Found her on Facebook. She's engaged. Everyone is pairing off, Kel."

Auntie Julie, our mam's sister, ambles over to us, leaning against the bar while she tries to flag the server down.

"It'll be your turn next, Kelly," she says, cheeks flushing from the wine she's been drinking all day. Mike and I were seated at the same table as her, so we witnessed it firsthand. "Are you seeing anyone?"

"No. And Mike insists I don't date," I say, finally grateful for the excuse.

But he chooses now of all times to change his mind.

"I'm actually thinking of lifting the ban," he says. "No point in Kelly being as miserable as I am."

He's frowning. A genuine frown that shows nothing but heartache.

"In that case—what do you think about him?" Auntie Julie points to a guy sitting at a spot a few tables away. He downs a pint, then slams the empty glass down on the table before whooping at the top of his voice.

"Who the hell is that?" Mike asks, straightening up.

"Maggie's son. He's lovely. Said he was hoping to meet a nice girl here today."

I don't know who Maggie is, but I'm not keen on meeting her son, either.

Mike scowls. "I bet he fucking did. But it's a no thanks to him. Ain't that right, Kel?"

I have to agree with him, because, despite everything, I want Mike to approve.

Not only is he such an important person to me, but seeing how he and Stacey's new husband are together breaks my heart. It's not a brother-in-law relationship that anyone would want, really. And the question sits heavy in my chest—would Mike be okay with Johnny?

"I'm not interested," I say. "Thanks anyway."

"Why, love? He's a good-looking boy."

"Yeah, but I'm... busy with uni and music and that."

"Ah, so you are seeing someone, then?" Auntie Julie asks, raising her pencil-thin eyebrows.

"No."

"I can see the twinkle in your eyes," she says. "Tell me more."

"She's not seeing anyone, Auntie Jule. Besides, if there's a chance that she'll end up with someone like Stacey, then I'm getting involved, whether she likes it or not."

My heart thunders in my chest.

What do I do? What do I say? Should I break the plan and tell Mike myself right now?

"Mike?"

"I'm just going to take a leak, Kel. I'll be back soon."

I watch him disappear through the double doors of the event space.

"What's going on then, Kel? Tell me because I can see it written all over your face."

But the scenarios play in my head. What if Mike disowns me? Doesn't want to associate with me any longer—and Johnny? What if he refuses to play on the same team as him?

It could ruin Mike's career—his chance for Team GB.

It could ruin Johnny's career, too.

"I need to go," I say to Auntie Julie, and I turn on my heel and amble out of the room towards the reception desk.

Because I need to cry in peace.

A DISHONEST MAN SHOULD not be a leader. I know this, which is why I ask Coach for a quick word before practice. I'm a dishonest man who is really fucking heartbroken.

I've been on edge since Kelly texted me, telling me that Bettsy needs to be okay with it. I mean, I get it, but also, I don't. Because what if Bettsy isn't okay with it? Because that part doesn't bear thinking about.

"Everything okay?" he asks. "With therapy and whatnot?"

"Yeah, not bad, thanks, Coach," I say, trying to soften the blow. "But I was wondering if I could ask a favour?"

I'm gearing myself up. Because the longer I go without talking to Bettsy, the longer I can live in the illusion that everything is okay, and nothing has to change.

Coach narrows his eyes at me. "What kind of favour? Because the last—"

"No, nothing like that. I've just been thinking about some things, and I wanted to ask you to relieve me as captain for a little while. I have a few things I'm working on... with Justine—" I lie. More dishonesty, but I can't even bring myself to tell him the truth. I'm a coward. "—and I just need some thinking space."

Coach stands up from his desk and moves himself around to where I'm standing, perching himself on the edge for a moment before he stands again, shaking his head.

"What's going on with you, Johnny? Help me understand."

And then I cry. Because I'm a fucking wreck.

I end up telling Coach all about Sarah and her antics, and then about my dad, but that's only half of it, really ... I tell him there's more.

"Johnny?" Coach prompts after a long stretch of silence, reminding me I'm in his office.

"I think I'm—it's about a girl," I blubber, staring ahead at the notice board behind Coach's desk.

"Ah, Christ. I thought these days were over when I moved away from junior hockey. This is above my pay grade, you know." He drops his head into his hands before standing abruptly.

"I know, Coach. But I'm in a mess. I don't have a clue what I'm doing."

"I don't think I want to hear any more about it," he says. "Do whatever you need to do, because we're right on the cusp of winning the Challenge Cup and the league title. What the hell are you playing at? I'd expect this sort of thing from Betts, but come on, Johnny."

I visited Justine this morning, and she did not help the situation one bit. All she gave me was her full-of-crap reflective listening.

"Koenig—what's your plan?" Coach says.

"Give Danny the 'C' for the time being. And I'll sort my shit out, I promise."

"The hell—is it that serious?"

"I can't go out there and lead a team of guys when I'm carrying a huge secret, Coach. Just please. Let me have some space and I'll fix it."

"Okay, I really do not want to know any more," he says, tightening his jaw. "But you're fixing it, right?"

"Yes."

Coach considers me for a moment before nodding.

"Just don't check out on me completely," he says. "Because we need you, Johnny. The guys need you. I need you."

I exhale and stand up, reaching for a box of tissues to dry my eyes.

"Thanks, Coach."

"So a broken heart, huh? It can kill a man. I've seen it before, and I'll see it again. You're not the first and you won't be—"

"Yeah, thanks, Coach. I get it."

Once he dismisses me, I head to the dressing room and wash my face, then I stare at my reflection in the mirror.

"Hey, there he is!" Prez says as I walk back to my cubby, his face dropping when he catches my eyes. "What's going on?"

"Forget it," I say. "I didn't sleep well last night. I'm tired, that's all."

An understatement of the century. I don't remember the last time I slept through the night. Not this year anyway.

"Bullshit," Prez says, moving to set a hand on my shoulder. "Talk to me, John."

I look him square in the eyes and open my mouth to say something—anything. Then the door to the dressing room swings open and Bettsy strides in.

"We're wanted upstairs," he says. "Something for the social channels and then a video review with Coach... you okay, mate?"

His eyes lock on mine and I push myself to nod.

"Yeah, fine."

But I'm anything other than fine.

Chapter 37

Kelly

MY BROTHER CHOKES ON his pre-nap snack when I phone him on Saturday afternoon. I timed my call perfectly, ensuring that it's just before his nap time because waking him up to ask him for a favour wouldn't go down well.

"And you want the tickets... for you?" he says, trying to suppress another chortle.

"I don't understand why this is so funny," I say.

"Because it's you asking me for tickets. I mean—who are you and what have you done with Kelly?"

"So, can I have one or not?" I say, chewing on the end of my pencil.

I've got my music score sheets spread out in front of me, reviewing a part of my third piece that I'm planning to play on Monday for my audition, except, I'm freaking out and I need one of Johnny's pep talks. One that'll ground me and give me a level head when I go to my audition on Monday—because right now, I'm a complete fucking mess.

I opened our texting thread at least six times before closing it again, reading over the last few lines of messages. My heart hurts.

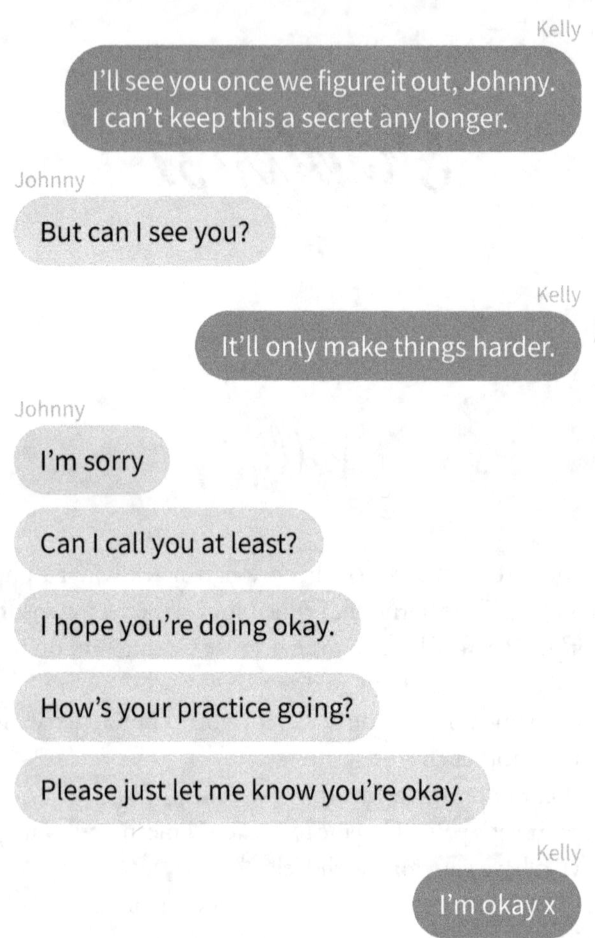

I'm as desperate to see him as he is me.

And it's only been two weeks.

But right now—this is the only thing I can think of as part of my plan. Just getting a glance of him in his natural habitat, and you never know, he may see me and realise that I am still here, and I support him. Because if I can do this, he can surely tell Mike.

"Just the one? Not bringing Tom or whoever? Or Darren?"

There's a playful jibe in Mike's tone, which pisses me off. "Why would you mention Darren?"

"Oh, I bumped into him the other day in town, and he mentioned—" My soul nearly escapes. "—that he still really likes you."

Phew.

I can live with that.

"Well, he can suck it. But the ticket, Mike..."

"Right. I'll be sure they're ready for you to collect from the box office. If they ask for a passcode, it's '*Bettsy is a legend'.*"

He laughs at his own joke, and I cringe.

"I only need the one," I say, pulling the conversation back to business.

"Sure, whatever. I'll fix it. But you best be coming to actually watch the game and not mope around in the bar area. Because we're making waves here, Kel. We're on fire, and Ffordey and the twins are—"

"—bringing the best out of the team," I say without even thinking.

A nervous laugh rumbles down the line. "How do you know how they're doing?"

Shit.

My eyes flick over towards my open laptop, a copy of Johnny's dissertation, work in progress, on the screen. I said I'd review it for him before Christmas, and this morning I finished—but it's put him right back in my mind. And his approach to leadership is in the forefront of my mind.

"I just pay attention to the social media feeds. I take an interest, you know."

And I'm obsessed with Johnny.

He makes a noise that has me under the impression that he doesn't really believe me, but he doesn't press anymore, opting to say goodbye in favour of his nap.

And it's only when I'm sitting in the post-call silence that it really hits me—I'm going to watch a hockey game.

I thought I'd feel better coming clean to the twins and my sister, but I don't. In fact, I festered for another week before concluding that the best thing to do would be to buy a one-way ticket back to Canada.

But then Vicky showed up and applied some hard love and I realised I can't keep hiding.

I understand how Vicky feels about Liam finally—or perhaps the other way around.

I need to tell Bettsy. And I need to tell him tonight.

It's the last leg of the Challenge Cup and we're on the cusp of bringing home the silverware.

The room is full of chatter as we ready up, and Bettsy sits in his cubby next to mine, winding tape around the blade of his stick.

"My sister's here tonight," he says.

And my ears perk up for a moment, wondering if he's talking about Stacey, but then he drops her name into the air and my stomach somersaults into my chest.

Kelly.

"Bettsy—"

"Yeah, she just called me out of the blue and asked me to put a ticket aside for her, but—"

"Bettsy—"

"—I didn't think—"

"Bettsy!"

He halts, mid-wrap of his blade, and looks at me, his eyebrows pinching together.

"What?"

I glance around the room again, and I figure if I'm going to tell him, then I may as well do it here with backup. Witnesses, maybe?

But then he glances down to my hands, where I'm clutching my notebook, and his face changes briefly, then he chuckles, and his smile drops.

"What's that?" he asks, pointing at the paper in my hands.

I look down at the page and my pulse thunders in my ears, and for a moment I think I'm about to pass out.

'Remember, I belong to you, Johnny—love Kelly xx (or Jelly since I'm feeling silly)'

I stare at it, and I honestly don't even know when she would have written it, but it sends both a red alert and a fucking flutter right to my heart.

"What is it?" he asks again, then he reaches for my notebook. "Jelly?"

"Bettsy—I need to talk with you."

But he grabs it from me, pulling it clean from my fingers, and dashes towards the showers, notebook clutched in his hands as he avoids the walls of bodies.

Fuck.

Kelly's writing, that's for sure. And let's face it—there've been plenty of opportunities for her to write inside it. The countless hours of studying together, or when she's been looking for a stat for me when we've been watching playbacks. She's the only person I've let touch it—except for now, but Bettsy has commandeered it of his own accord.

I follow him, finding him standing there in the entrance to the shower. I'm shaking and trying to remain stoic as I rack my brain for what to say next.

"Remember—I belong—"

"Don't," I say, trying to deter him from reading it aloud. And to be fair to him, he stops and glares at me.

"Jelly?"

"Betts—"

"Cap, are you...?"

"I'm in love with your sister," I say, hardly able to recognise my voice. It's a whole fucking mess, to be honest. I'm sweating and we haven't played a single shift yet.

I brace myself for the impact of Bettsy's fist, but it doesn't come. Instead, he looks between me and the notebook, then he bursts out laughing.

"You're kidding, right?" he says.

"Actually, no," I say, dropping my gaze to the floor briefly before looking him in the eyes.

"No?"

"No. I'm not kidding. And—"

"How long has it been going on for?" he says.

"Long enough for me to have told you already," I say. "I mean, I've been trying to find the right moment."

Bettsy studies me for a moment.

"Rather you than me," he shrugs.

"Rather you than me?" Hutch says, walking through the doorway to the showers, followed by Liam.

"What I mean is, she's annoying as hell, and I wouldn't want to share a bed with her."

"Who?" Hutch asks.

"My sister," Bettsy says

"She's *your* sister," Hutch adds.

"Which is why she's annoying, and I don't want to share a bed with her."

"Can you give us a minute?" I ask Liam and Hutch, waiting until they've left before addressing Bettsy again.

"I'm sorry. I should have had the balls to tell you sooner," I say. "But—I'm in love with her, bud. And I haven't even told her yet. I knew I had to make sure you were okay with it, and I've been trying to tell you but—"

"How did this even happen?" he says, pinching the bridge of his nose. "I mean—she's nineteen. She's smart for one—she wouldn't."

"It's a long story, but if you really want to hear about it, I'll tell you," I say. "But we didn't mean for it to happen. It just sort of... did. And now I'm in love with her, like, really fucking in love with her, man."

And I'm fucking crying again. Tears fill my eyes.

Bettsy steps forward and pulls me into a hug. "Johnny, stop it. I mean, is she into you, too?"

"I think so," I say.

"Well, shit."

He pulls back, standing there, holding his hands on his hips as he stares at me, probably thinking as much as I am right now.

But there's a scramble outside the door and a flurry of voices.

"Bettsy? Bettsy?"

He shoves my notebook into my chest as he hurries past me, and I follow, entering the dressing room to see Coach standing by the door, beaming, calling for Danny and Bettsy.

"Good news, boys. You've both been named on the preliminary roster for Team GB. I've just had the official word."

The entire room erupts in cheers and yells of excitement, and to my surprise, Bettsy seeks me out in the crowd, flinging his arms around me.

"All thanks to you, Johnny. You did this!"

"No, bud. You did."

I couldn't be any prouder than I am right now.

And relieved.

I'm really fucking relieved.

Chapter 38

Kelly

I GET A TEXT from Mike to meet him outside the dressing room after the game, with instructions to look for Vicky, Johnny's sister, as she'll get me to where I need to go.

I spot her when there are a few minutes left on the clock—just before the guys are ready to progress to the Challenge Cup finals—she beckons for me to head down to the barrier and then instructs some security guy to let me through.

The stench of cold and sweat hits my nose, but it's one of the few times where I can't focus on it enough to be repulsed. I'm shaking with anticipation because it's either going to be news that he's made the preliminary roster for Team GB, or that Johnny's told him—but Johnny couldn't have told him since they've both been out on the ice tonight.

"It's nice to see you again," Vicky says, flashing a smile. "We didn't get a chance to meet each other properly last time."

She looks at me with a glint in her eye and I see it straight away.

She knows.

But she grins and slips away, leaving me standing here, awkwardly waiting for the end of the game.

And then the final buzzer sounds and the nerves kick up a notch. Because I'm shaking now. Trembling with worry—and I hate surprises, so this is a nightmare.

The post-game awards begin, and I spot Johnny and his vacant smile as he involves himself in conversation with some of the guys from the opposition.

It's one of the smiles he does when he's acting. It's the smile of the 'Alternate Captain'—except there's an 'A' stitched on his jersey. My heart drops. He really *is* the Alternate Captain.

"And tonight's 'Man of the Match' award…"

I don't even pick up who wins it, because my head is spinning. Why would he give up his captaincy? And why didn't Mike mention it?

I run it over in my head, right up until the bench door opens, followed by the heavy sound of skates on the rubber matting.

Then he's there. Towering over me in his gear.

Tom would jizz in his pants right now, because Johnny is really fucking handsome—all hot and sweaty and tall. He's really tall.

"Hey," Johnny's voice cuts through the music that's blasting over the PA system.

I don't even know what to say to him, because I was expecting Mike to be the first one to greet me. But he looks… different, somehow. And he beams at me. His face lights up. And my stomach becomes so light it's floating.

He puts his helmet and gloves down on the floor next to us before tugging his jersey off, his underlayer tight over his torso. His eyes lock on mine as he hands it to me, damp with sweat and completely disgusting—but I take it from him.

"This is for you."

"For me?"

"Yeah. You came to a game," he says, still smiling.

"I wanted you to know that I'm still waiting for you," I say, my voice shaking.

"I'm really fucking glad," he says. "Because I told him. Long story short. He saw the note you left me and—"

"Oh, fuck."

"I was telling him anyway," he says, stepping right up towards me. "I told him I'm in love with you."

There's an emotion bubbling through me I can't even comprehend.

Did he just say—

"Did you just say—"

"I love you. I really fucking love you."

And sweaty hockey player or not, I step towards him, closing the gap. "And Mike?"

"Jelly!"

The word flies through the air, and I glance over at my brother. My cheeks flame red.

Shit.

"Mike, I—"

"I got selected for the preliminary roster, Kel!"

And there's an almost deafening roar of cheers and excited chatter as the rest of the team leaves the ice. Mike edges closer, pushing Johnny aside so he can scoop me up into a hug.

"Does he make you happy? Cap, I mean. Does he?"

"Yes."

He nods once, then turns to Johnny. "Do I need to remind you about the leg breaking thing... because—"

"Got it," Johnny snaps.

Then Mike steps away, joining the back of the line towards the dressing room, leaving Johnny and I standing alone, bar the support staff.

"I love you," he says again. "And I'm sorry for being such a fucking—"

"I love you," I say, and then he leans down and touches my cheek with his rough hand that he pulled right out of his glove—still moist and sweaty. But I don't care that he stinks. My lips find his sticky, clammy face, and I still don't care. I really don't. I don't know how long we kiss for, but I pull away, taking in a deep breath before speaking. "And I need you."

"Like, need me?" he says, in a voice that needs no explanation.

"Well, yeah, but I need a pep talk. For Monday. Because this is big, Johnny. And I need you."

"I got you, beautiful. Give me, like, twenty minutes and I'll be out."

What's weird is that when Johnny emerges from the dressing room and heads straight for me, I don't feel awkward.

And no one bats an eye when he lifts me up and swings me in a circle.

"Do you need the pep talk now or do you fancy celebrating with the team?"

"I—"

The nerves swim in my stomach because this is completely different territory. But he gives me a reassuring squeeze of the hand and I nod, letting him lead the way.

And celebrate we do.

We cheer Danny and Mike as they make it to the bar which Johnny selected for the evening.

"I gave Danny the 'C' for this reason," he says. "Because I know it'd be the icing on the cake for him, so to speak. Give him the boost he needs to be really seen."

And Johnny—the most selfless person I know, with a heart the size of the world, kisses me, right there, in front of everyone.

And no one pays us any attention—at least, I don't think they do. Because I'm all about Johnny.

Johnny

We've planned banners, balloons, and a cake donned with the word 'Congratulations' in orange letters—Kelly's favourite colour.

We're celebrating. Because Kelly's been selected as a reserve cellist for a national orchestra—which is a pretty big fucking deal.

"Please tell me Mike isn't planning a surprise party," she says, as we pull up outside her student place. "Because I can't handle it. I'm exhausted. I just want to go to bed."

"Just let him have his moment," I say, climbing out of the car and rounding to the passenger side.

It's the best both of us could hope for—that, and the fact that neither of my legs are broken.

Kelly's already out of the car, so I open the back door and pull her cello out, carrying it towards the front door as I trail after her.

We hear Bettsy's voice as soon as we step inside. A loud-whisper sort of noise which has Kelly rolling her eyes at me.

"Make sure you turn the lights off," he says, and there's a scrambling behind the closed living room door.

"I'll just drop off my cello into my room," Kelly whispers, trying to pry it from my hands.

"Oh, no you don't. Go in there and act surprised," I say.

I nudge her forwards, only dipping out momentarily from the route to place her cello inside her bedroom.

When I rejoin Kelly at the living room door, I pause for a moment, letting her take a breath.

"Johnny?" she says, tilting her head to meet my eyes.

"Babe?"

"Imagine where we'd be now if I got that place at the music college. Do you think it would have changed things much?" she says.

"Who knows. But you're onto something better, right? Sometimes life does that. When you think it's the worst news in the world, it's actually setting you on the path that's meant for you."

My mind drifts to what could have been for me. A big career, probably a load more money—but nothing compares to what I've got now. Because this has no tangible value. This is fucking priceless.

Kelly is priceless. And without all the shit that got me here today, I'd not be where I am— with her.

I make an over-exaggerated announcement that we're about to enter.

And the whoops, cheers, and party-poppers ascend, celebrating how incredible Kelly is—and I'm so fucking proud of her—demonstrating how tenacious she is. And that's only one of the reasons I love her.

Epilogue

Johnny

KELLY SINKS DOWN ON top of me as my phone rings.

"Ignore it," I say, encouraging her to start a rhythm by grabbing her hips. "Just ignore it."

Shifting my hand from her side, I run my thumb over her clit, just enough to tease her.

She grinds down on me and I can't think of a time where it felt this good—apart from the other times, but still.

"Johnny, it's ringing again," Kelly says, running her hands up and down my chest to get my attention.

But it has the opposite effect. Her touch ignites me and spurs me on. I grip her firmly, breathing, "Just keep going, forget about it."

"John—"

Impatience gets me, so I grab her hips and roll her onto the bed, working my hips to build a rhythm that has her squealing beneath me.

"Do you like that?" I ask, breathing into her neck. "Do you like the way my dick fills that tight little hole?"

"Oh, my—I wasn't expecting..."

"Shh. Unless you're begging me for more, I don't want to hear it," I say, a wicked grin breaking out across my face.

Her mouth forms the perfect 'o' and I wonder if this is too much—until she licks her lips gently and nods her head.

"You're going to come for me soon, yeah? And I'm going to fill you up, beautiful. I'm going to fill that tight pussy of yours because it's mine, remember?"

Christ, the dirty talk I've been trying to master is flowing now, and it's getting me hot. I think I'm going to explode really fucking soon.

"It's yours, Johnny," she says, moaning beneath me.

And I reach for her clit again, kissing her neck and whispering right into her ear as I adjust my position, so she's pressed into me.

My hand shifts and I grip her neck, ever so gently.

"Look at me and tell me you want it. Tell me you want me to fuck you like you're mine."

Her eyes flutter and she moans, and I try my hardest to keep the rhythm up as I edge closer to paradise.

"I want it, Johnny. I want you to come inside me. Please, come inside me."

"Yeah, that's it. You're taking it so good, baby. You feel fucking incredible—have I told you that? And I want you to come while I'm buried inside of you—while I'm giving you what you want."

And she cries out, my hand keeping her head aligned with mine so I can look right in her eyes as she comes apart, her pussy tightening around me as she comes. And I feel it. The love between us in such a way that has me spending my load right inside of her.

My favourite place to come.

"Johnny—"

"Hmph."

"Your phone is still ringing," she says.

I loosen myself from her and reach for my nightstand, not even bothering to keep the sheets clean at this point.

"Okay—what?" I say, putting my phone to my ear.

"Finally," Vicky says, exasperated. "John, I need a favour."

"Is everything okay?" The guilt in my chest turns up a notch.

"Can you come and give me away?"

"Excuse me?"

"Look—Liam and I are getting married. Please don't tell me I can't or whatever, but I want you to give me away."

"When?"

"In an hour."

Well, fuck me—again.

Part of me wonders if she's serious, but this is Vicky. She's impulsive. But I check anyway.

"Are you kidding?"

"No. Look, Liam and I—well, you know. But we're doing it. Today. And we'd love for you to be there. Please, Johnny?"

I shift my gaze to Kelly, who, hearing the conversation from the volume of the call, beams at me.

"Text me the details, and I'll be there."

I feel... odd. Almost like I knew this was coming, but also didn't fully comprehend that it would ever happen either. I leap out of bed and head towards the bathroom, because there's no way I'm going anywhere without a shower, and I'm expecting Kelly to be right behind me, but she's not.

"Are you coming, beautiful?" I ask, peeking around the door frame at her.

"Me?"

"Yeah, you."

"Really?"

"Yeah, you're my girlfriend. You're coming."

Shit. I've not said that out loud before, but I don't hate it.

I disappear back into the bathroom, turning the shower on and waiting for a second, letting the water run hot before stepping in. And a moment later, Kelly's familiar arms wrap around me from behind.

"I don't think you've called me your girlfriend before," she says.

I turn to face her and plant a kiss on her lips. "Is that okay?"

"Yes," she says. A troublesome grin forms on her face and she grabs the soap with a washcloth from the shower shelf. "How long do we have?"

She spins me around and starts lathering up my back.

"Not long—maybe say, half an hour?"

"That's enough," she says, dropping to her knees.

"What're you—oh fuck."

I have a feeling I know exactly what she's doing. And my dick, spent just a few moments ago, is hard again, begging for the attention that it's not going to be getting straight away.

"Lean forward a little," she says, pulling at my hips to bend.

I set my hands in front of me on the wall of the shower. Bracing myself.

Then I feel it. The washcloth right between my ass cheeks. Then she parts me and adjusts her position, the water from the shower beating down on us as she slips her tongue right onto my asshole.

She probes around, not penetrating me straight away, but teasing me. And it's enough to have me wanting to pull my hand away from the wall to jerk my dick.

Then her tongue flicks over my hole, and I gasp, almost choking on the air in my lungs as she works me right where I need it.

"Fuck."

"Is that okay?" she asks, taking a moment away.

And I grunt—it's all I can manage as I feel her tongue intimately exploring me in a way I wouldn't want anyone else doing.

"That's really fucking good, baby," I breathe. "But I need more."

I need to come.

And she knows exactly how to get me there.

She obliges, her touch gentle yet purposeful. I can sense her finger delicately exploring, gradually making its way inside. At the same time, her other hand firmly wraps around my shaft, sending a jolt of pleasure through my body.

"Yes," I hiss. Or at least I think I do—because I'm ignited. Hard, and eager for faster strokes.

I meet her hand on my dick, taking over the stroking as I chase the release that I know she's working me up to. Giving her a little more room to focus on the finger she's got buried inside me gets me there in a flash, and I'm groaning loudly, coming all over the wall of the shower.

"Fuck."

She gets to her feet and shimmies under the stream of water, washing herself before turning towards me.

"Any more thoughts on pegging?" There's a grin on her face that I can't help but mirror. Because I'm high on my second orgasm of the day.

"You can do whatever the hell you want to me if it's that good."

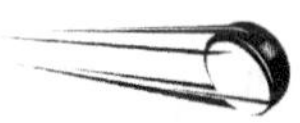

Liam ambles out of a side room in the registry hall, closely followed by Ryan as they make their way towards me in their matching suits.

"You remember, Kelly, right?" I say, pulling her right beside me and draping my arm around her shoulders.

"Yeah, nice to see you. Thanks for coming," Liam says.

"Where're the guys?" I ask.

"It's just us," Liam says.

"Well, and Jen. She's just in with Vicky. But—we're just doing this as a little thing. No big deal for now. But you can't tell Bettsy because he's expecting a huge stag-do or whatever it's called."

Both Kelly and I groan audibly. "We can't keep any more secrets," I say.

"It's not your secret to tell, anyway. Besides, Vicky and I are having a big event in the summer—with Jen and Ryan."

"A joint wedding?" I ask.

"Well, sort of. More like a two-day extravaganza."

I gape at him, but the sound of a door opening in the distance pulls my attention away, and Jen beckons me towards her.

"Come on," I say to Kelly, leading her away.

Vicky looks incredible. A huge white gown that is very... Vicky, and her hair in a wave over her shoulders.

"Thanks, Jen," she says. "I'll be fine with Johnny."

And Jen ambles out, steering Kelly away with her.

"Vic—"

"Do I look okay?" she says, tears forming in her eyes.

"You look beautiful. Like in an ugly way," I say with a grin.

"Thanks, Johnny."

"Are you sure you want me to—you know..."

"Of course I do," she says, stepping towards me, her gown billowing out behind her.

She really does look beautiful.

"Come here," I say, pulling her into a hug. She sniffs loudly and I glance down to see that she is trying hard to not sob. "Hey, don't cry. You'll probably ruin your make-up or something."

"You're different," she says, looking up at me, a smile creeping across her face. "You're happy, Johnny."

"Yeah, I guess I am."

"You're in love," she says, her eyes brightening.

"I'm in love, Vic."

There's a moment of stillness as we just stand there hugging.

It feels like everything we've gone through has led us up to this moment. I wouldn't say we were always close or anything, but we have a bond–probably more than a sibling thing.

Probably because we've both lived through the same experience of our parents. Except, Vicky had Liam. And it's only now, when I've opened my own heart up, I realise how much he must really fucking love her.

"So, you and Lee then?"

"Yeah. It's real, Johnny. There's no one else—"

"I know. I'm so glad that you've worked things out," I say.

There's a tap on the door and Jen pokes her head in. "They're ready for you, Vic."

Vicky nods and sniffs loudly, reaching for a tissue from a box set on a table next to the door.

"Are you really sure you want me to—"

"Yes. You're my brother. Besides, I don't have a dad anymore."

Her words stun me, but I find myself agreeing.

"Well, yeah. But I don't want to talk about him," I say.

"But you will, right? Tell me everything that happened between you both?" she says.

"Sure. Honest answer. I'll tell you. Because we made it, Vic. We made it."

She nods, both of us understanding the unspoken words between us.

We made it.

Thanks

Thanks for reading!

Visit www.alysjclarke.co.uk for bonus content and other exciting bits.

If you enjoyed this book, please consider leaving a review on Goodreads, Amazon, or sharing on your Social Media platforms.

About

Alys J. Clarke is the pen name of a British Author, who loves all things hockey. She lives in Wales with her husband and children and writes part-time.

To find out more, follow Alys on social media.
Facebook: Alys J. Clarke
Instagram - @Alysjclarke
TikTok: @AlysJClarke

Elite Hockey Series

The Import Slot (2023)
The Tape Job (2024)
The Alternate Captain (2024)
The Home Grown (2025)